"A masterful blend of romance, intrigue,
line of the novel, readers will engage with the compelling characters
who are forging paths through danger and lies to find their way to true
faith, hope, and love. Page-turning action combines with depth and
richness to create a full-bodied, rewarding read. After such a stirring
conclusion to this series, I can't wait to see what Crystal writes next!"
JOCELYN GREEN, Christy Award–winning author of
The Metropolitan Affair

"*Counterfeit Faith* is a story that raises the question: How do you handle life's adversities? The faith is evident through every page, and I
found myself encouraged throughout the story. Not to mention the
suspense woven between the pages that kept me reading until I hit the
satisfying end. Readers who love romance, suspense, and a graceful
amount of faith won't want to miss this story."
TONI SHILOH, Christy Award–winning author

"With clear and compelling prose, Crystal Caudill's *Counterfeit Faith*
is full of mystery, suspense, and romance. As one clue leads to another,
the reader is taken on a thrilling chase through Gilded-Age Philadelphia looking for answers until the satisfying end. A beautiful story of
faith, redemption, and hope."
GABRIELLE MEYER, best-selling author of *When the Day Comes*
and *In This Moment*

"*Counterfeit Faith* is a perfect blend of mystery, history, and romance.
Caudill once again weaves a masterful tale in Josiah and Gwendo-
lyn's story as they learn God is the creator of second chances, and He
breathes new life into those willing to surrender their plans for His.
An intriguing story I could not put down!"
TARA JOHNSON, author of *Engraved on the Heart*, *Where Dandelions
Bloom*, and *All Through the Night*

"In *Counterfeit Faith*, Crystal Caudill expertly weaves a story about counterfeiting, the Secret Service, and nineteenth-century children's homes while layering a romance between the pages that unfolds alongside the mystery. With a host of sympathetic and likable characters (and a few not so likable), a riveting plot that clips along at the perfect pace, and a relatable faith thread, this book will appeal to fans of Erica Vetsch and Michelle Griep. A completely enjoyable read."

KIMBERLY DUFFY, Carol Award finalist and author of
A Tapestry of Light

"This series has been perfection from book one, and it just keeps getting better! Caudill creates characters that are easy to love, and Josiah and Gwendolyn are among my favorites. The unique history (Gilded Age! Counterfeiters! Houses of refuge! The Secret Service!), the toe-curling romance, the witty and heartfelt dialogue, the edge-of-your-seat suspense, and the organic faith threads beckon readers to become immersed in this compelling story. If you have ever struggled to trust God, if you've ever echoed the gospel prayer of 'Help my unbelief,' then you will find your heart at home on these pages—at home, but not unchanged. Another fabulously entertaining and grace-filled offering from Crystal Caudill!"

CARRIE SCHMIDT, blogger at ReadingIsMySuperPower.org and
author of *Getting Past the Publishing Gatekeepers*

"*Counterfeit Faith* weaves fascinating historical details such as the green goods game and houses of refuge for children with questions of faith, family, intrigue, and suspense. A thoroughly entertaining read."

CAROLYN MILLER, author of the Regency Wallflowers, Regency Brides, Original Six, and Muskoka Romance series

COUNTERFEIT
FAITH

HIDDEN HEARTS
OF THE GILDED AGE
– THREE –

COUNTERFEIT
FAITH

CRYSTAL CAUDILL

KREGEL
PUBLICATIONS

Counterfeit Faith
© 2023 by Crystal Caudill

Published by Kregel Publications, a division of Kregel Inc., 2450 Oak Industrial Dr. NE, Grand Rapids, MI 49505. www.kregel.com.

Scripture quotations are from the King James Version.

Library of Congress Cataloging-in-Publication Data
Names: Caudill, Crystal, 1985- author.
Title: Counterfeit faith / Crystal Caudill.
Description: Grand Rapids, MI : Kregel Publications, [2023] | Series: Hidden hearts of the Gilded Age
Identifiers: LCCN 2022051252 (print) | LCCN 2022051253 (ebook) | ISBN 9780825447426 (paperback) | ISBN 9780825469503 (kindle edition) | ISBN 9780825477997 (epub)
Subjects: LCGFT: Christian fiction. | Novels.
Classification: LCC PS3603.A89866 C676 2023 (print) | LCC PS3603.A89866 (ebook) | DDC 813/.6--dc23/eng/20221028
LC record available at https://lccn.loc.gov/2022051252
LC ebook record available at https://lccn.loc.gov/2022051253

ISBN 978-0-8254-4742-6, print
ISBN 978-0-8254-7799-7, epub
ISBN 978-0-8254-6950-3, Kindle

Printed in the United States of America
23 24 25 26 27 28 29 30 31 32 / 5 4 3 2 1

To my LORD and Savior:
I believe; help my unbelief.

To Nehemiah:
You are my energetic, karate-loving boy,
who brings the cheesy and punny to my world.
May you always know how much I love you and appreciate your sharp mind,
and how often I pray for you. And may you never forget that
Jesus loves you more.

And straightway the father of the child cried out, and said with tears, Lord, I believe; help thou mine unbelief.

—Mark 9:24

Chapter 1

April 15, 1885
Philadelphia, PA

THE SHRILL VOICE OF THE Carpenters' Hall guide grated against Gwendolyn Ellison's raw nerves. Five tours in three hours and still Mr. Farwell hadn't shown. Of the dozen board members for Final Chance House of Refuge, he'd been the only one to believe her. The only one willing to secretly investigate her claims of abuse. Had someone at Final Chance discovered their clandestine meeting plans? Though she tried to appear the relaxed tourist enjoying a day at the home of the First Continental Congress, every muscle in her back and face ached with stone-hard tension.

The front door opened. Unseasonable cold swirled into the room, carrying with it the tap of shoes against the black and beige tiles. *Please be him.* She surreptitiously shifted her attention toward the sound. Just another tourist huddled in a woolen coat. Perhaps she'd missed Mr. Farwell's entrance and he was holding back for fear of being recognized by someone in the room. She edged closer to the fireplace, lit to ward off the chill brought in by the light snow, and searched the bright, open room. Half a dozen men wandered the space between the gilded-frame membership board, tall iconic columns, and congressional chairs, but none of them resembled the one she sought.

9

Her stomach churned. This was the last tour of the day. If Mr. Farwell didn't show, she'd be forced to return to Final Chance—and her position as matron over the girls' ward—unescorted and without answers. Once again, she peeked at her cupped hand to read the note he'd concealed inside the bouquet delivered to her office that morning.

Meet me at Carpenters' Hall, one o'clock. Tell no one. What I've uncovered is worse than you suspected and far more dangerous. We need to handle this carefully.

She swallowed around the permanent lump that had formed in her throat upon the note's arrival. What could be worse than the abuse of boys under the care of Final Chance's superintendent? And was the danger directed at them, or her, or both? Danger to herself—while unwelcome—could be tolerated, but toward the children? She wouldn't stand for it. Society might deem them worthless criminals, but they deserved to be safe and have a chance at reformation and an honest life.

As the tour herded toward the Sack-Back Windsor chairs once used by the Congressional delegates, Gwendolyn drifted toward George Washington's portrait hanging next to the window. She hoped to seem lost in admiration of the painting even though her scrutiny was fixed on the alley entrance. With Carpenters' Hall nearly boxed in and hidden by the businesses surrounding it, the wrought iron gate was the only way to access the property from Chestnut Street. Plenty of people bustled past the entrance, but the confident stride of Mr. Farwell never materialized. True, he could approach from the side alley, but the back door hadn't been opened in two tours.

Something must have happened. The watchmaker was punctual, without exception. To be nearly three hours late bespoke a calamity.

In a final grasp at hope, she surveyed the Hudson Street entrance.

A familiar, lone figure with folded arms and hat tugged down over his long face leaned against the wrought iron fence.

She sucked in a breath and gripped her collar.

Quincy Slocum, a former Final Chance inmate and seed planted by the devil himself.

No moral reformation techniques attempted in Quincy's three years at the institution had touched his conscience, yet he'd been released last year at sixteen without objection from anyone but her. Did he follow her now merely to satisfy a grudge, or had someone from Final Chance assigned him the task of silencing her after her pointed inquiries? Whatever the reasoning, his strategic position to allow him observation of either exit declared sinister intentions.

Gwendolyn rejoined the small tour group that now studied the banner that had been carried during the Grand Federal Procession. Wisdom dictated she not leave the premises alone, and that meant striking up a conversation that lasted until she reached the streetcar. Once there, Quincy wouldn't be able to act without drawing attention to himself.

As the guide concluded his speech, Gwendolyn appraised the prospects. The three single gentlemen were out of the question. Her position as matron over the girls' ward required an irreproachable reputation, and a lady did not engage with single men. The only other female in the group was a young lady of about fourteen, standing on the arm of a grandfatherly gentleman. Doe-eyed teen girls tended to have one important quality: the propensity to prattle.

When the building closed for the day, she followed the pair down the front granite stairs into the swirl of flurries brought on by winter's last grasp at spring. At the walkway, she matched pace with the girl. "What a fascinating tour. Did you enjoy it?"

The man raised an eyebrow at her impertinent intrusion and rebuffed her with silence as they walked across the Hall's yard toward the narrow alley.

Thankfully, his companion seemed eager to engage. "Oh yes! I particularly enjoyed learning about Mr. Robert Smith." Her wistful sigh hinted at girlish infatuation. "He was a true American hero. Imagine the suffering he must have endured as he stood in the frigid Delaware, building obstructions to thwart the British. It's so sad that he caught pneumonia and died before seeing the fruits of his sacrifice."

The designer of Carpenters' Hall certainly had a new admirer. The young thing continued to gush, allowing Gwendolyn the freedom to observe Quincy slink through the gate ahead of them. Would it be too much to hope he'd disappear somewhere and forget about her? When the girl's rambling dwindled to nothing, Gwendolyn engaged the gentleman. At least if Quincy tried to grab her as they walked through the entrance, the man would notice and be forced to act in her defense.

"And you, sir. What did you think of the tour?"

He raked Gwendolyn's appearance from the worn straw hat to the scuffed boots and pulled his ward to his other side, as if shielding her from a pickpocket attempting to cut her purse strings. Of course he'd assume the worst. While her position as matron and head officer was respectable for a single woman, it did not afford her anything better than the dull wool dress worn by most factory workers. Although, even if she did reveal that she oversaw the care and reformation of juvenile delinquents, he didn't seem the type of man to change his opinion of her.

"And just where is your escort, miss?"

She held her breath as they passed through the gate.

One step.

Two steps.

Three steps.

No hands seized her.

She released her breath in a hazy puff. "They abandoned me, sir, and I hoped your presence would serve as a barrier to unwanted attention until I reached the streetcar. I'm certain a gentleman such as yourself wouldn't deny a lady the protection of his presence."

"A woman who gallivants alone is no lady and deserves whatever advances are made upon her." He abruptly pivoted toward Hudson Street when they reached the corner. "Come, Penny. I'll not allow you to consort further with a woman of such low breeding."

Low breeding, indeed. He must consider himself a righteous Pharisee and her a repulsive Samaritan. She should've known better than to expect anyone but God to come to her aid. He was the only One whom she could rely upon.

A streetcar bell clanged, and she spun just in time to watch her transportation pull away. If she'd not wasted time with that Pharisee, she might've made it. Although she hadn't spotted Quincy yet, waiting for the next streetcar wouldn't be safe, and she'd never make it to the Second Street station before it left from there too.

Hang good manners. She lifted her hem and jackrabbited toward the departing car.

Appalled stares and muttered disapprovals met and followed in her wake. The car slowed as it approached the midpoint of the next square in front of Independence Hall. With a fresh spurt of determination, she sprinted onto Fifth Street.

Horse hooves rose up in her periphery, and the horses' startled shrieks pierced her ears. She snapped her gaze to the wagon ready to barrel her down. So much for Quincy being her biggest concern. She squeezed her eyes shut and braced for the impact.

A hand clamped around her arm and yanked her back onto the sidewalk as a whoosh of air revealed how close she'd come to being trampled.

"Careful now, Matron Ellison. I'd hate for a wagon to kill you."

Quincy. The malicious quality of his adenoidal voice could never be mistaken for a hero's. Her heart pounded against her chest worse than the agitated horses' hooves against the cobblestone.

Mustering a courage that could only come from God, she met the flinty glower of the boy whose features she'd always felt were too squished together for such a large surface. "I'd prefer my death to come by old age."

"Then you'd best be minding your own business. Asking questions is detrimental to your health. Just ask Mr. Farwell." Quincy forced his arm through hers in a mockery of gentlemanly behavior and propelled her down Fifth Street, away from the bustle of people—and the police station next to Independence Hall.

"What have you done to him?"

"You'll find out soon enough. I only wish I could be there when you find out his fate."

"If you've hurt him, I'll turn you over to the police."

"You should be more worried about yourself. I intend to make sure you understand the seriousness of your position." The fingers of his free hand stroked her arm as if she were a pet. "Maybe I'll start with setting flame to your skirts like the witch you always were." Quincy stopped walking, lost in the imaginings of his depraved mind. "Yes, that's what I'll do. Just a foretaste of what can happen if you open your yap."

There was no doubt he'd do it. He'd tortured animals that he'd claimed to adore. How much more delight would he take in harming his enemies?

"You wouldn't risk it. There are too many people around, and the police station's only a dozen yards away."

"You're right. It's too crowded here."

His free hand slipped underneath their arms to his pocket. The wooden handle of a knife emerged. In one swift movement, he shifted it into the fist beneath her pinned arm. He angled the blade's edge toward her and tugged her close. The point pierced through the wool of her coat and dress to scrape against flesh. Any movement contrary to his and she'd likely suffer a punctured lung.

"What say you? Shall we go for a ride?"

"I don't see as I have any choice."

"Maybe you got smarts after all." He guided her toward the hack stand outside the Philadelphia Library.

When two men jogged down the library steps and turned their direction, Quincy angled his body toward hers and tilted his cap to shield his face from view. For a breath, the blond man's eyes met hers, and hope for a rescue swelled within her breast. Then his focus skittered away, and he walked past, talking to his companion without a second glance. She should've known better than to hope. Heroes were in short supply in her life.

"At whose behest are you working, Quincy? I'll compensate you handsomely for telling me and then releasing me."

His derisive laugh proclaimed his refusal. "No questions. We've got eyes everywhere. Play by our rules and, aside from a few burns, there's no need to worry. But if you speak one word to anyone, even your precious little girls, we'll know."

He stopped at the first empty cab. "Christian and Carpenter Street." With a jab meant to remind her of the weapon he wielded, he released her arm and shifted almost against her back. "After you."

Getting in that hack meant submitting to torture—maybe worse, if he lost control. *My saviour; thou savest me from violence.*

"Get moving."

She'd move all right, but not inside. With one boot on the foot iron, she gripped the hack's frame and drew in a deep breath. May this horse be as unnerved as the ones that nearly trampled her. On a prayer, she rent a shrill scream that would lead either to her death or her salvation.

CHAPTER 2

UNNATURAL LIGHT GLINTED FROM A couple's entwined arms and distracted Secret Service operative Josiah Isaacs from his brother-in-law's ramblings about the Philadelphia Library's vast collection. The momentary light must've been the sun reflecting off a button. Josiah shook his head and tried to concentrate on Robert's words, but philosophy and classical literature failed to hold his interest. Why had he listened to his sister Abigail's suggestion that he take the day off work and go with her husband to the library? He had a routine for dealing with the anniversary of his wife's death, and while he loved his brother-in-law, Robert's subject matter failed to engage his mind like untangling a counterfeiting case would.

Light glinted again, and he squinted at the metallic object that quickly disappeared.

That was no button.

The familiar zing of warning coiled his gut into knots. A signal he'd learned not to ignore.

So as not to arouse suspicion, he evaluated the situation with a single glance. The man's unnatural, angled walk and tilted head betrayed an attempt to hide his identity. His companion's comely face, however, was clearly visible. Wide copper eyes stood out against her ghost-white pallor, and when their gazes met, unmitigated fear cried out to him.

Wherever the couple was going, it wasn't with her consent. Josiah snapped his attention back to Robert to avoid alerting the woman's partner that he'd noticed.

As soon as the couple passed, Josiah elbowed Robert. "Stay here. I might need you to run for the police."

Robert's thick brows shot toward his receding hairline, but Josiah pivoted to follow the couple without further explanation.

From the back, the man looked to be in that awkward age between youth and manhood. Likely he hadn't even grown enough hair to shave. Although, were anyone to call him a hobbledehoy, he seemed the type to knock out a few teeth to ensure the slur wasn't repeated. The woman's feminine frame posed no competition for his stocky build, and though her posture slanted away from his one-armed hold, the majority of her body remained unseemly close to his. If Josiah wasn't careful, she could be injured in any attempt to free her.

They stopped at the hack stand several yards away, and Josiah slowed his pace to watch them out of the corner of his eye as he pretended to study the Philosophical Society's building across the street. After a short exchange with the driver, the man shifted behind the woman, providing a clear view of their profiles.

And a knife.

Of all the days to play unarmed tourist with Robert. No one walked away from a knife fight unscathed. It'd be so much easier if he could just draw his Colt and tell Shaveless to drop the knife. However, the woman could easily become a shield for the criminal.

Josiah continued his seemingly distracted walk toward them. Just a few more feet and he'd be close enough to act.

"Get moving."

The knifepoint pressed against her back, forcing obedience—and the blade—into full view.

Perfect. With Shaveless's arm fully extended, the edge of his knife facing away, and his focus solely on the woman, the risk of injury was lessened.

Drawing on his years on the track and field team in university,

Josiah slid one foot forward and bent slightly at the waist. This was no hundred-yard dash, but preparation and speed would make the difference between winning or losing this battle. Every muscle tensed, ready to push him forward the moment she disappeared inside the cab. He forced steady breaths and concentrated on where the knife touched her back. She stepped onto the foot iron, and his hand edged forward despite his intent to keep an inconspicuous stance as much as possible. One more step; then he'd sprint and tackle.

Her other foot lifted, and her body pulled away from the blade.

Then she screamed.

His body shot forward without his leave, as if in response to a race gun's firing.

The horse spooked beside him.

Josiah pounded forward as the hack wobbled and the woman wavered backward toward the point. He pushed faster. Shaveless's head snapped toward him just as Josiah side-tackled him.

They thudded to the ground, but Shaveless retained a firm grasp on the knife's handle. He writhed beneath Josiah, and in a wild jab over the shoulder, nicked Josiah's cheek.

Instinctively, Josiah reeled back, saving himself from gaining an extra mouth hole but losing his grip on Shaveless in the process.

Shaveless rolled and thrust an elbow into Josiah's gut. Free of entanglement, Shaveless sprang to his feet and whirled toward Josiah, advancing with wide arcing slashes.

Josiah scrambled to gain his footing, but ducking and dodging kept him on the ground. How did he end up on the wrong side of this fight? If he didn't get to his feet soon, he'd garner enough holes to become a colander.

Robert's call for police assistance brought a wave of relief. He just needed to delay the fight long enough for help to arrive.

All at once Shaveless fell forward. The blade plunged toward Josiah, and he knocked his arm against Shaveless's arm. The knife flew from Shaveless's hand and clattered against the ground as the boy landed on top of him.

"Get off me!" Shaveless's command accompanied a kicking motion and a feminine yelp of pain.

The sound ripped a tide of righteous anger through Josiah, and he grabbed the boy's collar with one hand and landed a fist across his face with the other. Shaveless jerked sideways but returned a clobbering punch of his own. Lights flashed and ringing shrilled in Josiah's ears.

A shadow passed over his face as Shaveless reached for the knife.

Not a chance. They weren't starting that dance again. Josiah wrapped his arms around Shaveless's waist and rolled them in the opposite direction until the boy lay pinned beneath him. A fist crashed into Josiah's throat, and though it lacked deadly force, Josiah gasped for air.

Shaveless shoved Josiah aside and jumped to his feet again. He kicked Josiah's midsection. Josiah doubled over, and Shaveless followed up with another swift kick.

"Leave him alone!" The woman lunged forward like she planned to grab Shaveless's swinging leg.

With a well-balanced pivot, Shaveless redirected his kick and smashed his foot into her face. She fell back—dazed or unconscious, Josiah couldn't tell.

Police whistles pierced the air, and Shaveless dashed away before Josiah could stop him.

One police officer ran past him in pursuit of the boy, while a second stopped by Josiah. "What happened?"

"Call for an ambulance. The lady's been hurt."

The officer ran back to headquarters to do as bid while Josiah scrambled to the woman's side to check for life-threatening injuries. To his knowledge, the knife had never been close enough to harm her once the attack started, but that didn't mean she'd been without injury before his arrival. He was no doctor, but if he found blood, he knew he needed to put pressure on it until the ambulance arrived.

His ragged breath caught as he focused on her for the first time. He remembered having been gripped by her pale face and fear-stricken eyes, but now the beauty of her visage struck him as worthy of belonging in a Grecian temple. It was as if Aphrodite had taken on breath and walked off the page Robert had shown him at the Philadelphia Library.

Except this Grecian goddess looked like she'd been kicked down from Mount Olympus by a vengeful Hera. Dirt and debris imprinted Shaveless's shoe across her temple on the right side of her face. Based on her thin-pressed lips and deep furrows between her brows, she probably had one devil of a headache. Long soft curls knocked free from their confines spilled onto the ground like sheaves of wheat during harvest season.

Do your job and stop gawking. The woman could be bleeding.

He inspected the length of her, from the high neck of her worn, black wool coat, down her unfashionable but sturdy brown skirts, to the scuffed toes of her heeled buttoned boots. Thankfully, nothing indicated blood was seeping into the material, and her chest rose and fell in even—albeit shuddered—breaths. Once the ambulance arrived, he'd insist on traveling with her to the hospital to ensure she received proper treatment and an examination for a concussion.

"Miss, can you speak to me?"

Languid eyelids opened to reveal stunning copper orbs. Was there anything not breathtaking about this woman?

She blinked at him and then nearly collided heads with him as she shot up to a sitting position. "You're bleeding!"

He'd forgotten about the slice to his face, but now that she mentioned it, he noticed a dull throbbing.

She fumbled with the pockets of her coat and pulled free a lacy handkerchief. Before he could accept or reject it, she pressed the material against his cheek with as much tenderness as his middle sister, Abigail, would.

"You need a doctor. Hold this in place, and don't let up on the pressure."

Her no-nonsense tone surprised him, considering the shrill, panicked quality he'd heard only moments ago. Within seconds this woman had taken command of herself and the situation—headache or not. Josiah doubted even Theresa Cosgrove or Luella Darlington, the intrepid wives of his former Secret Service partners, could manage such a feat.

He commandeered applying the handkerchief and pulled away from the touch that zinged with unwanted attraction. "It isn't nearly as serious as you suppose."

She ignored his response and strode to the driver. "Sir, we require transportation to Pennsylvania Hospital."

Josiah followed. "I've already sent for an ambulance. We need to file a report with the police while we wait."

She sucked in a breath and stiffened. Though she attempted a relaxed countenance when she faced him, the pinched corners of her mouth and eyes gave away her anxiety. "Nonsense. Your health is of primary concern, and taking this hack will be more expedient than waiting for an ambulance."

Intuition honed over five years in the Secret Service twisted his stomach. Why did she fear going to the police? What did she know that she was afraid to share? "Perhaps, but that would greatly reduce my ability to get to know the damsel in distress I rescued."

A pretty pink blush crept across her cheeks. "I believe the fanciful intrigue of a mysterious woman is better than the reality you have before you."

"I'd like to judge that for myself." He bowed formally as if attending a ball instead of bleeding on the sidewalk. "Josiah Isaacs, at your service, Miss . . ."

Silence.

"Come now, my lady. I think it's only fair that since you know my name, I should be allowed to know yours."

"You'll forgive me if I remain silent on the matter. It isn't proper for a single woman to become acquainted with a stranger met on the street."

"Not even if he's your knight in shining armor?"

After being manipulated into making nine proposals, he knew better than to encourage any woman's fancy, especially as he had no wish to marry again. However, the same instinct that earlier told him to follow her urged him now to get her name, and charm was his best tool.

"Most knights require a kiss for their heroic acts. I only require a name."

Her eyes dropped, and that pink deepened to red. "I suppose that can be allowed." She took a deep breath and looked up with restored confidence. "I'm Gwendolyn—"

"Good heavens, Josiah! What will Abigail say when I bring you home?" Robert reached them, an officer at his side.

Gwendolyn's eyes rounded, clearly revealing that she now assumed Josiah was a claimed man. Normally he'd welcome the misunderstanding, but this time it chafed. If his charm lost its power over her, he'd be left with no recourse to find the information he sought.

"Abigail's my—"

"He got away, but I think I recognized him." The officer who'd pursued Shaveless interrupted Josiah's explanation. "You're lucky to have escaped, miss. Devil Quin's got quite the reputation at the station."

The clanging bell of the approaching ambulance prevented further conversation. Within the next minute the wagon stopped in front of them, and two men dressed in white uniforms hopped out. The doctor directed Josiah to the back of the wagon to have his gash stitched up. To his chagrin, Gwendolyn remained on the sidewalk, out of view. Though he was glad she couldn't witness him tearing up and clenching his jaw at the pain the four stitches induced, every minute apart from her strained his patience. As the doctor tied off his stitches, Robert, the other hospital attendant, and an officer rounded the back of the wagon.

"Is the lady still here?" The words pulled painfully at his stitches, and the doctor admonished Josiah for moving.

"I'm afraid not, sir," the officer said. "She refused an examination and declared she didn't want to press charges. If you ask me, she was afraid of Devil Quin finding her."

"Did you get her name at least?"

The doctor muttered under his breath about uncooperative patients.

"No, sir. She gave me the slip the first chance she got. I was hoping you knew her name."

That sealed it. Nothing weighed on him more than a woman in dire straits. He should know better than to get involved, especially since his attempts usually resulted in a coerced proposal and the need to break it, but this was different. Gwendolyn wasn't just in dire straits; she was in danger. Especially as long as Devil Quin prowled the streets.

"I'd like to be kept informed of your progress on the case." Josiah handed his business card to the officer, directing all information to be delivered to the Secret Service office. The more official the appearance of his involvement, the better.

Once they were on the streetcar home, Robert scrutinized Josiah's face. "I hope you have a story ready for that stitchwork of yours. Your mother and Abigail will faint dead away if they know the truth."

"You come up with a story. It hurts too much to talk." An ice pack and a good dose of medicine would go a long way in helping.

Robert rubbed his hands together. "What do you think of us being pirated away on the Delaware River and having fought our way free? I, of course, escaped unscathed due to my exceptional skills with a sword, but you received a nick due to your *almost* exceptional skills."

Josiah shook his head and allowed Robert to spin wilder and wilder tales. Eventually, Abigail would root out the truth, just as Josiah had every intention of rooting out the truth about the mysterious Gwendolyn. It shouldn't be too hard to find her. After all, how many Gwendolyns could there be in Philadelphia?

CHAPTER 3

THE PUNGENT SMELL OF MOLDING earth and stagnant water churned in the air as the girls under Gwendolyn's care splashed through mud puddles during their game of tag. Their pealing laughter stabbed at her headache like Quincy's knife, and she winced, praying none of the girls would notice. At least yesterday's escapade hadn't resulted in a boot-shaped bruise on her face.

Living full-time at Final Chance with the two other female officers hired to oversee the girls' ward made hiding secrets challenging in the best of circumstances. A bruise would've been especially difficult to explain away. It was bad enough that Gwendolyn's hours-early return from her half day off garnered an interrogation from her dearest friend, Officer Wilhelmina Grace. As much as Gwendolyn wanted to confide in Wilhelmina, yesterday proved how hazardous it was knowing too much, even if that knowledge was nothing more than vague suspicion. If only Mr. Farwell would contact her and provide some insight into what problem they faced. Then she might be able to fully protect those consigned to her care.

Her eyes bounced to each of the twenty-six faces that, for the moment, reflected the unrestrained joy of a carefree childhood. All too soon she'd have to end the charade and require all to don the undeserved shackles of their sentencing and return inside. It wasn't fair the courts deemed them criminals. They were victims of parental negligence and outright abandonment, not perpetrators of heinous

24

crimes. Petty theft. Vagrancy. All of it pointed to survival, not moral degradation.

Gwendolyn dodged a near collision with one of the girls and thudded against the tall wooden fence separating the girls from the boys. Another injustice and a curtain to the truth. The girls might be safe under her watch, but what sufferings did the boys endure on the other side?

"Matron Ellison!" Eight-year-old Lottie sang the name as she ran toward Gwendolyn from the furthest corner. "Tessa and Cara are crying." Lottie pointed to the base of the only tree in the small yard.

Twelve-year-old Tessa Murphy cradled her three-year-old sister on her lap as she peered through a rotted-out knot in the fence. Her mouth moved in shapes that suggested her brother was likely huddled on the other side. Pity for her newest Irish wards twisted Gwendolyn's heart worse than the gnarled tree they sat under. If only she could allow them to continue the forbidden communication—but to do so might bring the wrath of Superintendent King down on all their heads.

"Thank you, Lottie. I'll tend to them."

Lottie returned to her game of tag, and Gwendolyn lifted up a prayer for the new arrivals. The first day was always the hardest.

Foreign words rolled off the dark-haired Tessa's tongue with a lyrical beauty Gwendolyn wished she could understand, but the soothing murmurs of comfort needed no translation. Tessa mothered her huddled and hurting siblings with such strength and confidence that it must be a role she was familiar with filling.

The fence should be torn down and the siblings allowed to interact, not forced to endure the pain of separation during such a difficult time. But she was merely a matron, subordinate to a harsh man who hadn't a needle point's worth of concern for the children's emotional well-being. What caring Gwendolyn provided to these children had to fall within Final Chance's strict guidelines.

"Jude, I suggest you run along to play ball with the other boys before Officer Bagwell finds you breaking the rules."

There was another exchange of foreign words and then the sound of feet padding away. Cara wailed and lunged for the fence.

Gwendolyn crouched to eye level with the girl and brushed a tendril of Cara's dark, chin-length hair from her face. "It's all right, sweet one. You'll see him again."

Cara jerked away and buried herself in the protective arms of her big sister. Over Cara's head, Tessa threw daggers with her piercing blue eyes as if Gwendolyn were the reason their family's world fell apart. But Gwendolyn knew where the real blame lay.

Not that she could convince a daddy's girl that her father was the cause of her family's misery. However, time would teach her, just as it had taught Gwendolyn. A father's abandonment left wounds that never seemed to heal. Now the three siblings would suffer the same wounds because of Mr. Murphy's negligence. Wounds that Gwendolyn would try her best to bind up with hope, faith, education, and the fortitude essential for life in a world rife with struggles and disappointments.

"Come, dears. Let's wash your faces and then have a little chat in my office. I think it is time we become better acquainted. I want to hear about your family and life before you came here." She extended a hand toward Tessa.

Tessa's narrow chin lifted, drawing her whole body taut with challenge.

So, she was to be one of those.

Gwendolyn stifled the smile threatening to break. It wasn't that she relished the challenge of overcoming stubborn defiance but more that she looked forward to its reward. Of all the girls to pass through Final Chance, it was always the most challenging ones who claimed a special place in her heart and stayed in touch long after they'd left.

"I understand that you view me as the enemy, Miss Murphy, but I promise you, I only want what is best for you and your siblings. However, I don't know what is best until I learn more about your family."

"Best is with our *dadaí*. We don't belong here."

"You're right. You don't belong here."

Tessa blinked, obviously not expecting that response.

"Right now, you and Miss Cara belong in my office with a plate of cookies and warm glasses of milk. I'll not accept no for an answer. You can make this a battle of wills and lose out on the cookies, or you can go willingly and at least get a sweet treat out of the deal."

Tessa's brows dove into a sharp V. "I hate you."

"Well, I already love you and your siblings, which means I'm willing to be hard when it's in your best interest. Now you can either accept my assistance or get up on your own, but you only have until the count of three." Gwendolyn extended her hand again and waited. When Tessa didn't immediately take it, she counted. "One. Two. Three—"

Tessa huffed, shifted Cara into a better position, and stood on her own.

"Thank you." Gwendolyn dropped her hand.

The look Tessa delivered before marching past could melt stone.

Oh, Tessa. Just you wait. Friendship is about to bloom.

Gwendolyn clapped her hands to signal to the others their exercise time was over. The girls formed two lines—the younger Division A girls on the left and the older Division B girls on the right—with Tessa and Cara obstinately clinging together between them. Division B led the way into the green-wallpapered hall between the guest parlor and the classrooms and hung their coats on the waiting hooks. Officer Agatha Wood met them at the base of the stairs and collected the older girls for an afternoon of academic exercises. Though she greeted each girl with a happy smile and encouraging word, she could be a fierce taskmaster.

Behind Agatha, Wilhelmina awaited her turn to claim her wards, motherly pride glowing from her sepia eyes. Wilhelmina didn't have as genteel a face as Agatha, but her heart for the children made her the most beautiful person Gwendolyn knew. No one could resist her for long, and their friendship-turned-sisterhood was one of the dearest relationships Gwendolyn had. It was a wonder some young man hadn't come through and relieved Wilhelmina of her widowhood.

When Wilhelmina joined Gwendolyn, her smile fell into a severe line. "Superintendent King requires your immediate presence in his office, Matron Ellison."

A nervous shiver traveled down Gwendolyn's spine. Such formality between them was reserved for the presence of guests or as a secret warning. Since guests had to make an appointment days in advance and were escorted by either Gwendolyn or Superintendent King, the reason must be the latter.

"Thank you."

Wilhelmina squeezed Gwendolyn's arm before taking her charges into their assigned classroom. A physical touch too? Whatever the reason Superintendent King wanted to see her, it had to be bad.

First things first. The Murphy girls needed to be settled. She gestured toward the kitchen. "This way, please."

Tessa struggled down the long hall, constantly stopping to bounce Cara into a higher position on her hip before continuing. Gwendolyn allowed the girl her pride without comment, though she longed to ease her burden.

The scent of baking bread swirled around them like a comforting blanket as they entered the kitchen. Mrs. Flowers stretched on tiptoes over the worktable to retrieve a large pot from the ceiling hook.

It must be another soup night. The fourth this week, which meant supplies were dwindling. Gwendolyn bit her lip. She'd promised cookies, but were cookies even available? After a glance around, she spied a towel-covered plate with two empty glasses waiting on a tray near the other door. Good. They were set for now. And if need be, she'd dip into her personal funds to ensure this small pleasure remained possible at a moment's notice for new arrivals.

"Mrs. Flowers, would you allow the Murphy girls to assist you until I return? Superintendent King has summoned me."

The rotund woman of sixty-odd years made a sign of the cross, leaving behind a streak of flour on her forehead, chest, and shoulders. "Lord have mercy on your soul. I'll say a prayer, I will."

"No need to be so dramatic, Mrs. Flowers. I wouldn't want to give these girls the wrong impression of him."

Her white brows shot to her equally white hair before softening with understanding. Superintendent King's harsh rules and manners might be better suited for criminals awaiting execution than children, but it was better if the girls believed a gentle man presided over the boys' ward.

"My apologies, ma'am. We'll be right as rain here in the kitchen until you get back. Won't we, girls?"

A shy Cara peeked out from behind her older sister, and Tessa gave a doubtful grimace.

They'd be fine. Like everyone else hired at Final Chance, Mrs. Flowers had exceptional skills in dealing with children of an obstinate nature. Now if only Gwendolyn could master the skill of managing Superintendent King.

She exited the kitchen, traipsed into the expansive dining room, and ascended the stairs to the hallway between her and Superintendent King's offices. Outside his closed door, she brushed off a few pieces of grass from her skirts and tucked loose hairs that the breeze had freed back into her bun.

You can do this. You are his equal, no matter what the man thinks.

With a deep breath, stiff spine, and raised chin, she knocked.

"Enter."

Superintendent King stood behind his wide oak desk, hands behind his back and thick brows knitted together beneath his slicked black hair. One might call him handsome, if it weren't for his storm-cloud personality. A less congenial man she'd never met.

His coal eyes met hers. "Shut the door, Miss Ellison."

He refused to use her title except in front of the board, uniformly rejecting anything that might signify them as equals. But Christ called her to turn the other cheek. That meant not raising a fit over it, and showing Superintendent King the respect he didn't deserve. "What can I do for you?"

"Sit. Reverend Ballantine has brought news of a disagreeable nature."

To her left, Uncle Percy rose from a chair, formally dressed in his suit reserved for somber pastoral duties, hat in hand, and regret etched deep into the lines around his mouth and eyes.

No. He shouldn't be here. Not unless something had happened to . . .

A band formed around her chest and tightened until she couldn't breathe, couldn't even squeeze out the remainder of the thought. She glanced at Superintendent King, who regarded her with scorn. He probably expected her to faint.

She clasped her hands tight in front of her. *Show no weakness.*

With a deep breath, she prepared herself for the worst. "Has something happened to Mother or Aunt Birdie?"

A sympathetic smile touched Uncle Percy's lips but quickly fell away. "No, my dear. They are well. The news concerns Mr. Farwell."

Praise the Lord, Mother and Aunt Birdie weren't the reason for his visit, but what had Uncle Percy to do with Mr. Farwell? Her gaze dipped once again to his funeral attire. The breath choked out of her and then returned in quick sips that made her dizzy.

"Sit down, Miss Ellison. Only a man would be expected to meet such news on his feet."

Defiance warred with the trembling starting in her legs. Thankfully, Uncle Percy took the choice out of her hands by wrapping his arm around her shoulders and guiding her to the chair he'd vacated.

Kneeling on one knee, he encased her hands in his. "Mr. Farwell died this morning from injuries sustained during a robbery yesterday."

The words struck with the force of Quincy's boot. This couldn't be what Quincy meant. Surely not murder. Mr. Farwell had to be alive. Hurt, maybe. But alive. "No. You're wrong. It can't be true."

Uncle Percy's hand tightened around hers as if it might shield her from the next blow. "I'm so sorry, my dear. The family called me in to pray over him and stay with them until his last breath. He passed a few hours ago."

The information sliced at her, leaving her courage to bleed out onto the floor and her body to slump against the chair. What had Mr. Farwell discovered that was worthy of murder? What did his killers think she knew? Her eyes strayed to Superintendent King. Was he surprised and distressed by Mr. Farwell's death? Or was he among the people who wished them dead?

His dark countenance gave nothing away.

"I want you to know he cared deeply for you and had asked for permission to propose."

A proposal? But she'd only recently dared call him a friend. Thoughts of marital affections had yet to even be conceived. Was it merely a ruse to cover up their frequent meeting?

"When you didn't arrive for supper last night, we assumed you were with him."

A cold chill froze her veins from head to toe. Uncle Percy's statement had been innocent, but the insinuation jeopardized her job at the least and her life at the most.

Superintendent King huffed. "Don't look so terrified, Miss Ellison. Your job is safe. The entire board knew of his pursuit and turned a blind eye in hopes you'd exchange the title 'matron' for 'Mrs. Farwell.' What you should be concerned about is that the robbery occurred during broad daylight between here and Sansom."

So close? Had it been a crime of opportunity when they saw him deliver the flowers? Or had they planned it, and the location, to send a warning that she wasn't safe anywhere?

"I'm establishing a new policy," he continued. "No one is to leave Final Chance alone. You'll have to conduct your weekly half days off here or be escorted by a gentleman. Although I can't imagine who. I cannot spare an officer for your use."

In other words, he sought to constrain her movements.

"I'll escort you each Wednesday. Have no fear." Uncle Percy patted her hand.

"Good." Superintendent King gave a curt nod. "I'll leave you to comfort Miss Ellison while I inform the rest of the staff. Good day, Reverend." In a rare show of gentlemanly behavior, he gave a slight bow toward her. "My condolences on the loss of your future plans. Take as long as you need before returning to your duties." He strode out of the office and shut the door behind him.

She faced Uncle Percy, seeking the strength and wisdom he always provided. Should she confess to him all that had transpired over the last twenty-four hours? Show him the note locked inside her desk

31

drawer? Mr. Farwell had been murdered for his knowledge. Could she risk the only father figure who'd stayed in her life? Before she could further talk herself out of it, she rose.

"Would you come with me to my office?"

"Of course. Whatever you need."

When they reached her office, the door was standing wide open. Dread threaded its way through her limbs. Only she and Wilhelmina had a key to her office, as it connected directly with her bedroom. She entered, half expecting to see it ransacked. Instead, the only item that was out of place was the tipped-over vase containing roses and baby's breath that Mr. Farwell had had delivered with the note. Water spread across the surface of her desk, soaking into her paperwork and dripping over the edges onto the wooden floor.

"Oh no!"

Though it was likely too late to save the documents, she snatched a dress from the rag pile she'd been sorting earlier and rushed to her desk. Uncle Percy followed suit and attended the puddle on the floor.

Had someone broken in? Or had Wilhelmina simply forgotten to close the door? The flowers lay piled on their side inside the vase as if it had simply tipped over. But it didn't make sense. The bouquet had been perfectly balanced earlier. She righted the vase and flowers.

And there it was, previously hidden beneath the mess. Undeniable evidence someone had broken into her office.

A single mutilated rose lay atop a facedown picture frame, snapped into three separate pieces with its petals shredded and scattered around. The intruder had speared a soppy note to the wooden picture stand with a thorn. Ink bled across the paper's surface in ominous warning.

Tell no one. Ask no questions.

She wadded the note, fearful Uncle Percy might see, and lifted what should have been a family portrait. Instead, a large crack in the glass had allowed water to seep in and destroy the image, making the threat complete. The world swayed, and she fumbled for the chair behind her as her legs gave out.

"Gwendolyn!" Uncle Percy reached her just as she missed and hit the floor. "Good heavens, are you all right?"

She peered into the concerned hazel eyes of her mother's brother. The only man who'd proven good men did exist. When Father abandoned them, her uncle had taken them in, funded her private education, and then secured her position here when she'd graduated. He, Aunt Birdie, and Mother were all the family she had left.

But she couldn't abandon the children of Final Chance, either. Unlike her father, she wouldn't give up just because circumstances were difficult. But what could she do? Who could she turn to? She couldn't further risk her family's lives by sharing the threat.

Make haste to help me, O Lord.

Chapter 4

"I found her." Pinkerton Ignazio Morelli's voice on the other end of the telephone line came through distant and fuzzy.

Finally. Josiah blew out a breath and stretched for the notepad on his desk. He tucked the earpiece awkwardly between his head and shoulder and used the small table he'd placed beneath the wall-mounted telephone to write his notes. Bless Mother's overreach. Despite her installing the telephone against his wishes while he was out of town, he now welcomed the privacy it provided. Granted, listening ears could still partake, but no one he'd have to deal with at the close of the conversation. Unlike at the Secret Service office.

He leaned in toward the mouthpiece, thankful to have a discreet Pinkerton friend willing to take on special projects for him. "Go ahead. I'm ready."

"She is Gwendolyn Ellison, and she is matron of Final Chance House of Refuge, off Twenty-First and Spruce. For you, I did a little extra digging. She is thirty, has a good reputation, and *libera*. A good match for you, no?"

Josiah didn't have to sit across from Ignazio to see the waggle of his brows or the knowing smirk that accompanied his words.

"I'm only interested in tracking down a reluctant witness."

"*Vedo.* Just like the other nine girls you saved from trouble. They held no interest for you."

"I can't help that my rescuing them made them think I was in love

34

with them. Nor could I help that they devised ways to ensure I had to propose in order to protect their reputations."

"You could *not* rescue them."

"I can no more ignore a woman in trouble than you can a cannoli at the Italian market."

"Ehh. Possible, but not probable." Ignazio's shoulder shrug and turn of the hand were so common when he spoke that Josiah didn't even have to see it to know it occurred. "So no personal interest that she has one half day leave every Wednesday from noon to ten?"

"No personal interest whatsoever." Professional might be a different story if he needed to convince her to press charges against Quincy "Devil Quin" Slocum. "Thank you, Morelli. I'll follow up from here."

Ignazio's easy laugh rumbled across the lines. "I know you will. As always, I'm happy to help you find your next *fidanzata*."

"I'm not looking"—the line clicked—"for a fiancée." Josiah pinched the bridge of his nose.

His skin might be as thick as a rhino's, but that didn't mean the endless jokes were welcomed. Didn't anyone understand what it cost him to propose to these women? He wasn't interested in marriage. He just wanted to protect the women in his path who hadn't a brother, father, or husband to step in when they needed help. With the exception of his marriage to Shauna, every proposal had occurred because those same damsels in distress had turned into conniving fortune hunters and trapped him. Maneuvering each of them into breaking the engagements had taken considerable ingenuity. A man's reputation could suffer without much consequence to his daily life. A woman's ruined reputation could be a sentence worse than death.

The telephone line reverted to the operator. "Is there anything else you need, sir?"

"No, ma'am. Have a good afternoon." He hung the receiver on the hook and studied his hastily scribbled notes.

It had taken four days and owing Ignazio another favor, but victory was his. Gwendolyn Ellison was a mystery woman no more. Now what to do with the information? She refused to press charges, but in truth, the courts didn't need her testimony to convict Devil Quin, not with Josiah's preventing the kidnapping and gaining a wound in the process. His word would stand well enough. Still, the familiar zing of warning turned into coiled knots each time he thought of her, and it unsettled him. The sensation was too close to the days leading up to the telegram announcing the train accident that stole his wife from him.

On the wall, the illustrated Wanamaker calendar mocked him. April fifteenth and twenty-fourth loomed large like two knock-out punches. First the anniversary of Shauna's death, and then the wedding anniversary they never celebrated. Combined, the dates left him reeling through a darkness that he couldn't shake. Ten years later he stood between the two dates, having survived the first with a slice to the face and wondering how to endure the next.

Perhaps the impending anniversary was the true reason behind the warning zings. Ignazio had to have set eyes on Miss Ellison before giving his report and would've mentioned if she appeared injured or in danger. His mind was simply groping for anything to focus on instead of the renewal of grief so strong it drove him to the brink of insanity. Distraction was the only way to deal with the emotional turmoil this week brought.

Although—he skimmed his thumb over the serrated flesh on his cheek—the forced jaunt with Robert on Wednesday had provided more of a reprieve than his usual strategy of burying himself in counterfeiting cases. His mind circled back to Miss Ellison. Had the incident been random? Or had she been targeted specifically? He'd never forgive himself if he dismissed a true warning and the woman suffered for it.

Josiah puffed out a breath, reached for the small cedar box he kept on the corner of his desk, and opened the hinged lid. Affixed to the inside, the wedding photo of his spirited Irish beauty joined him in defying convention to smile back at the camera in their wedding clothes. He enclosed Shauna's small gold band with his hand and brought it to his lips. If only it could be her warm, soft skin his lips touched and not the cold, stiff metal she'd left behind.

"What would you have me do, Shauna? Am I just missing you? Or is Miss Ellison truly in need of help?"

He could almost hear her laugh and see the wag of her auburn head. "Worry's a long road that has no turning. If you're so afeared, get yourself up and go see her. It'll chew on you until you're nothing but cow's cud."

She'd probably even pull him from his chair and push him toward the door. He smiled despite the ache in his heart—and in his cheek. Though he'd had the reputation of being a charmer long before they met, she'd never held it against him. She knew his heart beat only for her, and like she did before her death, she would understand his concern now only stemmed from a passion to protect those unprotected.

Mind made up, he rose from his chair. He'd visit Final Chance House of Refuge to ease his mind about Miss Ellison's safety, surprise Shauna's brother Conor with a visit, and then check in with District Chief Hayden Orton about whether progress had been made on their several cases.

Little feet pattered outside his office, and he paused next to his chair. The door flew open, and a petite, blonde, curly-headed girl in a bright yellow pinafore led the way in, followed by a nearly identical sister and a toddling dark-haired miniature of their mother.

"Uncle Joe!" Rose sprinted across the room, circled his desk, and jumped into his arms before he had the chance to set the ring back in its place. "We came to sup—sup—" Her face scrunched up as she tried to form the word. "—Surprise you!" A wide grin broke across her face at her success.

Josiah tweaked her nose as he sat back down and then shifted her so that her twin sister, Lily, could climb up on his other leg.

Violet toddled to his feet and reached toward him. "Up."

Careful not to knock the other two off, he set the ring on the desk and lifted Violet to snuggle against his chest. "What a wonderful surprise! How are my favorite flowers today?"

"Mommy bought us new ribbons! See?" Rose turned her head and shook it so the red ribbon bounced.

Lily, ever the quieter one, dipped her head to show off a white version in her hair.

"Violet got purple, but she pulled it out already. I told Mommy she was too little, but—"

"Mind your manners, Rose." Abigail stood in his doorway, hand resting on her extended abdomen. After giving her daughter a pointed look, she dazzled Josiah with a full-toothed smile. "How's my little brother? Vanquished any pirates today?"

Violet accidentally bumped against his tender stitches, and he winced. "Not yet, but the day's still young." He stretched around the girls to press the bell that would alert his housekeeper, Tillie, to bring coffee, although the woman probably already had a cart full of treats for the girls on the way. "You look radiant, Abigail. I'd rise to greet you, but I wouldn't dare risk bruising a single one of these beautiful flowers."

With a quick kiss to each of their heads, he squeezed the girls a bit tighter than usual. Would he love them any more were they Shauna's and his children? It was hard to imagine such a possibility, but surely the love a father felt for his own children was unsurpassable. The knife of lost dreams twisted in the festering wound Josiah feared would never heal.

Abigail picked up the open cedar box and offered a sympathetic smile as she studied the picture. "Having a hard day?"

"It'll be ten years on Friday."

She nodded silently as she brushed the faces in the photograph.

Of all his family members, Abigail was the only one who didn't pretend Shauna never existed. Father had seen his marriage to a poor Irish immigrant as a political disaster and staunchly refused to acknowledge the union. Mother had waffled between supporting her husband and supporting Josiah, but as the tension between father and son grew, she'd withdrawn and refused to take sides. Her lack of defense felt like a betrayal, but Shauna had repeatedly told him to offer grace. Esther Isaacs was stuck choosing between being a God-honoring wife and a God-honoring mother.

Josiah blew out a breath and tried to shake the melancholy. "So what really brings you by? Have you come to chide me about not attending church this morning?"

"I never chide. If you feel any guilt, that is the Holy Spirit at work, and I find that ignoring Him too long has undesirable consequences."

"Are you trying to threaten me into attending?"

"Of course not. My threats come in the form of introducing you to my single friends, few as they are becoming."

"Har, har, har, Abigail. Very funny." It wasn't that he hated church, just that he felt like a fraud each time he walked through those doors. Faith had no room for doubt, yet his doubts about the goodness of God strangled him every time he joined the family in the pews. It was easier to pretend those doubts didn't exist when outside those stone walls. "Have you finally decided on a name for the wee one?"

"What's a wee one?" Rose's nose scrunched.

"A little one, a baby." He hadn't meant to use Shauna's words, but it happened without thinking on these harder days.

Lily's soft voice cut in before Rose spoke. "Mommy's gonna have a baby, and I get to hold it."

Tillie entered the room with a cart of lemonade and plenty of treats. Immediately distracted from the conversation, the girls scrambled from his lap and raced to the goodies. They reached Tillie before she was able to arrange the delicacies on the low table he kept in the corner of the room for their visits.

After standing and thanking Tillie, Josiah placed Shauna's ring back inside the box. "So, what will you name this one? Zinnia? Petunia? Azalea?"

Abigail's laugh tinkled as she swatted at him. "I'll have you know Robert's praying for a boy, and it will be a very practical name, like Adam or Joshua."

"Are you sure Dogwood or Cedar wouldn't be more appropriate, given the bouquet you already have?"

She chuckled and shook her head as she watched the three girls vie over an assortment of leftover confections. After a moment, she heaved a sigh and turned to him. "I wish today's visit was to announce a name, but I come bearing ill news." She gestured for him to sit back down.

Though his stomach roiled at the thought of something being wrong, he urged her to take the chair instead. "You know very well I can't sit when a lady is in want of a seat." After she settled, he crossed his arms and stared at her. Nothing about her demeanor indicated anything unusual with her health. If anything, she glowed like she did with every pregnancy. But just to be sure—"Are you and the baby well?"

She waved the concern away. "Yes, yes. Of course. It's Conor. Have you spoken to him recently?"

Josiah frowned. "A couple of weeks ago. I was just about to pay him a visit."

"Good. He needs you." Anguish twisted her mouth as she clasped his hands and squeezed. "The children were arrested for vagrancy two Fridays ago and sent to a house of refuge."

All the starch went out from his legs, and he thudded against the desk. Why had no one told him? They were his nieces and nephew. Conor, his last connection to Shauna. The man must be devastated. How could anyone arrest three-, ten-, and twelve-year-olds for vagrancy when they had a home? A father who loved and cared for them? It wasn't the same standard of living Josiah was accustomed to, but Conor flatly refused any help. The Murphy family had always been a prideful lot, Shauna being no exception.

"I'm sorry, Josiah. Mother just told me an hour ago."

Heat charged through his veins where only moments ago a chill had taken hold. "And how long has she known?"

"A few days after the arrest, but don't be angry with her. She needed time to convince Final Chance's board to accept them. They've never admitted a child as young as Cara before. Then she had to use her pull with the magistrate to transfer the children from Philadelphia House of Refuge to Final Chance. She didn't want to raise your hopes until she was certain it could be done."

"She should've used her influence to have the children returned to Conor."

"Josiah! You know it's not as simple as that. If you'd stop to see past your bitterness, you'd know what she did was a mercy. Final Chance is a small house of refuge, but they've had no complaints or investigations into the treatment of the children. Mother will be able to look weekly into their care. In fact, one of the board members recently passed, and she hopes you'll consider taking his position. It would allow you to personally ensure the children's well-being."

So despite sharing weekly lunches with him and being perfectly capable of telling him herself, Mother had sent Abigail to coerce him. He loved Mother dearly, but he would not be manipulated. "I'm a Secret Service operative. I don't have time to be on the board of one of Mother's pet projects."

"Not even when that pet project is responsible for what's left of Shauna's family?"

A low growl rumbled in the back of his throat before he could stop it. "That was cruel, Abigail."

"Perhaps, but it's true." After a moment of silent reprimand, her face softened into compassion. "I know you're hurting. The anniversary week of Shauna's death always turns you into a surly shadow of yourself, but Conor and the children need you. You've always been their champion. Mother's done what she can, but you and Father are the only ones in the family who can charm the world into believing your ideas are theirs."

Harrumph. Abigail was just as capable of charming a person into compliance as he or Father. But even without her prompting he'd never have been able to sit idle while his nieces and nephew remained separated from their father. Conor's situation would require Josiah to shove aside his grief and take action.

"I can't join a charity board. My job with the Secret Service won't allow the time for it." When Abigail opened her mouth to continue arguing, Josiah lifted his hand to stop her. "But I'll go talk to Conor and uncover what happened. Depending on who is involved, I might be able to use some of my own connections to sway the magistrate's ruling. Whatever it takes, you can rest assured that I will not stop until Conor and the children are reunited."

Abigail beamed at him like he'd slain a dragon. "I knew you'd help." Her gaze shifted to the girls, now lined up on the settee with treats in hand and crumbs on lap. "I just can't imagine them being taken from me and placed into such a cold, unloving institution."

"Thank you for coming to me." He brushed a rogue tear from her cheek. "You'll forgive me for not staying longer?"

She smiled beneath his touch. "Go save them, Josiah. They need you."

He kissed each of the girls on the way out of the office and grabbed his coat from the hall tree. It appeared he had more than one reason to visit Final Chance, and he wouldn't delay a moment longer.

CHAPTER 5

LORD, HAVE MERCY ON OUR souls.

Gwendolyn rubbed her temples as Cara screamed at the top of her lungs, her Irish accent too thick to make deciphering her words possible as they ricocheted off the office walls. Moody and defiant teenagers Gwendolyn could contend with, but this poor, wretched tot? What was she to do with her? How was she to comfort her? Cara was getting worse through the adjustment period, not better. Six times this morning alone, Wilhelmina had to step away from her duties to remove the hysterical girl before she upset the others.

"I'm at a loss as to what to do." Wilhelmina bounced the girl on her hip, face as flushed and hair as frazzled as her ward's. "She won't eat. She cries until she falls asleep, and she's wet the bed every time I've laid her down. We've gone through eight sheet sets in four days."

There was nothing for it. Whatever else she'd hoped to accomplish today would have to be set aside. "Leave her with me."

Gwendolyn reached for Cara, but the child pulled away and screamed louder.

So much for being considered gifted with children. If anyone who'd ever thought as much saw her now, they'd question her position as matron entirely. Gwendolyn bit her lips together and eyed the way Cara molded against Wilhelmina as if they were one. Sliding her arm between the two, she pried Cara away and shifted the girl into her arms. The screams funneled directly into her ears and made them ring.

"If Cara hasn't settled by supper, I'll send for Tessa." Superintendent King wouldn't approve of the tactic, but some rules were meant to be broken.

Wilhelmina nodded with evident relief before she escaped out of the room and firmly shut the door on Cara's wails. Lucky woman.

"Well, Cara. It's just you and I today. How about a story?"

Her cries didn't pause for even a breath.

That was just as well. A girl her age wasn't likely to be interested by Elizabeth Gaskell, Jane Austen, or the Brontë sisters. Although there might be a copy of Grimm's or Hans Christian Andersen's fairy tales in the schoolroom. She'd have to remember to check when the other girls went outside to play. For now, something else would have to suffice.

She scanned the room in a desperate search for something, anything, to quiet Cara. The desk covered in carefully organized paperwork contained nothing of use, and neither would her medical cabinet. Two piles of donated clothes lay on her floor—the rag-bin worthy and the possibly repairable. People who thought donating their trash was a noble thing should be forced to live off such dismal provisions. Then they'd change their tune, and maybe the quality of their donations. At least she could always count on the Philadelphia Quilter's Society to send wonderful blankets and occasionally rag dolls. And their latest delivery still sat unopened on a chair in the corner.

Awkwardly, Gwendolyn wrested the box open with one hand. Victory! She grabbed the topmost doll and held it up for Cara's inspection.

Cara snatched it from her hand and then flung it at the floor. Her wails crescendoed. "*Bábóg!*"

Drawn out like it was, the word almost sounded as if she cried for a bottle. Did children her age even drink from one? Not in Gwendolyn's limited experience, but it couldn't hurt to try. Mrs. Flowers had a bottle in the kitchen from when they'd nursed half a dozen abandoned kittens to health. The trick would be traveling downstairs without disturbing Superintendent King. The man was already in a raging tempest after their emergency meeting with Treasurer Wells in which they were told to increase the children's manufacture of products or tighten the already emaciated budget.

Gwendolyn pressed Cara's face against her shoulder, trying to muffle the cries as she peeked into the hall. Empty, and his door appeared closed. Good. Maybe that meant he was busy with the boys on the other side of the building. With as long and fast a stride as she could manage, she carried Cara toward the stairs.

Before she'd made it to the top step, Superintendent King stomped into the hall. "Can't you quiet her?"

"That's what I'm attempting."

"If you don't learn to care for that child properly before Tuesday's board meeting, I'm going to demand she be transferred elsewhere. She's disrupting everything."

It was God's mercy she held Cara. Otherwise, she might've taken up boxing gloves and knocked some sense into the man. How would he feel if he were in these children's position? The Murphy family had been ripped asunder, forbidden to speak to each other, and now he wanted to ensure they'd never be reunited?

"She's just having trouble adjusting. I'll have Cara settled shortly." *Lord, let it be so.*

"See that you do." He stormed into his office.

The door slam echoed down the hall and briefly stopped Cara's crying.

"That man is an evil leprechaun."

Granted, he neither wore green nor had red hair. And he was tall, not short. All right, so *leprechaun* didn't fit the man at all, but she doubted Cara would understand a reference to a basilisk.

Cara started crying *bábóg* again as Gwendolyn resumed her trek to the kitchen. Sweltering stove heat and the sharp scent of yeast working through dough greeted them as they entered the long, narrow room. Mrs. Flowers looked up from her position over one of the several pots bubbling on the stove. Watered-down soup. Again.

Gwendolyn's lips pinched. One problem at a time. "Would you put some water in one of those bottles we fed the kittens with?" Superintendent King insisted milk was too expensive and needed to be reserved for the Ladies' Committee's visit.

Though Mrs. Flowers arched a brow, she complied. All the while, Cara continued her vocal demands. When they offered her the bottle, she took it, considered it, and then chucked it at the floor. Glass shattered around their feet and water splattered onto Gwendolyn's dress. Enough was enough.

She thunked Cara onto the center of the empty worktable and then stood back with her hands on her hips. The sudden movement startled the girl into silence. "Cara, you cannot break things because you are mad. You will sit here in silence until I've cleaned up this mess."

"Bábóg!" Then she started to cry again.

Heaven help her. Gwendolyn had never met a more singularly focused person in her life.

"I'll clean it up." Mrs. Flowers dropped a towel over the mess and gave a sympathetic nod toward the girl. "Those little ones just don't know any other way to express their hurts. She needs to be held and comforted."

Isn't that what Gwendolyn had been doing? "And what do you propose would comfort her?"

"Act like she's your child and not someone else's burden thrust upon you."

Guilt twinged her conscience as she regarded the snot-nosed, red-faced child. Cara wasn't a burden; she was just a scared, lonely girl who needed someone to hold her while she cried out all her emotions. That's what Mother had done night after night for months when Gwendolyn finally realized Father was never coming back. No words. Just strong arms wrapped around her, rocking her while crooning, "I know." Cara needed understanding and patience, not someone commanding her to be quiet. Pulling a stool out with her foot, Gwendolyn scooped Cara into her arms and rocked her with low murmurs.

Jane, the oldest female inmate, entered the kitchen. "Matron Ellison, there's a gentleman in the receiving room who wishes to speak with you."

Probably another curiosity seeker. Why people thought it a form of entertainment to visit houses of refuge, asylums, and even prisons was beyond her. These were broken, hurting people. Not animals in a zoo. Cara sniffed against Gwendolyn's chest. Pushing the visitor off on Superintendent King when he was in a foul temper would do the reputation of the institution no favors, but she was finally making progress with Cara.

"Did he give his name?"

"Yes, ma'am, a Mr. Josiah Isaacs."

Cara started wailing again. Good heavens. She squeezed Cara tighter and rocked faster.

What was she to do? He wasn't supposed to have found her, even if a small part of her thrilled at the knowledge he had. Her fantasies— about a daring knight, a whirlwind romance, and the achievement of everything she'd long accepted as forfeited—were just that. Fantasies. Reality was the rule of life, and his appearance posed a very real threat. No one in Final Chance could know about her outing or the misfortune that almost befell her.

Jane raised her voice to be heard over Cara. "I told him he had to make an appointment, but he insisted he would see you now and that you'd wish to see him as well. I didn't know what else to do but come to you."

"You did right, Miss Jane. Please prepare a tray with coffee." She'd need something more bracing than tea to face what awaited her. "Here, Mrs. Flowers. Can you please take Cara?"

Cara's grip around Gwendolyn's neck tightened, the girl's words changing to "I go" on repeat.

Gwendolyn pried one of the arms just loose enough to breathe. Maybe taking Cara would make for an easy excuse to shorten the meeting and send Mr. Isaacs on his way. "Only if you stop crying."

Though the tears continued, her screams dropped into shuddering breaths.

Thank thee, Jesus.

Mrs. Flowers repaired Gwendolyn's appearance as best she could around the clinging Cara before Gwendolyn walked to the receiving room door at the front of the building. This room was a child's first impression of his or her new home, and her favorite. She'd fought with the board for the funds to redecorate it, disguising the request as a way to impress and influence potential investors and visitors. In truth, she wanted the children to feel warm and welcomed no matter the circumstances that brought them here.

Lord, mayest Mr. Isaacs be so impressed that he forgeteth to ask anything at all.

Unlikely, but He was the God of miracles. She took a deep breath and opened the door.

Though cloudy outside, natural light from the front window reflected off the golden yellow walls above the deep green painted paneling and brightened the space with a cheery glow. Gwendolyn forced a matching cheery smile and searched each seat of the well-worn parlor furniture for Mr. Issacs. The long settee that had supported countless huddled siblings remained empty save the pillow used to hide the threadbare spot near the armrest. The two armchairs, as well as the three parlor chairs—all draped with blankets over their backs to hide either stains or other areas of thinning material—stood empty. Her smile slipped. Where was he? She widened her search to each corner of the room.

As she turned to her right, Cara lunged from her arms, crying out, "Uncle!"

At least, that's what it sounded like. Gwendolyn was too busy scrambling to maintain her hold on the child to be certain.

Cool hands grazed hers as Cara dipped toward the floor and then swooped upward.

Gwendolyn straightened to avoid being kicked, and her gaze collided with eyes the color of tortoise shells. Her breath caught, and heat suffused throughout her body as the full face of her rescuer came into view. This was the man who'd risked becoming a cutting board to save her? Good heavens, she really must have been distraught after

Quincy's attack not to have been struck dumb then. She wasn't above taking note of a good-looking man, but this one made Michelangelo's *David* resemble a crudely carved stick—even with a two-inch line of stitches cutting across his perfect cheek. Maybe especially because of the stitches.

"Miss Ellison." Her name rolled off his lips in a formal, staid tone, but it set a field of butterflies loose inside her.

Compose yourself, woman. You're not a weak-kneed schoolgirl. He's just a man.

It took two attempts to clear her throat before she could speak without sounding like she'd swallowed a frog. "I apologize that Cara escaped my hold."

"Think nothing of it. I happen to enjoy rescuing damsels in distress. Isn't that right, *a stór*?" As he tapped Cara's nose, he gave a dimpled smile that made Gwendolyn want to puddle at his feet.

Cara curled against Mr. Isaacs and rested her head on his shoulder. Had the girl been a cat, Gwendolyn had no doubt she'd be purring. Certainly the man couldn't have the same effect on a three-year-old girl as a thirty-year-old woman, could he?

The words Cara said when she lept from Gwendolyn's arms resurfaced. "Did she call you uncle?"

"She did."

"But you're not Irish."

He chuckled. The evidence of crow's feet around his eyes suggested he likely was a man given to many smiles and much laughter. Yet, if she wasn't mistaken, a hint of sadness dampened the brightness of his eyes.

"My wife was, God rest her soul. Cara, Jude, and Tessa are her brother's children."

Well, that explained it, but now what was she supposed to do with the man? His seeing Cara went against policy. Families weren't permitted to visit any child until after the first two months, and then only for two hours once every other month after that. The purpose was to remove the children from the negative influences that led them to their placement to begin with, but surely this Mr. Isaacs, who bore the fresh wounds of a hero, wasn't a bad influence. At the very least, Gwendolyn owed him a few minutes with his niece, even if the others couldn't be included.

"My condolences on your loss. Please, have a seat."

He refused to sit until she did, so she selected the chair with the hole in the seat cushion and used her skirts to hide the gouge in the leg. What was she supposed to say to him? She couldn't ask him to leave the premises like she would any other family member who demanded to see a child. Yet every moment he stayed, she risked Superintendent King discovering her disregard for the policies he set in place, or those who threatened her to expand their threats to include Mr. Isaacs.

Mr. Isaacs claimed the chair opposite her and arranged Cara so she was tucked against him. Boyish charm curled from his temples in the form of dark blond hair as he tilted his head to whisper something to Cara. She patted his sideburns like she hadn't just spent the last five hours screaming and crying, and actually smiled.

Heaven help her. Did the Bible's warning about strange women with honeycomb words apply to this man? Was she treading too near the door of temptation that would lead to discontentment with her current life? She cleared her throat yet again. "What can I do for you, Mr. Isaacs?"

"Several things, actually."

She stiffened. Of course he came with demands. Had she really been so blinded by the heroics that she forgot she lived in the real world instead of a fairy tale? Those were for naive girls, not women who'd lived long enough to know nothing was free, no good deed went unpunished, and that people—men especially—were not to be trusted. It was time to take control of the demands before he got the idea that he had a carte blanche.

"Allow me to be candid, Mr. Isaacs." She clasped her hands on her lap. "I will pay for your medical bills and provide a small reward, but I cannot afford to give you what you deserve. Final Chance is a charity, and, as such, my wages do not allow much in the way of setting money aside for paying rescuers."

His dimples disappeared. "I don't want a reward. What I did was of my own choosing. Any decent man would step in to save a woman from being kidnapped at knifepoint."

Jane rumbled in with the coffee cart and came to an abrupt stop.

"Kidnapped at knifepoint?" The girl's wide eyes darted to Mr. Isaacs's stitches and then to Gwendolyn. A visible swallow indicated she'd heard more than enough to piece together a disastrous rumor.

How was Gwendolyn supposed to manage this mess? She'd offended her rescuer, and now Jane, bless her soul, posed a threat.

Gwendolyn rose and stayed Mr. Isaacs with a hand when he tried to rise as well. "Thank you, Miss Jane. I will serve Mr. Isaacs." She knew better than to make a big deal of what was said, but to say nothing was just as risky. "This conversation is confidential and not to leave this room. Do you understand?"

Jane nodded, though her eyes took on an excited gleam.

Not a good sign. Fine, she'd attach a punishment that might give the girl pause. "If I hear any rumors bandied about the premises, your office duties will be replaced with laundry management." She waited until the girl gave her horrified acknowledgment. It was probably wrong to use her knowledge of the girl's hatred for the chore against her, but everyone's safety depended on silence. "Please see if Officer Grace requires any help with the younger girls. If not, you may assist Mrs. Flowers with supper preparations."

"Yes, ma'am." Jane left in a hurry, closing the door behind her.

Propriety demanded it be open, but the conversation required it closed. Gwendolyn chewed on her lip as she poured a cup of coffee for Mr. Isaacs. An open door would at least allow her to determine if Jane eavesdropped, and it prevented Superintendent King from accusing her of misconduct and reporting her to the board. Decision made, she asked Mr. Isaacs's preference as she opened the door wide and checked the hall. No Jane.

"Would you like milk or sugar in your coffee?"

"Just coffee, please." After he shifted a sleeping Cara into a safer position, he accepted his drink.

Gwendolyn returned to the cart and dumped three spoonfuls of sugar into her empty cup, filled it halfway with the milk reserved for guests, and then added coffee. Perhaps the rare treat would calm her nerves. She just needed to figure out how to get Mr. Isaacs to leave the premises without further offending him or providing information that placed either of them, or the children, in more danger.

CHAPTER 6

JOSIAH OBSERVED MISS ELLISON WITH a scrutiny he generally reserved for interacting with suspects. Although, considering the circumstances of their meeting, her refusal to press charges, and her position of authority over his nieces, he probably had more of a right to scrutinize now than on any previous case. Though her movements were smooth, even refined, compared with the shabby surroundings, something wasn't right. They were too measured. Too controlled. Just like her breathing. Her wary glance ticked like a metronome between him and the door, almost as if she expected trouble to enter at any moment. One didn't grow up surrounded by sisters and not recognize a forced composure meant to hide true feelings.

Miss Ellison returned to the chair next to him with her coffee-flavored milk in hand and sat as rigid as a steel beam on the edge of her seat.

He set his own cup on the side table where his saucer awaited and shifted to rubbing Cara's back. "Are you unwell, Miss Ellison?"

Her copper gaze returned to his, and a false smile covered the nervousness. "I am afraid I have offended you. Please forgive my impertinent assumption that your rescue came with expectations. I owe you a debt of gratitude that can never be repaid. Wednesday might have ended very differently without your intervention."

Even her speech had turned formal and clipped. "There is no need to apologize. I suspect you experience a lot of tit-for-tat expectations in your line of work." Conversations with Mother had long ago revealed that the politics of government and charity work weren't so different.

A pretty blush highlighted Miss Ellison's high cheekbones. "Your understanding is more than kind."

"However, I do wonder why you refuse to press charges?"

The cup in her hand began to shake, and she set it down on its saucer. Her glance once again flickered toward the door. Whatever the reason, she did not feel free to speak of it here.

"I am sure if they catch Mr. Slocum, your testimony will stand without a need for mine."

If they caught Mr. Slocum? How had she known the boy's name when all that had been said on the street was Devil Quin? Josiah only knew the boy's real name because of his connections within the police department. Evidently it was time to take more of an interest in the attack on Miss Ellison.

"You must understand, Mr. Isaacs," she continued, "Final Chance cannot afford any negative publicity. We are dependent upon donations and the sales of goods produced by the children. If I were to become the cause of undue attention, I would lose my position."

The explanation was sound, even probable. Had she not referred to Devil Quin as Mr. Slocum, he might even be able to convince himself she spoke the full truth. However, the zinging sensation only increased. She hid something important that scared her, and he'd never been able to walk away from a woman in trouble.

"I understand your predicament, Miss Ellison. You have my assurance that when he is caught, I will provide a testimony that ensures he will never again threaten you."

A doubtful smile graced her lips. "Thank you."

Cara shifted on his lap, the even breaths of sleep pressing against his chest with each rise and fall. While he might not be able to obtain answers about Miss Ellison's situation at the moment, he could discover the truth behind the unjust imprisonment of his nieces and nephew.

"If I might request one favor of you, I'd like to understand why my nieces and nephew were arrested for vagrancy. They have a perfectly fine home off Naudain Street and a father who cares for their every need."

At this, Miss Ellison seemed to slip into a more comfortable version of herself. "That is a question better posed to Mr. Murphy as I cannot disclose the particulars of their case. However, I can assure you the children receive the best possible care. Each child is provided with clothing, food, education, exercise, and spiritual guidance throughout their consignation to Final Chance. They are trained to join respectable professions that will afford them a lifetime of stability and support. Though a difficult situation, God will use it for their good and His glory."

It sounded like a spiel she gave to every concerned family member who walked through her doors. "That's all well and good for general information, but this is my family. I need to see them with my own eyes. To see exactly where and how they are cared for." Cara shifted in her sleep, and his heart pinched. "They've already been through so much. There has to be a way to return them to their father, who loves them."

Miss Ellison heaved an audible sigh. "I wish I could give you what you seek, but it goes against our policy. Family is strictly forbidden from access for the first two months. It helps the children to adjust to their new circumstances. However, if you were to make an appointment as a potential investor—"

The mischievous tone gave him the impression she was conspiring against the policies rather than attempting blackmail. The mischief expanded to tilt her lips and gleam in her eyes as she continued.

"—You would be provided a tour of the premises. In addition, an interview with a few of the children is provided upon request. Of course, your guide selects which children so as not to disturb their routines more than necessary. I'm afraid Superintendent King is unavailable on Friday mornings, so you would have to tolerate my choices should you schedule during that time."

This woman was beautiful and brilliant. "I'm afraid my only availability occurs on Friday mornings, so you'll be the one forced to endure my presence."

The hint of a smile bloomed into something that knocked him back to the early days of courting Shauna—both unnerving and exciting. "Shall we say this Friday at ten? I believe Jude is in between classes and work at that time."

"Friday at ten is amenable to me."

She rose from her seat like the conversation was over and he was dismissed, but he wasn't ready.

"Before I take my leave, may I know how the children fare? I'll be visiting with Conor next and wish to assure him."

Miss Ellison's focus dropped to Cara, something akin to an ache of love dampening her earlier smile. Tenderly she brushed a hair from Cara's face and sighed. "Cara is struggling to adjust. She spent most of this morning crying—screaming, to be more precise. Something about a bábóg?" Her face scrunched as she tried to form the foreign word.

Had he not heard the girl scream for the special doll during his many visits to the Murphy house, he too would be stumped by the Gaelic word. "She wants the doll her mother made her. Was it not brought with her?"

Miss Ellison's brow furrowed and her eyes grew distant, as if she were examining some invisible list. "No, they were arrested while roaming the streets and never returned home. Unless she lost it while wandering, it must still be at the house."

They were found wandering the streets? But that didn't fit. Conor would never allow the children out of the enclosed square where they rented the back portion of a row house. It was too dangerous even with knowing most of the neighbors. Had he lost sight of why those rules existed, what with his wife's death only a few months ago?

"I'll check with Conor. If it can be found, I'll bring it by tonight before I return home."

Relief released the creases in her brow, and she sank back into her chair. "Thank you. I know Cara will appreciate it even more than I. As for Tessa, she and I had a difficult start, but I believe we have come to an understanding."

Code for his willful niece being begrudgingly compliant. Oh, the headaches Tessa must have caused Miss Ellison already. The Murphy women could make hurricanes change course. For Miss Ellison to have already achieved begrudging compliance spoke of her own strong nature, a quality that he suspected any matron would need in order to oversee the care and discipline of children placed here against their will.

"Superintendent King presides over the boys' ward, so I cannot personally speak to Jude's adjustment. However, since I've not heard his name discussed in a negative manner or read any reports of misconduct concerning him, I can assume he is adjusting as well as can be expected."

A thunderous male voice echoed down the hall.

Her face blanched, and she shot to her feet, almost knocking her half-drunk cup off the table's edge. "If you'll please pass Cara to me, the next few minutes will pass better than otherwise."

Though her tone remained even, the fear he saw in her matched their first meeting on the street. Josiah rose and gently transferred Cara to Miss Ellison's waiting arms. Thankfully, the girl was so worn out she didn't do much more than whimper and resettle. Josiah shifted his stance so he could easily defend against or cordially greet anyone who entered.

Moments later, the Grim Reaper's cousin stomped through the door. "I forbid this secret meeting."

"There is nothing secret about it." Josiah shifted to block direct access to Miss Ellison just in case the man proved to be the kind to strike out. "I came to inquire about the operations of Final Chance, and Miss Ellison has been kindly indulging my questions."

The man's eyes narrowed to a point and stabbed beyond Josiah's shoulder to where Miss Ellison stood. "And you did not think to send for me as agreed upon?"

To her credit, Miss Ellison's voice did not waver or rise. "I thought about it, yes, but determined that your foul mood would not cast a favorable light on our institution. It appears I was correct in my assumptions. Mr. Isaacs was just commenting on how impressed he is with Final Chance."

"Mr. Isaacs, is it?" The man's sharp gaze sliced toward Josiah. "Any relation to Mrs. Esther Isaacs?"

"She is my mother."

Miss Ellison gasped behind him. No doubt she recognized her precarious position should he choose to reveal Wednesday's attack or today's discussion with his mother. She had nothing to worry about, but he knew better than to reassure her of his secrecy in front of this thundercloud.

"It's at Mother's suggestion that I've come to evaluate Final Chance House of Refuge as an investment opportunity. Although, given the temperament of the man who is supposed to be over the boys' ward, I'm not sure that would be wise."

"We're not a nursery, Mr. Isaacs. We're a place of reformation for delinquent children. Mollycoddling will only lead to reprobates whose evil hearts will destroy the peace and prosperity of our good city."

"Please forgive Superintendent King." Miss Ellison stepped forward. "His manners are not always so out of sorts. I assure you, Final Chance is a wonderful, kind, and safe place for the children who are committed here."

King could learn some kindness and gentleness from the woman he worked with. Josiah faced Miss Ellison and gave a formal bow. "I think it is time I take my leave. Good day, Miss Ellison." Though the man didn't deserve such common decency, Josiah turned to King and offered him a respectful bow of his head. "Superintendent King."

The man did not follow him out the door and instead remained behind. Before Josiah even exited the building, King's voice railed at Miss Ellison, quickly joined by the wails of Cara. Every fiber in him desired to walk back inside, grab his nieces and nephew, and force Miss Ellison to join him in leaving the property. Final Chance was no place for a lady or children.

CHAPTER 7

THOUGH THE ARREST REPORT FOR the finished Donovan counterfeiting case still needed to be written, Josiah leaned back in his desk chair at the Secret Service's office, flicking a weighted bandalore out and back. At least he had the office to himself. Hiding his frustration behind a joke and a smile today would be impossible. How the devil was he going to convince the judge that Conor was a sober, hardworking man after last night's fiasco?

Josiah understood Conor's hopeless desperation after the loss of first Shauna, then his wife, and now the children, but drink wasn't the answer. Conor himself taught Josiah that lesson after yanking him from beneath a pile of empty bottles. Yet after an hour of searching for Conor last night, Josiah found him at O'Malley's Pub, so deep in his cups he could have drowned. Though if he'd actually been in water, he might have smelled better. And the man's ceaseless, superstitious muttering about some curse on the Murphy name proved that Conor was beyond reasoning with.

The bandalore flicked out and back again with enough force to tighten the slipknot around his finger and turn it purple. Josiah loosened it, but the next flick only put him in the same predicament. Maybe he should give more credit to Conor's supposed curse. What else could explain meeting the judge responsible for the children's placement in Final Chance on the street while Josiah helped a drunken Conor

59

stagger home? Amidst Josiah's efforts to intervene, Conor had gifted the judge a black eye.

Josiah missed the return of the bandalore, catching the wooden circle in his chest instead of his hand. "Conor, you fool. How am I supposed to fix this now?"

He dropped his feet to the floor and wound the string around the axle with violent jerks. While Conor sobered in a jail cell, Josiah was left without hope of overturning the children's sentencing. Even his family's private lawyer had declared it a lost cause.

Once the string disappeared into the groove, he shoved the bandalore in a drawer and paced. He needed a distraction from his inability to help those he loved. His eyes skimmed over his orderly piles of paperwork.

Maybe another look at the Fantasma case would work. They had little information to go on other than that the counterfeiter belonged to the Italian community in Philadelphia. Whoever was behind the rash of violence and counterfeit banknotes, they were more ghost story than man. Certainly one person couldn't be responsible for all the crimes attributed to Fantasma, but reputations could be a powerful weapon. The few people brave enough to whisper the moniker trembled with fear as they made signs of the cross and pleaded for Josiah to preserve their lives by asking no more questions. He might as well walk down Christian Street in a police uniform for all the good undercover questioning did him.

The main office door opened, and a gangly man entered the room, pulling a younger version of himself by the ear.

He immediately spotted Josiah and stalked toward his desk. "Are you an operative?"

"Yes, sir. How may I help you?"

"My son's committed a crime, and I want him to pay the consequences." The boy shuffled forward at his father's prodding.

"The police station is your best course of action then."

"I tried that. They sent us here because you're the one who deals with counterfeits."

Josiah regarded the boy who rubbed his red ear while staring at the floor. He couldn't be more than twelve, a perfect age for shoving counterfeits on the public but not much else. The consequences would be minimal but hopefully enough to teach the boy a lesson on dishonesty and theft. "What's your name, son?"

"Tim Benson, sir." His voice squeaked.

"Well, Mr. Benson, the first step in correcting a defect in character is admitting you've done wrong. Care to take that first step and tell me what crime you've committed?"

Tim reached into his pocket and laid a folded note on the desk. As he spoke, he shifted from foot to foot. "The shop ain't been doing so good. I heard Ma worrying about us having to sell it. When we got that in the mail, Pa threw it away, but I thought maybe it might help us, so I answered it."

Josiah opened the handwritten circular for the sale of counterfeits and shook his head. The only thing the boy was guilty of was being conned. The green goods game was a decades-old swindle used against dishonest business owners willing to purchase counterfeit money by mail. Those interested received a sample of the counterfeiter's "work," which was universally a genuine banknote. Convinced they were purchasing high quality facsimiles, the would-be criminals paid by mail—only to get nothing but empty pockets in return. Since it was a crime committed against other criminals, it rarely went reported. Even when it was reported, since there wasn't production or use of real counterfeits, the crime fell under the Postal Inspector's jurisdiction as mail fraud.

"Did you receive a response?"

"Yes, sir." Tim reached into his other pocket and pulled out another letter and a folded banknote.

Josiah examined the letter. Just as he suspected, a price list with the address and fictional name of the distributer, Jacob Marley. One would think a boy who so closely resembled Tiny Tim would recognize the Charles Dickens reference.

"Did you purchase anything?"

"No, sir. Pa found out before I did."

Josiah laid the documents aside to later add to the dozen circulars collected weekly to pass on to the Postal Inspector. "You are fortunate, Mr. Benson. While you attempted to commit a crime, you were not successful and thus may be allowed off with a warning."

Tim's head jerked up with a hopeful gleam in his eyes. However, the elder Mr. Benson appeared to be as mean-spirited as Scrooge. "So there is to be no punishment?"

"As I said, he didn't commit a crime, so I cannot charge him. However, as his father, you are able to teach him the error of his ways. I recommend extra chores around the store or perhaps taking on a job somewhere else if he is so eager to help out with the finances." Josiah addressed Tim. "While your heart was in the right place, your methods could have resulted in a serious crime that would've forever altered your life. Instead of sending you home with your father, I could be escorting you to jail and then a house of refuge where you would spend at least a year away from your parents."

Josiah's heart wrenched at the image of his nieces and nephew those words conjured. If he could save even one child from that life, he would.

"When a person produces, buys, or uses counterfeit money, he or she is committing deception and thievery. Innocent people are hurt. People like your mother and father, the very people you were trying to help. Do you understand?"

Tim nodded solemnly.

"Good. You'll accept your punishment like an honorable man and learn from your mistake?"

"Yes, sir."

Tim left with shoulders and head bowed as his father spouted off consequences. The poor boy wasn't going to enjoy himself for a good long while, but at least his life wouldn't be irrevocably changed.

Josiah examined the letters again and shook his head. How anyone, even a child, fell for such a scheme was beyond him. The address was real though, and one he recognized. He rubbed his eyes, hoping what he saw would change.

It didn't.

What was Final Chance's address doing on a green goods circular? No one there should be involved in that scheme. The familiar zing tensed his shoulders and squeezed him like grapes in a wine press.

It was *a genuine note, wasn't it?*

He reached for the "sample" banknote. An ill-formed dog and misshapen woodchopper's hat taunted him. Not only was the note as genuine as a wooden nickel, it was obviously a Fantasma reproduction. Regardless of whether the counterfeiters were planning on swindling their customers like a normal green goods game or this was a genuine attempt to sell their goods, the case now fell under Secret Service jurisdiction.

What kind of home for "delinquent" children was Final Chance? Only two possibilities of explanation for the address rose to mind, neither of which boded well for the institution's reputation. Either someone on the outside had an inside connection that allowed them to launder correspondence undetected, or the institution itself was involved.

The office door opened, and Hayden Orton—his former partner, now superior—entered. "There's a boy receiving a stern lecture from his father about the immorality of purchasing counterfeit money in the hall." Though he didn't frame it as a question, it was clear he expected details.

Josiah didn't trust himself to speak more than a few words. His family was likely caught in the crosshairs of this new case. "Green goods game."

Hayden nodded before shrugging out of his coat and tossing a telegram on Josiah's desk. "Our cases are about to stall. President Cleveland's new solicitor decided we are inciting criminals to commit crimes. Effective immediately, all operatives are banned from purchasing counterfeit money."

As if discovering Final Chance's potential involvement in a green goods game wasn't bad enough. "Please tell me you're jesting."

"Have you ever known me to jest?"

Since the man was as serious as smallpox, that was an emphatic no. Josiah sank into his chair, massaging the bridge of his nose. "I'm supposed to meet Wilcox tonight for a substantial purchase and introductions. Backing out now will look suspicious."

"We'll have to come up with a new strategy. I sent a reply acknowledging receipt of the ban."

Meaning Chief Brooks wouldn't buy a claim of ignorance should Josiah go through with tonight's plan. Did the Murphy curse extend to him by marriage? Because it was beginning to feel very real.

Hayden continued. "Knowing Chief Brooks, he'll be fighting the ban with every tool at his disposal. I wouldn't be surprised if he pulls Drummond into the politics of it."

A lot of good that did them now. "I'll send a message to Wilcox through one of our contacts that I have to pull out tonight. If we're lucky, he'll accept whatever excuse I give."

"Make it about a woman, and he'll believe it, coming from you."

Josiah's gaze landed on the green goods letters. There was only one person he knew who worked inside Final Chance, and she'd been scared—like someone who knew something she shouldn't. "Actually, that excuse wouldn't be a lie. Today's green goods letter came with a bogus Fantasma banknote and the address of the institution where Miss Ellison, the woman I told you about, works. She knows something, and I intend to find out what."

CHAPTER 8

"MATRON ELLISON, YOU'RE NEEDED IN the boys' infirmary."

Gwendolyn looked up from her third attempt to squeeze money out of a budget that had nothing left to give. Officer Crane's carefully manicured hair grazed the top of the office's doorframe as he stood awaiting her compliance. With a giant hooked nose and gangly limbs more akin to those of an awkward teenager than a thirty-something man, it was no wonder the children called him Ichabod behind his back. Gwendolyn stacked the hopeless ledgers on the corner of her desk and rose.

"Is one of the boys sick?" Anytime retching was involved, Superintendent King delegated the child's care to her.

"Hibbard got into a fight and didn't fare well."

"In a fight? With whom? Is the doctor needed?"

"Superintendent King said you'd do well enough." He stepped aside and allowed her entry into the hallway.

"You still need to tell me who fought Hibbard." She glanced over her shoulder when he remained silent. "Officer Crane, I require an answer."

He rubbed his neck for a moment, shortening his strides to what must be an uncomfortable pace in order not to overtake her. As they reached the double doors that led to the boys' ward, he answered. "I don't suppose you need to know. Superintendent King will deal with the particulars."

Of course he'd refuse to tell her. Superintendent King stayed out of her dealings with the girls' ward if she stayed out of his with the boys'. At least, that was how it was supposed to work. "Hypocrite" must be his middle name.

She yanked the boys' ward door open. "Female on the floor!" She waited, allowing time for any half-dressed scamps either to finish dressing or shut a door.

The only sounds came from the infirmary, where Hibbard groaned.

Superintendent King stepped into the hall. "The floor is empty. You may enter."

"Unless I'm needed, I'll be supervising mealtime." Officer Crane retraced his steps to the stairwell hall.

If Officer Crane retreated, Superintendent King really had to be in an intolerable mood. With a prayer for forbearance, she walked past the dormitory hall on her left and straight to the infirmary. A single, dim gas lamp illuminated the windowless room that housed two beds, a simple washstand, and a myriad of basic medical supplies scattered across the nightstand in the corner.

Superintendent King relocated to the other side of the bed, giving her clear view of Hibbard curled into a ball beneath a sheet and clutching his chest. Blood caked in his hair and seeped from cuts on his face, mingling with tears that rolled from nearly swollen-shut eyes. His shallow breath brought on a mewling cry that mangled her heart.

"Good heavens! How was the fight allowed to go on long enough to do this?" She snagged a rag off the supply table, dunked it into the water basin, and rushed to the fourteen-year-old's side.

"Had I been there, it wouldn't have been allowed." A growl undergirded Superintendent King's response.

She glanced up from mopping the rag over Hibbard's face to look at Superintendent King's snarled lips. Visible ticks jumped along his jaw, and his fingers alternated between stretching and clenching. Good. If the man was this angry, then perhaps Officer Bagwell would finally get the reprimand he deserved. He might even lose his job for his failure to stop the fight, especially if he'd been participating in his favorite pastime—looking at himself in a mirror—rather than watching the children.

Hibbard whimpered beneath her touch.

Whoever did this deserved a throttling. She didn't have the skills or knowledge of how best to help him. "Hibbard needs a doctor."

"We don't have the funds for an extra visit."

"Then I'll pay for it myself. He might have broken ribs or other injuries we can't see."

"No. We deal with it here. Final Chance cannot afford any negative publicity."

That masquerade of an excuse might work for other unsavory events, but not this time. She'd been praying for guidance on what to do since Quincy's attack. Now the answer whimpered next to her.

God, granteth me wisdom so that none may suffereth again.

Hibbard needed help, and unless she convinced Superintendent King, that help would never arrive. "There'll be no negative publicity if action is taken against those responsible and a full report made to the board next week. We owe it to Hibbard to get him the medical care he needs. I'll personally pay every penny of the expense. Just please go get Dr. Munich."

Superintendent King considered Hibbard. For one long minute he stood motionless. Then, with the air of firm resolve, he pivoted and marched out of the room.

Thank thee, Jesus.

Once certain she couldn't be heard, she leaned toward Hibbard. "Who did this to you?"

Terror screamed out from the one eye that wasn't completely swollen. He sobbed when he tried to shake his head, his jaw hanging not quite right. She dropped to her knees beside him and searched his pained face. Final Chance's secrets couldn't remain behind locked doors. She needed answers, and Hibbard needed justice.

"I must know who did this. You needn't speak; just make a noise to answer yes. Can you do that?"

He groaned.

"Did one of the older boys do this to you?"

Silence.

"One of the younger ones?" It was unlikely, but not impossible.

Again, silence.

"Was it one of the Final Chance officers?"

He moaned.

She closed her eyes. Hibbard was supposed to be safe here, to have refuge from the trials of life, and to have a second chance at becoming the young man God called him to be. Whichever officer did this deserved to be an inmate of Sing Sing.

"Superintendent King?" As foul-tempered as the man was, she could not see him partaking in such extreme, unrelenting violence.

Hibbard's silence was a relief.

"Officer Crane?" The man was an awkward tree, but she'd always imagined him gentle.

Silence.

That left one. "Officer Bagwell?"

Hibbard tugged the sheet up further, as if shielding himself from the very man, but made no noise.

"I need you to make a sound. I cannot do anything if I don't have confirmation."

A throat cleared behind her.

Gwendolyn twisted to find Officer Bagwell standing in the doorway like a Pharisee, all pomp and thinly veiled threats. The rag balled in her fist, and she shifted to her feet so that she stood as a shield between Hibbard and the man who'd likely beaten him. Although Officer Bagwell's bushy whiskers hung over his mouth and hid any evidence he'd heard her accusation, she didn't doubt he had.

"Superintendent King sent me to assist you."

"Thank you. Would you retrieve a cloth with some ice in it from Mrs. Flowers? It should help with the swelling." Anything to get that man out of the room.

Suspicion painted his countenance, but he complied.

Praise the Lord. Whatever it took, she wouldn't leave Hibbard alone with that man, even if it meant defying the rules and sleeping in the boys' infirmary.

As soon as Officer Bagwell's steps faded down the hall, she tried again. "Was it Officer Bagwell?"

Hibbard closed his eye and said nothing.

"Please, Hibbard. Without your word I have no proof to take to the board."

He tugged the sheet over his head, and no matter what she said or how she pressed, he gave no answer.

Officer Bagwell returned and remained at her shoulder the entire time she tended to Hibbard. The longer he stayed, the more agitated Hibbard's breathing became and the louder his pained whimpers grew. At long last, Dr. Munich arrived and ushered them into the hallway while Superintendent King remained inside the infirmary.

While Gwendolyn paced, Officer Bagwell examined his appearance in the glass reflection of a framed portrait. Dissatisfied, he groomed his overlong mustache and then ran the same comb through his hair. Lord forgive her, but she hoped snot joined the pomade to slick back his curls. Apparently returning to help Officer Crane with the mealtime duties was not as important as preening.

Hibbard's yelp of pain cut through the door.

That's it. She yanked the picture frame from the wall and confronted him. "Where were you when Hibbard was being so thoroughly beaten?"

He straightened and tucked the comb away. "If you must know, I was using the necessary."

Heat spread across her cheeks, and not just from embarrassment of the indelicate lie he provided. "It is your responsibility to keep a watchful eye on those boys at all times."

"Are you saying I should drag all twelve out to the privy every time I have a need?"

"No, but I will hold you accountable for Hibbard's condition."

"Hibbard is responsible for his own suffering. He had no business questioning Gareth. Gareth's reason for imprisonment here is no one's business but his, and Hibbard deserves the consequences of putting his nose where it doesn't belong. I recommend you heed his lesson."

"Is that a threat, Officer Bagwell?"

"Of course not. Just wisdom. The way we run the boys' ward is necessarily different from that of the girls. We'll handle all indiscretions as we decide best." He adjusted his vest and lifted his chin. "I'll check on Hibbard later."

Gwendolyn watched his retreating back, anger boiling over like an unwatched pot of potatoes. Though she had no proof, she was as certain of his striking Hibbard as Mr. Farwell's death not being a robbery. Danger or not, she would find answers, and God willing, it would be something she could take to the board and be believed with.

The door opened and Dr. Munich stepped into the hall with Superintendent King. "I recommend transferring Hibbard to Children's. His broken jaw needs surgery."

Superintendent King frowned. "Surely that isn't necessary."

His aversion to the idea likely had more to do with finances than anything else, but she had no such reserves. She'd drain her savings if it meant Hibbard would recover out of Officer Bagwell's reach. "Do whatever you think best, Dr. Munich. I will personally pay for any treatment Hibbard needs."

"That is kind, but Children's Hospital is free for all colors and creeds. I cannot force you to send him, but the boy's mouth may never function properly again if he doesn't go." Dr. Munich looked to Superintendent King in expectation.

He remained silent.

What was holding him back? The hospital was only one square northwest of them, and finances were no longer a concern. "If we do not get Hibbard the proper treatment, the board will hold you and me personally responsible."

Superintendent King drew a long breath before nodding. "Should I summon an ambulance?"

"My gig should suffice, but if you have something we could use to transport him to it, that would be best."

"We have a cot in the donation closet."

"That should work." Dr. Munich addressed Gwendolyn. "Stay with Hibbard until I return. I've administered a draft for pain, so if he isn't sleeping yet, he will be soon."

Superintendent King and Dr. Munich left, allowing Gwendolyn to settle next to Hibbard and watch the rise and fall of his breathing. No one deserved such brutal treatment, especially not a child. Whatever Mr. Farwell had claimed was worse than this needed to be exposed. During tomorrow's half day off, she'd begin her search for answers.

CHAPTER 9

As she did every time before she left for her half day, Gwendolyn peeked into Wilhelmina's class. Groups of three huddled around the few cast-off McGuffey Readers she'd convinced a pawn dealer to donate. Cara sat at the front table, arm clutching the rag doll dropped off by Mr. Isaacs and thumb stuck in her mouth. She didn't appear to be listening to Wilhelmina's lesson on the alphabet, but it was still an improvement over the constant wailing.

Even Tessa had eased her defiance after Gwendolyn conducted a private meeting with her yesterday. It seemed conspiring together against the institution's policy to allow her and Jude to see Mr. Isaacs served as a bonding opportunity. Tessa promised to inform Jude that they would need to pretend they didn't know their uncle when he toured the premises. May God forgive the deception, but the children needed to see Mr. Isaacs as much as he needed to see them.

At least that secret only risked her job. The one she hoped to uncover today had her repeating her own version of Romans 8:38 and 39 as frequently as her heartbeat.

I am persuaded that neither death, nor life, nor Final Chance secrets shall be able to separate me from thy love, oh God, which is in Christ Jesus, my Lord.

She might've taken liberties with the verse, but Uncle Percy insisted praying the Scriptures had the power to change the one who prayed it. And she needed that power to transform her fear into courage.

72

Taking her cue from the chiming hall clock, Gwendolyn closed the door. There'd be no checking on Agatha's sewing lessons today. She needed every possible minute to scrounge for answers. Before leaving, she checked the thermometer outside the window. It appeared winter had vacated the lap of spring at short notice and summer had taken its place. Eighty degrees at noon? She selected a light shawl, pinned her straw hat in place, and faced the door. Though the expectation of a warm day awaited, a shiver stole over her. The last time she'd ventured out, Quincy had followed her and a rather heroic man had been injured. Would Quincy be waiting to follow through with his threat today?

Again she prayed her prayer and then allowed Jesus's peace to thread through her before stepping outside.

Uncle Percy awaited her at the curb, and a glance around revealed no one of Quincy's build lurking amongst the Twenty-Second Street pedestrians. Worries abated, she accepted Uncle Percy's arm. "Thank you for sacrificing your afternoon to escort me."

Uncle Percy patted her hand. "Do not fret, my dear. I'm always here for whatever you need. Where are we heading to first?"

"Children's Hospital. Hibbard Wilcox suffered significant injuries yesterday, and I'd like to check on him."

As they walked, Uncle Percy peppered her with questions about what happened. She shared Mr. Bagwell's version of the story until safely away from the institution, then, after checking for eavesdroppers, shared her true concerns.

"Accusing Officer Bagwell is a heavy charge, Gwendolyn. Do you have any proof beyond your suspicions?"

"Nothing that would suffice for anyone but myself."

"Then I caution you against sharing your thoughts with anyone else. You wouldn't want to discover Gareth actually was the attacker and you, guilty of slander."

She pressed her lips together. There was wisdom in his statement, yet she couldn't quiet the certainty that Officer Bagwell perpetrated the abuse occurring at Final Chance. Would Uncle Percy change his mind if he knew about the threats? Unlikely. She had no idea who'd issued the note. And aside from the intangible quality of his Christian faith, Uncle Percy was a man of logic and facts. He wouldn't help her in her investigation; instead, he'd be concerned and escort her to the police, who then would either say they'd look into it, or worse, brush her off. Then he, Aunt Birdie, and Mother would be left unprotected when those trying to intimidate her realized she'd defied their warnings.

Before Gwendolyn could decide whether to tell Uncle Percy, they arrived at the bottom steps of the four-story, tan stucco hospital. Perhaps the best choice was to wait to see what she uncovered today. The more evidence she presented to Uncle Percy and the police, the more likely she was to be taken seriously.

She climbed the stoop stairs, passed beneath the large canopy overhang, and entered the building. The receptionist directed them to the boys' surgical ward on the second floor, where nurses in white capped uniforms tended the half dozen patients. Gwendolyn surveyed the room, seeking out Hibbard. One nurse rocked a toddler not much smaller than Cara, while another made choo-choo sounds as she and an older boy pushed a toy train around on the floor. It was harder to see the faces of the children who were lying in beds.

The resident physician approached them. "May I help you?"

"I'm Matron Ellison of Final Chance House of Refuge. Hibbard Wilcox is one of our wards, and I've come to check on him."

The physician nodded and led them to a small, narrow bed in the far corner where Hibbard lay with nearly his entire head wrapped in thick bandages. Her throat tightened at the pitiful image he presented. How could anyone hurt a child like this? His swollen black and blue eyes remained closed as Gwendolyn pulled the chair from the end of the bed to his side.

She struggled to speak as she watched the covers rise and fall with his shallow breaths. "Will he recover?"

"He will, but it'll take time. His jaw was dislocated and broken in several places, and the surgeon had to repair a tendon. It appears he took a pretty good beating. Thankfully, none of his broken ribs punctured a lung."

Uncle Percy stood at the end of the bed with folded arms. "Did he happen to indicate who did this to him?"

The physician shook his head. "No, and he's not likely to say anything for the foreseeable future."

"When Hibbard is cognizant enough to write, could you send for me? I'll need a written account of what happened to add to his record."

"Of course."

The physician left them, and for a long time she sat praying over Hibbard, hoping against reason he would wake and give her some sort of usable evidence that Officer Bagwell was to blame. Eventually, she had to concede nothing would come of this visit other than the knowledge Hibbard was being cared for better than he would have been at Final Chance. God willing, her next stop should be more revealing of Final Chance's secrets.

When she rose, Uncle Percy offered his own prayer for healing and then escorted her out of the building in silence.

Outside, he led her to the nearest streetcar stop. "Hibbard's condition is quite disconcerting."

Disconcerting was putting it mildly. "Regardless of who delivered the blows, it should never have been allowed to reach that point. Officer Bagwell should be held accountable for the failure of his duty to oversee and protect Hibbard."

"It is certainly something that needs to be addressed. Will you bring it up to the board?"

It would only further upset those who would see her removed from her position, but the children needed an advocate. One who wasn't afraid. "I will."

"Good. I'll be praying for you and for Hibbard."

"Thank you. If you wouldn't mind one more stop, I'd like to visit the Farwell residence to offer my condolences." And discover if someone in that house knew what Mr. Farwell had discovered that was worth being killed over.

He consented to the additional errand, and when the streetcar stopped to allow boarding, Gwendolyn chose an outer seat in the back row. If Quincy or someone else followed, she'd notice.

With a resolve that both thrilled and terrified, she watched the buildings shift back and forth from row houses to businesses. They passed through the sulfuric odor of the gas works, over the train tracks that led to Broad Street Station, and eventually turned onto Arch Street. She smiled despite the seriousness of her errand. An air of old-time gentility lived here where the hum of city life was quieter. Mansion-sized row houses wore uniform brick fronts, wrought iron stoops, green shutters, and a sense of nobility that fit the merchant princes of Philadelphia.

The reserved and cordial Mr. Farwell had matched his surroundings perfectly.

Her pleasure turned to regret when they disembarked from the streetcar and walked to the house on the corner. Tightly drawn curtains cut off the mourners inside from the outside world. Had Gwendolyn not brought Mr. Farwell into her suspicions, would he now be sitting in the front parlor ready to greet his guests? Uncle Percy led her to the door, where black crepe draped the knob, and quietly rapped. Though they stood on the stoop for several minutes, knocking louder in case their entreaties had not been heard, no one answered. Like the man himself, the house was still as death.

And so was her search for answers.

"I'm sorry my dear. It appears the house has been closed up."

"It's fine. I'll—" She took a deep breath and straightened her shoulders. Giving up wasn't an option. "I'll try again later."

He patted her hand. "Would you like to visit Wanamaker's until your mother and Aunt Birdie finish their shift and then come home with them? I have some things I need to see to at the church before dinner."

Visiting Wanamaker's would save him some of the time she'd already wasted so much of. She didn't need to purchase anything, but walking around to view the company's art collection was cheaper than a trip to the art museum. Perhaps she'd even treat herself to a stop at the soda fountain and then see if there were any books that might shed some light on how to best investigate secrets without being detected.

"Thank you, Uncle Percy. That is a wonderful idea."

Halfway to Broad Street, someone called her name.

Behind her, Mr. Isaacs jogged down the steps of a house identical to Mr. Farwell's. A serious man stood at the top of the stoop, watching her as if he suspected her of some great misdeed. Mr. Isaacs's countenance was far more congenial, despite the stitches in his cheek, and it turned her ragged emotions into a flurry of butterflies. Here was her own real-life knight, and by his expression as he evaluated her escort, he wasn't done playing protector.

He nodded at Uncle Percy and then endowed her with a heart-palpitating smile. "I'm relieved to see you have a safer companion with you this week, Miss Ellison. Although I'm not opposed to providing another rescue from villains should you need it."

His wink almost made her giggle. Good heavens! She, a sober-minded old maid, almost giggled. She shook her head and caught a glimpse of Uncle Percy's disapproving frown.

"Gwendolyn, who is this man, and what does he mean by 'provide another rescue'? When was the first?"

All butterflies and giddiness fled with the breath that gusted from her lungs. With Mr. Farwell's death, all questions of why she didn't come home for her weekly visit last week had been forgotten. Her family had been spared the truth of the very real fact she might never have come home again. While Uncle Percy did need to know about the threat to the family now that she'd chosen to pursue answers, she'd prefer for the details of her particular experience never to come to light.

"That is a story best saved for the privacy of our home." After she'd had a chance to concoct a safer version.

"Gwendolyn," he admonished.

Maybe introductions would distract him. She released Uncle Percy's arm and stepped back. "Uncle Percy, may I present to you Mr.

Josiah Isaacs? He's the son of Esther Isaacs, one of our board members." She hoped the connection to Final Chance made their unconventional interactions easier to digest. "Mr. Isaacs, this is my uncle, Reverend Percival Ballantine."

The gentlemen shook hands, and at the conclusion, Mr. Isaacs flexed his fingers with upturned lips. "That's quite the grip you have, sir. It's good to know Miss Ellison will not be in need of my protection after all."

Why did the man have to bring attention back to that? "As you can see, I am in good hands. Now, I'm afraid my uncle has an appointment, so if you'll please excuse us, we must be on our way." She turned and tried to urge Uncle Percy back toward Broad Street, but he remained rooted to the spot.

"I will have an explanation, Gwendolyn. As your only father figure, it is my right to know of any distressful situations you've encountered. Either you or Mr. Isaacs may explain, but I will have my answer now." His glare shifted between her and Mr. Isaacs, signaling that he'd brook no deceit or foolishness.

Mr. Isaacs appeared nonplussed and perhaps even eager for her response. Fine. She'd give a short variation of the story, enough to satisfy for the moment, without giving the full illustration of Mr. Isaacs's heroism. "While conducting errands last week, I ran into a bit of trouble, and Mr. Isaacs stepped in to ensure an unscrupulous character moved on without further incident."

Though Mr. Isaacs's brow arched, he said nothing to contradict or add to her story.

However, Uncle Percy knew her too well. "I don't want a news clipping, my dear. I want the whole novel."

"You'll be late for your appointment. I'm sure the storytelling can wait until after dinner." Her smile felt as forced as her words.

"My appointment is with a book. I'd much rather hear your story."

"It's not one that should be told on the street where anyone can hear it."

"Then let us tell it in the comfort of my parlor." Mr. Isaacs gestured toward the stoop where his companion still stood. "I'll be happy to share with you anything your niece does not."

The traitorous man.

Uncle Percy hooked his arm through hers and urged her forward. "I'd be much obliged for your hospitality and your information."

When they reached the stoop, Mr. Isaacs spoke to his friend. "It appears my plans have changed. I'll meet you at the office when I'm finished here."

Dark eyes met hers and held. After a moment, an almost imperceptible tilt of his lips softened his serious face. "I'd be careful if I were you, Isaacs. This one has a good potential to become number ten."

Mr. Isaacs let out an ungentlemanly snort. "I'll see you at the office."

The man nodded at them in acknowledgment before passing onto the sidewalk toward Broad Street.

Mr. Isaacs opened the outside door and gestured for them to pass through the vestibule to where a butler held open the interior door. "After you."

While etiquette justified his coming in behind them, she couldn't help feeling that Mr. Isaacs was intent on preventing her escape from the impending conversation. Her stomach churned as, against her resistance, Uncle Percy's strong hand at her back pushed her inside Mr. Isaacs's home, where the bright glow of electric lights illuminated the narrow foyer.

Her thoughts scattered and her mouth gaped. Only four years ago had Philadelphia lit Chestnut Street from river to river with lights, and few businesses had been able to afford the upgrade since. Mr. Isaacs must indeed be rich to have installed such new technology inside his home. No wonder he wasn't concerned about a reward. Her paltry offering probably wouldn't have paid for even one of the ornately carved chairs he directed them toward. Even his maid's black dress and white apron appeared to be the finest quality available. Gwendolyn might as well be a bedraggled street urchin in comparison to the surrounding finery.

"Should I serve coffee, sir?"

Mr. Isaacs declined, dismissed the maid, and gestured for his guests to take a seat.

Gwendolyn snapped her mouth closed and ducked her head, praying he hadn't noticed her shameful gawking. She sat on the upholstered chair that had nary a stain or broken thread and winced. She'd been so proud of her improvements to the Final Chance parlor. Now embarrassment trampled her confidence. Most people probably viewed the receiving room in no better light than she did the miserable donations Final Chance regularly received.

Mr. Isaacs claimed a spot on the plush settee opposite her, rested his arm across its intricately carved back, and crossed his outstretched legs at the ankle. The man looked as contented as a cat in a spot of sun as he regarded her with expectancy.

She hated to disappoint him, but his part in the story was over. He didn't need the details, and she wouldn't give them freely. "May my uncle and I have some privacy, please?"

He arched a brow. "Are you afraid I'll share something you don't want your uncle to find out?"

Of course she was. "Is that a no?"

The corner of his mouth hitched up in a smirk like he knew she'd purposely evaded answering. "It is. I recommend you take that seat there, Reverend." He gestured to the green velvet armchair. "The story is not for the faint of heart."

Uncle Percy took the proffered chair and pinned her with a glare that revealed he'd not missed her evasiveness either. "Then let us have it, Gwendolyn, or I'll be forced to take a stranger's word above your own."

Her throat tightened as she glanced between the two men. How to get them to understand? "I can't tell you. They'll kill me and anyone who knows."

Chapter 10

Miss Ellison's proclamation might have taken the reverend by surprise, but it only confirmed Josiah's conviction that she was a victim of, and not a participant in, the counterfeiting schemes connected to Final Chance. No wonder she'd been opposed to reporting the attack. Stories of Fantasma's retribution described stalwart men groveling for mercy. Any woman—even one such as Miss Ellison—would faint dead away.

Or maybe it was except Miss Ellison.

The same resolute eyes that met him when she tended his wound swung toward him now.

"You've already suffered enough injury on my account. I'll not further risk your life."

Thunderation! The indomitable courage radiating from her and the conviction behind her words stirred the cold ashes of his heart, uncovering and blowing to life an ember of admiration unlike anything he'd felt since Shauna.

And it terrified him.

He cleared his throat to dispel the feeling and focused on the problem at hand. Miss Ellison needed an ally, and he could provide that. "I think I've proven myself capable of handling dangerous men."

"A single knife-wielding villain is nothing compared to a group attacking without mercy."

Reverend Ballantine jolted to his feet. "Gwendolyn, I demand to know what's going on."

"Not until he leaves."

Josiah shook his head. Her stubbornness might aid her in her job as a matron, but it would not serve her here. She needed him, whether she realized it or not. "Your niece was almost kidnapped at knifepoint by Quincy Slocum."

He ignored the reverend's slack-jawed response and discarded his nonchalant position to lean forward until his face was level with hers. "Whatever threats have been made, you needn't fear. It's my job to deal with unscrupulous men, and I'll not allow you to refuse my help or protection."

"Your job?"

Hayden was going to give him a dressing-down when he returned to the office, but revealing his profession was the only way Josiah could see to get Miss Ellison to trust him. He reached into his vest pocket and pulled out his credentials book with the five-point silver star. "I'm a Secret Service operative investigating Final Chance House of Refuge."

She blinked at him. "Investigating? At whose behest? Did Mr. Farwell come to you before they killed him?"

Josiah frowned as he returned his credentials to his pocket. Farwell? Wasn't that the board member Mother told him had recently passed and whose position she wanted him to take?

Reverend Ballantine sank into a chair next to his niece. "Will you please explain what's going on? What has Mr. Farwell's death to do with this?"

She glanced between Josiah and Reverend Ballantine.

Josiah clenched his jaw to keep from speaking. He'd learned long ago that if he gave a person room enough to speak, the person would likely fill the silence with more information than he'd originally sought.

After a moment, she released a sigh that sagged her shoulders. "There have been whisperings between the fences. Siblings talking to each other and then coming to me about abuse in the boys' ward."

A muscle in Josiah's cheek jumped. Jude. He was supposed to be safe at Final Chance. Miss Ellison herself had assured him Jude received the best possible care. Was he even now sporting bruises?

As if she could read his thoughts, Miss Ellison's pained gaze lifted to his. "So far, I've heard nothing of Jude being hurt. I'm sure Tessa would have torn down the fence to get to him if he had. At the very least she would have raged at me. As long as he doesn't share his sister's vocal spirit, he should remain unharmed." Tears slipped down her cheeks, evidence of the helplessness and regret tearing at her soul. "You'll see him Friday. Just please encourage him to do whatever he's asked without a fight. It will save him from a heavy hand."

"That's why you believe Mr. Bagwell beat Hibbard." For a man of the cloth, Reverend Ballantine's face looked murderous. "And the board has done nothing about this?"

"I approached them last month, but my concerns were dismissed as unreliable rumors from children who would say and do anything to hurt the reputation of the people in charge of them." Understandable bitterness seeped into her tone. "Mr. Farwell was the only one willing to give the rumors any credence. He promised to look into it quietly so as not to ruffle any feathers. Last week he sent me a note telling me it was worse than I thought and asking me to meet him at Carpenters' Hall. He didn't expound, just said it was something that needed to be handled carefully, but then he never showed."

Reverend Ballantine shook his head. "Because of a robbery. Not foul play."

The reverend might deny the connection, but Josiah didn't like the way the pieces fit together.

Miss Ellison's chin dropped, and she began to wring her hands. "You're wrong, Uncle. Before we even knew what happened to Mr. Farwell, Quincy hinted at knowing and threatened me with the same should I continue asking questions. Mr. Isaacs intervened and suffered a slice to the face as his only reward."

Silence stretched between the three of them as Reverend Ballantine scrutinized the red line on Josiah's cheek.

Josiah shifted in his seat and averted his face. He'd joked with his family and Hayden that the scar only made him more charming to women, but in honesty he hated the attention it brought.

Eventually, Reverend Ballantine spoke. "It seems I owe you a debt of gratitude, Mr. Isaacs."

"What I did, I did because it was right. Gratitude is unwarranted." Before anything else could be said in regard to his actions, Josiah changed the subject. "So far, Quincy Slocum has slipped through all attempts to locate him. It would be unwise for you to travel anywhere alone, Miss Ellison. After reading his file, I expect another attempt."

"I well know that, but it's not just my life that's been threatened." Her tongue skimmed her lips. "Someone inside Final Chance threatened my family's lives as well."

The news confirmed his suspicions of an inside job, and the threats to Miss Ellison's life elevated the case to a priority investigation. Fantasma could not be allowed to attack another victim.

"And then there are the children. They already suffer abuse. What will happen to them if it's discovered that you're investigating Final Chance?" Panic seized her composure and seemed to drag her mind into horrific imaginings.

He reached across the space and took her gloved hand in his. "Nothing will happen because whoever is behind this won't find out. You'll not say anything?"

She shook her head.

He turned toward Reverend Ballantine. "And you?"

"Of course not! But something must be done."

"We're working to find answers. At this point, we have no evidence that can be used to arrest anyone." For abuse *or* counterfeiting. "We're not even sure who is involved."

Miss Ellison brushed a tear away with her free hand. "All I know for sure is Quincy. I suspect Officer Bagwell is as well, but like you, I have no proof."

But she could get it. Easier than anyone else he could rope in as an informant for the case. She had unobstructed access to the building and the people. If she were a man, he'd have no hesitation in asking her to take an active role in uncovering the truth. But she was a woman. A very beautiful one, even with her pale face and eyes growing puffy from crying. The heart that beat within her proved tender yet courageous, just like his Shauna's. If he asked her to help him, he had no doubt she would. He could see it in her face, in the way she spoke about the children, in her actions to ensure he saw his family. She wasn't a woman who backed down from danger, regardless of the possible cost to herself.

And that was the true problem. Already her position in the situation placed her in great peril. Asking her to become further involved would place him in the same category of miscreant as Quincy Slocum. Worse, because he knew her love of the children would drive her to say yes. He couldn't do it. Wouldn't do it. The best he could ask was that she not reveal his true motives when he joined the Final Chance Board of Directors.

He withdrew his hand from hers. "I'll get proof. I just need assurance of your silence as I investigate."

Miss Ellison drew in a breath that infused her posture with steel. "You have more than my silence. I'll help your investigation in any way I can."

"No, Gwendolyn. Your silence is enough." The authority in Reverend Ballantine's voice should have stopped anyone, but Miss Ellison proved as stubborn and courageous as Josiah suspected.

"It's not, Uncle. I know God has called me to seek answers and protect the children. He made it abundantly clear yesterday as I tended Hibbard. Discovering Mr. Isaacs is an officer investigating Final Chance only confirms it."

"God is calling you to hand this matter over to the authorities and step back. There is no place for you in this investigation." Reverend Ballantine implored Josiah with the wave of a hand, "Tell her all you need is her silence."

Miss Ellison barreled over any attempted response. "I live and work at Final Chance. No one else will have better access to potential information than me. Please, Mr. Isaacs,"—she grabbed his hand, and her eyes pleaded with a desperate sort of courage—"allow me to be a part of your investigation. I promise I'll be an asset, not a burden. I'll do anything for those children."

"Not anything, Gwendolyn. I don't want you sacrificing your integrity or"—Reverend Ballantine flicked a glance at Josiah—"innocence under the misguided notion that you're protecting the children."

The familiar implication scraped like wool against a burn. The reverend probably read social columns and was well acquainted with the sensationalists' versions of Josiah's nine broken engagements, many of which toed the line of slander for the scandals they falsely insinuated. The world might believe Josiah held romantic intentions with every woman he met, but he'd never taken advantage of one. Not even when they'd pursued him like Potiphar's wife pursued Joseph. He was in the business of helping women, not hurting them.

Indignation flamed red in Miss Ellison's face. Though she dropped Josiah's hand, she leveled a fierce glower at Reverend Ballantine. The spitfire didn't have to say another word for Josiah to know Shauna would have loved Miss Ellison. He smiled despite the insult of a moment ago.

"I am no doe-eyed schoolgirl incapable of discerning between right and wrong, Uncle."

"Your father claimed he knew what he was doing too, but look where it led him. I'm telling you, Gwendolyn, there are more dangers than you understand by partnering with this man."

"And I'll risk them all. I'm not my father, Uncle. He's gone and can stay gone for all I care, but I won't abandon those under *my* care just because someone tells me to walk away."

"You can't make up for the mistakes of your father by doing this."

"I'm not trying to." Miss Ellison pivoted toward Josiah. "What do you say, Mr. Isaacs? Will you work with me to bring an end to whatever's going on at Final Chance?"

A man could get lost in those eyes and lose all sight of reason. A perilous proposition. Partnering with the extraordinary Miss Ellison would be far more dangerous than any criminal he'd ever pursued. Attraction thrummed to life too easily around her. Three meetings and already she came to mind almost as often as Shauna. It was disloyal to his wife.

"No." He didn't need a person on the inside, even if the value of it could not be denied.

Reverend Ballantine blew out an audible "Praise God."

Miss Ellison rose to her feet and gave one of those "I know you think you're right, but you're wrong" smiles that every woman seemed to come equipped with. "I understand. A woman has no place in protecting those she loves. It's not as if God used Deborah and Jael to deliver Sisera into the hands of Israel."

The challenging glare she sent to both of them made Josiah's throat bob. While he only vaguely recalled the details of the Bible story, he did remember something about a tent stake through the head. Apparently Miss Ellison knew how to wield her weapon well, even if she was wrong to so easily toss aside her uncle's concern.

"You are no Old Testament character, Gwendolyn." Reverend Ballantine folded his arms and squared off with her.

"Of course not. Women have no place in God's calling. Just ask Mary, Elizabeth, or Lydia. Their contributions meant nothing."

All right, so she wasn't exactly like Shauna. While Shauna could paint masterpieces of humor and wit with her words, Miss Ellison's sarcasm was more direct and cutting.

"Gwendolyn, you cannot use God's Word as a weapon against me."

"Can't I? 'For the word of God is quick, and powerful, and sharper than any twoedged sword, piercing even to the dividing asunder of soul and spirit, and of the joints and marrow, and is a discerner of the thoughts and intents of the heart.'"

"Fine, you want biblical truth? 'Children, obey your parents in the Lord: for this is right.' Your father may no longer be in your life, but I have long filled that position, both spiritually and financially. You must heed me when I say becoming involved is not in your best interest. Trust me."

Like two dogs in a show of dominance, Miss Ellison and Reverend Ballantine stared each other down. The tense silence stretched until Miss Ellison folded her hands over her skirt and dipped her chin in what appeared to be resigned submission.

"I understand your concern, Uncle Percy, and yours, Mr. Isaacs, but the reality is I am already involved. Today's jaunt to visit Hibbard and then Mr. Farwell's residence is not likely to go unnoticed. Regardless of your beliefs, I do feel God has called me to be a defender of these children, and I will pursue answers to that end. I'd rather do it with your blessing"—her gaze shifted from Reverend Ballantine's to his—"and with your support, Mr. Isaacs, but I'll not go against what God has called me to do."

Josiah rose to his feet and ran a hand over his face and neck as he paced to the mantel where Shauna's mischievous smirk mocked him from a picture frame. She knew he couldn't allow Miss Ellison to work alone, especially not with the threats and his need for whatever information she uncovered. How was it he always ended up in these situations? Hayden was right. Miss Ellison made the tenth time he'd been cornered into making a decision he didn't want to make by a beautiful woman in need. Thank God this time didn't require a marriage proposal.

He released a long breath and straightened. This was a case. That's all. His heart belonged to Shauna and always would. Working with Miss Ellison, no matter the enticement, would not change that. Any admiration or attraction would disappear the moment she did. He knew his weakness. This would work.

"Miss Ellison, you leave me no choice but to accept your proposal." When he turned, her relieved and hopeful smile contrasted with the dark scowl of Reverend Ballantine. Josiah ignored the tension in his gut and focused solely on Miss Ellison. "However, I am the one in charge. You will obey my directions in the interest of ensuring your protection. Is that understood?"

"As long as your directions don't break God's law, then we are in agreement."

He nodded. "I need to return to the office, but we'll meet this evening before you return to Final Chance to discuss how we will proceed."

"Do you know my home address?"

"I do." And he hadn't needed Ignazio to get it.

Reverend Ballantine ushered Miss Ellison toward the door. "Please wait in the foyer. I need a private moment with Mr. Isaacs."

Miss Ellison gave them a wary glance before exiting and shutting the parlor door.

The reverend strode to Josiah and dropped his voice. "I know your reputation, young man, and I will not see any harm come to Gwendolyn's tender heart. You will conduct any and all meetings in the parlor at my house under my supervision. Nothing is to be hidden from me. Gwendolyn is not to be one of your victims of romance. She deserves something real and lasting, not whatever paltry dalliances you have to offer. Am I clear?"

"Yes, sir."

Josiah had run into protective fathers before, but it never failed to frustrate him to be considered so reprehensible. After seeing them both safely to Wanamaker's, Josiah crossed the street to the Secret Service offices in City Hall. Before he met with Miss Ellison again, he wanted to know everything he could get his hands on about Final Chance and this Mr. Bagwell.

Chapter 11

Steaming bits of potato shot from the pot as Gwendolyn smashed the boiled chunks with more vigor than the task required. Was it really necessary for Uncle Percy to malign Mr. Isaacs's character in order to convince her to abandon "this ridiculous notion" that God called her to lay her "life and reputation" on the line by partnering with the city's foremost bachelor and "rake"? The potatoes sucked at the masher as she pulled up, releasing the kitchen tool with a gurgle and a spray of starch spittle.

Gah! She swiped away the mess on her apron and thunked the pot back onto a warm burner.

An old newspaper article, folded so that the story about Mr. Isaacs's last failed engagement stood prominently on the page, slid into her periphery.

"Percival told me what's happened." Mother tucked a tendril of gold and gray hair behind her ear and tilted her head so the concern behind her amber eyes burrowed deep into Gwendolyn's conscience. "Are you sure that working with this Mr. Isaacs is the best choice?"

Uncle Percy must have sent her in hopes she'd succeed where he'd failed. "He's an officer of the law, Mother. Don't you think it wiser for me to work with the police than on my own? Because you know I will seek answers. To me, those children are as much my own as I am yours. Would you not move heaven and earth to protect me?"

The heart-weary wrinkles on her face deepened as she lifted a hand to cup Gwendolyn's cheek. "You always have been a champion for the less fortunate. I would expect no less of you, but must you partner with *that* officer? Surely there is another within the department to whom you can apply for help."

Gwendolyn didn't want another officer. Despite Uncle Percy's digging through a year's worth of newspapers and producing nearly a dozen articles about Mr. Isaacs, she couldn't give credit to the disparaging remarks. Mr. Isaacs might have flirted a little on the street, but nothing out of the ordinary or suggestive of anything indecent.

"From my experience, Mr. Isaacs is a gentleman and a family man. He is not the type to go carousing or seducing women in helpless estate. Even if he were, do you not believe me capable of withstanding flirtations?"

"I just don't want you forming an attachment to a man who may break your heart." Though Mother didn't say it, the ever-present hollowness in her once-vibrant gaze declared she knew that pain as well as anyone.

"Working with him doesn't mean I'll form an attachment." At her mother's skeptical brow lift, Gwendolyn added, "Even if I did form an attachment, those children are worth any and every heartache. Can you please support me in this?" She squeezed her mother's arm, hoping to convey the importance of her blessing to her. Standing firm against Uncle Percy was one thing, but defying Mother would break her heart worse than any man could.

Mother gave a weak smile. "Sometimes you have so much of your father in you that all I can do is say yes. Just please promise you won't hide anything else from us. If your father had been forthcoming instead of keeping secrets, our lives might have been different."

Gwendolyn's throat tightened. "I promise. No secrets."

"Good." Mother took a shaky breath and then assumed a more confident stance. "Then let's serve dinner and put all unpleasant thoughts aside for the remainder of the evening."

Dinner was its usual lively affair, apart from the unspoken tension in the room. Aunt Birdie, as animated as she was eccentric, flung half a serving of potatoes across the room as her spoon waved in admonition of the two boys she had found nosing around the women's underpinnings department. Even the stuffed finch pinned in her hair seemed to flap its wings in agitation, and at one point Gwendolyn was sure the thing would take flight and join the potatoes. Once Aunt Birdie finished her enthusiastic storytelling, they shared in cleanup duty and then moved to the parlor to await Mr. Isaacs's arrival.

Though all feigned engagement with their personal occupations, Gwendolyn noted Uncle Percy turned even fewer pages in his *Sermons of the Rev. C. H. Spurgeon* than she did in her copy of *Treasure Island*. Even Mother kept scratching through her writing and reaching for a new piece of stationery. If their wait went on too much longer, they'd run out of paper. Aunt Birdie was the only one who seemed able to focus. She moved about the corner of the room, perfecting her dramatic reading of Genesis chapter one for the children on Sunday.

The mantel clock struck a quarter past nine, and Gwendolyn's focus returned to the front door. If Mr. Isaacs didn't arrive within the next five minutes, she'd have to leave without speaking to him. She could not afford to draw attention to herself or earn a reprimand by being out past curfew. Though she stared at the door for several more minutes, no one knocked. Did Mr. Isaacs's absence prove Uncle Percy's condemnation of his character correct? She didn't think so, but it didn't change the disappointment weighing on her as she abandoned her novel and rose from the settee.

She joined her mother at the writing desk and squeezed her shoulder. "It's time for me to leave."

Mother looked up with a strained smile, her hand quickly covering the salutation of her letter. "Already? But he's not come."

Gwendolyn struggled to keep her face passive at her mother's odd behavior. It wasn't like her to hide her correspondence. "All the same, it is time. Will you come with Uncle Percy to services at Final Chance on Sunday?"

"Of course." Her mother rose, turning the paper over as she did so, and embraced Gwendolyn. "I'll even bring you a small tin of Whitman's Chocolate for comfort."

While she appreciated Mother's consideration, the secretiveness behind the concealing of the letter unsettled her. "Who are you writing to, Mother?"

She straightened away. "No one important. Just"—she tucked a rogue tendril behind her ear and cast a worried glance toward Uncle Percy before answering—"an old friend who might be coming to visit us soon."

"Do you really think that wise, Kate?" Uncle Percy folded his arms as he regarded Gwendolyn's mother. "Especially now with all this trouble."

"That's why I'm writing, to postpone the visit. We'll discuss this after Gwendolyn has made it safely back to the refuge."

Silent tension coiled around the room.

And they were upset with *her* for keeping secrets? "Mother, what—"

A sharp rap on the front door interrupted her words.

Of all the times for Mr. Isaacs to make his appearance. Mother looked far too relieved as Uncle Percy strode toward the foyer. She scooped up her papers and closed the secretary before Gwendolyn could do anything more than frown. "I think I'll retire. Good night, everyone."

"Don't you want to meet the rake you're so worried about?"

Uncle Percy cleared his throat. Next to him stood Mr. Isaacs.

Gwendolyn groaned inwardly. Yes, Mr. Isaacs indeed had impeccable timing—for rescuing damsels, and for mortifying them as well. Experience had taught her that bringing attention to such embarrassing statements only increased the awkwardness. It was best to barrel on ahead as if nothing had happened.

"I'm afraid you've come too late for a meeting. I was just preparing to leave. If you please, Mr. Isaacs, this is my mother, Kate Ellison, and my aunt Bernadette Ballantine. Mother, Aunt Birdie, this is Mr. Josiah Isaacs."

The corners of his mouth twitched, and the amusement in his countenance revealed he recognized her diversion tactic. He gave each lady a deep bow. "It is a pleasure to meet you. A rake such as myself is not usually welcomed into the parlor of such fine company."

Gwendolyn's face flamed while her mother sputtered.

Aunt Birdie had no such compunction. "It's our pleasure to have such a fine-looking young man call upon our Gweny. It's been too long since a man elicited her feisty defense."

Cries of "Birdie" filled the room, followed by the robust guffaw of Mr. Isaacs.

"Careful, Mrs. Ballantine, a woman who makes me laugh like that is at great risk of stealing my heart. As you're a married woman, that just wouldn't be fair."

"Oh, I like him." Aunt Birdie elbowed Gwendolyn in the side. "Bears watching, mind you, with those words sweet as honey, but so long as you take Red, he'll give you no problems. Isn't that right, Mr. Isaacs?"

"I suppose it depends on who Red is."

Aunt Birdie cackled as she went to her cabinet of crafting oddities and pulled out a red-handled awl. She placed it in Gwendolyn's hand with a firm nod. "If he misbehaves, just jab him or give his other cheek a nice matching line. Red kept Percival in line. I imagine he'll do just fine for Mr. Isaacs."

"I can assure you I will be on my absolute best behavior around your niece." His chuckles filled the spaces between his words and forced a reluctant smile from Gwendolyn.

"With Red, you will." Aunt Birdie punctuated her statement with a crisp nod, her bird echoing the movement.

Gwendolyn snickered and ignored Uncle Percy's scowl and Mother's unsure appraisal of both her and Mr. Isaacs. After twirling the ice-pick-esque tool in her hand, she pointed the tip at Mr. Isaacs. "You're late." The quarter-until-ten chime emphasized his tardiness and urged Gwendolyn to grab her shawl from the hook. "And now *I'm* going to be late."

Before she could reach it, Mr. Isaacs lifted it and held it open for her to slide beneath. "Allow me to offer my deepest apologies. Another case needed my attention, and I was unable to get away until just now."

She hesitated a moment before turning her back to him and allowing him to lay the shawl over her shoulders. "Apology accepted, but I'm afraid now we cannot meet privately about the situation until my half day next week."

Once she had her shawl on, Mr. Isaacs shifted to her front and folded his arms. "I cannot allow you to return to Final Chance without some instruction. A hack is waiting outside for me. I can advise you as I deliver you to Final Chance. You'll be safe and arrive on time."

Uncle Percy reached for his hat. "I'm coming."

"I'm afraid there is only room for two."

When Uncle Percy began a string of objections, Aunt Birdie placed a finger over his mouth. "Gweny is well protected by Red, and it's a ten-minute ride by hack. Not much can happen in ten minutes."

"I beg to differ."

Aunt Birdie's mouth quirked as if a memory triggered her agreement. "Well, Gweny is too practical for such tomfoolery. We can trust her."

"It's him I don't trust!"

"Don't worry, Uncle." Gwendolyn wiggled the awl. "Red will be my defender."

With a quick kiss to Aunt Birdie's cheek, a wave to her mother, and a squeeze to Uncle Percy's hand as she brushed past him, Gwendolyn made her escape. Mr. Isaacs circled around her to reach the hack first and lifted a hand of assistance, bowing as if she were the Queen of England and not some lowly charity worker. What sort of man who lived in a house like his would lower himself to her level, let alone treat her as an equal or better? She'd never experienced someone so noble before, but could she really trust the sincerity of his act? Gwendolyn settled onto the seat, careful to angle the awl so it didn't poke the man but remained easy to use should he prove to be everything the newspapers asserted.

After providing the driver with directions, Mr. Isaacs slid onto the bench next to her with gentlemanly decorum, keeping a good foot between them. Not even when they jerked into motion did his leg brush against hers, and it was absolutely shameful how much that disappointed her. For mercy's sake! What business had she in wishing that her leg would brush a man's—especially a man who'd had nine engagements and a marriage? It had to be the cool spring air scented with blooming cherry blossoms. Nothing revitalized her dreams of a husband and family more than the pink, white, and purple blooms combined with the would-be attentions of a handsome man.

Well, he would be handsome if she could see him clearly in the dark interior. Instead, she only saw shadowed glimpses of his face when they passed a streetlamp.

Mr. Isaacs shifted next to her. "So I'm a rake, eh?" Humor laced his voice.

"I'm afraid my uncle and mother give more credit to the gossip-mongers than they are due."

"Am I to assume you are not in agreement with them?"

"I prefer to make judgments through personal acquaintance. That's not to say I trust you—only that you have yet to give me a true reason to fear you. But should you get any rakish ideas, Red is faithfully waiting to take action."

His chuckle caused her heart to flutter, and she was suddenly glad that if she could not see his face, he could not see hers.

"Well, be sure to keep Red on hand even at Final Chance." The humor fell away, and a businesslike tone replaced it. "I'm only at the beginning stages of my investigation and cannot give you any warnings as to specific persons to avoid. It is of utmost importance that you go through your days as you would have before any threats or suspicions shadowed your experience. I don't want you to do any snooping around. I don't want to upset those involved and risk their making another attempt on your life."

"Is there anything I *can* do?" It sounded as if he wasn't going to use her help after all.

"Make me a list of all those employed by Final Chance, connected to the board, or anyone who regularly visits. That includes those who bring deliveries, donations, or have any other connections you can think of. I'll need to know what their positions are and all their responsibilities."

"I'll do my best to have it by the time you arrive on Friday."

"Anything you can provide will be helpful. I'd also like to find a way to be in the building as often as possible. What activities would give me that sort of access without appearing suspicious?"

"You could volunteer with the Ladies' Committee to visit each week, but I don't believe you'd make a convincing woman." Although it would be amusing to see him attempt to wear a corset, bustle, and bonnet. "Other than that, Sunday afternoon services with the children are all I can think of. Services are open to the public, so no one would question if you joined us."

"Church services? At Final Chance?" By the underlying horror in his tone, she assumed Mr. Isaacs must not be a religious man.

"Yes. Unfortunately, except for services and an odd meeting, the presence of male board members is fairly scarce. Service attendance is really the only weekly activity I can suggest without bringing awareness to your investigation."

The rough fabric over Josiah's elbow grazed Gwendolyn's cheek as he rubbed the back of his neck and blew out a heavy breath. "Just wait until Abigail hears I have to attend church for a case. She'll probably point to it as God's consequence for my ignoring His holy prodding."

"I can think of worse consequences. Although I do suppose being forced to sit and listen to the Word of God can be quite disconcerting. Especially when it pricks our conscience and makes us aware of how infinitely unholy we are without Christ as our Savior."

He huffed. "Spoken like a true reverend's niece. You've probably never doubted your faith a day of your life."

She almost laughed outright. "Doubt strikes even the most confident of believers, Mr. Isaacs. We all must wrestle with it at some point, but it is not our doubt that defines our faith. Faith redefines our doubts."

"Pretty words from a pretty lady, but one cannot doubt the goodness of God and still have faith. They are opposites."

His words so echoed her own during the first years after Father's leaving that all she could do was offer the wisdom Uncle Percy gave her. "Unbelief is the opposite of faith. Doubt is the struggle to believe God's promises when confronted with the darkness of this world. It's the wavering between accepting God and His unsearchable ways or believing what our limited experiences might tell us. You can still believe in God and doubt His goodness. It's what you do with that doubt that matters. Ignore it and you give it the power to destroy your faith. Confront it and ask God to help you, and I guarantee you your faith will come out stronger in the end. Tell me, Mr. Isaacs, have you gone to God with your doubts and asked Him to help you to confront them?"

The clop of hooves filled the space.

Oh, how well she understood his silence. Only by the grace of God and the encouragement of those who'd faced their own doubts had she overcome the ones left behind by her father.

His silence lingered, and the hack slowed to a stop half of a square from Final Chance. The wooden doors released from over their legs, and he climbed down to the sidewalk. Fear clawed at her, and she gripped Red tighter. Was he planning to eject her from the carriage and abandon her on the street? The walk wasn't far, but what if Quincy lurked in some shadow, waiting for her return?

Mustering what courage she could, she sat up straighter. "Have I offended you so greatly that you find the need to abandon me so close to Final Chance?"

The gaslight illuminated half his serious face when he turned to close the protective door. "You have not offended me. As you noted, we're close to Final Chance. I don't want anyone to see you with me, lest it put you in more danger."

Gwendolyn released a breath of gratitude to the Lord, but a new worry edged in. "What about you? Mr. Farwell was killed not far from here."

"The driver will return to retrieve me after he's seen you safely inside. We'll meet again on Friday as planned, but keep Red handy at all times. It brings me comfort to know you are protected."

No wonder so many swooned at his feet. His consideration knew no bounds. "Thank you. I'll be sure to keep Red nearby, but do give serious thought to attending services with us. At the very least, you'll see the children. Have no concern about bringing your doubts to God. You'll be in good company, as I'll be bringing my own."

"You are a singular woman, Miss Ellison. Be safe." He nodded at her and then waved the driver on.

The hack moved only a few feet before Mr. Isaacs melted into the shadows of late evening, almost as if he were more specter than man. She leaned over the half door for a moment and tried to discern where he'd gone but then quickly settled back into the seat. It wouldn't do for the man to think she'd set her cap for him—even if he did stir up feelings she wasn't quite sure what to do with. One thing she did know: he needed her prayers, and those she would give without reserve.

The ten o'clock bells of a distant church clanged as the hack stopped in front of Final Chance. By the time she unlocked the front door and crossed the threshold, the last gong reverberated into a fading echo. It was the closest to being late she'd ever been. She locked the door and turned to find Superintendent King standing in the receiving room doorway with the visitor schedule in hand and a scowl on his face.

"Come in and have a seat, Miss Ellison. It's time we had a talk."

CHAPTER 12

A WHITE-GLOVED WAITER REMOVED THE gold-rimmed oyster plate and matching fork from the place setting in front of Josiah and replaced it with a bowl of green turtle soup. Josiah nodded his thanks, even though he'd prefer to be dining on Tillie's simple fare at home rather than the extravagant meal at the Continental Hotel's restaurant. Mother rarely chose something so public for their weekly luncheons, but since the children's arrest and her subsequent concealment of it, she'd insisted on eating in public. The woman was as good at avoiding uncomfortable conversations as Father was about forcing them.

"Where is your mind today, Josiah? I don't believe you've heard a single word I've said." Mother set her spoon on the edge of the plate and pinned him with an accusatory arch of the brow.

He wasn't about to admit his mind had been jumping from Miss Ellison's words about faith, to the uncomfortable attraction taking root, to grief over Shauna's death, and then to concern for his nieces and nephew. None of the former were topics he wanted to broach with his mother, and the latter was sure to cause conflict. Not that a little conflict would hurt if it gained him answers.

"Forgive me. My mind was distracted by the fact that my nieces and nephew are in an institution for juvenile criminals and that my mother hid it from me."

A nearby table of women quieted and made subtle turns in their seats to better hear the conversation. Though he didn't care a whit what others thought of him or his family, he did care about his mother, and maintaining a positive public appearance was of utmost concern to her. He blew out a frustrated breath. Maybe he had a bit more of his father in him than he cared to admit. Yes, the conversation needed to happen, but he should be more diplomatic in his approach. Being perturbed with her did not give him the right to be cruel and lance her with a tactic he knew would embarrass her.

Ever the politician's wife, she maintained her composure and patted her mouth with a napkin—ostensibly to disguise her response from the nosy buzzards at the next table over. "I never kept it secret. I only waited until I was certain I could get them transferred to Final Chance."

Except she sent Abigail to tell him instead of informing him herself. He could press the issue, but now was not the time. "I'm sorry, Mother. I shouldn't have spoken so. We'll save this discussion for another time. However, if you could choose a subject other than fashion for the remainder of our dinner, I would greatly appreciate it."

The busybodies' chairs scraped over the marble-tiled floors as they returned their focus to the conversation at their own table. They were probably already twisting what little they heard into tittle-tattle for the next society column.

Instead of choosing a new topic, Mother absently stared at her soup. As the silence stretched into the next course of lobster à la Newburg, regret at bringing up her duplicity pricked his conscience. They might have their difficulties, but he knew her misguided choice came from a place of love. Allowing her to prattle on about fashion would have been much better than the awkwardness between them now. As he tried to think of a tolerable topic that would restore her joyful mood, she finally spoke in a quiet voice.

"Will you visit Shauna's grave tomorrow?"

Josiah froze with a bite of cream-coated lobster midway to his mouth. The question itself was extraordinary coming from his mother, but the fact she'd spoken Shauna's name aloud was practically miraculous. Without taking the bite, he lowered his fork. The emotions that welled up at the sound of Shauna's name finally on her lips were such a mix he couldn't be sure if it was bitterness, relief, joy, or grief that rose to the surface most.

He cleared his throat before speaking, but his voice still came out froggy. "Yes. At one." The hour of their wedding. Visiting her at that time on their anniversary just felt right. Like a renewing of his vows.

"May I go with you?"

Had he been attempting a bite, the fork would have clattered to the plate and drawn the curiosity of the whole room. Was this even his mother? Maybe this was some political ploy to boost his father's reputation. Josiah scanned the room for any one of the numerous newspaper men who'd hounded his private life over the years. Finding none, he returned his attention to his mother. The vulnerability in her face suggested there were no ulterior motives, but years of rejection couldn't be erased in a single moment.

"What's brought about this change? You wouldn't even say her name a week ago."

Her chin dipped. "It's something the Lord has been working long and hard on my heart to bring about. I'm sorry that I didn't show you or Shauna the love you deserved. I put the approval of others above my own son and God's calling to love others as myself. Helping the Murphys is my attempt to do better, but I want to love you better too. To get to know the woman who so thoroughly stole your heart." She gave a soft chuckle even as a tear slipped down her cheek. "She must've really been something special to win your heart. Countless women have sought it. Nine almost had it—"

"None ever came close to having my heart. It's always beat for Shauna alone, and it always will."

Her mournful smile spoke her regret. "Then she was lucky, and I missed out. Is it too much to ask for your forgiveness and a chance to get to know her through you?"

Josiah sat back in his chair, the full weight of the conversation hitting him like a sandbag and knocking him into an uncontrollable flood of emotions. He'd gotten used to keeping Shauna's memory away from the scorn of his family. Even Abigail knew of only a few sweet memories. But this is what Shauna had prayed for and what he'd given up on praying for. How could he deny his mother forgiveness?

"No. It's not too much to ask, but I'm not ready to share my visits."

Her smile wobbled. "I understand. Small steps. I'll gladly listen to any stories you might wish to share about her. Whenever you're ready."

"Thank you, Mother. That means more than you know."

The rest of the meal passed in quiet conversation. Small tidbits about Shauna slipped out. Her fear of crickets, disdain for potatoes, and love of Irish lore. Although he still felt the weight of grief, a bittersweet aftertaste lingered, like a finely made dark chocolate. Little bites were all he could stand, but they left behind a sweet pleasure he hadn't anticipated he would feel so deeply in finally being able to share Shauna with his mother.

When they walked outside, Saul, his housekeeper's son, sat next to the driver of Mother's personal carriage. Josiah frowned. The boy was supposed to be in school. He hadn't hired Tillie and Elias to save them from the streets just to have their son grow up without an education.

Upon spotting their approach, Saul hopped down. "My teacher got sick and sent us all home early. Mam was gonna make me help with the wash, but Pappy sent me to give you this." Judging by his grin, the boy felt elated at his escape from the dreaded chore. "The restaurant man wouldn't let me in, so when I saw Mrs. Isaacs's carriage, I decided to wait for you here."

There was little doubt in Josiah's mind that Saul saw the proprietor's dismissal as an excuse to extend his errand and avoid the laundry tasks awaiting him at home. Josiah should reprimand the boy, but in truth, he couldn't blame him. If he were in Saul's position, he too would do whatever he could to avoid washing laundry.

"Thank you, Saul." Josiah released Mother's arm and accepted the letter. If Elias sent a note across town, he must have deemed it important. His butler had a good eye for separating the frivolous from the urgent. Josiah looked for a return address or even a stamp indicating it came through the mail. Nothing. "Was this hand delivered?"

"Yep, by a Mr. Crane or something like that."

He broke the wax seal and found Superintendent King's signature at the end.

Mr. Isaacs,

In observance of mourning for the passing of Mr. Farwell, Final Chance is closed to the public until further notice. Your tour has been canceled. Should you require further information about the institution, you may ask your mother or write to me. Matron Ellison is no longer at your disposal.

Superintendent King

Familiar unease wrung his gut until he regretted his food choices. Farwell had been dead for more than a week and King was just now closing Final Chance? The suddenness of the closure, his canceled tour, and the direct reference to Miss Ellison did not bode well for his investigation. Had King discovered Miss Ellison's partnership with him? Josiah had watched her enter the building last night, but anything could've happened to her after that.

"What is it, dear?"

Josiah worked to keep the concern out of his voice, although it was difficult given the images of a beaten Miss Ellison flashing through his mind. "Superintendent King decided to postpone my tour of Final Chance. Indefinitely."

Mother pulled the letter from his hands and harrumphed as she skimmed its contents. "That man may be good at his job, but he's an intolerable grouch. Miss Ellison is a saint for dealing with him on a daily basis." She handed back the letter with a calculating glint in her eyes. "Final Chance may be closed to the public, but as a board member, I can drop in unannounced. What do you say to taking your tour now?"

Some of the tightness unwound, and the images abated. He needed to see her again, but provoking King's ire would only further risk Miss Ellison's safety. This needed to be handled carefully. "When is Mr. Farwell's funeral?"

"Tomorrow morning." A sly grin spread across Mother's cheeks. "Superintendent King will be representing Final Chance, as only one administrator can be absent from the building at a time. I'm sure Miss Ellison is grieved that she could not attend. A visit from me would be welcomed."

"I knew Abigail's deviousness had to come from somewhere."

Mother pressed a hand to her chest and feigned dismay. "I am never devious. Strategic, yes, but never devious."

He chuckled as he bent to kiss her on the cheek. "I love you, Mother." When he straightened, he handed her up into the carriage. "By all means, strategize freely, and then send word of your plans for tomorrow as soon as they are settled. I have some strategizing of my own to do."

While it would be a relief to see and speak with Miss Ellison himself tomorrow, he could not wait that long to verify she was safe. He checked his pocket watch as Mother's carriage pulled away. Three o'clock. Perfect. Speedy and his pack of newspaper hawkers should still be working the corner of 13th and Chestnut. The street urchins were always eager for a chance to earn a few coins they didn't have to share with the ruthless man over them, and Josiah had just the job for them to keep coins in their pockets and food in their bellies.

CHAPTER 13

THE EXCITED CHATTER OF THE boys and the girls bounced off the garden walls and filled Gwendolyn's heart with joy. Garden preparation day was always her favorite day of the year. More so this year with Mr. Bagwell taking to bed with a headache and Superintendent King's absence due to his attending the funeral. Superintendent King might have spoiled her plans to give Mr. Isaacs a tour and a visit with his family, but God had seen fit to give her a day to bend the rules and allow all to work together.

She watched the younger children playing in the girls' yard and then the older children turning soil and removing weeds within the walled garden. While there was the typical grumbling and complaining, everyone seemed to be enjoying themselves more than usual. Siblings who'd gone weeks, even months, without talking to each other bantered, whispered, and stole secret hugs. Even Mr. Crane seemed to enjoy himself as he instructed the older boys on how best to wield their shovels and conversed with Agatha as they supervised. Wilhelmina orchestrated a game of blindman's buff with the younger ones, who could play until it was their turn to work and give the older ones a break.

This was how an institution dedicated to reformation should be run. God didn't design the world for men and women to be separated, but to support one another, working in community. Of course, He hadn't originally designed food to be obtained through such hard labor either, which made today a perfect illustration of how choosing to break the law had long-term consequences. This weekend's Bible study on creation and sin would likely have new meaning to many of these children as they felt the soreness from today's work for many days to come.

Gwendolyn knelt next to Tessa and Jude and dug her hands into a clump of soil. "Have you ever planted a garden before?"

Jude eyed her warily and remained silent, but Tessa no longer held such reserve around her. "We had a box with dirt and seeds in it once, but the birds ate the seed, and the cat turned it into a privy."

"That naughty cat sounds like one I used to have—only he ate my aunt's favorite bird." She scrunched her face at the memory of the aftermath as she tossed the weeds to the side and reached for another clump. "All he left behind was the beak and the feet. My aunt looked at his fat belly and screamed and sobbed for days. She forced me to give him away after that."

Grief she hadn't expected welled in her throat. That kitten had been a gift from her father two months before he left. Losing Clover had been like losing her last connection to him.

"Why you be helping us? Aren't you too good for this?"

Jude's disdain wasn't surprising, considering none of the other staff worked in the dirt. So often these children were made to feel that they were worthless. A lie she worked hard every day to expose.

"No one is good, Jude. We all are sinners who deserve the just punishment of God. Even me. I might have a position of authority over you by the world's standards, but in God's eyes you and I are made equally in His image. If working in the dirt alongside you will reflect God's love for both of us to you, then I will gladly do it. Even if there are worms crawling about." She pulled one free of the clump and flung it away with an exaggerated face of disgust.

Jude scrutinized her with a frown, as if taking the measure of her words.

Lord, may he seest thou instead of me.

Tessa elbowed Jude in the side, a grin splitting her face as she gestured with her head to somewhere behind Gwendolyn and whispered, "Uncle Joe's here."

Gwendolyn spun to verify Tessa's claim and lost her balance.

Mr. Isaacs grabbed her arm, but not fast enough to prevent her from toppling sideways into the damp soil and knocking the straw hat off her head.

Cool mud clung to the side of her face and likely the full length of her dress. Heat hot enough to dry the mud crept into her face as Mr. Isaacs displayed a bemused smile. What a way to greet the man. Why hadn't Speedy mentioned Mr. Isaacs's plan to come today when he'd brought the note with the instructions of how to call for help? Had she known he would keep his appointment, she would have waited to help with the garden and maybe even worn her best dress.

She pushed from the mud and accepted his and Mr. Crane's help to get to her feet. Jude grabbed her hat, leaving his muddied handprints all over the wide brim before handing it back to her.

Not that her hands were much better. She cringed at the handprints she'd left behind on both men's coats. "Oh, no! I'm so sorry. I've made a mess of all three of us."

"A little dirt never hurt anyone." Mr. Isaacs held a handkerchief out with his clean hand. "You, however, have quite a bit more than a little. Are you all right?" His appraisal sent somersaults rolling in her stomach.

She refused the handkerchief. It would take more than a square of cloth to clean up her appearance. "Other than the damage to my pride, I am unharmed."

"Truly?"

The word with the arched brow implied more than concern over the fall. Speedy had asked after her welfare when he delivered the note, but her reply must not have satisfied Mr. Isaacs. Though the concern likely was born out of duty to his job, it warmed her to know he cared. "Truly, but I'm afraid a trip to my room is prudent. Officer Crane, Officer Wood, will you please supervise the garden work? Jude, Tessa, please clean up and inform Mrs. Flowers we have a guest."

"Two, actually." Mr. Isaacs stepped aside to reveal his mother standing at the gate between garden and yard.

Jude and Tessa scampered past Mrs. Isaacs into the girls' yard like she wasn't among the most important guests to grace the property and snagged Cara before disappearing into the building.

Of all the times for Mrs. Isaacs to make a surprise visit. The unexpected presence of board members, especially on a day like today, rarely boded well. Even Officer Crane and Agatha straightened their postures and sobered. So much for a perfect, carefree day. Mrs. Isaacs likely came with an eye for improvement on a budget that couldn't be supported. She was a kind woman but had no concept of frugality or the realities of running a nearly impoverished institution.

Gwendolyn gave the best curtsy she could manage with mud-caked hands and mustered a poor copy of the smile Mr. Isaacs had so easily conjured earlier. "I apologize for the improper welcome, Mrs. Isaacs. We're behind on planting the garden, and I decided we could delay no further."

"Don't give it another thought, Matron Ellison." Mrs. Isaacs waved off the explanation as if the situation were nothing more than a wisp of extinguished candle smoke. "Catching you working with the children is just another testament to your good character. If you wouldn't mind cleaning up, though, I've come to check on the newest wards and give my son a tour of the facilities. He's considering joining the board."

After reiterating her instructions to the officers, Gwendolyn led the way into the building. Mr. Isaacs opened the door for her, and she directed him and his mother to wait in the receiving room while she cleaned up. After scrubbing every fleck of dirt from her hands and face, she wavered between her usual staid, somber ensembles and the long-abandoned dress in the corner of her wardrobe. The light blue skirt with a bodice of blue ribbon and black scrollwork was better suited for a day out with a beau than a stuffy meeting with a board member. However, after her embarrassment in the garden, the bit of extravagance would restore confidence in her role as matron. Decision made, she dressed and hurried down to the kitchen to retrieve the tea cart.

"Land sakes! You look like one of them porcelain dolls." Mrs. Flowers stared at her from the stove, wooden spoon dripping broth and causing sputtering and sizzling on the hot burner. "Who are you all done up for?"

"Mrs. Isaacs has paid us a surprise visit. Is the tea cart ready?"

"Yes, ma'am. Tessa delivered it to Mrs. Issacs and her son near ten minutes ago." A spark of suspicion lit her expression. "You wouldn't be putting on airs for him now, would you? I haven't seen that dress since Robert Rankin stopped courting you."

"Don't be ridiculous. Mr. Isaacs is a widower, and I have my hands full enough with the children here. This is simply an attempt to negate the disastrous state Mrs. Isaacs found me in upon her arrival."

"Seems to me a widower is prime for the enticing, and with that fancy dress you just might convince him you fit in with that hoity-toity family of his." She turned to continue stirring the pot. "Can't say I blame you for wanting away from this place, especially after losing Mr. Farwell, but I never imagined you'd go after one of their ilk."

Was it really so hard to believe that Gwendolyn wished only to make an impression upon the wealthiest board member—one who also happened to be in charge of the Ladies' Committee? The woman had substantial power over how the facility ran just by her family's political influence. "If Mr. Isaacs has anything to do with my appearance, it's merely to encourage him not to look too closely at the struggles of Final Chance. He's considering joining the board, and he's a fair sight more observant than his mother."

"Oh, you have no worries there. He won't be observing anything but you. Mark my words. Now you best get going. You've kept them waiting long enough. Do be sure to show them the kitchen so I can get a good look at him."

Gwendolyn bit her lip as she strode down the hall. She didn't have time to change again, but she truly hadn't dressed to impress Mr. Isaacs. Well, not intentionally. Mostly. Maybe a little. Oh, for heaven's sake, had she?

Stopping at the mirror by the receiving room door, she looked herself in the eyes. "Stop behaving so foolishly. You're a matron. He has a job to do. So do you, and that's that." The whispered reprimand did little to stop the increasing pace of her heart as she turned the doorknob and stepped inside to peals of laughter.

Mr. Isaacs lay belly-up on the rug with all three Murphy children leaning over him and plying him with wiggling fingers. Robust and genuine laughter filled the room as he writhed on the floor under their touch. His movements were too exaggerated to stem from their attempts, but the children's delight in his reaction made it obvious why he pretended. Mrs. Isaacs was too focused on watching her son with a wistful sort of smile to notice Gwendolyn's entrance.

The intimate scene made her feel an intruder, but at least it confirmed her original thoughts. Mrs. Flowers was wrong. It didn't matter what Gwendolyn wore. Mr. Isaacs only had eyes for the children and his case. Feeling more at ease, she clasped her hands and waited until someone noticed her presence.

It didn't take long. Jude spotted her and elbowed the girls with whispered warnings to stop. All joy and merriment vanished from their faces and were replaced with varying amounts of hostility, disappointment, and resignation. It dampened her own spirits to see that her intrusion brought about such feelings, but she couldn't help that her role would always be viewed as the enemy. It was the double-edged sword of her calling—to love the children with her whole being even though the majority of them would likely reject her. She gave them an encouraging smile, though she well knew it wouldn't make a difference.

Mr. Isaacs sat up, his hair poking out every which way and his breathing labored from the exertion of playing with his nieces and nephew. Her smile grew of its own accord. Had his appearance been immaculate, he couldn't have appeared more handsome than he did now. The disorderly love, guileless smile, and joy-filled laugh that enveloped all those around him drew her in like a moth to the flame. She knew better than to be attracted to him, but she just couldn't help it. The Murphy children were lucky to have an uncle like that in their lives, and one day—if he wasn't one already—Mr. Isaacs would make a wonderful father.

She concentrated on the task at hand. "Thank you for your patience. Again, I apologize for soiling your clothes and for my appearance when you arrived."

Mr. Isaacs's tortoise eyes swung her direction, and his smile dropped. He didn't even acknowledge her apology but stared at her like she was a hog dripping mud on an Oriental rug. She swallowed and tried to smile, but his obvious disapproval of her attire hurt. He must think of her as no better than a fortune hunter.

"Don't give it another thought," Mrs. Isaacs said. "Josiah knocks women off their feet all the time. It's the getting back on them afterward that's more troublesome." Her scrutiny swept the length of Gwendolyn's attire. "However, it appears you've recovered extraordinarily well. I didn't realize you owned something so . . . vibrant."

There was a twist of censure to her tone, and Gwendolyn cringed. Obviously Mrs. Isaacs agreed with Mrs. Flowers's assessment of Gwendolyn putting on airs.

A tinge of red colored Mr. Isaacs's cheeks before he shot to his feet and completed a quick repair of his appearance and the children's. "All right. It's time to mind our manners. Onto the settee, if you please."

Tessa sat on the end and patted the center. "Sit here, Uncle Joe."

He complied, and the other children vied for the best spots, with Cara claiming his legs and Tessa and Jude snuggling against each of his sides.

Why did a widower, especially one so far above her station in life, have to fit so perfectly with the long-set-aside dreams of her future husband? One would think after the painful end to her near engagement with Robert she'd know better than to entertain even a passing fancy.

She prepared the specialty tea reserved for Mrs. Isaacs's visits and handed the woman a full cup while taking only a half cup for herself. Even that much was an indulgence she didn't often allow. Though she shouldn't torture herself so, Gwendolyn sat in the chair next to Mrs. Isaacs and faced the settee where Mr. Isaacs cuddled the children. What could she say that wouldn't appear flirtatious or contrived? It couldn't be about the case. Even if he had shared about it with his mother, it wouldn't be wise to speak in front of the children, especially the younger ones.

Yesterday's newspaper lay on the floor. Perfect. "Thank you for providing a daily subscription to the newspaper, Mr. Isaacs. You can be certain I will make good use of it."

"Excellent. Did Speedy share the details of the arrangement?"

"Oh yes, but I made a few changes. I hope you don't mind." While Mr. Isaacs's plan for Speedy and his friends to watch the building for trouble was sweet and helpful, he missed the most practical application. "He appeared hungry but refused any charity, so we struck a deal. He will deliver the newspapers directly to me at the kitchen door during the noon meal so that he can eat a plate of whatever we're serving in exchange for delivering our mail to the post office afterward."

The ploy was perfect for hiding communication, as long as the newspaper and its contents made it into her hands before anyone else's. She held his gaze to ensure he understood her meaning.

His tilted smile reappeared. "That's very generous and wise of you. I'm impressed."

She hid the embarrassment of his praise and the appreciation she saw in his eyes behind a drink from her cup. The plot was merely a similar trick to the one she'd used while an officer and still courting Robert.

Mrs. Isaacs coughed and set her teacup on the side table. "I'm afraid we're on a strict schedule. Josiah has an appointment at one o'clock. Before you provide a tour, Jude mentioned something about a child sent to the hospital?"

Gwendolyn snapped her attention to Jude, who now cowered behind Mr. Isaacs. Had he seen what happened? "Yes, Hibbard Wilcox. Superintendent King and I are going to give a full report of the incident on Tuesday."

"Is the delay so that you can align your stories to make it less reprehensible?"

She bristled at the accusation. "Of course not. If you'll recall, it was I who came to the board with concerns for the children's well-being last month. Superintendent King was the one who squelched the possibility of maltreatment, despite my objections. I have not yet come forward about Hibbard myself because I lack the proof required to support my suspicions."

"Are you insinuating the child was beaten by one of our officers?"

"As I said, I have no proof. Hibbard's jaw was so thoroughly broken that he cannot chew, let alone speak the name of his attacker."

"Oh my word." Mrs. Isaacs's hand fluttered to her chest.

"I'm joining the board." Mr. Isaacs's arms encircled his little family and pulled them closer. "I can't have them living in an abusive place. I'd like to conduct an official investigation, but I need the help of all of you." He eyed each person in the room, ending with Jude. "Did you see what happened to Hibbard?"

"No. But I know it weren't Gareth like they say. They was best friends."

Mrs. Isaacs scooted to the edge of her seat and claimed a regal command. "I agree an investigation must be conducted, and I trust no one better than you. Cara, Jude, Tessa. Are you in agreement to work with Matron Ellison?"

Two of the three children looked at each other. Cara played with her rag doll, oblivious to the entire conversation. One at a time, they nodded at each other. Then Tessa spoke. "We will."

"Good. Now, how does this work, Josiah? I'm afraid I'm out of my element."

"Matron Ellison and I need to search the building, but I don't want anyone to discover what we are doing. Do you think you can keep watch for Superintendent King's return and distract him if necessary?"

"Of course."

"The children should rejoin the group, or else their extended absence will be noted." Gwendolyn addressed Tessa and Jude. "I need you to listen to what the other children are saying when they think no one else is around. Jude, you'll tell Tessa anything you hear. Tessa, you'll be responsible for coming to me. Is that understood?"

"Yes, ma'am."

There was a bit too much enthusiasm coming from the children, but the officers would simply attribute it to the special day all were having.

She dismissed them outside and then settled Mrs. Isaacs with her tea in the donations room across the hall. The window there would allow her to see if Superintendent King entered through the boys' ward entrance while still being able to maintain watch here.

When Mr. Isaacs opened the door to the foyer, he prevented Gwendolyn from passing through. "Are you certain you wish to take the risk? There is no harm in telling me no."

The faces of Hibbard and Mr. Farwell flashed through her mind. A child lay in a hospital bed and a good man lay in the ground because of evil men. How many more would suffer if she did not act? With a quick prayer for protection and success, she strode past him. "We'll begin in the boys' ward."

CHAPTER 14

As HE FOLLOWED MISS ELLISON, Josiah swallowed hard and adjusted the paper collar around his neck. His mother might not have approved of Miss Ellison's dress, but Josiah couldn't imagine one suiting her better. And that was part of the problem. If she'd been any other woman, he could disregard the physical attraction with more ease than people gave him credit.

But nothing about Miss Ellison could be disregarded. Not her beauty, not her kindness toward the children, not even her compassion when confronted with his doubts. Determined to shove the unsettling feelings aside, Josiah lengthened his stride until he walked next to her.

She cast him an apologetic smile. "I'm afraid I haven't completed the documents you requested. Superintendent King wasn't pleased when he discovered I scheduled your tour for a time when I knew he would be gone, and he's been very demanding on my time ever since."

"Are you concerned for your safety?"

"No. He's an insufferable man, but I don't believe him capable of laying an actual hand on me or the children. His crime is in not opposing it." She stopped in front of a door at the end of the corridor. A kitchen, if the smell of baked bread and something frying were any indication. "I'd like to introduce to you Mrs. Flowers before we continue forward. She handles most of the deliveries and generally knows all the gossip. If there are whisperings of goings-on, she likely knows something about it."

And it also meant that if she suspected any investigations, she wouldn't keep quiet about it. "Then I suggest you be very careful around her."

Miss Ellison shrugged. "You don't spend nearly ten years with the woman and not learn how to keep a secret from her. It's you who should be worried. She already believes the reason I'm wearing my best dress is to impress you. That isn't why, by the way." The last of her words rushed out faster as color rose high in her cheeks. "Your mother is the one whom I wished to impress. Especially after finding me in the mud. I want to assure you I have no romantic intentions toward you. I'm not the type of woman who chases after a man."

He blinked and then choked on a laugh. Of all the things to spill from her mouth. He hadn't considered his presence to be a factor in her choice of dress to begin with. Everything he'd seen her say or do was for the sake of others, not personal gain.

Her eyes widened, and the red spread to cover her entire face. "Oh, good heavens! Forgive me."

She didn't give him a chance to respond but opened the door and scurried into the room with a hand to her cheek and her eyes downcast.

A plump woman with a frizzy cap of white hair—presumably Mrs. Flowers—turned from the stove, took one look at Miss Ellison, and arched a brow at him. "Whatever you said, you best apologize, young man. Matron Ellison is a lady and should be addressed as such."

Her manner and heavy Southern accent warned that she'd probably have no compunction against swatting him with a spoon if he didn't comply, regardless of the fact he had nothing to apologize for.

He turned toward Miss Ellison and gave a slight shake of the head when she opened her mouth to speak. "My apologies, Miss—"

Mrs. Flowers gave a reprimanding cough.

"—Matron Ellison. It is never my wish to make you uncomfortable. I think your dress very becoming of a matron, regardless of whom you were trying to impress."

Miss Ellison's mouth clamped shut, and she angled away. He hadn't meant to further embarrass her but to ease her discomfort. The best choice now was to get the attention off her.

He approached Mrs. Flowers, took her hand, and kissed it as he bowed. "Final Chance is lucky to have such an astute and proper lady in its kitchens. I am sure the children here leave well-fed and well-mannered under your excellent tutelage."

A giggle erupted behind him, and when he looked over his shoulder, Miss Ellison had her hand over her mouth and tried to spin away from view.

"I don't know if I should be miffed that you would try to butter me up or giddy that you did." By the saucy tilt to her smile and shoulders, Mrs. Flowers most assuredly felt the latter. "I give you leave to like him, Matron, so long as he behaves." She gave him a stern but jovial look before shooing him away. "Off you two go. I've got a mess of work to do before the dinner crew comes and destroys my kitchen."

Josiah couldn't help but grin.

It increased until his cheeks ached when Miss Ellison walked past Mrs. Flowers and Mrs. Flowers whispered, "He's a charmer. If you're not interested, see what he thinks about courting an older woman."

Once they exited the kitchen and made it halfway across the dining hall, Miss Ellison cleared her throat. A tinge of pink still colored her cheeks. "Please forgive Mrs. Flowers if she offended you in any way. She can be a bit spirited at times."

"I like her. I feel all the women I've met at Final Chance thus far are spirited and to be admired."

Her head tilted with innocent confusion. "Who else have you met?"

Though he shouldn't, he claimed her arm. "Just you."

Her lashes flitted, and her dainty mouth formed an "oh" before she dropped her chin like a woman suddenly gone shy. To both his relief and chagrin, she did not pull away from him.

What was he doing flirting with this woman? It was his anniversary, for heaven's sake. He should be mourning that it wasn't Shauna next to him, not enjoying himself on the arm of another woman. He glanced sideways at Miss Ellison, and his heart jolted in his chest—disturbingly similar to the way it had within the first week of his meeting Shauna and every time he looked at her afterward.

Some in his family called it the Isaacs Intuition. Generations of Isaacs had claimed to know from first sight who their spouses would be, including himself and each of his sisters. But that couldn't be what this feeling was. He didn't need, let alone want, another wife. His heart belonged to Shauna alone. Didn't it? He firmed his jaw against any other possibility. He was a one-woman man, forever and always, and that woman was Shauna.

"This is the boys' ward." Miss Ellison pulled away and unlocked a set of double doors that led to a dimly lit L-shaped hallway.

Relieved he could again shove aside his troubling thoughts, Josiah dove headfirst into the investigation. "Are the doors always kept locked between the two areas?"

"Except at mealtime. Down that side hall, there is another set of stairs that leads to the sleeping quarters. The doors prevent the children from sneaking into each other's quarters and protect their privacy."

"It seems to me that it provides protection for those who would want to hide their behavior from the unexpected visits of others."

She blew out a heavy sigh as she relocked the doors behind them. "Often what is meant for good is twisted for the purposes of evil men."

"Have you considered there might be more than abuse going on behind these locked doors?" He'd been careful to keep any mention of counterfeiting out of their conversations, but if she was really going to partner with him in this, she needed to know what she should watch for.

Her shoulders slumped, and she clasped her hands behind her back as she began walking again, her eyes focused on the scuffed wooden floors. Her denying him the chance to reclaim her arm relieved him of any guilt he might have felt at not doing it of his own accord, but it pinched that she rejected his attentions.

"Mr. Farwell suggested as much, but I never got the opportunity to hear what he discovered. I have no notions of what may be going on, but I suspect you do." Disappointment etched her face as she regarded him. "Abuse is rarely investigated unless there are other motivations that finally bring the police about."

The pained cynicism behind those words spoke of experiences he wished he could erase. "While there might be other reasons I am here, I want to assure you that if it were within my job's scope to investigate purely on the suspicion of abuse, I would."

"And that's the problem. It's always someone else's job, and so nothing ever gets done. I'm glad the Murphys' presence brought your scrutiny to Final Chance. The other children will benefit so long as your investigation removes those who are hurting them too."

"I hope it will, but if it doesn't, you'll come to me. I'll ensure the board listens and takes action to protect all the children, not just those related to me."

Nothing in her expression indicated his words brought her comfort or hope, but she nodded in agreement. "What is it that I need to be looking for to help with your case?"

"Anything related to counterfeiting or writing letters." He gave a brief explanation of the green goods game and what supplies it might require.

"I hardly think counterfeiting is occurring here. We don't have any printing equipment. We barely have the essential tools for the products the children do make."

"And what would those things be?"

"Brass nails, shoes, the occasional chair, all sorts of clothing, and sometimes we earn extra money by assembling spelling books and Bibles. I suppose there could be some counterfeiting amongst the indentured children, but I doubt it."

"Indentured? I didn't think that was done anymore."

She stopped at a door at the end of the hallway. "It has its purposes. Our arrangement provides the children with security and a future that prevents them from returning to what brought them here."

After trying the knob and finding it locked, she pulled out her keys and began testing each one while she spoke. "Of course, the parents— if the children have any—must grant permission. Most of them do as it provides for their children in ways they cannot. Each owner and place of business are thoroughly vetted before meeting board approval.

Terms are agreed upon for a set time where the children will be provided room, board, and an apprenticeship, while Final Chance is paid a small stipend for the labor the children provide. We regularly visit to ensure they are being treated fairly and kindly and that they are working hard and not slipping into old habits.

"When the children reach twenty-one, they are released from the indenture, and new deals may be struck with their employer, or they may strike out on their own. It's not a perfect system, but the majority of our children go on to be productive, healthy individuals. A few have even begun families of their own now." Pride filled her countenance until she frowned at the lock. "That's strange. None of my keys is working."

She tried again, the furrow between her brows increasing with each successive failure.

"May I?" He held out his hand.

She complied.

As he worked each key into the lock without success, Josiah asked, "What's in this room?"

"It's just another larger work space for special projects. Usually furniture or books waiting to be collated, folded, and bound."

And yet the door was locked so that not even Miss Ellison, matron of Final Chance, had access. Maybe he shouldn't have been so quick to reject the lock-picking lessons Ignazio offered a few years back. "Is there anywhere else the key could be?"

"Officer Crane might know, but my guess is Superintendent King has it locked in his office or on his person."

If he had his guess, this room was the key to finding evidence, but it might not be the only one. Though it galled him to leave the room behind unsearched, there was still much of the building to see before King returned. After he procured a lesson on picking locks from Ignazio, he'd return.

CHAPTER 15

Miss Ellison took him through two other workrooms and the boardroom—all devoid of anything suspicious—and finally into the records room. For a moment she hesitated at the open door, then shut it and locked it.

"Do not get any inappropriate thoughts, Mr. Isaacs. I merely locked the door in case anyone should come down the hall. This room is strictly off-limits to visitors."

"I promise you, I'll be on my best behavior. I know the risk you are taking with your reputation."

She nodded her acknowledgment before moving to a table at the center of the room and lighting the lamps at either end. Considering how bright the room was with the afternoon sun pouring in, he didn't understand the need. Not until she closed both sets of curtains.

"Board members are only allowed access under the supervision of Superintendent King and for specific purposes. Other visitors are strictly forbidden." She walked to a wall of filing cabinets nearly as tall as she was. "These first two contain the information of current children organized by last name. Where no last name exists, they are placed in the section labeled Ellison."

"Your name? But why?"

She wouldn't look up and instead traced a finger on the surface of the desk. "Everyone deserves a family. Even if the children reject me, I always adopt them as my own. It's their choice if they keep the name once they leave here, but I give it to them freely, along with my love and prayers. The world may despise and turn its back on them, but where it is within my power, I try to show them that they are loved and wanted."

Josiah stared at the woman before him. She couldn't be real. "Do you have any defects, Miss Ellison? Because I'm quite certain you are as close to perfect as anyone who ever walked this earth."

"Then it is quite obvious you don't know me well, for I am full of defects. One of them being a propensity to ignore the wisdom of my elders and work with a man known to the world as a rake." She shot the hint of a flirtatious smile at him, and it struck with a startling resemblance to Shauna's.

She'd been a master of flirting covertly while she worked as a maid at the house he'd been visiting at the time. The mix of restraint and teasing in her smile had always drawn him in and enticed him into an irresistible game of reciprocation.

And apparently that game was just as irresistible with Miss Ellison. "You may count it a defect, but this rake counts it as a blessing."

Her restrained smile bloomed, and she quickly turned away. "These cabinets hold all the information for those who have passed through Final Chance. We maintain records of their indenture, jobs, marriages, births, and anything else we can discover. Some write us letters, but mostly we obtain our information through the newspapers. The clippings are added to their files."

"You said Quincy Slocum was an inmate here. Do you have his?"

She opened a drawer, flipped through files, pulled out a thick one, and set it on the desk. Then she wandered to the other side of the room, arms wrapped around her middle.

Josiah opened to the picture sitting on top of the stack of paperwork. A menacing glare pierced through the dirt and grime on Slocum's face as he stood with arms crossed over ragged clothes too small for his bulky frame. Though he wore boots, his toes stuck out the front of one, and the leather peeled away from the sole of the other. The attitude of a boy too far gone reached out from the photo and declared pride in his foul deeds.

Josiah slid the picture aside, turning his mind to the admittance form. He'd planned on skimming to the list of crimes, but the line declaring Slocum's name arrested his interest. Quincy Ellison Slocum.

"He was one of yours?"

Miss Ellison released a heavy sigh. "He was, and he's the only inmate I've ever advocated to have transferred to an adult facility. I held out hope for him until"—she bit the top of her lip—"he took liberties with two of the girls. He's the reason we lock the doors now."

The edge of the file crumpled in his grip. "Was he not arrested and prosecuted?"

"The girls refused to testify, so I had no proof. Their pregnancies were attributed to their criminal histories, and they were transferred elsewhere. I kept in touch with them for a while, but eventually they ended up on the streets and . . ." She just shook her head and shrugged her shoulders.

The anguish written on her face mirrored his own. It wasn't right. Someone on the board should have done something. They'd denied those girls justice and tossed them to the streets to be devoured by evil.

"Quincy took unnatural pleasure in causing others pain. I lost count of how many fights he started, but I could never get the board to remove him. Half the board agreed with me. The other half insisted we just needed to try different techniques with him. When his sentencing ended, they washed their hands of him. They claimed he'd break the law soon enough and would be sent to prison then. I believe they were afraid of retaliation."

From what little he'd seen of the boy, Josiah understood their fear and felt some of his own. But with Slocum's grudge against Miss Ellison, it was not fear for himself that rose up to choke him. "I don't want you setting a foot outside without someone with you. Thank God I was leaving that library at the same time he was trying to cart you off."

"I thank God indeed. It's by His grace and mercy alone we stand here now. Quincy could have just as easily killed you as he could have me." She moved to the opposite side of the table and laid her soft hand over the top of his.

Had it been another woman, he might have thought her forward, but this was more than a mere game of attraction. Her eyes held earnest compassion, gratitude, and concern. Her intentions were as innocent as a lamb but completely bewitching. If he didn't end this moment of enchantment, he might never escape whatever charms she'd cast over him.

"If you're going to hold my hand, you had better start calling me Josiah."

Her eyes widened. She jerked back so fast he feared she might tumble to the floor. Color flooded into her face as she fumbled with where to look. "I didn't mean . . . I'm sorry. I—"

"I was joking." He clasped her hand, squeezed it, and then quickly released it. It had been a risk to touch her, but assuring her he was not offended mattered more. "I know you didn't mean it in any way beyond sincere friendship."

"Still, it should never have happened. Unfortunately, when my emotions run high, I tend toward impulsive behavior. A trait completely unbecoming of a matron and one I normally keep under tight control. Please forgive me, Mr. Isaacs. I meant no disrespect."

"Gwendolyn." Her name rolled comfortably off his tongue as if it were a cherished name he'd said all his life. He might regret the removal of a boundary between them, but he could no more keep it in place than she could lessen her compassion for others. "I'd like for us to be friends."

"Is it even possible for you to be friends with a woman?"

Her face and tone were so serious, he laughed outright. "I can't say I've ever succeeded at that, now that you mention it, but I'd like to try." If he could do it with any woman, it would be Gwendolyn. She held no expectations. No goal of obtaining his wealth or the power of his family name.

Creases appeared in her brow as she peered at him. "Just friends?"

"As long as you promise not to corner me into a proposal, then I promise not to propose. Friendship is all I desire."

She bit her lips together, her mind obviously working behind those copper orbs. Her hesitation made him antsy, but it instilled hope that theirs would truly be a friendship without expectations or ulterior motives.

The front door opened and shut, rattling the framed portraits on the wall. Miss Ellison—Gwendolyn now, he hoped—scooped up the file, gestured for him to move toward the wall, and then turned out the lamps. Darkness crashed over the room, and she barely made it to his side before the doorknob jiggled. A key scraped in the lock, and the door opened to within an inch of Josiah's nose.

"Who's in here?" King's thunderous voice came from the other side. "I smell the lamps. You cannot fool me."

Josiah gulped. How was he going to talk his way out of this one? There was no tale he could spin that would put being caught with Gwendolyn in a room with the curtains drawn and the door locked in an acceptable light. With his notoriety, the consequent ruination of her reputation would probably cause her to be fired from her position. How was he going to fix this?

Pounding rattled the front door, and Superintendent King grumbled before yanking the door shut.

A moment later, Mother's voice rang out. "Superintendent King, I demand to speak with you and Matron Ellison at once."

"You'll have to make an appointment. We have other tasks to attend."

"Unless you want to add searching for another job to that list, you'll speak with me now. I know about Hibbard Wilcox."

"Then I suggest you wait for us in the receiving room."

"I think not. I want the truth. Not whatever contrived stories you concoct before meeting with me. We'll go together, or I go straight to Chairman Abernathy."

The strained silence lasted several breaths before Superintendent King acquiesced. "This way, if you please."

Their steps moved down the hall.

Gwendolyn cracked the door and, after a moment, shoved Slocum's file into Josiah's hand. "Go. I'll meet them in the donations room like I've been working there the whole time."

Outside, they split directions—Gwendolyn toward the girls' ward entrance and Josiah into an alley across the street where he could access the room he'd rented for Speedy's observation of Final Chance. They'd need to be extra vigilant after today's near disaster. Whether Gwendolyn accepted his friendship or not, her safety would be his responsibility.

Josiah left Speedy's, satisfied that the boy understood the gravity of his job, and returned to the office to scour Slocum's folder for leads. Slocum was more of a threat than he'd given him credit for, and Slocum's failure to be transferred from Final Chance indicated he once had—and maybe still had—someone in his pocket there.

Hours later, Hayden entered the office. "What are you doing here? I thought you took a half day off."

Josiah looked up from the papers strewn across his desk and frowned. "What time is it?"

"Nearing five o'clock."

The air leached from his chest, and he thudded against the back of his chair. For the first time in nine years, he'd missed his one o'clock graveside visit. And it was all because of a sudden weakness for another woman. Josiah thunked his elbows on the desk and dropped his head until he gripped fistfuls of hair.

What am I doing?

CHAPTER 16

A COLLECTIVE GROAN OF PAIN rose from the children as Uncle Percy instructed everyone to stand for closing prayer. Two days of intense gardening left even the most hardy begging for some of the cream Mrs. Flowers made for aches and pains. Gwendolyn barely contained her own moan as her feet, legs, back, muscles—well, everything, really—protested the movement. She must not have contained it well enough, because Mother squeezed her arm and cast a sympathetic smile before dipping her head for prayer.

Gwendolyn followed suit. *Thank thee, Lord, for another day of protection. Goeth with my family and the children, keepeth them from harm, and prepareth me for whatever is about to happen.*

She peeked an eye open and glanced over her shoulder toward the visitors' benches once again. Every male member of the board was in attendance, and at their head sat Chairman Abernathy and Mrs. Isaacs. They'd marched in mere moments before services began and claimed seats directly behind Superintendent King, sending a clear message they were here on business. Gwendolyn stole a look at the man on Mrs. Isaacs's opposite side. Regardless of his motives, at least Mr. Isaacs had come.

He stood in respectful reverence with hat in hand and head bowed. Perhaps something in Uncle Percy's sermon stirred his soul, settled his doubts, and renewed his faith in God. She smirked at the foolish thought. Wrestling with doubts took time. A single sermon wasn't likely to move Mr. Isaacs.

Or should she call him Josiah?

It should be a simple no. To be caught using his Christian name would be scandalous, especially with an infamous reputation such as his. But he wasn't what the world claimed. He was noble, courageous, caring, and loving. Everything a man should be. She wanted to call him Josiah, to form a tentative friendship with him. To be that friend who ministered to his obviously scarred heart. And to her shame, she wanted a chance to see if something more could develop. To hope that her dream of a husband and children wasn't lost to her after all.

Josiah's head lifted as if he'd heard the whisperings of her mind. A roguish grin twisted his lips, and he winked.

She snapped her attention forward, her face warming with embarrassment. Everyone's heads were lifted, and Mother was staring at her. Apparently the prayer had ended and she'd been caught neglecting her duties to ogle a man. Sweat beaded between her shoulders and dripped down her back as she tried to focus on Uncle Percy's blessing of dismissal.

The children dispersed to their assigned officers to return the dining hall to its proper order before mealtime. Visitors not associated with the board or the minister's family exited without speaking to or hugging the children. It was as if they sensed today was not a day to approach her or Superintendent King for special permissions.

Disregarding her trepidation, Gwendolyn joined Superintendent King at his side. They ran Final Chance together, and together they must face the trials set against them.

Though the room was full of people, only the sounds of scuffling feet, shifting benches, and the occasional whispered direction dared scrape against the palpable tension.

Chairman Abernathy strode forward and greeted them with a curt nod. "Matron Ellison, Superintendent King, your presence is required in the boardroom, as well as that of Gareth Ellison and Officer Bagwell."

So this ambush was about Hibbard. Finally the board recognized the peril they'd left the children in by ignoring her claims. Unfortunately, with their coming today instead of Tuesday, she didn't yet have proof to contradict Officer Bagwell's story. She needed a moment alone to pray and beg God for help. "If you'll allow me a few minutes to see the other guests out and lock the doors, I'll join you directly."

"Reverend Ballantine has his own key to the premises. He'll see to those needs. The board requires your immediate attendance."

She nodded as the rest of the group proceeded toward the boys' ward.

Mother grabbed her hand and prevented her from following. "Gwendolyn, we need to talk. It's important."

"I can't, Mother. Not now." She tried to tug away and follow before Chairman Abernathy accused her of dallying. "Can't it wait until Wednesday?"

"Our visitor is already at the house. He arrived before he received my letter asking for a delay."

He? That snagged her curiosity. Mother had been writing to a man?

"Matron Ellison, do you not know the meaning of *immediate*?"

Gwendolyn pulled her hand free. As much as she wanted answers now, they would have to wait. "Mother, please. I promise we'll talk Wednesday, but I must deal with this now."

She rushed to catch up as Gareth and Officer Bagwell walked toward the boardroom. By the time they entered the room, all twelve board members sat around the large table, leaving her, Superintendent King, Officer Bagwell, and Gareth to stand around like hangmen facing their executioners. Gwendolyn clutched her throat and swallowed against the mental image. But she couldn't stop herself from thinking that even if Mrs. Isaacs were on her side, there was no guarantee that the board wouldn't side with Superintendent King's persistent claim that she was unsuited to be matron of Final Chance.

Someone coughed from the corner of the room and drew her attention. Josiah leaned against the wall with crossed arms and legs and gave her a barely noticeable nod. To anyone else he looked to have not a care in the world, but she was quickly understanding the laissez-faire stance served as a deflection from his true purposes. From his position, he had a clear view of everyone in the room while going unnoticed himself. His gaze lingered on hers, infusing her anxiety with a calming strength and a reminder of the truth. This meeting was not about her suitability but rather the lack of Officer Bagwell's. Hibbard needed justice, and she would do her best to ensure it.

Two of the board members entered carrying chairs and set them against the wall before claiming their own at the opposite end of the table.

"Shut the door and take a seat." Chairman Abernathy rose from his place at the head of the table and positioned himself in front of Superintendent King in such a way that his height advantage would provide a physical reminder of his superiority over them.

Gwendolyn started to sit in obedience but stopped when Superintendent King grabbed her elbow.

"We'll stand, thank you."

"Very well. Why was I not immediately notified of Hibbard Wilcox's condition?"

"Everything was handled in accordance with policy." Even in the face of his superior, Superintendent King maintained his arrogance. "The doctor was sent for, treatment provided, the offending party identified and duly punished, and a report written and added to each boy's file. Matron Ellison and I are prepared to give a full report of the incident on Tuesday, as required."

"Mrs. Isaacs was presented with two very different versions of what happened. I'd like clarity on the matter and require individual written accounts of what occurred. Mrs. Isaacs, Mr. Hunt, will you please escort Superintendent King, Matron Ellison, and Officer Bagwell across the hall and provide them with writing materials. Ensure that they do not speak to one another. We will interview Gareth in here."

While from the outside the scheme appeared a sound way to adjudicate, Gwendolyn saw it for what it was. Superintendent King and

Officer Bagwell had already aligned their stories to hide the truth. Her account would be discredited in an instant. Gareth's version was the only one that might tip the board's opinion in her favor.

Officer Bagwell shoved the boy into a chair. "You heard what the reverend said this morning. You best stick to the truth or suffer the consequences of your sin."

Gwendolyn stepped between Officer Bagwell and Gareth. "You cannot threaten him into telling your version of the truth!"

"There is only one truth, Matron Ellison, and we intend to find it out," Chairman Abernathy said.

Mr. Hunt ushered her out of the boardroom and into one of the workrooms, where Mrs. Isaacs directed them to sit at separate tables. After writing their accounts of what happened, the three delivered their papers to Mrs. Isaacs, who then delivered the narratives to the board and left Gwendolyn and the others to wait in silence with Mr. Hunt until Treasurer Wells retrieved them.

This time Superintendent King and Officer Bagwell took the proffered seats, forcing Gwendolyn to sit as well, when she'd rather pace the room.

Chairman Abernathy lifted their accounts from the table and shook his head. "The only significantly different account is yours Matron Ellison, and as you were not a witness to the fight, it cannot be counted as an accurate retelling of events. By the boy's own mouth and testimony of Officer Bagwell and Superintendent King, Gareth Ellison is guilty. Finding his punishment insufficient for the damage inflicted, the board has voted that Gareth be transferred to Eastern Penitentiary."

"But he's a child!"

"Gareth chose to fight with the intensity of a man, and therefore he will be punished as such."

"Look at his hands! There are no cuts or bruises. They are not the hands of one who battered another boy nearly thirty pounds heavier than himself."

"The boy confessed."

"And you would take the word of a boy under the threat of his supervising officer when you didn't take the word of those two girls Quincy violated?"

"This is not the same, Matron Ellison." Chairman Abernathy's tone shifted, as if addressing a simpleton. "I understand you have a soft heart toward these children. 'Tis a woman's weaker nature to ignore the evil presented in lamb's wool and believe in innocence that doesn't exist."

"I did it, Matron Ellison, and I'd do it again." Gareth lifted his chin in defiance as he stood under the controlling grip of Treasurer Wells.

It was all bravado. It had to be. "At a very minimum, Mr. Bagwell should be held accountable for the severity of Hibbard's condition. If he'd been present with the children like he was supposed to be, the fight would've ended without serious injury."

"I told you, I was using the necessary."

"If you'd not delayed—"

"That is enough. We'll revisit the policies for leaving children unattended at a later point. For now, we've finished what was required of us. I'll complete the obligatory paperwork, and Superintendent King will personally see to it that Gareth is transferred into the hands of wardens better suited to dealing with brutes. Until then, Gareth is to be kept in isolation lest he influence the others."

"At least talk to Hibbard and hear his version of the story before sending Gareth away."

Superintendent King scoffed. "The boy can't even talk."

"No, but he can write."

Chairman Abernathy nodded. "When he's recovered enough, I'll see to it myself. Now, with this business settled, we adjourn until Tuesday. Gentlemen, Mrs. Isaacs, thank you for sacrificing a portion of your Sunday."

Chairs scraped, and murmurs filled the room as the group filed out. Gwendolyn couldn't rise from her seat even if she tried. The weight of her failure wouldn't allow it. That boy had been threatened into confessing, and, in truth, she couldn't blame him. After seeing what happened to Hibbard, the boy must be scared out of his mind to defy Officer Bagwell.

"You may console yourself with the fact Gareth will no longer be under Officer Bagwell's oppressive hand, as you so illustriously put it in your account." Superintendent King stood in front of her, looking down his nose like she was a roach to be squashed.

She rose to her feet and squared off. She would not give him the satisfaction of towering over her any more than what he could do naturally. "You have failed in your duties, Superintendent King. We're supposed to protect these children from harm, teach them skills that will give them hope and a new future, and show them Christ's love. What do you think is going to happen to Gareth when he's thrown into a cell with a murderer or thief who decides their new cellmate is the perfect target for their frustrations? There's a reason houses of refuge exist. Children don't belong with hardened criminals."

His nostrils flared. "Then he shouldn't behave like one. You heard him. He had no remorse."

"What I heard is a boy who's too afraid to oppose the threats issued to him by the very people who are supposed to protect him."

"You've said quite enough, Miss Ellison. I recommend you return to your side of the refuge and stay there." He pivoted and stalked out of the room.

Alone, she closed her eyes and allowed the war between anger and grief to play out down her cheeks and in the ache of fisted hands.

"That was both brave and foolish."

She startled at the sound of Josiah's voice and spun to face where he still stood in the corner, forgotten by everyone.

He strode forward and heaved a sigh as he took in her countenance. Shaking his head, he pressed a handkerchief into her hand. "I suppose we are all prone to rash words at times, but challenging that man— regardless of if he's involved—is a reckless gamble. I didn't take you for a gambler."

"I'm not, but some risks are worth taking." She glanced around the empty room to ensure she hadn't missed anyone else and then took a resolved breath. "If you're still amenable to friendship, I think I'm in great need of one."

"You had my friendship whether you accepted it or not."

If anyone could restore her faith in there being good men left in the world, it would be him.

"Then I'd be grateful if you called me Gwendolyn. In private, of course."

"As long as you call me Josiah." When she held the handkerchief out, he enclosed her hand with his and wrapped her fingers back over the material. "Keep it as a reminder that you're not facing this alone." He smirked. "And to maybe hold your tongue around men who have the power to harm you. I've learned the hard way that I cannot always protect those I care about. So help me, please? No more challenging the board or Superintendent King."

"I'll do my best, but I've already warned you, sometimes my passions override my self-control." Case in point, accepting his friendship.

"We'll discover the truth and protect these children. It just takes time." When she nodded, he glanced toward the door. "Do you think you can get me Hibbard's and Gareth's files? I'd like to look into their mutual connections."

"Yes, but I'll need them back as soon as possible."

"Of course. I'll wait for you outside."

It felt duplicitous, sneaking into the record room and removing the files, but if it was the only way Gareth and Hibbard could receive justice, she'd do it. She checked the hall, locked the door, then slipped out front to where Josiah waited at the corner, outside of view of anyone in the building. He scanned their surroundings before accepting the files and concealing them inside his coat.

"If you need anything, one of Speedy's crew is right there." He waved at the building across the street and a small head peeked out an open window on the top floor. Josiah gave a mock salute, which the boy returned before ducking back inside. "If you feel unsafe for any reason, just motion at that window. Speedy knows how to find me, and he has his name for a reason. I'll see you on Tuesday, but look for a note before then." He lifted her bare hand toward his mouth but kissed the air above it like a gentleman. "Goodbye, Gwendolyn. Be safe."

He released her hand and strode away, leaving a flurry of foolish fantasies in his wake.

CHAPTER 17

JOSIAH'S EYE TWITCHED WITH EACH tap of Hayden's pencil against the desk. Was it really necessary for the man to process his thoughts as if he were a telegraph operator? During the hour Josiah had spent scouring Gareth's file for connections, the man must have tapped out the equivalent of the entire Constitution, including all fifteen amendments.

Josiah pressed a finger to his ear to dampen the sound and opened Hibbard Wilcox's file.

Name: Hibbard Wilcox

Tap. Twitch.

Arrival Date: 1884 November 5

Tap. Twitch.

Crimes: Breaking and entering, passing counterfeit—

Tap. Twitch.

Josiah thrust back against his chair. "For pity's sake, man. Stop that infernal tapping."

"Sorry. This new policy is frustrating me to no end." Hayden laid aside his own paperwork and tilted his chair back against the windowsill. "The Billy Wilcox case is dead in the water unless we observe him making a sale or counterfeits, and I'm at a loss about what to do about Fantasma. The man's more myth than reality. I can't find one clue to his actual existence."

"There's always the possibility that someone fabricated the story to build up fear in the community. Isn't Felicity bringing lunch? I bet if we asked her, she'd be more than happy to investigate it from a newspaper standpoint."

"I don't want her near anything related to Fantasma. She wouldn't stop until she had an answer."

In contrast to his gruff tone, a smirk edged the corner of Hayden's mouth, and pride twinkled in his eyes. Once the bane of the Philadelphia office's existence, Felicity had won the heart of its most serious operative during the Philadelphia Mint burglary investigation two years ago. Though now married to Hayden and a soon-to-be mother of two, she continued to write and investigate articles for her family's newspaper. More than once, the Secret Service had pulled her in to gain access to information and people they could not access on their own.

"You're right. She'd probably end up on an ice-cream date with a suspect again. Although I'm not sure ghosts eat ice cream."

Hayden's chair legs thudded back to the floor. "Felicity is not helping on the Fantasma case, nor do I want her to know anything about it. It's exactly the type of trouble she likes to stick her nose into."

A knock at the office door preceded the woman's entrance.

"Not a word, Isaacs. Do you hear me?" Hayden impaled him with a glower before rising to greet his wife.

To give them privacy, Josiah returned to examining Hibbard's file. Well, that was something. The boy had been arrested for passing counterfeits last fall. Depending on who provided Hibbard the money, that might be how Final Chance received their counterfeits. There weren't many details about the actual crime, but as Detective Morrows had been his arresting officer, it shouldn't be too hard to get them. All Josiah had to do was invite his long-time bachelor friend over for one of Tillie's roast dinners.

Josiah skimmed the rest of the page until his eyes snagged on the name of the boy's father, Billy Wilcox—the same Wilcox Josiah had been about to arrest before the new policy sent his case to a careening halt. Likely the boy got his money from his father—and his father was no Fantasma. If anything, the two were rivals, although Wilcox's work didn't offer much of a competition given the lack of skill behind his bogus notes. Still, the connection was worth following up.

A wicker hamper of food dropped onto the corner of his desk and broke his concentration. Felicity smiled down at him, her usual supply of pencils poking out from her bun. A notebook dangled from a ribbon wrapped around her wrist. The vivacious woman was such an opposite to the serious operative she'd married. Their relationship made little sense, but their love for each other, though reserved around observers, was evident. And it never failed to send a pang of longing through Josiah.

She opened the top and began removing plates and silverware from the hamper's contents. "I hope you like corned beef and cold potatoes. I even found fresh strawberries at the market for dessert."

"What? No ice cream?"

From behind her, Hayden directed a scowl at Josiah.

"If you want ice cream, you'll have to make a trip to Bassetts on your own afterward. I can't go past the butcher without the smell making me regret having eaten."

"I wouldn't want that." He winked at her, more because he knew it annoyed Hayden than for any other reason.

She shook her head as she plated the corned beef. "I've been thinking about your problem with that new policy. It says that counterfeits can't be bought with Secret Service funds, but it doesn't say anything about personal funds, does it?"

"You cannot buy counterfeit money with personal funds without committing a crime, Felicity." Hayden pulled out a chair and indicated she should sit while he plated the food.

"Even if the purpose is to expose criminal operations?"

"Whether division funds or personal funds, the intent is the same. We cannot incite criminals to commit a crime."

"But what if they've already initiated the sale?" Josiah rose from his seat and rummaged through the filing cabinet for the green goods letters, a loophole plan taking shape. "Technically, the offer to sell has already been made, and we didn't instigate it."

He found Tim Benson's letters, including the partially written one stating he'd like to purchase some tens. If they had him finish the letter demanding the exchange be done in person, then they'd be able to identify at least a few players in the green goods game, obtain much needed evidence, and back out of the purchase before breaking the policy. It wasn't perfect, but anything he could do to bring the case to a close quickly, he would. Gwendolyn and the children wouldn't be safe until it was over. Not to mention every delay forced him to grow more acquainted with the woman who broke down barriers faster than he could rebuild them.

Josiah explained the plan as they ate. He'd have Tim Benson finish the letter, both as a way for the boy to redeem himself and to prevent any incongruity that the counterfeiters might notice. Then Hayden would act as the boy's father to conduct the transaction, as Josiah had been around Final Chance enough to be recognized should one of its employees be present. Not that any of them knew his real profession. He'd been quiet on that front, and Mother had explicit directions not to publicize it either.

"Is there anything I can do to help?" Felicity set her empty plate on the desk and leaned forward with a hopeful gleam in her eye. "Hayden's mother keeps shooing me out the door during Martha's naps. She claims having two children changes everything, and I need to enjoy my freedom while I can."

Josiah chuckled as he imagined Abigail giving the same advice if she could. She loved her children, but occasional bemoanings to the tune of "no time to herself" did escape.

"Actually, there is."

Hayden folded his arms. "Don't make me pull rank on you, Isaacs. I'll file a formal reprimand if you even suggest it."

Surely the man gave him more credit than that. "I don't think an article on how private houses of refuge compare to the state-run Philadelphia House of Refuge is worthy of a formal reprimand."

"It could bring dangerous attention to her."

"One interview at Final Chance followed by an article in the newspaper covering multiple refuges isn't going to bring her unwanted attention."

"They'll be suspicious of a reporter suddenly taking an interest in Final Chance."

"No, they won't." Felicity's eager voice broke into the argument. "A competitor recently printed an editorial piece about the overcrowding of the Philadelphia House of Refuge and the need for either a larger facility or for other options to be provided. It would only be natural for me to follow up that article with one about private refuges."

Hayden's scowl deepened.

Felicity laid a hand on one of his crossed arms. "Come now, you know I'm right. Besides, if you tell me who I'm avoiding and what information I'm looking for, I can be better prepared."

"This isn't like other cases, Fel." He dropped his arms and faced her. "We don't have a clear understanding of who is involved or how dangerous they are. A boy was beaten so severely he ended up in Children's Hospital and underwent surgery."

"Oh my! How awful." Her hand protectively covered the barely detectable bump of their unborn child. "Has anything been done?"

"The board held a mock court where they blamed a child for the abuse. I'm certain that's not the truth." Josiah handed them the documents he'd confiscated after everyone left. "The testimonies provided by the superintendent and responsible officer are too similar to be true, as far as my experience with witnesses goes. Their wording matched almost exactly, like they scripted their stories before presenting them to the board. Even Gareth's version matched. When the board asked him specific questions outside the scope of the script, he kept his answers limited and vague. Once he's transferred to Eastern, I'm going to intervene and have him placed in a different house of refuge. He'll be out of their reach for punishment and shouldn't fear telling me the truth."

"All the more reason for Felicity not to get involved. If they have no compunction about hitting a child, they might strike a pregnant woman." Hayden's hand covered Felicity's so they shielded their child as one unit.

Josiah blew out a breath. Hayden was right, and it was wrong to even suggest Felicity get involved, especially in her condition. But the longer his gaze lingered on their joint hands, the more he saw Gwendolyn shielding the children of Final Chance with a lone hand. She deserved a second hand to join hers. A hand that didn't just join but covered and provided a first line of defense. More than a hand, she needed a person to partner with.

The image of her being his partner instead of Shauna choked him. He'd already missed his anniversary date with his wife, and now he was picturing someone else's face in solidarity next to his? What sort of unfaithful husband was he?

"I'm sorry." Josiah pushed away from the desk. "You're right. It's too big a risk. You enjoy the rest of the meal. I'm going to meet with Tim Benson and do some follow-up work on the Wilcox case."

He escaped the office with enough speed that he forget his hat, but the warm sunshine on his face would do him good. Maybe the sun would blind the image from his head and burn away the attraction he shouldn't feel. Maybe he'd be lucky enough to encounter Fantasma while he was out. A fight with a ghost might be the only way to get Gwendolyn out of his head.

CHAPTER 18

RECEIVING HIDDEN NOTES IN THE newspaper should cause anxiety and trepidation, not anticipation and delight. Yet here Gwendolyn stood by the back kitchen door, near bouncing on her toes as she waited for the customary tap. How had doing something that might cost her her reputation and job become her favorite part of the day? It wasn't as if Josiah revealed anything of substance about himself during his friendly communications—communications that were meant to disguise his inquiries about Final Chance. Even the admission reports she filled out for each child contained more intimate details than anything he'd shared. But she couldn't help hoping that trajectory would change. After all, his little touches and gestures of protection proved they were developing a real friendship, right?

Or was he only as good as his reputation and merely using her for the sake of his case?

A gust of doubt snuffed the bright flame of excitement, casting her confidence in shadows. Josiah might be a gallant man, but he was an Isaacs—one of the wealthiest and most influential families in Philadelphia. She was so far below his station that even his servants were better dressed. He had no reason to befriend her except to further his case.

Perhaps Mother was right to be concerned for Gwendolyn's heart. She had become attached to the man far too quickly, and it was a precarious position to place herself in. Contentment with her life as a spinster matron was a hard-fought battle.

Lord, forgiveth my traitorous heart that hopes for more than what thou hath provided. Helpeth me to be content. To not dream of more than friendship with Josiah. This is my place. These children, mine quiver of arrows. May I servest them well in thy name.

She watched the girls scuttle about the kitchen under Mrs. Flowers's direction. The younger group wiped counters and carried plates out to the dining hall while the older girls cut bread, plated food, or scrubbed pots. Somehow the chaos of sound and activity progressed with nary a squabble or spilled plate. Pride swelled in her chest, pushing aside the momentary melancholy. By the time the girls left Final Chance, they'd be able to work at one of the big houses with such efficiency that no one would be the wiser as to the origin of their education.

A tap sounded behind Gwendolyn.

Finally. She smiled as she grabbed the plate of beans and bread set aside for the delivery boys. So far, each of the last five days, a different boy had arrived with a newspaper in hand and a grumble in his belly. Apparently Speedy had a crew, and he was careful to make sure each got a turn for a hot meal. This time when the door opened, the youngest one from their motley band stood on the stoop, grinning up at her with a missing front tooth.

"Hello, Mouse. How are you today?" She exchanged the newspaper for the plate and joined him on the stoop.

He snuggled against her side, and she tried not to cringe at the thought of all the grime that was probably transferring to her clothes. But the unwashed, unkempt boy obviously needed the love and support of a mother in his life, and she'd not deny him what little piece of herself she could offer.

"Better today." Mouse drug his bread through the beans and shoved it into his mouth. His cheek bulged as he spoke between chews. "Speedy gave me his turn to come, seeing's how I ain't eat since Saturday."

"Good heavens, why not?" Three days without food was unthinkable, especially for a boy his age.

Mouse shrugged. "Ol' Pig Face said we didn't sell 'nough. Probably won't today neither. The Ghost stole our papers again."

Ghost? What a ridiculous notion. "I don't think ghosts have an interest in reading the newspaper."

"Maybe not real 'uns, but them boys that call themselves The Ghost sure are real 'nough. It ain't fair they rule the streets and no one does nothing 'bout it."

"Has no one gone to the police?"

"Who's gonna believe us? Exceptin' you and Mr. Joe, there ain't nobody who cares what happens to us. Don't you worry none though. Speedy knows how to keep us safe. Long as we give 'em our papers and pay their fee, they don't hurt us none." He shoved the last bite of beans and bread in his mouth, laid the plate on her lap, and then jumped to his feet. "Got any mail today?"

She pulled an envelope from her apron pocket and handed it to him. Though she'd see Josiah later today at the board meeting, she didn't want to risk someone noticing her passing him a note. "Have the other boys eaten since Saturday?"

Mouse shrugged. "Probably. They're better at stealing scraps than me."

"Wait here." Gwendolyn ducked back into the kitchen, found an unattended loaf of bread, and brought it outside. "Be sure to share this with the others, all right?"

"Yes, ma'am." Mouse gave her a gap-toothed smile, shoved the bread under his arm, and ran down the back alley.

Bless his soul. How her heart ached for Mouse and the rest of Speedy's group. What kind of world did they live in where men starved children or ignored their plight? Gwendolyn lifted a prayer for the boys' needs and turned to reenter the building.

Chairman Abernathy stood at the top of the stoop with crossed arms and a scowl hanging above that ridiculous woolly caterpillar beard that outlined his chin and jaw. The rest of his face remained clean-shaven, making her want to either shave the beard off or ink the empty space.

"Good afternoon, Chairman Abernathy. I'm afraid Superintendent King hasn't returned from escorting Gareth yet." Only her secret knowledge of Josiah's plans to rescue the boy from the penitentiary soothed her anger at the injustice of it. "Would you care to join us for evening meal before the meeting?"

She lifted her skirts to mount the steps, but he refused to move aside.

"Did I just see you give away Final Chance property to a vagrant?"

"He's not a vagrant. He's a delivery boy for the newspaper subscription that was generously donated to us."

"That doesn't change the fact that the bread was made solely for the inmates of Final Chance. Do you deny you gave it to him?"

"I do not. He's hungry, and it's our Christian duty to feed him as we are able."

"Anyone outside of this building is in God's care alone. We cannot afford to feed the street rats of Philadelphia."

While she understood his position, it was one loaf of bread. "Then take the cost from my pay."

"I will." Finally he stepped aside. "The inmates are waiting for the dinner blessing."

She dipped her head in deference to him as she passed and concealed the newspaper with a smooth slide. Should Chairman Abernathy confiscate it and discover Josiah's message, it might be enough for him to fire her.

As they entered the dining hall and she took her place at the front of the room, the exuberant conversations of the children quieted.

"Let us pray." She bowed her head, waited a breath for the children to mimic, and began the blessing, which the children joined her in reciting. Once they had finished, the scraping of forks against plates and quiet conversation filled the room.

"Would you care to join the officers?" She gestured to the clothed table that separated the inmates of either ward.

Chairman Abernathy glanced at a nearby plate of beans and canned tomatoes, and his face pinched like he'd stepped in horse manure. "No, thank you. I'll not waste Final Chance's resources."

"The children would benefit from your example. Was it not you who insisted we teach them that we are to eat whatever we are fed, as it's a blessing from God?"

It was difficult not to grin outright when his eyebrows and lips settled into matching flat lines. He strode to the head of the table and claimed Superintendent King's seat with all the disdain of a child forced to comply. With the tines of the fork, he poked at the gelatinous lump on the plate in front of him so cautiously it was as if he was afraid it might poke back. Gwendolyn smirked. The man probably hadn't eaten such meager fare since he was a babe and his mother spooned it to him.

"How are the children doing today?" Gwendolyn asked Wilhelmina as she took her seat.

"Lottie's fever broke, but I'm keeping her in the infirmary for another day."

"That's wise. Are any other girls showing symptoms?"

Wilhelmina continued her evening report on the children while Gwendolyn surreptitiously felt between each page of the newspaper in her lap. She needed to find the note and read it before the board meeting. If Josiah needed something, she wanted to be prepared. Midway through the pages, her fingers grazed the smooth texture of high-quality stationery. A thrill hummed through her, reaching her heart with a renewed melody of hope. Surely it wasn't wrong to hope for true friendship so long as she remained content with her situation in life.

She eased the note from its confines and into the folds of her skirt.

"The boys were subdued today." Officer Crane pushed aside his empty plate. "I think Gareth's removal has sent a clear message that violence—"

The boys' ward door crashed open.

Superintendent King staggered into the room with one hand clutching the back of his head. Blood dripped from his nose, and mud clung to his torn coat.

Gwendolyn shot to her feet. "Officer Crane, go for a doctor."

A cacophony of excited chatter erupted throughout the room.

Over the tops of heads, her gaze collided with Superintendent

King's. Pain glossed his eyes along with . . . Was that fear? He wavered, then crumpled to the floor.

Boys surged from their seats toward him. Although Officer Bagwell yelled orders to back away, it took Chairman Abernathy to create a path through the crush to reach Superintendent King. Gwendolyn dropped to her knees next to where he lay on his back with eyes closed.

"Superintendent King, can you hear me?"

He groaned and opened pained eyes that looked beyond her to Chairman Abernathy. "They took Gareth."

"Took Gareth?" His words shot through her, and she jerked back. "Who took him? Where?"

"Don't know. I was hit from behind." His eyes closed again, breaths coming in ragged gulps. "Then they beat me."

"Was Gareth hurt?"

"Maybe. There were too many to keep track of."

"Too many" meant a group. Just like with Mr. Farwell. It couldn't be a coincidence. Not with Gareth knowing the truth of what happened to Hibbard. Her heart raced faster than a thoroughbred. They wouldn't kill a child, would they? Surely not.

Hibbard's condition flashed to mind, and she stifled a cry.

A hand pressed against the small of her back, jerking her attention toward the toucher. Josiah squatted next to her, eyes scanning the prone Superintendent King. When had he gotten here? For the first time, she noticed the small cluster of board members standing behind him in various states of horror, anger, and shock. They must have arrived for the meeting.

"Where were you attacked?" Josiah asked.

"Twenty-Second and Sansom."

So close to the refuge?

"Could you identify them if you saw them?" Josiah pressed.

"No." A tremor shook the end of Superintendent King's answer, and his Adam's apple bobbed.

There was only one person she knew powerful enough to wield fear over adult men. "Quincy. Did you see Quincy among them?"

The material where Josiah's hand was resting bunched.

"Maybe."

"It was broad daylight. How could you not see?"

"That is enough," Chairman Abernathy barked. "Someone get Matron Ellison out of here. She's become overwrought."

A feminine hand wrapped around her elbow and insisted Gwendolyn rise to her feet. Josiah's hand fell away, leaving behind a seeping cold that made her shiver. Was it merely the loss of warmth, or did he have the power to hold her terror at bay? She glanced at him, but he remained focused on Superintendent King.

"Come along, dear." Mrs. Isaacs wrapped an arm around Gwendolyn's shoulder and directed her away from Superintendent King's supine body. "Perhaps we should check on the children. I am sure they are upset as well."

Gwendolyn blinked at the tables of abandoned half-eaten plates. Where had the children gone?

Wilhelmina. She must've had the foresight to remove them. What would she do without that woman? Gwendolyn drew in a deep breath and released it slowly. The children were in good hands. Her duty was to take control of the situation here.

"Thank you, Mrs. Isaacs, but I am well." She faced a congregation of mostly male board members with a stiff back and raised chin. They needed to see her strength, not confirmation of their bias that she was ill-equipped for her position. "Officer Crane has already gone for the doctor. Mr. Hunt, please take someone with you to summon the police. These criminals may still be lurking nearby. Mrs. Isaacs and Mrs. Hunt, will you please gather some pillows and blankets from the receiving room for Superintendent King's comfort? And please inform Mrs. Flowers we need ice and a basin of water."

Surprisingly, no one balked, and the more she dispensed orders, the calmer she felt. She'd work through the connection of Gareth's disappearance and Superintendent King's injuries later. For now, she needed control. Over herself and the world that shook around her.

CHAPTER 19

TURMOIL DOMINATED THE NEXT FEW hours. Once past her initial shock, Gwendolyn had turned into a seasoned soldier and taken command of herself and those under her authority. Though Josiah recognized the facade of relaxed control for what it was, her ability to shove aside fear and anger to confront the emergency with calm and reason impressed him. She and the other women attended to King's comfort and medical needs until Dr. Munich arrived. Then she seamlessly switched focus to assisting Chairman Abernathy with Detective Morrows and his small contingent of patrolmen.

Although Abernathy rejected her suggestion of organizing a search party, Detective Morrows wasn't the type of man to dismiss a good idea just because it came from a woman. Without giving away their professional connection, Detective Morrows assigned Josiah the task of leading the patrolmen and other willing board members. Forming pairs, they combed the surrounding streets and alleys for witnesses, evidence, or the boy himself. Less than an hour later, the sun set and put an end to their search.

When they returned to Final Chance, Detective Morrows exited and motioned for Josiah to join him by the privacy of the garden wall. "I gather you didn't find the boy?"

"No, and I don't suspect we will." The boy either had escaped or was dead, and although he hoped for the former, Josiah feared the latter. "Did you discover anything useful?"

"Perhaps. I'll drop by for breakfast tomorrow and share the particulars."

"Desperate for a home-cooked meal, are you? Breakfast is at eight."

Detective Morrows grinned and shook his hand. "You best get back inside lest you miss out on something we need."

Josiah entered the nearly full boardroom, where all listened to Treasurer Wells's description of the failed search efforts. At the other end of the table, Mrs. Flowers and Gwendolyn distributed coffee. Gwendolyn's head swiveled in his direction, and though outwardly she appeared composed and confident, her eyes seemed to cry out to him with deep sobs that could only be heard in the soul.

His arms ached to go to her and wrap her in an embrace that would release her pent-up grief to soak into his coat. Against his will, his heart had claimed Gwendolyn as his to protect and comfort. But friendship was all he could concede. And a secret one at that. Both their jobs required it, and he'd already foolishly succumbed to the temptation of publicly comforting Gwendolyn when he found her hunched over King, pale and stricken. To do so again would only expose them to gossip and censure. After a single nod to acknowledge her pain, he forced himself into the nearest seat.

Despite his attempt to avoid her, she brought him a cup of coffee. Apparently she'd read the nod as an invitation. Her fingers brushed his as the cup transferred hands. While she gave no outward appearance of being affected, his heart kicked into a trot. When she didn't move away but lingered within easy reach, it cantered. He white-knuckled the delicate handle to keep from touching her lithe fingers dangling at her side.

Thankfully, Abernathy's voice provided a distraction. "No one's to speak a word of this outside of these walls. Maintaining this institution's reputation is priority. Should we lose the support of our financiers, we'll have to shut our doors and send the children elsewhere. Donations are down significantly as it is. Even the loss of a loaf of bread can tip the scales toward closing our doors." He directed accusing, narrowed eyes at Gwendolyn.

The woman met his glare with a raised chin and flared nostrils. Josiah couldn't determine who was the bull and who was the matador, but there was a definite challenge issued between the two. Something had occurred in his absence, and it couldn't have been good. With Gwendolyn being emotional as she was at the moment, Josiah feared her passions might override sense.

Wells spoke. "We're not quite that destitute, but the cost of Superintendent King's care will substantially reduce what little funds we were able to squeeze from the budget last week. If we receive any more blows, then the loss of a loaf of bread may very well close our doors."

Gwendolyn's flexed fingers and the smug look from Abernathy declared he'd been victorious. She'd worked too hard to maintain her calm these last few hours. Josiah wouldn't allow her to toss it aside now.

Careful not to draw notice from anyone else, he prodded her foot with his until she looked at him. Her copper orbs were bright with furious zeal, and for a moment he feared she might lance him with her anger. But he maintained his stare and silently implored her to trust him and remain calm. He couldn't protect her and the children if she bucked his lead. After a moment, her eyes slid shut, and she drew in a deep breath. On its slow release, her eyes once again met his and seemed to say, "I trust you, but don't make me regret it."

He reached to reassure her, and her hand shifted to meet his.

What was he doing? They couldn't risk such liberties, in public or in private. At the last moment, he changed trajectory to his cup. He cringed at the hurt and confusion he saw in her expression, but it couldn't be helped. He had to protect both her reputation and his heart.

In an effort to gain control of his thoughts and the conversation, Josiah turned to Abernathy. "Why was Gareth removed from the premises? Surely the prison hasn't approved his transfer already?" Never in all Josiah's experience had the prison system moved that swiftly. The transfer request couldn't have been submitted any earlier than yesterday.

Gwendolyn spoke with a far steadier voice than he'd expected. "We received a message from Warden Spille this afternoon informing us all was settled, but it was up to us to escort him to the premises before the night shift. Superintendent King left almost immediately with Gareth."

"They didn't send a wagon?"

"No. He's just a child, so I don't imagine they consider him a threat."

The whole situation stunk worse than sewage at the peak of summer. At a minimum, an officer from the prison or local station would have assisted in the escort of a boy who'd supposedly beat a bigger boy to the point of hospitalization. The communication from the warden had to be counterfeit. The setup was too perfect. A narrow window of time to act, the requirement for Gareth to be personally delivered, and the attack occurring before the nearest streetcar stop or hack stand.

"May I see the note?"

Chairman Abernathy shook his head. "It's either been misplaced or thrown away. Neither Matron Ellison nor I could find it."

More likely someone had destroyed it. Tomorrow he'd pay a visit to Warden Spille and get answers.

Gwendolyn shifted next to him, causing her skirts to brush his legs. "I think we need to focus on who could have taken Gareth. If we find him, then our questions can be answered."

A rumble of mixed responses rose from the board members. Some called it the responsibility of the police, others a waste of time.

Mr. Hunt leaned back in his chair and rubbed his bare chin. "Wasn't Gareth a part of a gang of newspaper boys before his arrest? Is it possible he arranged the attack himself?"

"Newspaper boys, eh?" Abernathy faced Gwendolyn. "I don't suppose that boy you gave the loaf of bread to was one of Gareth's former comrades? Perhaps as payment?" He arched a brow, and the corner of his mouth tilted as if he'd trapped her. "It's well-known you didn't approve of the transfer."

Surprised exclamations rounded the table, and Josiah couldn't decide if Gwendolyn was going to faint or explode. First, her face blanched and she stumbled back, only stopping when his hand instinctively shot out to catch her. In the next breath, her face turned florid, and she leaned forward with both hands planted on the table.

"I gave Mouse that loaf of bread because he and his friends hadn't eaten in three days!"

He shouldn't be surprised at her generosity, but he wished she'd been more discreet in her distribution. If the board knew of Speedy's group making daily visits to the kitchen door, then their method of communication was no longer safe. Nor were Speedy and his crew. The counterfeiters would likely be on the lookout for them now.

"Then you don't deny giving away Final Chance property?" Abernathy asked.

She straightened and spoke, each word clipped. "It was one loaf of bread, and I said I'd pay for it myself. My actions had nothing to do with Gareth. I may disagree with the board's decision to send him away, but I abide by their ruling."

"It is simple enough to check into." Wells rose from the table. "I'll retrieve Gareth's file, and we'll compare the names of his former group with those Matron Ellison gave the bread to." He strode from the room with the confidence of a man certain he'd complete his mission.

But he wouldn't, because Gareth's file still rested in a desk drawer at the Secret Service office. As did Hibbard's and Slocum's.

Though Gwendolyn stood firm, the tics along her jaw and forced breaths revealed her anticipation of the adversity to come. Minutes passed before Wells asked Gwendolyn to assist him in locating the file. She moved stiffly past Josiah and joined him across the hall. A few more minutes elapsed along with the opening and shutting of drawers. At long last, they returned.

"It appears the file is missing, along with a few others." Wells scrutinized Gwendolyn with undisguised suspicion. "Hibbard Wilcox and Quincy Slocum, more specifically."

Abernathy smirked like a boxer about to deliver the winning blow. "I believe you have had personal objections in regard to how the board has treated their cases. Am I correct?"

Gwendolyn spoke nothing to her defense and instead just stared at one spot on the back wall.

"Answer me!"

"You are correct, but the files are not just my responsibility."

"Then do you know where the files are?" The words were measured and accusing.

If she looked at Josiah, someone was bound to pick up on it. Josiah found the first prayer in years worming its way through his thoughts and breaking through to the surface. *Please, God, guide her response. For her sake and mine.*

Gwendolyn closed her eyes before speaking. "They are unavailable and will be for some time."

The room erupted into disapproval and calls for an explanation.

However, it was Mother's voice that overrode them all. "Gentlemen, I've heard enough." She rose from her seat, forcing the men to follow suit out of deference. "Stress and exhaustion have stolen reason. Giving a starving child a loaf of bread does not equate with paying for an escape, and missing files do not mean misconduct. These unjust accusations will serve to do nothing but divide this board when we really need to stand in unity against any repercussions of Gareth's disappearance. I recommend we go home and allow the police to do their job. We'll reconvene in a week when we have more facts and less speculation to guide our decisions."

"While Mrs. Isaacs does not preside over our meetings, I agree with her assessment." Abernathy, who'd stubbornly remained seated, finally rose from his chair. "However, I'm forming a committee to review Matron Ellison's participation in Gareth's disappearance and the suitability of her continuance as matron of Final Chance. If interested, please remain behind. Otherwise, this meeting is adjourned."

Gwendolyn remained rooted near the door as the majority of board members passed her with wary glances or blatant cold shoulders.

In the end, only Josiah, Mother, Abernathy, and Wells remained behind to form the committee. Both men had made it to the top of his list of suspects when he'd examined the information provided by

Gwendolyn. Abernathy had the resources and power to use Final Chance as a front, and, as treasurer, Wells had access to the money and ledgers. One or both of them could be involved in the green goods game, but their presence on the committee boiled down to one goal. They sought to remove Gwendolyn from her position as matron. Or worse.

Before he could stop himself, Josiah moved to her side. The obvious sign of support would not be to his or Gwendolyn's favor. Thankfully, Mother was more politic in her movements, remaining firmly in place between the two groups.

Wells eyed Mother before joining her in the position of neutrality. "I believe in the maxim of innocent until proven guilty, Matron Ellison. So long as you cooperate, I see no need to fear for your job."

"I disagree. I suggest you use your half day tomorrow to apply for work elsewhere." Abernathy collected his coat and hat from the hall tree in the corner. "Though you'll continue your duties, you're under probation. Beginning tomorrow morning, any who are able to join me will examine all of your paperwork—personal and professional." He turned to the pale-faced Mrs. Flowers, who collected the cups and saucers as inconspicuously as possible. "You. See to it Matron Ellison isn't left alone between now and then. I'll not risk her destroying evidence."

"Yes, sir." The distressed cook stacked the remaining cups on a cart as she addressed Gwendolyn. "If you please, ma'am, I need to soak these cups before the coffee stains the china."

Gwendolyn nodded and waited with clasped hands for Mrs. Flowers to lead the way. The cart squeaked across the floor, and the china rattled in its pile. Just before they passed through the door, Gwendolyn's eyes sought his. He'd expected to impart silent comfort and strength to her, but instead she'd imparted them to him. How—with everything she stood to lose—could she have peace in a moment like this? It didn't make sense.

CHAPTER 20

THOUGH OUTSIDE THE NIGHT WAS cool and clear, a storm raged inside of Gwendolyn, stealing all hope of sleep and—more frustrating—peace. She'd clung to it like Jesus's outstretched hand as she left the boardroom. But, like Peter, she'd soon begun to sink beneath the lashing waves of fear and anxiety. Why, when she knew all the right prayers to pray and the verses to read? She should be sleeping like David, confident in safety because God watched over her. After all, hadn't people praised her stalwart faith and pointed to her as an example of a strong Christian? Hadn't she learned that no matter the trial, she could lean into Jesus? Yet here she sat, cross-legged on her patched coverlet with the lantern turned bright and Mrs. Flowers sleep-snuffling on the extra mattress wedged between the wardrobe and bed. Her mind, body, and soul felt more ragged than the scrap dolls made by the quilting group.

Tears dripped down Gwendolyn's cheeks and off her chin onto the thin pages of her Bible. Years of notes and prayers in the margins smudged beneath the watery pools. Were the imminent loss of her job the only consideration, she'd be heartbroken but hopeful for whatever plan God held in His hand.

But this? This was the maneuver of evil men who sought to shed innocent blood. Proud looks, lying tongues, and wicked hearts. Weren't these all things that the Lord found abhorrent? Why did He not act and at the very least intervene for these defenseless ones? Gareth didn't deserve to be attacked, let alone possibly killed. Hibbard should be running his mouth and taunting the other children during a game of blindman's buff. And Mr. Farwell. How he'd suffered because he'd been brave enough to help her!

Give ear to my words, O Lord. Thou art not a God that hath pleasure in wickedness: neither shall evil dwell with thee. Yet many are they that rise up against me. Against the children. How long, O Lord, will You wait to act? Are You not more powerful than they?

All through the night, her words mingled with those of David's psalms, wrestling with the truth of who God was and with the doubt that rose up in her soul. By morning, she was exhausted and clinging to verses of justice and vengeance with a threadbare faith that doubted whether God would execute either. God was who He said He was, but her faith was so weak.

Lord, I believe. Help thou my unbelief.

She rose from the bed, waking Mrs. Flowers when she tried to step over the woman.

"Is everything all right, ma'am?" Mrs. Flowers sat up, rubbing her eyes and then her stuffy nose.

"Rise and shine, my little duckling. It's time to face the day."

Though she made light of Mrs. Flowers's assignment to follow her every move, Gwendolyn chafed under the inability to use even the necessary unchaperoned. Even so, both women agreed they didn't want to give the board any reason to cast further accusations of misconduct. Her dismissal might be coming, but Gwendolyn would delay it as long as possible.

Chairman Abernathy and Treasurer Wells arrived before breakfast. No doubt they did so to avoid objections from the Isaacses, considering that they demanded to search Gwendolyn's private quarters, where she was "most likely to hide the files and other evidence of misconduct." Josiah and Mrs. Isaacs would've never allowed such an atrocity, but what recourse did Gwendolyn have? To object would only fuel their arguments for immediate dismissal or ensure her own attack when she left the premises this afternoon. Thankfully, they'd conceded to allow Wilhelmina to be the one to remove and examine each item in

Gwendolyn's wardrobe. It was bad enough for the men to see her unmentionables. To have them touch them would have been the ultimate humiliation.

"This is wrong," Wilhelmina whispered after she'd returned Gwendolyn's clothes. They stood at the door, watching as the men flipped through books and searched drawers. "We need to report this to the rest of the board. They're treating you worse than a criminal."

Gwendolyn wrapped her arms around her middle, too sick to her stomach to speak. Chairman Abernathy stripped her bed as if she'd hidden something between the sheets and mattress. She didn't care if both men were married and accustomed to such liberties. That was where she slept. Their actions went beyond reason. It was more a display of dominance than a true search. A reminder that she had no power here except that which they gave her.

"I will endure it for the children's sake," she finally said.

If either man was a part of the diabolical dealings, she'd rather they find nothing and realize she wasn't the threat they supposed. But then again, if they didn't find anything and assumed nothing was written down anywhere, they could silence her forever and think no one but Josiah would suspect the truth.

"How does enduring this help the children?"

"It buys me time."

Although Wilhelmina shot her a concerned frown, Gwendolyn did not expound. But she would. When, not if, Gwendolyn lost her position as matron, Wilhelmina would need to know what was going on and how to protect the children.

"What's this?" Treasurer Wells lifted the small diary she kept hidden in the space between the floor and wardrobe.

Gwendolyn tensed. Every bit of frustration with board members, children, and budgets, as well as confessions of wishing for more than what God had granted her, lay in those pages. Not to mention the later pages where she revealed her suspicions regarding certain people and her partnership with one very dashing and very undercover Secret Service man.

"It's my diary, sir. Nothing but the boring and idle thoughts of a woman."

He considered it a moment and bent like he intended to return it to its place.

"Keep it." Chairman Abernathy threw her bedding into a pile on the floor. "If she's hiding secrets, that's where we'll find them."

Wilhelmina's nails dug into Gwendolyn's arm as she hissed, "Say something."

"Have you finished with my room? I don't believe there is an inch left for you to examine."

He squeezed the pillow in one last attempt to discover something hidden and then tossed it against the wall. "I believe we are."

They strode between Gwendolyn and Wilhelmina into the private office.

With some reluctance, Gwendolyn followed. While Treasurer Wells tackled her desk, stacking anything resembling paperwork in a pile, Chairman Abernathy rifled through the donation piles and undid all her sorting. She turned her back on the invasion and locked her bedroom door.

"Officer Grace and I need to return to our duties with the children. If you have need of anything, I'll be downstairs."

Though her legs trembled as she walked, she managed a regal exit. Wilhelmina, however, exited more like a stampeding elephant. She waited only until they were far enough away for her voice not to echo into the office before launching into an interrogation.

"What is going on? They have no right to treat you this way, and yet you submit to it like a timid mouse! You are the matron of Final Chance."

"Meet me in the donations room." Josiah might not have wanted to trust anyone else in the building, but circumstances required a shift in strategy.

Wilhelmina abruptly stopped. "That bad?"

They only resorted to that room when the utmost secrecy was required.

"Worse."

Wilhelmina frowned but nodded. "Mrs. Flowers offered to watch over the girls while we ate breakfast, if needed. I'll get them started on their lessons and then join you."

Settling the children took longer than Gwendolyn hoped, and Mrs. Isaacs arrived before Wilhelmina. "Chairman Abernathy and Treasurer Wells arrived almost two hours ago and have already been through my private quarters. You can probably still find them in my private office."

Mrs. Isaacs looked aghast. "They've been through your private quarters? As in your bedroom?"

Good. Maybe there would be some repercussion for her humiliation. "Yes, and I assure you, they did a thorough job. Officer Grace held up my clothing piece by piece and shook them out while they watched to prove I did not hide anything. They confiscated my diary, but I assure you its contents are irrelevant."

Mrs. Isaacs huffed. "Their behavior is unacceptable, and I will not tolerate it. You may be assured of my support and the return of your diary."

"Thank you, ma'am." Gwendolyn blew out a breath, only mildly reassured. Already they'd had more than a half hour with her diary. Depending on where they started and if they skimmed, they could have already found the incriminating thoughts they sought.

Wilhelmina passed Mrs. Isaacs in the hall and her eyes widened. She tugged Gwendolyn into the donations room, locked the door behind them, and huddled in the farthest corner.

"What is going on, Gwendolyn? Mrs. Flowers said they're threatening to fire you."

"If I tell you what's going on, it will put your life in danger. All I need you to know is that if something happens to me or my family, it wasn't an accident."

Wilhelmina pulled back. "You're scaring me, Gwendolyn."

"I know, but if something does happen to me—if I don't come home tonight, or I get hurt—I need you to immediately notify Josiah Isaacs as quietly as you can. No one can know."

"Mr. Isaacs?"

"He's—" Gwendolyn bit her lip. She couldn't give away his role as a Secret Service operative, but she couldn't leave Wilhelmina without some sort of explanation. "He's working with the police in an investigation of Final Chance."

Wilhelmina's eyes widened. "You are too, aren't you?"

"I am. Mr. Farwell's death wasn't an accident. Neither were Hibbard's injuries, nor Gareth's disappearance. They all knew too much."

"And you're afraid you're next."

Gwendolyn clasped Wilhelmina's hands. "I gladly sacrifice everything to protect these children, but if something happens to me before the culprits are caught, I fear more children will be hurt, or worse. I need to know that you'll step in to take my place."

"Why wait? Let me help now. These children mean as much to me as they do to you."

Wilhelmina pushed until Gwendolyn couldn't deny the benefit of having another set of trustworthy eyes and ears within Final Chance. In as succinct a manner as she could, Gwendolyn shared the details of all that had transpired and what evidence she searched for, leaving out the specific details of Josiah's involvement.

"I suspect Superintendent King is involved, although I'm not certain after the beating he received. Officer Bagwell most certainly abuses the children, but that doesn't make him a counterfeiter. Treasurer Wells seemed an unwilling participant in today's search. That doesn't mean he's not involved, but nothing so far suggests his being so."

"And that leaves Chairman Abernathy." Wilhelmina sighed. "I never liked that man. I know he's not the only one who believes a woman's place is in the home, but his disdain for what we do in a ministry he volunteers for . . . it's just wrong. But if he sees the children as a tool to increase his wealth, then I suppose it makes sense."

"We've no proof of anything, counterfeiting or otherwise." Gwendolyn heaved a sigh at how little she and Josiah had been able to accomplish in the last week. "I've turned over everything the police have asked for, including the missing files. I can't clear my name by disclosing where they are to the board, because it will reveal Final Chance is under investigation. And since I've thoroughly searched this half of the building, I've come to the conclusion that any evidence we need is locked behind the boys' ward doors. There is nothing else we can do but watch and listen."

"But you've got the key. A little snooping might be all we need."

Gwendolyn wrung her hands. Josiah hadn't wanted her to take any unnecessary risks, but providing him with the files and notes he needed hadn't progressed the case forward. If anything, it had only given the board grounds to deny her access to the building. They were running out of time. And with the confiscating of her diary, how long would it be before those involved decided to move all the evidence to a more secure location?

The children of Final Chance needed her to take action, not funnel paperwork. "There's a locked room in the boys' ward that I don't have a key for. I'm certain it holds what Mr. Isaacs needs."

"That sounds like a reasonable assumption to me. With Superintendent King abed for recovery and Officer Bagwell overseeing his duties temporarily, they'll be too busy to notice if we break into it at night."

"There's no we to it, Wilhelmina. If there's to be any breaking in, I'll be the one doing it. They don't suspect you, and we need to keep it that way."

"But you don't know how to pick locks."

"And you do?"

"Did I never tell you?" Wilhelmina exuded feigned innocence. "My husband was a locksmith. There's not a lock in this building I can't get past if I've a mind to. I might not have disclosed that earlier for fear of being dismissed, but I've got the skills, and you've got the need."

"If I didn't absolutely trust you, I'd be terrified."

Wilhelmina smiled. "So, when do we break in?"

Chapter 21

Josiah's head jerked forward as the carriage rumbled over the train tracks, startling him awake. He rubbed his eyes and surveyed the passing businesses and above-stairs homes. By the sulfuric smell of the gas works, he was still blocks away from reaching Final Chance.

Exhaustion and worry over Gwendolyn had dampened his ability to focus all throughout the morning's blur of activity and information. He'd slept with his window open and his ears attuned for the moment Speedy would pound on his door to announce some calamity had befallen her. Though the pounding never came, he awoke at every sound in the night. If only he'd gotten the chance to speak to her before she'd left with Mrs. Flowers. Then he might've been able to provide her a weapon of some sort. Something to ease his mind over the danger she faced.

"Don't you be taking the Lord's job, Josiah. It's His to do the protectin', yours to do the trustin'." Shauna's voice rolled through his head, and he could almost feel the tap to the nose she'd always done to emphasize her admonitions.

But Josiah *had* done his job. It was God who'd failed. God hadn't protected Shauna from the train accident, and now Josiah wasn't sure he could trust Gwendolyn to God's protection either.

"It's Him who numbers our days, and there's naught you can do about it."

He ran a hand over his face and stared out the window. He hadn't given God this much consideration since Shauna died, and now he vacillated between praying to Him and being angry all over again. Although he supposed he'd never really stopped being angry, and that anger was the true crutch of his doubt. Gwendolyn's words rose to mind next, and it was as if the two women in his life that had an un-natural way of worming into his heart had joined together to beat Him with their Bibles.

"Doubt is the struggle to believe God's promises when confronted with the darkness of this world. It's the wavering between accepting God and His unsearchable ways or believing what our limited experiences might tell us."

Josiah bit the inside of his cheek. What was it about Gwendolyn and Shauna that drove him to God even when he didn't want to go?

God, both women seem to think You worthy of their love and devotion, but I confess I'm angry. Angry, hurt, and resentful that You did not intervene to save Shauna. You could have, but You didn't. And now Gwendolyn faces a different danger. Are You going to act this time? You say You are good. You say You are just. But I can't see it. Gwendolyn says to bring my doubts to You and ask for Your help to confront them. Well, here they are. I don't want to be angry anymore. I want to know I can trust You, but You're going to have to help me. I'm not sure I have enough faith left to be able to believe on my own.

The carriage stopped at the back of the hack stand as previously ar-ranged, and Josiah swallowed the mix of emotions that sought to choke him. He still doubted, but he held fast to a new hope that God would help him and protect Gwendolyn.

After Josiah disembarked, the carriage proceeded to the front steps of Final Chance two blocks away, where it would collect Gwendolyn. Josiah disguised his lingering by striking up a conversation with a driver waiting for his next passengers. The man hadn't been around during the previous attacks on Mr. Farwell and Superintendent King, but he'd heard secondhand about yesterday's attack from a fellow driver who had witnessed a portion of it.

"Do you think he'd be willing to speak to me? Share what he saw?"

"Nah. He was shakin' in his boots just tellin' me. Definitely won't tell no coppers." The driver arched a thick brow. "As they say, dead men tell no tales."

"I don't suppose he's afraid of Fantasma?"

"Sounds to me like you already know who done it then." He scratched at his scraggly beard for a moment, and then an amused smile tilted to one side. "Exceptin' Fantasma ran into a bit of opposition." After an examination of each face on the street and a special concentration on the alley corners, he leaned over. "You'll have better luck askin' one of them paper hawkers that showed up last week. If'n you can find them. They didn't show up today, and they be a wily bunch to find."

Josiah's gaze strayed down the street to the building across from Final Chance. He'd told the boys not to worry about Wednesday afternoons and evenings, but perhaps he should check in at the room he'd rented for them. If they'd tangled with Fantasma, they could be hurt, or housing Gareth if they'd gotten the boy away.

"Thank you. If your friend decides to gain a little courage, a reward is being offered. Just ask for Detective Morrows at the Fifth District precinct office."

By the gleam in the driver's eyes, that "friend" might be making a visit sooner rather than later. Josiah crossed the street and wandered toward Speedy's hideout with an eye for any activity suggesting an attack waited for him. Nothing indicated Fantasma was brave enough to conduct a third attack so near in time and distance to yesterday's. The carriage waited for Gwendolyn up ahead, and Josiah cut down the alley to enter Speedy's building from the back.

Unfortunately, the room appeared abandoned when he reached it. The pallet he'd provided was gone, along with the supply of food he'd sent yesterday evening. He'd check into Speedy's other locations, but instinct told him Speedy and his crew weren't going to be found until they wanted to be.

By the time he returned to the street, the carriage had left with Gwendolyn to meet him out of view of Final Chance. Keeping to the alleys to disguise his presence in the area, Josiah returned to the hack stand where the carriage waited with an anxious Gwendolyn peering around. A little levity might help break the tension they evidently both felt. He snuck toward the door from behind and popped into view with a "Boo!"

Gwendolyn screamed, and Josiah found himself chest to tip with the infamous Red.

"Josiah Isaacs, I could have killed you!" She released a heavy breath and set the awl in her lap.

He released a chuckle mixed with relief that she hadn't thrust forward. The two-inch point might not have killed, but it wouldn't have been pleasant. "I'm glad to see you stay well armed. I can't have the prettiest woman in Philadelphia accosted when I'm not around to protect her."

Her lips parted for a moment before slipping into a shy smile that she quickly hid by ducking her head. Soft pink climbed her neck, giving color to the cheeks that no doubt had been wan only a moment ago. He might not have meant to tease her in that manner, but he was glad he had.

"May I join you? Or would you rather sit there in the middle and have me follow behind in another?"

"Oh, of course. Please." She scooted to the far side, making room for him.

He climbed inside, forcing himself to give as much room between them as the carriage allowed. They didn't have far to go for their next destination, but he'd asked the driver to take a path that would make no sense to anyone who might follow them. The instructions were as much for their protection as they were to provide him an extended period of privacy with Gwendolyn.

"How are you, really?" He shifted so he faced her more directly. Though surprise had originally rounded her eyes at his appearance, it'd only taken a glance for Josiah to recognize the dark shadows beneath them and the furrows of stress in her brow.

She boldly wrapped her gloved hands around his, closed her eyes, and squeezed until his fingers ached. He tensed. Other women had taken such liberties before trapping him into proposals. But he hadn't expected such behavior from her.

After a deep breath, she opened her eyes. Whatever she saw on his face caused her to immediately drop his hands and jerk back. "I'm so sorry. Please forgive me. I shouldn't have done that." She sagged against the carriage's frame and looked away. "It was just a long night, and I needed to feel someone else's strength for a moment."

By thunder—this woman. Why couldn't she be playing coy? It would be so much easier if she were. Then he could shove aside the yearning to pull her against his chest and envelop her in his arms to shield her from the brokenness of this world. A desire he should only have for his wife.

But he'd promised to be a friend to Gwendolyn, and right now she needed a strength outside her own. Shauna would understand his providing some measure of comfort. As a friend. Nothing more.

He clasped her hands and gently squeezed. "You can have my strength whenever you need it."

Tear-filled eyes lifted to his. "Thank you." She freed a hand and wiped furiously at the streams making paths down her face. "I'm sorry. I promise, I don't usually cry so often."

Josiah captured a tear on his hand before lifting her chin and brushing another away with his thumb. "Tears don't scare me. I grew up with three sisters."

A small smile brightened her soul-weary face. "You are a good man, Josiah Isaacs. The world could do with a few more of you."

"I'm fairly certain there are a number of people who are relieved there aren't."

"Mostly fathers, but only because they don't realize what you hide behind that rakish reputation of yours. If they knew, you'd have to fend off as many fathers wanting suitors for their daughters as would-be fiancées."

The teasing light in her eyes sparked a warmth that spread through him. Laughter and flirtation. Two of his favorite things. "You're good for a man's ego, do you know that?"

"Don't get used to it. When I'm not tired, I'm much better at controlling my mouth."

At the mention of her mouth, his third favorite thing popped into mind. Kissing. He coughed. Now was not the time for thoughts like that. They were far too risky. Where thoughts led, actions followed.

With concentrated effort, he shifted his focus to safer and more serious topics. "How did the search go this morning? I'm sorry I couldn't be there."

His meeting with Detective Morrows had provided a few snippets of useful information, but it was largely an excuse for the man to fill his belly. Not that he blamed the man for contriving a way to enjoy Tillie's cooking. Josiah's other errands had been far more productive, including confirming that Warden Spille hadn't sent the note. The man hadn't even had time to look at the transfer request yet.

"The board collected anything they considered potential proof of my misconduct. Of course, they didn't find the files, but Chairman Abernathy and Treasurer Wells did find my diary and 'lost' it before your mother could have it returned to me."

A rock formed in his stomach. "I take it you wrote about my profession and my reason for being at Final Chance?"

She glanced to where she still clung to his hand, as if afraid he might take his offer of strength back. "It was supposed to be my safe place to process my thoughts. I never imagined they'd tear apart my bedroom and go through my wardrobe."

"They did what?" The indecency of it set his blood to boiling. "You should have required they obtain a warrant."

"And give them another reason to suspect me? Or to resort to violence? I'd rather they come in under my watchful eye so I could know what they walk out with than find out later."

"I don't like it. What if they come into your room at other times?"

"Then they'll find it as they left it. I've informed Wilhelmina what's going on, and henceforth I'll be sleeping in the extra bed in the officers' quarters. Have you discovered anything about Gareth?"

"He did, in fact, run with a group of newspaper boys, but their names weren't listed in the file. A driver I spoke with suggested Speedy's crew was involved in yesterday's altercation, but the room I rented for them is empty." The carriage pulled to a stop outside Children's Hospital. "Our best hope is to learn what we can from Hibbard. Do you think he'll speak with you?"

"As long as he's recovered enough to write. Especially when I explain what we're investigating."

Josiah opened the door, let down the foot iron, and aided Gwendolyn to the ground. She squeezed his hand and then let go, leading the way to the hospital wing where Hibbard was recovering.

The nurse who greeted them frowned in confusion. "I'm sorry, ma'am, but we released Hibbard Wilcox to Final Chance's care last night. We'd advised against it, but Superintendent King insisted."

"When was this?" Josiah demanded.

She walked to a desk in the corner of the room and referenced a file on the top of a stack. "Nine o'clock. Normally we don't release any patients after six, but with Hibbard being an inmate and Superintendent King his warden, we weren't permitted a choice."

Gwendolyn shook her head and turned toward him. "That's impossible. Superintendent King was attacked shortly before seven. By nine he was in bed—and heavily medicated." Fear and panic sparked in her eyes, and her breath quickened. "They're covering up their tracks. Eliminating anyone who can testify against them."

Josiah squeezed her hand, willing her to calm. Facts. He needed facts, not a jump to a conclusion, no matter how right it appeared. "What did this man look like?"

"It wasn't my shift, but Nora was here." The nurse strode to another woman tending to a child in the far corner of the room.

After a moment of quiet talk, Nora returned in the nurse's stead, looking as if she were approaching a guillotine. "I wasn't on duty last night; I was just visiting one of my patients during off-hours. Doctor McKenna is the one who released Hibbard to Superintendent King. Or at least to the man who said he was Superintendent King."

"You're not in trouble, Miss Nora, but I need you to describe the man to me. Can you do that?"

"He was about yea high." She lifted her hand midway between her height and Josiah's height. "Stocky, probably 'bout fourteen or fifteen stone. His hair was cut close to his scalp, like he was trying to hide his bald spot at the front."

That was the most encouraging news he'd heard all week. "By any chance did the man have a tattoo of a woman just above his wrist?"

At this, Nora's whole face pinched. "Maybe. His sleeves covered it, but I recall him shaking hands with the doctor and the sleeve shifting up a bit. It looked like a tattoo, but I can't say what it was of."

Some more good news. "Thank you, Miss Nora. We'll leave you to your fine work."

Although Gwendolyn sent him a questioning look, he waited until they were back in the relative privacy of the carriage. "I believe the man who impersonated Superintendent King is Billy Wilcox, Hibbard's father."

Gwendolyn's body thudded against the seat back. "Do you think Hibbard's safe, then?"

"As safe as he can be for the time being. I'm going to take you home and then check Wilcox's usual haunts. Once I've ascertained Hibbard's location, I'll come to let you know."

She smiled in acquiescence, but her hand found his again and held tight for the entire ride to Reverend Ballantine's home.

CHAPTER 22

THE PAD OF JOSIAH'S THUMB caressed the inside of Gwendolyn's wrist, both calming her anxiety and sending her heart racing. She'd invited him into this intimate gesture, practically begged it of him, and now she second-guessed the wisdom of it. It simply wasn't fair for his hand to be such a strong anchor in her tempestuous world. God alone should be her anchor and her source of strength, but Josiah's physical presence, gentle understanding, and care for her well-being felt like a tangible extension of God's love. And like an infatuated schoolgirl, she craved the tangibility.

Infatuation was like opium: dangerously habit-forming but providing no real satisfaction. It was a facsimile of love. What she felt now—in the midst of her exhaustion on every front—wouldn't last. She needed a nap. A chance to put her head on straight, pray to her real anchor, and think through how to face the challenges awaiting her at Final Chance. With the time being only half past one, she should have several hours alone to rest before having to face her family's questions and demands for updates. She especially needed to be ready to combat any comments or concerns about the certain man holding her hand as if they were betrothed.

When they stopped in front of the house, Josiah offered his arm. "Allow me to walk you to the door. I want to see that you are settled and safe before I leave."

She tamped down the exhaustion-induced thrill at having him near her for even one minute more and unlocked the door. "Everything should be quiet." She stepped inside. "I'm the only one—"

The words fled at the sight of an unfamiliar hat hanging on the hook.

An equally strange voice called from the parlor. "Kate, is that you?" A very male voice.

Gwendolyn's breath caught in her throat. Mother's visitor.

With all that had happened, Gwendolyn had forgotten about Mother's attempt to prepare her. Given the man even called Mother by the family name rather than her Christian name, they must have grown quite close indeed. Was it possible Mother was considering remarriage? Her parents hadn't officially divorced, to her knowledge, but it only took seven years of abandonment for it to be approved without the presence of both spouses. Father had been gone seventeen. Mother could have easily submitted the paperwork to the courthouse years ago and Gwendolyn never be the wiser. Was that what mother was trying to prepare her for? A new man in their lives?

"Gwendolyn?" Josiah's hand touched the small of her back, and he peered at her as if he feared she might faint.

Maybe she would, and she'd much rather he catch her than a stranger. "Would you come in with me? I forgot Mother has a visitor, and I'm afraid I've never met him. I don't know what kind of person he is, and if he's the only one here . . ."

"Say no more. I'll not leave you alone."

Though she wanted to grab his hand again, she didn't dare take such a liberty here. With stiff movements, she hung her shawl and Josiah's hat on an empty hook. *Lord, preparest me.* After one lingering look into Josiah's concerned eyes to steel her nerves, she plastered on a smile and stepped from the foyer into the parlor.

A skeleton of a man fumbled for a crutch and rose to his feet.

No, not feet. A foot. He had only one leg.

And one eye. The other was covered by a swathe of fabric that not only hid the missing eye but also the rippled scars that spidered down his face and neck. She couldn't see them, but she knew they were there.

They had been branded on him during the fire that had claimed his leg and made him a local hero.

And then turned him into a fraud and an addict.

"Gweny, is that really you?" Her father staggered forward, reaching for her.

"No." She stumbled back.

It couldn't be him. Not after so long. After so many broken promises.

Her gaze flicked up and down the threadbare clothes, pausing at each undeniable feature that proved even further he was her father. Each breath came quicker than the last. Dizziness buzzed to life.

Why had he come back? Why now, of all times?

His crutch tapped against the wood floor, and his wistful smile pleaded with her to forget the past and enthusiastically welcome him home. "Gweny. My little Gweny."

"Don't." Though a giant could lie head to toe between them, she continued backward. "Don't call me that."

He stopped pursuing her. Anguish rippled his face where his scars did not. "Please, Gweny. Forgive me."

She'd passed the point of being able to speak. Her chest heaved and gasped for air as all the bad memories she'd shoved aside crashed over her. Nights of paranoia that made her and her mother hide the knives. The fits of rage when Mother tried to restrict his medicine consumption. The destruction he left in his wake as he searched for the empty bottles he was certain had been full.

Yes, she missed her father. But only the father from before the fire. This man who was back now . . . She couldn't live through that again. Couldn't believe mother would.

She bumped into Josiah's chest, but even he could not anchor her. Not this time. The edges of her vision blackened, creating a tunnel where all she could see was the monster who'd stolen her father.

Feet pounded down the stairs, and Uncle Percy's voice sounded miles away. "Gwendolyn, you're home."

She swung her ever-narrowing vision in his direction, but all she saw was the letter in his hand.

Letters. Mother had been writing letters. To her father.

And she didn't tell me.

Her tunneled vision slipped to Uncle Percy's wide-eyed face. The slow dawn of realization lit her world in a red haze of pain and betrayal. "You knew, didn't you?"

"Gwendolyn, I—"

"Didn't you?!" A sob broke loose, and her legs gave out.

Arms wrapped around her waist and eased her to the ground.

"Breathe, Gwendolyn. Slowly." Josiah's breath fanned against her ear.

She gasped, trying to obey. The air rushed back out as quickly as it came. Breath after breath. But Josiah kept talking, low and soothing.

"That's it. Nice and easy."

Slowly her vision expanded, and she became aware of Josiah rubbing circles on her back as he practically held her in his lap.

"Get her a glass of water."

Uncle Percy moved to obey, but she croaked out a "no" to stop him. "We're not staying."

"Don't be ridiculous," Uncle Percy said. "This is your home. We need to discuss this. Your mother—"

"Lied to me. You all did." Her gaze shifted from Uncle Percy to her father, but she refused to allow it to linger. "I can't stay. I need space. Time." She pushed away from Josiah, but he swooped back in to assist her when she wobbled.

Uncle Percy approached her with hands palm out as if calming a skittish horse. "Stay here. We'll give you all the space and time you need. I know it's a shock—"

"A shock? No, Uncle Percy. A shock is when you drag your feet over a carpet and then touch the doorknob. This—" Her eyes bounced around the room from Uncle Percy to the letter desk to the man standing in her parlor like he belonged there. "This is the destruction of my sanctuary. How long has Mother been writing to him? How long have you been lying to me?"

"If you'll talk to your mother—"

"No. I can't." She faced Josiah, apparently the only person left in her world that she could trust. "Please, Josiah. I need to leave. Can you help me?"

He nodded. "Of course."

"You can't leave with him. Not in your state. He'll take advantage of you." Uncle Percy grabbed her arm and tried to jerk her away, but Josiah wrapped her in a protective embrace.

"I vow to God I will not take advantage of her." His arms squeezed in affirmation. "I'll take her to my parents' house on Rittenhouse Square. She'll have all the space she needs, and her reputation will remain intact. When she's ready, she'll reach out to you. Until then, I ask that you respect her need to be left alone."

Tears streamed down her face again, and she allowed Josiah to lead her out of the house in an awkward walk that had her tight against him.

Once aboard the waiting hack, he pulled her to him and brushed a loose hair from her face. "Who was that man?"

"My father."

Then the dam broke loose, and she sobbed all over again, this time fully aware of the way Josiah held her and the comfort he brought, even as her heart was being torn asunder.

Chapter 23

The new floral carpet Mother had installed in the drawing room dampened the sound of Josiah's pacing considerably but not enough to keep the servants from stopping in to see if he needed anything. After the fourth one came in to offer him coffee, he finally acquiesced and dropped onto the padded wicker chair next to Mother's tea table.

He should've known Mother would still be at Final Chance and Father hobnobbing at the Philadelphia Club. Praise God Celestia was home. His baby sister might barely be a woman in his eyes, but with her impending marriage and move to Germany in just a few months, he had to trust she could meet any of Gwendolyn's needs. After all, she'd proven herself quite competent on the *Golden Gestirn* when she and Aldrich Weise encountered a counterfeiter and murderer working onboard.

The maid poured his cup and then removed to a nearby corner of the drawing room to anticipate any need for a refill. Normally, he'd talk to the new girl—it paid to make friends with the staff—but not today. He rested his elbows on his knees and scrubbed his face. He really needed to determine Wilcox's whereabouts, but with Gwendolyn's complete undoing, he couldn't bring himself to leave. What if she asked for him? She obviously shouldn't be left alone, but with the possible exposure of his Secret Service role, he needed to act quickly on what little information he'd gained.

Celestia swept into the room in her silvery-blue tea gown, looking every bit the ethereal being her name suggested. "Miss Ellison's asleep and probably will be for some time. The poor thing said she hadn't slept in two days." She took a seat, and after waving off the maid, poured herself a cup of coffee. "Who is she to you? The only time you bring a woman here is after you've proposed. But if she's your next fiancée, she didn't seem happy about it."

"We're not betrothed. Nor will we ever be." The words tasted sour, but he refused to consider anything more than friendship.

To do so meant betrayal to Shauna and the love they'd shared. Something once in a lifetime. Soul deep. Eternal. Gwendolyn clinging to him and sobbing enough tears to flood the Schuylkill River changed nothing.

Celestia smiled behind her cup. "Never, hmm? That's impressive coming from a man with a record like yours."

He knew she only jested, but the turmoil roiling through him made it impossible to respond with his usual humor. He shoved from the chair to his feet. "I have work to do. If she wakes before I return, will you reassure her that I've not abandoned her?"

Celestia blinked and lowered her cup. "Of course." He turned away, but she grasped his sleeve. "She's important to you, isn't she? And not like those other girls. She's really important to you. Like Aldrich is to me."

When had his baby sister grown so perceptive? He refused to look at her and instead focused on the opulent arrangement of flowers and feathers in the center of the room. "She's a friend, and that's all she can be. Do you understand me? Don't make this out to be any more than it is."

"I understand that you're hurting," she said slowly, "and that you're scared. But that doesn't make Miss Ellison any less important to you. I'll take good care of her, Josiah. You needn't worry."

When he faced her, compassion and wisdom beyond her twenty-two years shimmered in her dark blue eyes.

"Thank you, Celestia. I'll be back before dinner."

"I'll inform Cook to expect both of you."

He nodded and then set to his first task. There was a great deal he wanted to accomplish before dinner, for he would not leave Gwendolyn alone to contend with his father.

The sound of a door closing startled Gwendolyn awake. Soft light snuck into the unfamiliar room through the sides of curtains that stretched to the heavens.

Where was she? She blinked against the grit in her eyes and tried to make sense of her surroundings. A fire illuminated a grand room that must belong to a queen. Maroon and cream papered walls reached to a ceiling nearly twice the normal height. Intricate filigree moldings were carved into the mahogany cornices that matched those on the four posters of the bed and the fireplace mantel.

Her mind finally cast aside the quilt of sleep and remembered. Not only was she in one of the Isaacs's guest bedrooms, but she also wore one of Miss Celestia's nightgowns. Gwendolyn groaned and rolled to her back, only to sink farther into the mattress that wanted to eat her. Above her, a dozen cherubs flew between flowers and clouds, flaunting just how many pointless details old money could buy. She could only imagine the titter she'd set off with the servants by waltzing through the front door, clinging to Josiah and sobbing into his shirt like he was her personal handkerchief.

She closed her aching eyes. How was she ever to face him again? Not only had she humiliated herself, but she'd also humiliated him in front of his sister and staff.

If only she'd not gone home and found her father. Her stomach twisted at the memory of seeing his battered and desiccated body, so different from the last time she saw him—yet still the same in so many ways. Why had he come back? More important, why had her family hidden him from her? How long had Mother been communicating with Father? Shouldn't they have told her and at least allowed her the choice to write him too if she wished? She probably would have said no at first, but what girl in her position wouldn't hold on to hopes of one day having her father back in her life? Even if the one in front of her could never live up to the idealized version of the father of her childhood—before the fire and pain drove him away.

Gwendolyn pressed the cool palms of her hands against her tear-swollen eyes. *One problem at a time, Gwendolyn.*

As distressing as her father's return was, it wasn't nearly as bad as the problem she and the children faced at Final Chance. That situation required her full concentration. Father made his choice to walk away seventeen years ago, forcing her to wait beyond hope for his return as a changed man. It was his turn to wait for her to make a choice about how to proceed. And she'd not make that decision until the villains of Final Chance were arrested and her children safe.

Which meant she needed to renew her search for answers instead of wasting the rest of her half day in bed.

She wiggled to a sitting position in the massive bed. Once again, the difference in her and Josiah's social status smacked her in the face. The room overflowed with knickknacks and paintings, each probably costing a year's salary. Josiah might genuinely want to be friends, but after their connection through Final Chance ended, he'd realize she didn't fit into his world. It hurt to even think about, but the Lord had promised to be a lamp—not a sun—unto her feet. He would illuminate one step at a time and no more. She knew herself well enough to recognize the wisdom in keeping that truth at the front of her mind. It was likely that if she knew the full extent of what they faced, she'd lack the courage needed to move forward.

The door opened, allowing more light to pour into the room. "Begging your pardon, Miss Ellison, but Miss Celestia thought it best to wake ye with enough time to dress for dinner."

Dinner? Had she really slept that long?

Her stomach rumbled as if to confirm the time.

The way her eyes ached and her head throbbed, she wasn't fit to be seen by a rat, let alone the Isaacs family. "If you'll give them my regrets and perhaps order a hack for me, I'll not impose on the family."

She had enough coin on her for a ride and something to eat from a street vendor. Then she'd head back to Final Chance early and make plans with Wilhelmina on what their next steps should be.

"Nonsense. I've already informed Cook that you and Josiah will be joining us. All we have to do is prepare you." Miss Celestia appeared behind the maid and strode into the room wearing an evening dress of pink silk and gold lace. Trailing behind the train of her bustle was another maid with an equally expensive dress draped over her arms.

With a sinking feeling, Gwendolyn glanced at the chair where she'd laid her own dress before climbing into bed. Empty. Certainly this woman knew what a catastrophe it would be to put Gwendolyn in anything but her sturdy work dress. It was bad enough she'd borrowed a nightgown that would make her the envy of every woman she knew. Women like her did not dress above their station.

The first maid turned up the lights, and Gwendolyn raised the blanket to shield her chest. "I'm quite capable of dressing myself. If you'll just return my dress, please."

"I'm afraid not. My father has certain expectations—" Her sweeping glance seemed to evaluate more than Gwendolyn's lack of expensive clothing. "And your dress is a bit common for his taste."

Was it the dress or her that he'd find too common? It really didn't matter. She knew her place. "Common or not, it is my experience that wearing attire from above my station has rather unpleasant consequences. I believe it is best to beg your pardon and excuse myself from the meal."

Gwendolyn tossed aside the covers and swung her feet toward the furthest side of the bed. In a wiggle that discarded any hopes of her appearing dignified, she scooted across the ocean-sized bed and stood. Once her feet hit the floor, so did the folly of her plan. Just where exactly did she plan to go? All she had on was Miss Celestia's nightgown. She couldn't exactly traipse through the house to find her dress.

"I see why Josiah likes you. You've got spunk, and you'll need that in this family."

Gwendolyn swiveled toward Miss Celestia so fast her feet squeaked on the polished floor. "I am not after a marriage proposal from your brother. We are friends, and likely only until his dealings with Final Chance are over. I'm well aware of my place in society, and I'll not humiliate him any more than I already have. Now, please. Return my dress."

Miss Celestia tilted her head and a slow smirk crept across her face. "And what will you do if I don't?"

"I can't come down to dinner in your nightclothes, so I'll remain here and miss the meal. Eventually your brother will force you to return my dress."

Miss Celestia chuckled. "You're perfect for him."

"I told you. I'm not seeking a proposal."

"You don't have to seek it. It'll come eventually. What you do with that proposal is up to you. However, I've seen enough for me to believe you two belong together. Call it Isaacs intuition. We have a long family history of knowing exactly whom God intends us to marry almost as soon as our eyes fall upon them."

Gwendolyn covered the thin material over her chest with her arms. "Love should be based on more than just a feeling."

"Oh, I agree. Feelings should be tested and pushed against. The euphoria of new love passes, and something must remain as a solid foundation to build your lives upon. Or at least, that's what Mother always taught us. You and Josiah must test those feelings yourselves, but I want to prepare the way for Father's acceptance of the idea." Miss Celestia tugged Gwendolyn's hands into her own and squeezed. "It's one dinner in a borrowed dress. I'll take all the blame should Father say anything. Please say you'll wear it and join us for dinner. It will please Josiah so much."

Gwendolyn drew a breath and cast a glance at the light blue silk and white lace. The colors would suit her nicely, and perhaps consenting to wear the dress would detract attention from her earlier behavior. Or it would confirm her to the family as one of those women who sought Josiah as a husband. Her heart made a traitorous flutter.

Lord, leadeth me.

When no answer was forthcoming, she sighed. "Fine, but I am not one of those women."

Miss Celestia's smile widened in triumph, and she clapped her hands like a child granted a treat. "I can't wait to see Josiah's face when he sees you! This is going to be so much fun."

Why did she feel like she'd just been duped into the biggest mistake of her life?

Chapter 24

Neither Billy nor Hibbard Wilcox was anywhere to be found. Rumor had it the man was hiding from Fantasma after rescuing his son. Wilcox was wily enough to ensure Hibbard would be safe from another attack, but that left Josiah without a witness or information for now. Hopefully Ignazio would have better luck discovering their whereabouts.

Discovering Speedy's was another story.

Josiah fidgeted with his hat as he wandered past yet another new mansion being built on the fashionable Rittenhouse Square. Had Gwendolyn not been left alone too long already, he would've continued his search for the missing crew of newspaper boys. Even their snake of a newspaper boss didn't know where the group was and spat curses about what he would do when the boys came back begging for jobs. Josiah had no concerns about that. They were too smart to give "Ol' Pig Face" another day of their lives. But why hadn't Speedy sought out Josiah or left a message at Josiah's home? He thought they'd built a rapport.

A lamplighter worked the street, indicating to Josiah that the hour was later than he would've wanted. He'd be lucky to have time to wash his face before dinner, let alone change into evening attire. Probably for the best. Gwendolyn would likely be uncomfortable enough in her simple clothes at the formal family dinner. His not changing might provide her a measure of comfort. The real trouble would be diverting Father's ire from the breach of house rules. He loved Father, but he could be a difficult man when his ideas were opposed. It served him well as a politician, but it created a constant source of friction when related to Josiah's choices in wife and profession.

Josiah crossed the street to the three-story brick home, built when Rittenhouse Square had been at the edge of the countryside.

The butler opened the door with a bow. "Nicolas is waiting upstairs with your clothes, sir."

"Thank you, Richard. Is Miss Ellison still resting?" He passed his hat and outer coat to a maid's waiting hands.

"No, sir. She, Miss Celestia, and Mr. and Mrs. Isaacs await you in the parlor."

Josiah glanced at the closed pocket door leading to a far too quiet parlor. Celestia he expected, but Mother and Father too? What sort of inquisition had Gwendolyn already endured? And why was it now quiet? He should have come back sooner. "Thank you. Please inform Nicolas I'll not be requiring his services tonight."

Richard's brows rose for a quarter second before he regained control of his countenance. "Very well."

When he entered the parlor, Mother and Father were engaged in soft conversation on the settee, leaning into each other like newlyweds. On the opposite side of the room, Celestia stood at the table with her large book of star maps open and was pointing out constellations to . . . Gwendolyn?

A desert formed in his mouth, and he had the good sense to close it before anyone took note of its gaping.

Powder blue silk and white lace wrapped around Gwendolyn's frame in swaths of fabric that gathered into a bustle and poured onto the floor in a train of embroidered flowers. Even her hair had been swept up into a collection of curls and baby's breath. She looked every bit the part of a society woman that Father would approve of.

Which was exactly the point.

When Celestia had said she'd take good care of Gwendolyn, she'd meant she'd take good care of hiding who Gwendolyn was from their father. He clenched his jaw against the rising frustration. Celestia meant her actions for good, but Gwendolyn was perfectly fine just as she was. Whether high society woman or matron of Final Chance, she was worthy of his father's respect and admiration. She didn't need a House of Worth dress to declare her so.

"Josiah, why aren't you dressed for dinner?" Mother rose from the settee and reclaimed his attention.

He greeted her with a kiss and nodded his father's direction.

Father responded with a disapproving frown. No doubt Josiah's suit showed evidence of the disagreeable places he'd visited in his search for Wilcox and Speedy.

"I only just returned and didn't wish to delay dinner any further. Miss Ellison has a curfew she must abide by."

Celestia practically skipped to his side and kissed him on the cheek. "Isn't Miss Ellison beautiful in that gown?"

Gwendolyn watched from across the room, twisting a handkerchief in her gloved hands. She probably didn't even realize that she pressed her lips together or that she stood stiff as stone. Whatever had been said in his absence had sent the confidence he admired in her skittering to a mouse hole.

He might not always know what to do with her or the feelings she stirred within him, but in this moment he knew exactly what they both needed.

He abandoned his family and clasped her hands in his, giving them a reassuring squeeze. Her anxious face lifted toward his, and the longing to kiss away the furrow on her brow arose. Acting on that impulse would certainly scandalize his family, and it only made him want to do it more. But he was a gentleman, at least on most days, and he settled for kissing her hand. Although a true gentleman would have stopped at the air above her knuckles.

"My sister is only half right. You are beautiful, but it isn't the dress that makes you so. It's you who makes the dress the envy of every woman. I've never met a more breathtaking creature."

Her tremulous smile wobbled into a grin, and the tension in her stance melted away, leaving in its place the familiar adoration that he'd seen so often from Shauna. It should scare him, but instead the realization washed him with warmth.

Was it so bad? This part of him that wondered if there could be more than friendship. That perhaps his cup wasn't quite as empty of the ability to love as he first supposed. He'd cherished being married. The laughter, the companionship, the ability to lean into someone else. He missed all of it. Ached for it.

And he stood for the first time able to imagine having it again. With Gwendolyn.

God, is it even possible? Am I wrong to want it?

His mind balked, but something else within him shushed it and encouraged him to marinate in the possibility. If Shauna were answering the questions, he knew what she'd say. Yes, it's possible, and, no, it isn't wrong. She'd want him to be happy. But was Gwendolyn just part of his usual damsel-in-distress weakness?

Yes, she was a woman in need, but she was also a woman with her own incredible competence. Her physical beauty certainly attracted him—especially now in a dress meant to encourage attraction—but her spirit was proving to be far more captivating. She was a woman who saw him for who he was. Not the reputation he had nor the wealth that so many sought. More than that, she had a strength of faith and character that bolstered him. Their situation hadn't allowed them the opportunity to simply enjoy each other's company, but the potential was there—enough so that he could see the hopeful twilight of a new future after the dark night of ten lonely years. One that might bring with it the sunrise of marriage once more.

She looked beyond him and then back again. "Thank you, Josiah. This dress wasn't my choice. I don't want you to think—"

"Don't give it another thought. I know my sister's proclivity for interfering and how impossible it is to refuse her. Besides, I know your heart." He stepped to her side and rested her arm on his. "Shall we join the others so we can eat and get you home in time?"

"If I weren't so famished, I'd ask you to take me back to Final Chance now. I don't think your parents are happy that I'm here."

"Nonsense. They're just stodgy. Come along. Father's notorious for having several courses, even for family meals. You'll leave so full that you won't eat for days."

She smiled at him again, and the answer to his marriage questions pushed tentatively through the soft soil of his uncertainty. As she squeezed closer to his side, the tender seedling of possibility unfurled in the rays of hope, setting roots that, given time, might become something enduring.

They rejoined the family side by side. Celestia's sparkling smile announced she thought her scheme was going to plan, the little imp. Although he might just have to thank her one day.

Mother's gaze dipped to their linked arms with a coolness that could make ice shiver. "Dinner is served, and as we do not have a round number, you'll escort Celestia. I'm sure Miss Ellison doesn't mind following behind."

The room's temperature shot up in an instant. Apparently her singing Gwendolyn's praises at Final Chance did not equate to her providing a welcomed invitation to join the family, for an evening or otherwise. All her talk about wanting to do right by him and by Shauna only applied to the dead, it seemed. Why had he thought she'd really learned to support his choice to see beyond class?

"She most certainly does mind following behind."

"No, Mr. Isaacs, it's quite all right." Gwendolyn held on to a smile as false as a Fantasma note. "I know my place." The last came on a whisper that accompanied an attempt to slip her arm from his.

He held fast. "You are the equal of everyone here." To his mother he said, "I have two arms and am capable of escorting both Celestia and Gwendolyn."

Mother sucked in a sharp breath. "Really, Josiah, her Christian name? You've only known each other a week!"

"Two weeks."

"It's the Isaacs intuition," Celestia sang.

"Not after nine times, it's not." Father cut a critical eye toward

Gwendolyn. "I'd supposed you one of Celestia's friends, but I see I was mistaken. Whatever your intentions are toward my son, I'd reconsider them carefully. He may propose, but he'll not marry you."

Gwendolyn stiffened and pulled away before he could stop her. "I have no wish for a proposal or any other romantic escapades you might attribute to me. We are friends. That is all."

Father scoffed. "That's what they all say . . . before they wheedle a proposal out of him. I warn you, any attempt to place him in a compromising situation will only ruin your own reputation. He has none left to maintain."

Josiah drew a breath through clenched teeth. He would be the better man. He would not resort to harsh words. At least, not until after he'd seen Gwendolyn safely home. Then he'd return to openly speak his mind.

"It's a shame you think so poorly of your son, no matter what you may think of me." Gwendolyn's defense of him came swift and sure, making him proud despite his anger. "Mr. Isaacs is a man any father would be proud of if he took the time to know him beyond what the papers say. Thank you for the hospitality of this afternoon and evening. Miss Celestia, it was a dream to have worn your gown, but I think it best I take my leave. Would you be so kind as to send a maid to help me change while you dine?"

"Of course." Celestia looked to Josiah for help, but there was nothing for it.

Remaining here any longer than necessary would only push him beyond the limits of his restraint.

Gwendolyn curtsied and walked out of the room with more dignity than his parents had offered her.

And this was why he and Shauna never entered the Isaacs residence after they were married. And it would be the same with him and Gwendolyn. For a man who served the people, Father had no tolerance for those who did not meet his pompous standards. A feat Josiah was beginning to doubt even God could reach.

Mother barely waited long enough for Gwendolyn's footsteps to be heard on the stairs. "What are you thinking, Josiah? She's the matron of Final Chance!"

Thankfully, Celestia had the presence of mind to close the door. "That was poorly done, Mother. Father. Did you not raise us to encourage those beneath us?"

Josiah gripped the back of a wicker chair until the bumpy surface bit into his hands. "There is no 'beneath' us, Celestia. That would require us thinking better of ourselves than others. Neither wealth nor status defines a person's worth. Gwendolyn Ellison is good enough for me because of who she is as a person. Whether she be my friend or more, I won't allow her to be treated like that again."

"You have a blind spot with fortune hunters, Josiah." Father crossed his arms. "If I can intimidate even one of them from duping you, then I've done my job as a father."

"I don't believe her to be a fortune hunter, Magnus, but she is responsible for the care of many children who need her." Mother faced him, concern and sympathy softening her countenance. "I'm protecting you both. Miss Ellison loves those children like no other I've met. Your courting her is going to get her fired. Then you'll feel obligated to propose, only to realize you don't really want to marry her. We've seen it played out time and time again. There's nothing I want more in life than to see you happy, but you're not ready to marry again. And those children need Miss Ellison. I won't allow you to jeopardize that. I had a hard enough fight today to ensure the review board treated her fairly. Tread carefully with her. For both your sakes. We're not monsters. We just want to protect you."

How he wished he could believe that was their motivation, but their rejection of Shauna was too thorough. Too grounded in her objectionable social status and background as an Irish immigrant.

"Good night, Mother. Father. Celestia. Give Cook my regrets for missing one of his magnificent meals." He pivoted and strode toward the door. Once Gwendolyn was changed, he'd make his apologies for his family, take her somewhere to eat, and do his best to tend to the hurts inflicted.

When he opened the door to exit, Mother's abject voice rang out behind him. "We love you, Josiah. Please understand that."

CHAPTER 25

WOUNDED PRIDE AND CHRISTLIKE HUMILITY were not garments Gwendolyn enjoyed wearing together. Both feelings chafed as she carefully hung the dress that had, for a few moments, made her feel like Cinderella. The prideful thing to do would be march down the front stairs with her nose in the air and rub theirs in the fact that her value wasn't determined by their words but God's. She was a daughter of the King. A bride for the Prince of Peace. Jesus had paid a far greater price for her than what the Isaacses had paid for that dress.

Unfortunately, the same King and Prince called her to be a servant, humble and willing to turn the other cheek. Objectively it wasn't wrong for her to walk out the front door, but her motivations being in the wrong place made it wrong for her. The humblest thing she could do was leave quietly through the servants' entrance and hail a hack. Even so, she couldn't quite bring her heart into completely innocent motivation. A good part of her harbored the hope that her quiet exit would heap coals upon the Isaacs's heads.

Poor Josiah. Her family might have its challenges, but at least they didn't behave so poorly toward a guest.

Her conscience pricked. Hadn't her own family spoken of and treated Josiah just as poorly last week?

She blew out a breath. *Forgiveth me, Lord. We art all sinners and judgeth unjustly.*

As she followed the maid toward the servants' entrance, the mouth-watering scent of delicacies, the likes of which she'd only read about, wafted through the air. Her stomach protested and begged her to sneak into the kitchen and pinch just a bite of whatever it was that smelled of rich meat and something buttered. They passed the kitchen door as a maid carried out a silver tray with a lid over the top, denying even her eyes the chance to feast. It was probably for the best. Mrs. Flowers would only be able to provide leftover broth and stale bread this late in the evening.

A man in a formal suit opened the back door for her.

"Thank you. Would you please inform Mr. Josiah Isaacs that I've seen myself home?"

"Nonsense." Gwendolyn startled at Josiah's voice behind her. "I'm escorting you to dinner and then Final Chance."

"I'll be fine. You should eat with your family."

He huffed. "Not tonight. I'd never be able to hold my tongue, and I'll not let you return to Final Chance without a decent meal." Then to the servant, "Is the carriage ready?"

"Yes, sir. It's pulled around front, as requested."

When they'd passed through the door, she asked, "How did you know I'd leave this way?"

"I didn't." He tucked her arm into his and directed her toward the gate. "Celestia's maid informed me of your secret escape. I expected you to stand your ground and walk out the front."

She ducked her head. "I wanted to, but I felt the most Christlike thing to do was honor their wishes and disappear."

"And that is one reason you are a better person than I am. Now all I want to do is propose to you just because they don't want me to."

Her face jerked toward his. "Josiah! That's a terrible reason to propose. Besides, you promised you wouldn't."

And as much as she'd allowed herself fantasies of a Cinderella story, after tonight there was no question about their future. He wasn't her prince, and she wasn't a rags-to-riches princess.

"I promised I wouldn't as long as you didn't corner me."

Her heart thudded in her chest, and her eyes felt wide as saucers. "But I've not cornered you, so there's no need to propose."

His silent sweeping of her face left her unsettled. Surely he wasn't considering it?

They turned the corner of the house and a grand closed carriage waited for them with a coachman and two footmen dressed in full livery. Cinderella's fairy godmother couldn't have done better. She stifled a chuckle. She and Josiah best not stay out too late or the whole outfit was liable to turn into a pumpkin, mice, lizards, and a rat. Thank goodness this wasn't a fairy tale. Glass slippers sounded dreadfully uncomfortable. Still, she couldn't help but smile when the footman bowed and handed her up like she was matron of the house instead of a house of refuge. The inside was plush and even smelled of fresh flowers, unlike the typical hack odor of must and body sweat. As terrible a day as it had been, this night would be one to remember.

Josiah climbed in, pulling the door shut behind him, and claimed the spot next to her instead of the opposite seat. His arm slipped behind her and rested atop the back cushion.

Gwendolyn sucked in a breath. What was he doing? It was far too intimate a gesture, especially since he'd just jested about proposing. It had been a jest, hadn't it?

He tapped on the ceiling and then angled toward her as the conveyance rolled into motion.

A passing streetlamp illuminated a gleam in his eyes that she wasn't sure what to make of.

"Are you so opposed to the idea of a proposal that you won't even consider one?"

Her heart pounded. "Is that what you're doing? Proposing?"

His breath blew out with enough force to cause her bangs to dance, and he deflated into the corner of the carriage. Though his head tilted back against the paneling, he didn't angle away or remove his arm. "I'm not proposing, but it infuriates me that my parents would treat you so. They were the same way with Shauna. To them, when considering marriage, a person's character has weight only after her social standing and bank account have been taken into consideration."

Gwendolyn swallowed. Other than their first meeting at Final Chance, he'd not mentioned his deceased wife. And she'd been content to forget he'd had one—to forget the fact that another woman had truly claimed his affections, not just the illusion of it. A pang of jealousy swept over her, but she tamped it down. She was his friend. Nothing more. And friends were confidants in time of need, voices of caring reassurance. What kind of friend would she be if she didn't encourage him to unburden himself?

"You said she was Irish, and since her nieces and nephew were rescued from the street, I assume she wasn't from a wealthy family?"

"They weren't rescued. They have a home. A father who loves them. An uncle who would have stepped in had I but known." He pinched the bridge of his nose and then ran his hand down his face. "But, yes. Shauna was a maid in one of the houses I visited once upon a time. A maid, Irish, and according to my father, a complete political disaster."

Bitterness and anger rested behind those words, and her heart hurt for him. She'd never had the joy of loving a spouse or the heartbreak of her family not accepting him, but she could imagine how difficult it would be. "How long did you court before you married?"

Light peeked inside the carriage as they passed another lamp, and it illuminated a smile that spoke of great love and a good dose of mischievousness. "One month. I knew by the second time we spoke that she was the one."

The way his smile lingered and silence fell, he'd fallen into the memories of their whirlwind courtship.

An ache to be loved like that—to be the reason that a man's face lit up and that he drifted into pleasant memories—spread through her. It would've been wonderful if it could've been Josiah. Now, however, it was evident that more than social barriers stood as an impenetrable fortress between them. The realization hurt more than it should, considering it was regarding a man whose acquaintance she'd made only two weeks ago.

But was it any wonder? He was such an easy man to be around.

Someone who made her feel safe. Feel a strange sense of home when she knew she'd soon be homeless. He stirred a longing in her to be held, caressed, and kissed by him in the same way Father had Mother before the fire destroyed their world.

If only that were enough to overcome what stood between them. But Mrs. Isaacs's words of wisdom to her children held truth for Gwendolyn too. Feelings were something to be tested and pushed against, and she didn't have to push hard to know where her heart stood. Love built on the feelings of butterflies and romantic fantasies wasn't really love at all. It was a mist quickly burned away by the first harsh rays of life. What she felt would never survive the hostility of their families or her inferiority in living up to the perfect image of his dead wife.

How fortunate she was to realize it before she'd completely surrendered her contentment in spinsterhood. Although, if—when—she lost her position as a matron, maintaining that contentment was going to be a battle far worse than the first time she'd fought for it. Especially when that loss came at the hands of evil men.

Lord, help thou my unbelief.

"She would have loved you, you know."

Josiah's voice jolted her back to the moment. He appeared to be focused on her, although it was difficult to tell with the passing of light and dark.

"I can't imagine a wife loving her husband being alone in a carriage with another woman."

He laughed. "Definitely not. She would have been spitting mad and run you out with a broom and colorful images of your destruction."

"As she should."

"Perhaps." He straightened. "But she's been gone ten years, and I'm starting to wonder if she might give her blessing over a second chance at marital bliss. Especially with someone like you."

His arm shifted from behind her, and his hand traced her arm until he found her hand to clasp.

Gwendolyn swallowed hard and twisted to face the window. Two weeks. It wasn't enough time for him to know his mind. These were just feelings during a time of high emotion and stress. Feelings she couldn't and wouldn't trust.

"Where are we going?" The purposeful change of subject came out strangled and high-pitched.

His hand withdrew from hers, and she closed her eyes against the loss. Her subtle rejection felt as heavy and painful to her as it must have him.

Unless it had just been words without meaning. A jest taken too far. Or revenge against his parents.

He was silent for a whole measure before his words emerged in a staccato beat. "To Orton's. I sent a note ahead. He'll have food, and we'll discuss the case."

Though he probably couldn't see it, she nodded. Her throat was too thick for her to speak, and she refused to look at him and encourage any notion she might desire something more than friendship between them.

The remainder of the ride passed in an uncomfortable silence. They stopped at the end of brick row houses where light poured from parlor windows onto shared covered porches. It was quaint in comparison to Rittenhouse Square, but it sang a quiet melody of happiness, home, and family. Rittenhouse Square might be where the rich lived, but this was what she longed for. Simplicity and a family to share it with. She peeked at Josiah, but thankfully he was distracted by the footman opening the door.

Josiah exited first and handed her down. "I didn't mean to make you uncomfortable with my talk of marriage."

Friends talk about hard things with friends. Be a friend. "Shauna would want you to be happy, but perhaps you should approach marriage more cautiously this time. Make sure the woman is a good fit for you and your family."

"I don't care a whit what my family thinks." He claimed her arm and escorted her toward the door.

"But you should. Your first marriage brought strife. Let your second one bring healing to your family."

"After tonight, I don't think healing is possible."

She paused at the first step. "Don't be upset with your family for their reaction. They want what's best for you."

"And what if what's best for me is you?"

His persistence sent her heart racing. The earnest supplication in his expression and the way his thumb caressed her arm made her waver. "I—"

The door opened. "You're lucky your note arrived when it did. I was about to polish off our dinner leftovers."

The distraction brought on by the serious man who'd been on Josiah's stoop last week broke off the unformed statement.

By the sudden V that formed on the man's brow, her distress must be evident on her face. He stepped back and waved them inside, his eyes noticeably darting between her and Josiah.

With a fortitude that could only have come from God, she shoved aside Josiah's question and focused on her host. "Please forgive our intrusion. I didn't know we'd be keeping you from eating."

"Don't listen to anything Hayden says. It would've been his third helping." A vibrant woman with her hair held up by pencils poked Hayden in the stomach. "If he's not careful, he's going to end up with a bigger belly than me."

Josiah, too, must have pushed aside their half-finished conversation, for he tilted his head to the side and seemed to consider Hayden's weight. "Too late. I'd say he's a good five months along."

The woman laughed.

Hayden scowled. "Are you going to make introductions, or will I be forced to do them myself?"

Josiah stepped next to Gwendolyn as if he hadn't just upended her whole world moments ago. "Miss Ellison, may I present to you my friend and superior, Hayden Orton, and his wife, Felicity. Hayden, Felicity, this is Gwendolyn Ellison, matron of Final Chance House of Refuge."

"It's a pleasure to meet you, Mr. and Mrs. Orton."

"It's Hayden and Felicity. I insist." Felicity nudged Josiah aside and tugged Gwendolyn forward. "I hope you like fried pork tenderloin."

Gwendolyn's stomach made an embarrassingly loud grumble.

"Good, it sounds to me like you do."

The woman's congenial laughter eased some of the tension in Gwendolyn's shoulders, and the rest of it dissipated when they entered the kitchen and a baby cooed at them from a bassinet in the corner. Baby snuggles were a rare treat and the perfect distraction from Josiah's regard. While Felicity plated the warmed tenderloin, Gwendolyn held and cooed at five-month-old Martha. Unfortunately, the distraction only lasted a few minutes. Felicity reclaimed her daughter the moment the food was served.

Hayden didn't waste time diving into conversation about the case. "Josiah said he's explained the green goods game to you and what to look for. Is that correct?"

This kind of conversation she could handle with confidence. "He did explain, but I've found no evidence of it. Not in the girls' ward, at least."

Did she dare share about her and Wilhelmina's plan? It wasn't likely to be well received, but they were running out of time.

"You're biting your lip, which means you're hiding something." Josiah leaned back in his chair and crossed his arms. "Speak, or I'll be forced to charm it out of you."

A corner of his mouth tilted as if he hoped she would choose the latter option.

And like a puppy chasing a tossed stick, her heart pattered with traitorous excitement.

Stop it, Gwendolyn. This is serious, not a game. And proceeding without their knowledge would be unwise. "Wilhelmina and I plan to sneak into the locked room tonight. Superintendent King is bedridden, and the other officers will be preoccupied with preparing the children for bed. It's our best opportunity."

"Absolutely not." Josiah remained nonchalant in his stance, but the vehemence in his voice revealed him anything but relaxed. "It's too risky."

"They have my diary. They know an investigation is underway. What if they remove the evidence tonight while everyone's sleeping?"

"I'd rather the loss of evidence than your life. It's my job to take the risk, not yours."

"I agree," Hayden said. "Not to mention Josiah's been practicing picking locks since you discovered the room last week. He'll check the room tomorrow while there with the review board. If necessary, and only if necessary, you'll provide a distraction that will allow him the time to poke around. Nothing happens tonight. Your lives are worth more than the risk. Do you understand?"

"But aren't the children's lives worth even more?"

"Please, Gwendolyn." Josiah clasped her hand and waited until her eyes found his. "You can't help the children if you are dead."

"We won't be caught."

"But if you are, the children will be in *more* danger. Waiting until tomorrow is the safest plan."

"If they remove the evidence before we get in there, we'll never catch them."

Josiah sighed and seemed to weigh his words before speaking, "Are you afraid that somehow God's plan for these children will be defeated if you do not act?"

Was that not the very thing she wrestled with? It appeared evil was conquering God's goodness and that it would win if she didn't do something. But hadn't God often allowed the wicked a period of success in the Bible?

And hadn't that rule of the wicked always come to an end?

"Lord, I believe. Help thou my unbelief."

Josiah's hand squeezed hers, and he rewarded her with a soft smile. "I'm glad I'm not the only one who struggles. I choose to stand in faith with you, but please be patient. As much as you love those children, God loves them more. Don't take the risk tonight. Promise me."

Though she wanted to avoid the promise, she couldn't deny the feeling God wanted her to wait as well. "Fine. I promise."

But would that promise cost them the evidence they needed? And could her faith sustain her if it did?

Chapter 26

Although Gwendolyn gave him her word, Josiah struggled to keep anxiety at bay the next morning. It didn't help that his mother requested to ride with him and spent the better part of the journey excusing her behavior toward Gwendolyn as an act of protection for them both. No matter how he tried to stare out the window and ignore her, she kept pushing the subject.

"Josiah, stop giving me the cold shoulder and listen to me."

"Unless it has to do with the case, I have no desire to hear anything further. You've made your excuses, and all it's done is reveal that if Shauna were still here, nothing would've really changed. Neither she nor Gwendolyn is rich enough or connected enough to be allowed the Isaacs name." He glared at her until her gaze dropped to her lap. Good. Maybe now she understood and would begin to feel some sort of remorse.

For two blessed minutes, the only sound was the rumble of the wheels against the road, the hawkers they passed, and the nagging worry in his head.

"Do . . ." Mother cleared her hoarse throat. "Do you want to give her the Isaacs name, and I mean really want to? You're not just saying that because you feel trapped or believe you can rescue and protect her?"

Josiah closed his eyes against the weight of her question. Last night he'd felt almost certain of it. But this morning? Every time he'd caught a glimpse of Shauna's face in a picture frame as he readied for the day, guilt plagued him. He still loved Shauna. That wasn't going to end. Yet he was considering marriage to Gwendolyn? Even if it wasn't disloyal to Shauna, it would be to Gwendolyn. What woman wanted to share her husband's heart with another? And setting that familiar Isaacs zing of certainty aside, could he really say that he loved her? The potential was there. But did he love her now? Should he walk away before he hurt Gwendolyn with his inability to love her and her only?

"I don't know, Mother, but I want the chance to find out without her being trampled on by my family. She's a good woman, and she deserves to be treated with respect and dignity."

"You're right, of course. I owe her, and you, my apologies. But may I urge you to be cautious and certain before you propose?"

He almost laughed. Hadn't Gwendolyn said near enough the same thing? "I'll be cautious, but I warn you, Gwendolyn has already urged me to find a woman who's a good fit for my family."

"And she didn't suggest herself?"

"After last night, I think it's obvious she knew that quality would exclude her."

Mother touched his arm, sympathy crinkling her face. "Have you considered that was her gentle hint she doesn't want a proposal at all?"

A band around his chest tightened. Is that what she'd intended by the statement? Or was he right to assume the deflection came as a result of his family's treatment of her? She never did respond to his insinuation that she was what was best for him. They'd returned to Final Chance in amenable silence, mostly because she'd ended up dozing. But she hadn't objected when he suggested she use his shoulder as a pillow after her head had banged the wall during a nasty dip, or when he'd brushed the hair out of her face when she'd startled awake at their arrival. Surely if she were so opposed to his affections, she would have rebuffed him.

"I guess I'll find out when the time comes to ask."

Their arrival at Final Chance provided no opportunity for Josiah to slip away and search the locked room while the children were at breakfast. Abernathy and Wells were waiting outside and directed them straight to the boardroom, where the table was covered in paperwork, ledgers, and stacks of letters. If a single sheet of paper remained anywhere in Gwendolyn's office or personal quarters, he'd be surprised. However, nothing resembling a diary lay on the table or ever turned up as they passed the morning examining pointless paper after pointless paper.

The only interesting thing he discovered was Gwendolyn's talent for meticulous note-taking and negotiating deals in order to procure items not covered by her budget. Had she been male, she might have become a highly sought-after estate manager. If King's records were half as organized, there would be a counterfeiting paper trail strong enough to identify and arrest Fantasma himself.

At the sound of the tea cart rattling down the hallway, Josiah set his paperwork aside and stretched until his back gave a satisfying pop. How long would this witch hunt last? This continued search was a tiresome front that needed to end. "I don't see anything here that suggests Matron Ellison needs to be fired. If anything, I'm convinced it would be to our detriment to lose such an organized person."

Abernathy huffed as he continued scouring receipts and comparing them to ledgers. "She's too organized, which means she is fully capable of hiding anything she doesn't want found."

"If I wanted to hide something, I wouldn't make my notes so easy to decipher." Gwendolyn's voice rose over the rattling cart she pushed into the room.

The lingering anxiety over her absence dissipated on an exhale. Weariness darkened the skin beneath her eyes, but she appeared unharmed.

"What are you doing here? I thought I made it abundantly clear you're not to be present as we review your paperwork."

"That may be, but you're preventing me from doing my job. We received an unexpected and substantial donation of groceries a few minutes ago, and I need my kitchen record book in order to note the items and quantities. There is also the matter of a monetary donation." She gestured to a boy who waited in the hall. "I didn't dare touch it myself for fear of being accused of stealing."

A lanky, dark-haired boy of about ten shuffled into the room like he was a canary forced into a room of cats. His eyes darted from face to face as he clutched a large envelope to his chest. When his eyes met Abernathy's glare, he backstepped into the tea cart, making the cups and pot clack.

His eyes rounded. "*Perdonami.*"

"*Non preoccuparti.*" The Italian phrase slipped naturally from Wells's lips.

Josiah frowned. The Italian phrase for "Don't worry about it" was simple enough that even Josiah used it on occasion with Ignazio, but Wells's superior pronunciation set him ill at ease. Was Wells the connection to Fantasma that Josiah sought?

Wells rose from his chair and approached the boy. "*Dammi la busta, per favore.*"

The boy extended the envelope to him.

"*Grazie.*" Wells pushed him toward the door. "*Sei libero partire.*"

He scurried out, appearing relieved to be dismissed.

"I didn't realize you spoke Italian. Where did you learn?" Mother asked.

"My wife is Italian, and I learned so that I might win her affections. She misses Italy, so we often speak it at home." His smile showed his pleasure at comforting his wife.

Or was it satisfaction at so easily explaining away his Italian connection? "There's a large Italian community near Christian Street. Do you ever go there?"

"My wife refuses to shop anywhere else and has made many friends in the area. I go on occasion, but my business keeps me tied to Market Street."

Just because Wells had an Italian wife who frequented the area didn't mean he was guilty. But it also didn't mean that Josiah shouldn't dig around in the man's personal connections to the Italian community.

Wells opened the envelope and thumbed through the contents. "It appears our donor was quite generous. I'll count it to be certain, but I estimate there's more than one hundred dollars here."

"Praise God." A victorious smile cut through Gwendolyn's weariness as she faced Abernathy. "See? God has returned the cost of that loaf of bread more than a hundredfold. He is a generous gift giver."

"That doesn't change the fact that you gave Final Chance property away. Knowing your father's history, I'd say you're well on your way to the penitentiary yourself."

Gwendolyn's smile faded, but her chin lifted. "I did not and do not condone my father's choice to steal from your company. Nor do I follow in his footsteps."

There was a theft connection between Gwendolyn's father and Abernathy? He looked to Gwendolyn for some explanation, but she was too busy staring her accuser down to pay Josiah any mind.

"Is that what this has been about?" Mother stood, hands on her hips. "A grudge against Matron Ellison and her family?"

"This review board concerns her suitability to remain matron of Final Chance." Though he addressed a lady, Abernathy assumed a stance not unlike a boxer intimidating a competitor.

Josiah rose and shifted closer to his mother and Gwendolyn. A table might separate them from Abernathy, but he wasn't taking any chances.

Mother refused to be quelled. "I've found no evidence of misconduct, and I don't believe we'll find any, no matter how long we search. My vote is Miss Ellison stays."

"And I vote she be fired." Red crept into Abernathy's face, and fists formed at his sides.

Josiah edged in front of his mother. "You have no grounds to do so. I vote she stays."

"I have to agree with them, Abernathy." Wells deposited the envelope into his coat pocket. "Matron Ellison had nothing to do with

Gareth's disappearance, and her paperwork is immaculate. Even if she did give a loaf of bread away, it's not enough to fire her. Besides, she agreed to cover that cost herself. I say she stays and we get back to our real jobs. I've wasted enough time on this wild goose chase."

"That makes three against one, Chairman Abernathy. Even if Superintendent King voted to fire her, it would be three against two." Mother crossed her arms and lifted a brow in challenge. "Accept defeat and be glad that we have such a competent matron running this institution during Superintendent King's recovery."

"You are not the chairman of this board, Mrs. Isaacs, and you would do well to remember that."

"And you would do well to remember that your position is voluntary. You may step down any time you wish. Considering your past history with Matron Ellison's family and your obvious determination to take it out on her, I recommend you do so sooner rather than later."

"My father established this institution, and I will not allow it to fall into hands that are unwilling to hold its staff to the highest standard."

"Then perhaps you should live up to your own standards instead of partaking in behavior unbecoming of a gentleman."

"Good day, Mrs. Isaacs. Your husband can expect a visit from me very soon."

"Why not join us for dinner on Sunday after services? I believe your father has already accepted our invitation. I'm sure he'd be intrigued to hear my perspective on how you handle the board. After all, it was at his suggestion that I joined."

Abernathy stormed out of the room with nary another word.

Wells selected a ledger labeled "Kitchen" from the stack on the table and extended it toward Gwendolyn. "Your position is secure for now, but I'd be careful concerning Chairman Abernathy. He's a ruthless businessman and a dangerous enemy. He might not have fired you this time, but he'll find a way eventually."

Gwendolyn clutched the ledger to her chest. "Thank you for your vote of confidence, Treasurer Wells."

"As long as you do your job, you'll have it. Good day."

The moment the front door closed, Gwendolyn sank into a chair. "Praise God that's over."

"Your position is secure for now, but this is far from over." Josiah couldn't help but wonder if Abernathy's enmity toward her connected solely to the past or if it had ties to the green goods game. "What is Chairman Abernathy's connection to your father?"

Gwendolyn's eyes flicked toward his mother as she rose to her feet. "I need to record the donations before they are put away. We can discuss this another time."

"I, too, would like to know the answer to my son's question, Matron Ellison. I think it is quite pertinent to your future."

Gwendolyn closed her eyes for a moment and released a slow breath. "I really do need to record the donations, as it is holding up Mrs. Flowers's ability to serve lunch to the children. The short of it is my father was an accountant for the Abernathy consolidation firm. Circumstances led him to embezzle money. He was caught when his accounts were audited, and he went to jail. If you want further details, I suggest you speak to him. Although I cannot guarantee he'll speak the truth."

Josiah hated it, but he had little choice. "I'm afraid I'll need to."

She dipped her chin in controlled acknowledgment, but the pain left behind by her father's actions couldn't be hidden. Her entire body seemed to pull inward in an attempt to hold her emotions at bay.

"I'm sorry." He brushed his thumb along her cheek and found a tear. Without thinking, he leaned in to kiss it away.

Mother cleared her throat.

He jerked back, upset both with his mother for her interruption and with himself for his lack of self-control. He had no right to comfort Gwendolyn in such a manner.

Gwendolyn pulled from his touch, her eyes refusing to meet his, and spoke with a croaky voice. "As long as I'm not there, I'll be fine. Eventually I'll face him, but not until this mess with Final Chance is over. I can only handle so much at one time."

"You should return to your duties, Matron Ellison. We'll collect your papers and return them to your office." Mother spoke crisply, no doubt mortified that Josiah was again attaching himself to a family that would cause scandal.

Familiar confidence steeled Gwendolyn's posture and voice as she addressed his mother. "Thank you, Mrs. Isaacs, but allow me to help. I'm sure you son has other tasks to attend to. It would be an honor if you joined us for lunch afterward. All the officers and children will be in attendance."

Josiah helped them stack the paperwork and waited until they'd left to remove his lock-picking tools. The time to test his newly acquired skills had arrived.

CHAPTER 27

THE HUM OF VOICES COULD still be heard through the doors leading to the dining hall, covering the noise of the picks clicking together as Josiah tried and failed to catch the pins. This lock was proving considerably harder to pick than the ones Ignazio had him practice with. Sweat slicked his hands, and his fingers trembled with the concentration of trying to work without being caught. Ten minutes he'd been working already. Ten minutes of kneeling with bated breath and growing anticipation of someone opening the boys' ward door and spotting him.

After losing the pins again, he shot to his feet and started to pace. He needed to calm his nerves and steady his hands. Ignazio had warned him that picking locks became a completely different beast when the threat of being caught entered the scene. He hadn't been exaggerating.

With deliberate deep breaths, he relaxed long enough for his heart to stop pounding in his ears. He knelt again and blew out one last slow breath.

God, I'd appreciate it if You'd help me along here.

He slid the tension wrench into place and applied the requisite pressure for it to turn, then squeezed the rake pick into the narrow space above the tension wrench. Now came the more difficult part. He closed his eyes, concentrating on the feel of the pick against the pins as he worked the tool up and down.

One caught. Then another.

Second after excruciating second passed between the successful hooks of each pin.

Finally, after an interminable amount of time, all six pins rested against the pick's wavy surface. Now the trick was to get them all to lift to the correct height to allow the plug to turn.

With each wiggle, tension hardened his shoulder muscles into painful rocks. Sweat reappeared on his palms, slicking his grip. The end pin slipped, and he forced himself to remain still and calm before attempting to catch it again.

The door at the end of the hall opened enough to allow the din of conversation to escalate but no further. Almost as if someone had been stopped before going all the way through the doorway.

"But Officer Bagwell gave me permission." A boy's voice carried into the hall.

Time was an expired commodity. Josiah gave the pick one good shove and wiggle.

The plug refused to budge.

Josiah tried again.

Still nothing.

Please, God. I need You to do this for me.

He pressed against the tension wrench and the plug ground against the bottoms of the pins, forcing them clear of the shear line. The knob turned, and the door opened. He scrambled inside, shut it with a gentle click, and twisted the lock back into place.

His heart pounded so loud that he didn't hear the boy's humming until he passed directly outside the door.

Thank You, God.

He'd made it in, but he didn't have much time. Lunch had to be at least half over by now.

A sweeping glance of the wide space didn't reveal anything immediately obvious as something deserving of a locked room. One long table cut through the center with pieces of furniture in various stages of completion. Two finished chairs and four stools stood in the corner along with cans of stain waiting to be applied. At the table against the far wall, collated spelling books sat in stacks to be folded, sewed, and bound. Josiah flipped through each one to ensure nothing was hiding from plain view, but they were exactly as they appeared—the future punishment of children everywhere.

No matter where he searched or how many times he flipped through individual papers, he found the same thing. Nothing.

Either this room had never held anything related to the green goods game, or whoever was involved had already acted. Josiah wasn't sure if he should be relieved Gwendolyn hadn't interrupted the removal or concerned that his cover had apparently been exposed.

Never had Gwendolyn been so glad to see a person leave. She parted the receiving room curtains just enough to watch Mrs. Isaacs ascend into the carriage fit for a queen. How had Gwendolyn ever fancied herself Cinderella in that ostentatious contraption? It was better suited to Marie Antoinette—at least, before her head rolled. The sheer layer of the curtains wavered under the force of Gwendolyn's exhale.

Naively, she'd believed Mrs. Isaacs's insistence on helping restore Gwendolyn's office to order had been motivated by genuine concern. Indeed, for nearly an hour she'd had Gwendolyn fooled as they returned the paperwork to the office and then ate lunch together. Mrs. Isaacs had drizzled their conversation with sweet-honey praise over Gwendolyn's skill as a matron. They'd spoken in happy congeniality about the children, matters of Final Chance, and even Gwendolyn's years of education at West Penn Square Seminary for Ladies. The exchange had given her hope that perhaps the family might accept her should Josiah truly choose her as he'd insinuated last night.

But then Josiah had stopped by the office soon after she and Mrs. Isaacs had left the midday meal.

He'd pulled her into a corner and effectively cut off his mother from observation by giving her his back. It was entirely too intimate a gesture, especially with an audience.

"Josiah, not so close. Your mother—"

"Didn't I tell you I don't care a whit what she thinks? I need to talk with you privately, and this is the best I can manage."

"You should care."

"What I care about is your safety." He'd caressed her face and, to her shame, she'd leaned into it. "Mother doesn't know about the other aspect of my investigation, and I can't risk her overhearing and asking questions. Whoever is involved already removed everything from the room, which means they know about the investigation or the evidence was never really there. I need to follow up on some other leads, but I'll be back every day at random times. I want them to know you are under my protection."

"Is that really wise? They killed Mr. Farwell for helping me, and I've just barely maintained my career. If you show up every day, not only will they target you, but they'll also think you're courting me."

"And what if I want to? What if I want to see where this leads?" His fingers had entwined with hers, stealing her breath and almost her reason.

Almost.

"Not until the children of Final Chance are safe. I can't leave here as long as I know they are at risk. The moment we start courting without board approval, I'll be in breach of contract and Chairman Abernathy can fire me without the board's consent."

"Then I best leave and get to work on following those leads. For the children's sakes and for my own. Because I do want to court you, Gwendolyn. More and more every day."

He'd left then, consigning her to endure the condescension of his mother. While Gwendolyn might be good enough for Final Chance, she'd never be enough for Mrs. Isaacs's son, and the remaining quarter hour had passed with veiled reminders of Gwendolyn's station in life and Josiah's inability to commit to a woman.

But he had.

He'd committed to Shauna for ten years past her death. Was it really so wrong for Gwendolyn to hope he might form that same commitment to her?

To Mrs. Isaacs, it was a resounding yes.

"Did I really hear her insinuate that you should remain a spinster your whole life?" Wilhelmina joined her at the window to watch as the carriage rolled away.

"What? You didn't find her compliments on my exceptional skills flattering?" Gwendolyn turned from the window and did her best not to let the sarcasm drip from her voice. "She hopes I might remain Final Chance's matron for another thirty or forty years."

"Thirty or forty years! You'd be as shriveled as she. She must be miserable in her marriage to wish such a thing upon you. You can only be a matron if you're unmarried."

"I think it has less to do with her marital bliss and more to do with dictating her son's. She certainly wouldn't be quite so eager to keep me as matron if it weren't for the fact he asked to court me."

Wilhelmina's squeal accompanied a clap of her hands. "I knew there was more to his visits than interest in Final Chance. What did you say?"

"I can't risk losing my position until I'm certain the children are safe. He searched the locked room. They've already removed everything."

The excitement faded from her friend's face. "He searched?"

"Josiah's the officer I'm working with."

"But he's an Isaacs. The only work they do is tally up their investments and spend their profits."

"Well, this Isaacs works, and the evidence he needs wasn't in the workroom."

"And you won't court him until the corruption here has been removed?" Wilhelmina studied her for a moment. "But you do want to court him, don't you?"

"I love these children too much to choose my happiness over their safety."

"Well then, that settles it. We'll have to find where they hid the evidence." Wilhelmina smirked. "I can't have my friend turning into an old, shriveled hag before she finds love and romance."

"Are you sure your willingness to help isn't because you want my job?"

"Well, of course, I want your job. What else is *this* old, shriveled hag going to do with the rest of her life?"

"You're not old, shriveled, or a hag. You deserve love and romance as much as the next person."

"Ah, but I've had it once. I'm contented to wait until God sends my own version of an Isaacs to whisk me off my feet. Although I'd be content with someone whose family was a little less pretentious."

Gwendolyn laughed at Wilhelmina's jest. "I suppose when you have such great wealth, you can afford to be pretentious."

"Well, we can't even afford new shoes, so we certainly can't afford to be pretentious. Although you might marry into it very soon."

"I'd rather be as poor as church mice than wealthy and pompous, but it won't matter unless God deems it to be His will and the children are safe."

"And to that end, we should get the children in bed so we can begin our snooping." Wilhelmina directed Gwendolyn toward the hall with a gentle push. "That evidence has to be somewhere in this building. I mean, it would be so easy to hide papers like you described in a place like this. There's paperwork everywhere."

"We'll start by searching the file room after everyone's asleep. If I were hiding something, that's where I'd put it."

Chapter 28

So much for proceeding cautiously. Was he really so incapable of reason around a woman that he couldn't keep his hands or declarations to himself? Josiah tossed his hat onto the hack seat and pressed his fingers into his scalp. He did want to court Gwendolyn, but the moment he left her beguiling presence, guilt slammed into him like a train into a streetcar.

Courting led to marriage and marriage to becoming one with another. But Shauna had already been his one and only. Pursuing a future with Gwendolyn meant he'd have to learn to push Shauna aside. To forget their cherished memories and pretend he didn't have a divided heart.

It would mean losing Shauna all over again.

The hack stopped in front of Abigail's, and he blew out a breath. He should go straight to Wells's business. But this panic, this struggle to breathe, left him unable to focus on remaining inconspicuous. And he certainly couldn't face Gwendolyn's father until he had his own emotions about the man's daughter under control. The only option was to talk with Abigail. Growing up, Abigail had been the one he'd run to, and Shauna's death had only strengthened that bond. If anyone could help him to see reason again, it would be his sister.

Thankfully, it was nap time for the girls, and she met him in the parlor within minutes of his admittance to the house.

"I told Gwendolyn I want to court her." He blurted it almost as soon as the door closed.

"All right." Abigail spoke slowly, her observant gaze taking in his pacing. "And by your panic, should I assume Gwendolyn said yes when you wanted her to say no?"

"No. Yes. I don't know." He raked a hand through his hair and tugged. Why did this have to be such a mess?

"I'm not sure I know who Gwendolyn is. Is she one of those girls you help that tends to trap you into a proposal?"

"No. I mean, I am helping her, but she's not seeking a proposal. She's barely agreed to court me, and only once this mess with Final Chance is over."

"Final Chance? As in the house of refuge?" Abigail sat on the plush settee and patted the seat next to her. "I'm afraid you're not making any sense. Why don't you start from the beginning and tell me about this Gwendolyn and what's going on?"

He couldn't sit and instead continued to pace as he shared everything from their first meeting to his declaration less than an hour ago. "Shauna was the love of my life. My one and only. She's my wife, and yet this desire for another has risen. My head says she'd want me to be happy, but I feel like I'm betraying her."

"Oh Josiah." Abigail reached out and caught his hand. "You're correct about one thing. Shauna would want you to be happy, whether that be single or married again. Come here and sit. Hard truths should never be taken while standing."

"You're just tired of watching me pace."

She smiled. "My neck *is* getting a bit of a crick."

It was just like her to force him to be still when everything in him jittered and screamed to move, but years of this tactic had taught him the wisdom of giving Abigail his full attention.

He dropped onto the spot next to her and released a breath that could have sailed a ship across the Atlantic.

She took both his hands in hers and regarded him with such compassion that he knew he'd made the right choice in coming. "Choosing to look beyond what you had with Shauna to something new doesn't make you love her any less or make you unfaithful to her. Through no act or will of your own, your marriage bonds have been broken. You are released from your pledge to love only her. You have fulfilled your vows. They are complete and finished."

"But I still love her and miss her."

"I imagine that will always be true, but that doesn't tie you to loving only her for the rest of your life. Shauna has moved forward into her new role as the bride of Christ in heaven, and by God's blessing, He's brought someone else into your life who could potentially be part of a new future for you here on earth."

"But this isn't fair to Gwendolyn. I cannot shove everything I feel for Shauna aside and pretend it doesn't exist."

"Your marriage to Shauna cannot and should not be ignored or buried in your memories. What you had together has influenced and shaped your life. If Gwendolyn is the right woman, she'll accept it. Don't get me wrong. You need to be honest with her. You're going to have to work through things with her that you didn't with Shauna, but the right woman will have a big enough heart to accept Shauna's role in yours."

"And if Gwendolyn doesn't?"

"Then God used her to open your eyes to the fact you are free to find happiness, maybe even love, separate from Shauna. That doesn't mean you shove Shauna's memory aside. It means you live life forward with a heart open to new possibilities without Shauna being the basis for your decisions."

Abigail's words settled over him like water on drought-packed soil, standing on the surface and slowly sinking in. It was a lot to take in. More than he could handle in one sitting, but it still brought an odd sense of relief. His love for Shauna was there, but there was a subtle shift in knowing he'd done his job as her husband. His role was no longer the same. Instead of an active love that continued to grow, death had necessitated his love become passive and nostalgic. They no longer walked side by side. She lived on the eternal plane while he remained on earth.

And he was tired of walking alone.

"Don't be afraid to explore the possibility of a future with Gwendolyn, but take it slower than you did with Shauna."

"Are you insinuating that I'm rushing things?" He smiled in spite of the heaviness that weighed him.

"You and Gwendolyn are going to have to decide that for yourselves, but you do have a tendency to sweep women and reason right off their feet." She squeezed his hand. "That being said, this decision to begin living forward is a process. I want you to be happy, Josiah, whether it be as a single man or a remarried one. But whichever you choose, take the decision to God first. For there is no sense in doing anything if God isn't a part of it."

"Thank you, Abigail. I'll keep that in mind, but I wouldn't be opposed to your prayers as well."

"You have them, and I'll be praying for Final Chance too. They're so blessed to have you as their hero."

"I haven't vanquished any villains yet."

"No, but you will."

The dilapidated hack slouched away from the Italian quarter like it felt as defeated as Josiah. He'd taken a risk in searching the workroom and then visiting Abigail before he tailed Wells. This time his gamble had cost him far more than he'd gained.

Wells hadn't returned to his business or gone home. Even if the man's reason was benign, something about it didn't sit right with Josiah. Defending Gwendolyn's position as matron did not make Wells innocent. It was to his benefit she remain within Final Chance. She'd be easier to control—and eliminate should he decide she knew too much. All he had to do was alert his inside contact.

Who was likely Bagwell, King, or both. Gwendolyn had vouched for the character of Officers Grace and Wood as well as Mrs. Flowers. Josiah wasn't as quick to dismiss their possible involvement as she was, but he'd yet to find anything that might suggest their participation in anything related to counterfeiting or abuse. Of course, he hadn't found much to suggest anyone was involved in counterfeiting. Soon, someone was going to demand justification for the pursuit of this case.

But something was going on to make it worth the risk of killing a man, beating and kidnapping children, and threatening Gwendolyn. And that green goods letter had listed Final Chance as its receiving address.

They needed a response to Tim Benson's letter.

Josiah scrubbed a hand over his face as he ran mental calculations. The letter hadn't been posted until Tuesday. At best it would have been delivered yesterday. The soonest a response could be expected was tomorrow, and that was if the counterfeiter had responded and the post office had been expedient. But it was more likely he'd never receive a response. With Gwendolyn's diary confiscated and now missing, along with the attack on Gareth and the empty workroom, the counterfeiters had to know they were under investigation. Others had halted and moved operations for less.

With the way things were coming together against him and Gwendolyn, he needed to move quickly. Get eyes on all his suspects and hopefully catch a glimpse of something that would lead to an arrest. But he couldn't do it alone. Normally he'd request police cooperation, but he had no evidence to argue for the use of their resources beyond hunches. He could persuade Detective Morrows to make a concentrated effort on ferreting out Quincy Slocum—although Slocum was almost as much a ghost as Fantasma. Ignazio was already investigating a case of his own and tracking down Hibbard and Wilcox on the side. That left Josiah with only Hayden for available and experienced help.

They could each take a man to follow—Wells or Abernathy, but that still left him with little time to search for Speedy's crew, maintain regular visits to Final Chance, and pursue that discussion with Gwendolyn's father. Not to mention he still needed to determine how to track the movements of the men inside Final Chance. Then there were the other cases still open on their desks. Headquarters wouldn't tolerate ignoring them for long, especially with this case's lack of concrete ties to counterfeiting.

I could use a little help here, God. I can only do so much.

He exited the hack on City Hall's south side, the only fully occupied section of the perpetual construction project. Why the Secret Service chose to rent an office here he'd never understand. Already more than ten years had been given up to construction, and the hollow square building enclosing a four-acre courtyard still was far from completed. It might be a piece of art with all its carved marble and French Renaissance elements, but it was never as quiet as an art museum. Inside, he had to skirt around a group of tourists reading one of the free brochures Wanamaker provided to its customers about the "hanging" staircases. The six stories of wide spiral stairs without any visible supports were an architectural feat, but not one he trusted. He stuck close to the walls as he climbed to their offices on the topmost finished floor.

When Josiah opened the office door, a familiar but unexpected voice carried from the back room.

"I'll tell you a secret. Morning sickness has been a blessing in disguise. Theresa hasn't gotten into one scrap of trouble for six weeks. It's a new record."

Having Broderick Cosgrove around would be a boon, so long as he was here to work and not just visit his family.

"Enjoy it while you can, friend," Hayden warned. "After the morning sickness ends, a fresh wave of energy arrives that will have you chasing your wife's coattails to keep up."

"If morning sickness and Theresa's name are in the same sentence, then it sounds like I owe you my congratulations." Josiah offered his hand and clapped Broderick on the shoulder with his other when the man rose from his chair.

"Congratulations or regrets, I'm still not sure which. If the baby ends up being just like his mother, then I might end up in an early grave." His wide smile and easy laughter revealed the prospect of impending fatherhood was joyful no matter whose personality the baby took after.

"It's definitely congratulations. I seem to remember something in the Bible about happiness and the man who has a quiver full of children." Josiah gave a mock bow. "Worse comes to worse, you can shoot the little rascal off to his grandparents for a few weeks. My mother can never get enough of her grandchildren."

"I'll keep that in mind."

Josiah claimed the extra chair and asked the question that he hoped was an answer to his recent prayer. "How long are you in town?"

"A couple of weeks. We wanted to tell my parents in person, and Dr. Pelton cautioned us that with Theresa's health history we should stay close to home once she begins to show. Since my cases have shriveled with this new policy, we figured the time was now."

"Any chance you're interested in working while you're here?"

"My paycheck certainly wouldn't mind it. What do you have for me?"

CHAPTER 29

IT TOOK THE REMAINDER OF the evening to negotiate, but between Broderick's and Hayden's connections, they'd worked out a plan that allowed Josiah the freedom to continue pursuing other leads.

Although Abernathy still had a strong potential to be involved, his newly discovered grudge against the Ellisons provided enough doubt to lower the priority of being tailed by a Secret Service operative. One of Broderick's detective brothers agreed to do the job for free after some private agreement that resulted in Broderick grumbling about the opera. In exchange for first rights to the final story, Felicity's family agreed to provide the use of their sneakiest gopher boy and a journalist. Since Officer Grace, Officer Wood, and Mrs. Flowers posed the least risk to civilian safety, whoever the newspaper sent would follow the three on their half days off. That left Josiah, Hayden, and Broderick to share the duty of following Wells, Bagwell, Crane, and King. As the latter three only had half days outside of the building once a week, it shouldn't be too hard to manage.

With King still abed, Josiah spent the next morning conducting another futile search for Speedy and his crew. Two days missing wouldn't normally concern him, but with their possible connection to Gareth's disappearance, the urgency to find them thrummed as strong as his need to protect Gwendolyn. Still, Speedy was as good at hiding as Fantasma. It helped that people largely ignored the grimy faces of street children. Had Josiah a picture of Speedy to show around, even the people who daily bought their papers from him wouldn't be able to identify him. There seemed to be a universal belief that if one didn't acknowledge the existence of the person from whom one purchased a paper, then there was no personal obligation to help or to even know the name of that person. Let the city officials and politicians deal with the issue. It bothered Josiah to no end. He might not be able to save every child on the street, but he tried to help them as much as they'd allow.

Josiah returned to his house midmorning, and as Elias greeted him at the door, asked, "Any word from Speedy's crew?"

"Nothing, sir, but Reverend Ballantine and Mr. Ellison have arrived. I've put them in your office, and Tillie's already served coffee."

"Thank you. Unless a message arrives concerning Final Chance, Speedy, or Miss Ellison, we're not to be interrupted."

It was with great trepidation that Josiah approached his own office. He'd anticipated this meeting would be challenging both on a personal and a professional level, and he'd wanted every advantage he could claim. The way he'd left with Gwendolyn on Wednesday hadn't won him any goodwill from the overbearing uncle who'd played father for so long, and the questions Josiah needed to ask of Mr. Ellison weren't likely to garner any with him either. Yet these were both men that, should things with Gwendolyn go as Josiah hoped, would one day be a part of his family. He prayed all would go better than he anticipated.

When he entered his office, both men were examining the wall-mounted telephone. Mr. Ellison flicked the silver bell beneath the transmitter, and it gave a dull ring.

"It's much louder when the hammer hits it from the inside." Josiah closed the door and pretended not to notice their sheepish faces at being caught gawking. "The voice quality isn't as clear as if we were in the same room, but I confess I've found the contraption to be worth the annoyance it can bring. It's nice to save time on urgent matters, but I still prefer face-to-face conversation. Especially when difficult topics need to be addressed."

He gestured for both men to take a seat and waited until they were comfortable before claiming his own behind the desk.

"How is Gwendolyn?" Reverend Ballantine asked.

Mr. Ellison visibly swallowed before looking away. Josiah couldn't imagine what it must have felt like to experience Gwendolyn's reaction as a father. Especially if he'd anticipated a warm reception.

"She's choosing to focus on the problems at Final Chance at present. The unexpected nature of your arrival came at the same time as the threat of losing her position, the disappearance of two boys, and the attack on Superintendent King. The combination has been a bit much for her."

"More disappearances and attacks?" Reverend Ballantine leaned hard against the back of his seat and scrubbed a hand over his neck.

"What do you mean, more? Is Gweny in trouble?" Mr. Ellison sat up straighter, all vestiges of shame gone in the face of a concerned father.

"She's at risk but determined to protect those under her care. She and I are working together on an investigation into counterfeiting and child abuse at the institution where she works. You can be assured I am doing my utmost to protect her."

"How, exactly, did what occurred on Wednesday entail 'protection'?" Reverend Ballantine must have recovered his senses with all the suspicion and accusation his tone carried.

"My sister, Celestia, tended to her needs at the home of my parents while I continued my investigation elsewhere. When I returned, I transported her to my colleague's home to eat dinner and discuss the case. She was returned unharmed and untouched to Final Chance by curfew."

That's all he'd say on the matter. Any discussions about courting and marriage would need to be broached later, and with Gwendolyn's permission. Family was important to her, and he'd not strain their relationship any more than it already was. Both of their families were going to have to work through disapproval and prejudice as he and Gwendolyn moved forward. Today's meeting was about Abernathy's connection to the Ellisons.

"Chairman Abernathy caught Miss Ellison providing food to children outside of Final Chance a few days ago and is actively trying to have her dismissed. He insinuated that she was well on her way to the penitentiary, like her father."

"Abernathy? As in Abernathy & Sons Consolidation Firm?" Mr. Ellison twisted in his chair to face Reverend Ballantine. "You got her a job working in the charity run by *them*? What were you thinking?"

"Unlike you, I was thinking about her future. I'm the only father she's known these seventeen years."

Mr. Ellison visibly winced, but Reverend Ballantine roared on.

"It's me who put Gwendolyn through school. Me who gave her and Kate a home. Me who consoled her when man after man ended a courtship because your history clung to her like sewage. When Gwendolyn decided she wanted a position serving children who, like her, had been failed by their fathers and needed a second chance, I used my connections at Final Chance to get her the job. It's by God's grace and mercy alone that Alfred Abernathy Sr. was willing to hire her. No one else sees anything but your crimes when they look at her, and they always will, what with your return."

Josiah gritted his teeth, torn between gratitude and anger that no man had yet recognized Gwendolyn for who she was separate from her family. "A man worthy of her wouldn't care what her father's past is."

"Then there isn't a man worthy of her yet." Reverend Ballantine scowled at him.

"There will never be a man worthy of her by his own rights, but I know of one man who sees Miss Ellison for the jewel she is." There went not declaring his interest, but he didn't regret it. Even if the Reverend looked ready to jump from his chair and challenge Josiah to a duel.

"With the way Gweny clung to you when she saw me, she knows who that man is and deems him worthy. Am I wrong, Mr. Isaacs?"

Josiah faced Mr. Ellison. Instead of open hostility, he was met by the one-eyed gaze of a man who seemed to both mourn and give silent approval.

"I can't speak for Miss Ellison, but it is my hope that she'll find me worthy one day."

He nodded and then leaned back in his chair with a challenging glint in his eye. "Did she tell you what I've done?"

"I'm going for a walk. It was bad enough living through it. I'll not tolerate listening to it." Reverend Ballantine stalked from the room, closing the door behind him just shy of a slam.

Mr. Ellison released a sigh heavy enough to sink to the bottom of the Schuylkill. "So much for the good reverend being an example of forgiveness to his congregation. Not that I can blame him. I've not yet forgiven myself, even if the good Lord has."

"I suspect embezzlement isn't your only crime."

"I committed some petty theft after I left, but there are crimes against my wife and daughter that I fear only God can forgive. His grace and mercy should be sufficient for me, but I confess I want their forgiveness more than I want my own life."

Josiah listened as the man poured forth a story of heroism turned tragedy. While working for Abernathy & Sons, Mr. Ellison served as a volunteer firefighter—long before the city organized a paid fire department in 1871. During a fire in 1864, he'd rescued a sleeping woman and child from inside a building. As they escaped, the building collapsed, and a burning beam crushed his leg and caught fire to his clothes. His fellow firefighters pulled him free, but he remembered none of it. They'd almost lost him to shock and then infection. By a miracle—or curse, as it often felt—he'd survived. The year that followed was a blur of blinding pain and experimental surgeries to bring him back to be some sort of functioning person—if what he became could be called that.

"I wasn't in my right mind enough to make the comparison then, but I can now say I feel a kinship with Frankenstein's monster. Not only am I gruesome to look at, but I shouldn't be alive. It would have been better for my family if I hadn't survived.

"I spent all our money on opiates trying to escape the pain. If we couldn't afford it, I blamed Kate. At times—" He looked away and nervously tapped his thumb against the stump of his leg. "At times, I'd become so desperate I—" He swallowed hard and shook his head. "God, forgive me. But I hit Kate. Never Gweny, but she saw. There's nothing like watching your child grow scared of you. I was out of my mind and unable to control myself, but every time I looked in her eyes, I knew I'd become a monster."

That certainly explained Gwendolyn's reaction to his return. Josiah and his family may have differences and struggles, but not once had he feared anything worse than a paddling. "I assume you returned to Abernathy & Sons at some point?"

"In 1866. That was the year when Gweny started searching the newspapers for positions that would accept eleven-year-olds. In my stupor I didn't mind that Kate was working herself to the bone, but I couldn't stand the thought of Gweny dropping from school to work at a factory. I went back to Abernathy and begged for my old position. It didn't matter what I did; I was in pain anyway. Then I realized I could alter the account books and pocket enough money to buy a bottle of laudanum on the way home. After a few weeks of not getting caught, I started to increase what I took. Abernathy Jr. audited my books. When he accused me of embezzlement, I broke his nose and was publicly arrested."

A broken nose would certainly contribute to his already existing grudge against Mr. Ellison. "Is Abernathy the type of man you would suspect to sell counterfeit banknotes in order to make a little extra money?"

Mr. Ellison snorted. "And risk his family's good name? Not a chance. He's a mean businessman, but he's as straight as a die."

It wasn't evidence enough to strike him completely from Josiah's list of suspects, but with his limited resources, he wouldn't waste a man on tailing him.

"I want to know the truth, Mr. Isaacs. Is my staying with the Ballantines going to keep Gweny from coming home to visit her mother?"

"It's likely, at least for the time being. She had no warning of your arrival, and she's not ready to come to terms with it."

"I see." Mr. Ellison fell pensive.

Josiah allowed him the space to think by refreshing their cups of coffee. He made it to pouring a second before Mr. Ellison finally spoke again.

"I think it best that I return to New York. Kate already told me if she has to choose between Gweny or me, she'd choose Gweny. At least I'll be able to tell the Good Lord I tried."

Seeing as the man had been here less than a week, Gwendolyn must have gotten her implacability from her mother. Although, perhaps not. Josiah studied the physically broken man before him. It must have taken great fortitude for him to go through his recovery and then to reach out for reconciliation.

"What brought you back in the first place?"

"Obedience to God, I suppose. That and the hope He'd restore my family, just as He did my faith. Are you a believer, Mr. Isaacs?"

"A doubting one, but He and I are working through it."

"Good. Don't ever be afraid to wrestle with God. For fifteen years I demanded to know 'why me?' After all, I was doing the right thing. I was helping people, and yet He didn't protect me from that beam. Do you know what His answer was?" The mischievousness that sparkled in Gwendolyn's eyes on occasion Josiah now saw sparkling in Mr. Ellison's.

"To make you into a better man? Or perhaps a better witness to Christ, as some say."

"Neither. He told me He is the potter and I am the clay. It might be His good pleasure to give me an answer on occasion, but my faith isn't dependent on receiving a response. It's dependent on me declaring Him Lord of my life anyway." He leaned back in his chair and crossed his arms. "It's the most frustrating answer to learn to be content with."

Was this a gentle hint from God that he'd never receive the answer as to why Shauna had to die so young? Her immortal image smiled at him from the photo on the wall. The need for a why was fading quickly in the light of a future with Gwendolyn, but that didn't mean he'd stopped wanting one.

"Would you tell Gweny that I love her and I'm sorry? Not that she'll believe me, but I've quit the habit with the help of a doctor."

"For how long?" In Josiah's line of work, he'd seen many with the opium habit return to their dependence even after quitting.

"Three years. Managing my pain is . . . difficult. Worse on some days than others, but I've maintained it."

That was impressive. "Congratulations. That is something to be proud of. But you should tell her yourself."

The man shook his head. "I don't think she or Kate want anything to do with me."

Josiah wasn't often on the wisdom-giving side of conversations, but Gwendolyn deserved a chance to have her father in her life. "You're trying to reconcile with your family after seventeen years. It's going to take time, persistence, and patience. Your family has lost some chances for memories that you'll never get back, and there will be lasting scars and pain. But recovery is possible. Just like after the fire.

"I can't speak for Mrs. Ellison or the Ballantines, but Gwendolyn has a heart for the broken and hurting. She doesn't give up easily. She needs time to make it through what's going on at Final Chance before she attempts reconciliation with you. But don't deny her the opportunity before she's even had a chance to consider your return."

"Calling my girl by her Christian name, are you?"

Josiah hadn't even realized her name had slipped so easily from his lips. Heat crept up his neck, and he tried to determine the best way to backstep from the folly.

"It's all right, son. I won't tell ol' Percy if you don't. Gweny isn't a child anymore. If she says a man can call her by her Christian name, it's not my place to say nay." His head tilted, and he squinted his eye. "She did give you permission, didn't she?"

"She did."

"Then if there's potential for me to be in her life, it sounds like you and I need to become better acquainted. Regardless of the past, she's still my girl, and I aim to see she settles with a good man who can provide for her." His gaze wandered the room, and then he chuckled. "I don't think I'll have to worry too much about the latter."

Josiah liked his bluntness, and he was happy to return the favor. "No, sir. Should she and I enjoy a future together, I can assure you that I will shower her with every extravagance I can afford."

And oh, how he looked forward to that.

CHAPTER 30

GWENDOLYN STIFLED A YAWN WITH her arm and then set the coffeepot on the tray for Superintendent King's breakfast. From midnight to near four in the morning, Gwendolyn and Wilhelmina had searched the records room for anything resembling the paperwork and money that Josiah had described. Though there had been two of them working, they'd only made it through one of the four filing cabinets before exhaustion required them to abandon the task. They collapsed into bed only to have the sound of retching awaken them an hour later.

Isolating the first case of illness two days ago hadn't been enough. Four girls fell violently ill and spent the early morning hours at the back alley privy vaults with Gwendolyn assisting them. Praise the Lord, the night men had recently cleaned out the privies and hauled off the soil. By the time Gwendolyn returned inside, cleaned up the girls, and settled them in bed to be watched over by Wilhelmina, the day's activities needed her attention. Beginning with Superintendent King's already late breakfast tray.

"Is this everything, Mrs. Flowers?" Gwendolyn glanced over at the tray of oats, warmed ham, and portion of canned apples.

"He'll likely want some medicine to help with his headache, but I know how you feel about that."

Gwendolyn swallowed. Superintendent King was not her father. The few doses he'd required wouldn't make him a habitual user. She'd take the bottle with her but not offer it unless he asked for it. Even then she'd provide the smallest dose possible. She retrieved the laudanum from the locked cabinet in her office and dropped it into her apron pocket.

To her relief, Superintendent King sat at his desk in the office rather than in his bedroom. Though she'd always left the door open, kept her eyes averted, and exited as quickly as possible, it had been awkward and uncomfortable to enter his private quarters. "Are you improved?"

"Improved enough."

By the gravelly and low tone of his voice, it was only due to sheer stubbornness that the man was out of bed.

"We had a surprise donation of groceries yesterday, so enjoy the bounty. We'll stretch it as far as we can, but a man in recovery should be allowed a few extra pleasantries."

"What is it you want?" He jabbed the ham she'd set in front of him with his fork and sliced it into bites. "Bribery doesn't suit you."

Perhaps providing him with a knife wasn't her wisest decision, but she was determined to find answers. With his being attacked so severely, he couldn't possibly be involved at the criminal level. Perhaps he was under threat like her. If so, they could work as allies. Protect the children together and extract those who sought to harm them. She claimed the seat in front of his desk and took a breath.

"You know more than what you shared with the police. I could see it in your face when they questioned you. You recognized at least one of your attackers."

He shoved a rather large bite into his mouth and chewed in silence as he glared at her. After a gulping swallow, he reached for his cup.

When he took a drink and still didn't answer, she leaned forward. "Well?"

"Well, what?"

"Who did you recognize?"

"Miss Ellison"—the cup clattered onto the saucer—"I have done my utmost to keep you on your side of the building for a reason. It is my duty to oversee and protect all those under my authority. You included."

"Are you afraid of retaliation from Quincy?"

"Did you not hear me? If you continue this line of questioning, I cannot be held accountable for what happens to you."

"Is that a threat?"

"It's a warning. You've already got enough rope to hang yourself with. Don't make the mistake of tying the noose too." His menacing glower hollowed out her courage.

It was a foolish mistake to think they could become allies. They were not on the same side, regardless of whether he was an unwilling participant in the Final Chance plot. His desire for self-preservation would never allow him to voluntarily take risks for the sake of others.

"I've never been good at tying knots."

"I wouldn't be so certain. You seem to be quite adept at it. Heed my warning. Stop asking questions. We may have our differences, but I do not wish to see harm come to you."

"Nor I you. You can be assured that I'll ask no more questions." She'd simply continue to seek the answers through other means.

"Good. As long as you keep to your side of the ward, you'll have nothing to be concerned about." He grimaced at his plate. "I'll finish eating later. Please retrieve the laudanum or the Dover's powder from the infirmary."

"I brought some with me in anticipation of your need." She measured out a small dose and handed it to him.

Although he swallowed it without complaint, the face he made could've competed with any of the children's.

When he stood, his face blanched and fully evidenced his lack of recovery.

Stubborn man. She rushed to his side to steady his sway.

"I'm fine!" He flung out his arm to keep her away, knocking the stack of papers to the floor by accident.

"You will allow me to help you to your bed. We cannot afford for you to take a tumble and hit your head."

Once he was settled onto the edge of his bed, he jabbed a finger to the door. "You've helped quite enough, Miss Ellison. I can take care of myself from here. You are dismissed."

She fled his room and shut the door behind her. Papers carpeted the easiest path to the exit. Superintendent King would probably prefer her to walk around rather than touch his paperwork, but she had no doubt they'd be ignored and stepped on by Officers Bagwell or Crane. After collecting and tapping the stack into a neat pile, she set it on the corner of the desk. Four envelopes poking out from Superintendent King's Wanamaker planner caught her notice. She might as well post those for him, even if it risked his ire. There might be bills involved, what with it being the beginning of the month. The last thing they needed was for the gas to be cut off or for the night men to skip a week of emptying the privies. This week especially.

As she walked down to the kitchen, she flipped through the envelopes. Just as she suspected. The gas company and the company they used for the removal of night soil were two of the addresses. The other two must be new potential donors. Gaetano Russo and Tim Benson. Hopefully they had deep pockets. Even with Final Chance's generous donor of late, every penny mattered.

She handed the envelopes to Mrs. Flowers when she entered the kitchen. "Would you add the return addresses to these and ensure they get posted? There are several bills and donation letters that I don't want delayed."

"Yes, ma'am." Mrs. Flowers tucked the letters into her apron and returned to ladling out bowls of broth. "Would you like me to deliver the broth to the girls, or you?"

"Would you, please? Now that Superintendent King is settled, I told Wilhelmina that I would take over her class for the day since she's taking care of the sick girls."

"Yes, ma'am. Just to warn you, I've already heard Miss Cara making a fuss."

"Of course she is."

Why was it always the days with the least amount of sleep when everything seemed to go wrong? At least she knew two things for certain. Superintendent King knew about the threats to her safety, and he was afraid of whoever was behind the abuse at Final Chance.

After spending most of the early afternoon with Gwendolyn's father and then her uncle, Josiah felt he had an even better understanding of the Ellison family. It was no wonder Gwendolyn was such a compassionate and strong woman. She'd endured much and, by the grace of God, become a better person for it. Now more than ever Josiah wanted to walk alongside her and be her support as she navigated through this new set of challenging circumstances. He wanted to watch her faith—their faith—grow through the experiences.

When he arrived at Final Chance for his promised visit, Josiah found Gwendolyn in a corner of the exercise yard swaying with Cara in her arms. By the way her mouth moved in that slow way of a lullaby, Cara was doomed to be asleep soon, if she wasn't already. Gwendolyn hadn't yet spotted him, her attention focused on a group of young girls playing Ring Around the Rosie. But he didn't mind basking in the swell of emotions the image evoked.

For years he'd envisioned a scene similar to this featuring Shauna, and it had always brought with it the grief over what could have been. But this time the hopeful anticipation of what might be expanded in his chest. A future life with Gwendolyn. The thought was enough to make him grin like a fool for the whole world to see.

He ambled over, watching the way the breeze made a tendril of her golden hair dance to the melody of her lullaby. She really had no idea what a striking image she made.

When she finally spotted him, Gwendolyn greeted him with a smile that matched his own. "What has you so happy?"

"It always makes me happy to see two of my favorite girls together." He brushed the sleeping Cara's cheek and watched as pink tinged Gwendolyn's. It was fun courting her, even if he was technically supposed to wait. "Where's Tessa?"

"There's a stomach ailment traveling through the girls' ward at the moment. She's in bed with three others. The good news is it only lasts a day or two, so she'll be back to her feisty ways soon enough."

"I'm glad to hear it. And you? Are you well? Have there been any more threats?"

"I'm fine as far as illness goes, but Superintendent King knows about the threats and probably more. However, he refuses to tell me anything and warned me to stay on my side of the building. He insists he's trying to protect me."

"I think it's time we remove you from Final Chance. I don't like how vulnerable you are."

She arched a brow at him. "I'm no more vulnerable than these children. I'll not leave them."

He'd expected that answer. "Please, promise me that you'll not cross him."

"I'll do my best to not upset him, but his is not the only threat I've received."

His breath knotted in his lungs. "Who else?"

"Your mother, after your bold behavior yesterday." She smirked as she continued to sway. "Oh, she likes me well enough as matron, but I'll never be good enough for her precious boy."

The knot unraveled and freed his breath. "Whatever she said, ignore it. I'm the one who's not good enough. Diamonds, rubies, and sapphires are nothing more than common stones compared to you. I don't even deserve to stand on the same ground as you."

She laughed so heartily Cara startled. "You are an incorrigible flirt."

As Cara resumed sleeping, Josiah shifted toward Gwendolyn's free shoulder and leaned in to whisper. "Just wait until you finally consent to court me. Then I'll show you how incorrigible I am with kissing as well."

Her face jerked toward his, and their noses brushed. "Josiah!"

He didn't pull back. A mere breath separated them, tempting him with the intimacy he longed to have with a woman once again. With Gwendolyn. A quick peck and she'd know. Maybe even decide that it would be worth the risk to begin courting now.

"Are you being the rake everyone warned me about?"

"Most rumors have at least some truth, but I am no rake." Just to prove it, he pulled away, though he desperately wanted to give her a kiss. "Just a man alive with dreams and hopes of a future with you."

She stepped away, putting between them the space he knew they needed. "You don't know how to move slowly, do you?"

"I suppose I don't, especially given the enticement, but I'll endeavor to do better."

"Thank you. We both need to be sure of what we're doing. There's a lot going on in our lives that can create a false illusion that we belong together."

False illusion? "I see."

Something in his tone must have revealed the sting of her words. She gaped at him as if she were the one who'd been wounded.

"I don't think you do." She glanced around.

Josiah realized they'd gained the attention of several girls. A few of the older ones were more surreptitious in their observance, but the younger ones outright stared.

Gwendolyn nodded to the tree that would disguise at least some of their interaction. Once safely hidden behind its trunk, she squeezed his hand. "The truth is, I do want to be with you. I want to test that this friendship is really meant to move beyond. But we need to be patient. Not only is this investigation with Final Chance a hindrance, but there's also your parents, mine, and even Shauna standing between us."

"Shauna doesn't stand between us."

"I'm not so sure about that."

The elation and freedom he'd felt earlier deflated on a breath.

And Abigail said hard truths shouldn't be taken while standing.

He leaned against the tree for support and scoffed. "What will it take to convince you to give me a chance to prove it?"

"Time. Patience. For both of us to work through our personal struggles and make sure we're not running to each other simply as a means of running away from our families. Marriage is a commitment, not an escape."

Gwendolyn's practical wisdom left him no room to argue. There was a lot to overcome. For both of them.

But he knew what she didn't. Marriage brought a support like no other to make it through the hard things. To face those family challenges with someone who saw them from a different perspective. Someone who could gently push for forgiveness and reconciliation even when the other didn't feel like it. That's what Shauna had done for him, and what he would do for Gwendolyn.

Lord, go before me.

He cleared his throat. "I spoke to your father this morning."

"Oh." She shifted from the sparse shadow of the tree into the open sunlight as if seeking to escape the dark memories that mentioning her father conjured. "How did it go? Did he . . . was he . . . overly medicated?"

The weight of fear and pain behind those words made him ache. "No. Your father said he worked with a doctor and has broken the habit."

"I'm glad to hear it."

"But you don't trust that to be the truth?"

She looked at him over Cara and gave a sad smile. "No. He did a good job of hiding it from us until he got caught stealing. When he came home from Eastern Penitentiary, we had so much hope that he'd be broken of the need for opiates. It only took one day for it to become apparent we were wrong, and only a week before Uncle Percy had to intervene.

"While I was in classes, Father attacked Mother because she wouldn't buy him extra medicine. Uncle Percy stopped him before he did any lasting damage and forced him to leave with a promise not to return. Until Wednesday, I hadn't seen or heard from him in seventeen years, and I'm honestly not sure how to move forward."

Time and patience were torture in moments like this. Were they married and at home, he could rock and comfort her like she did now with Cara. But at her request, all he could offer her was the comfort of friendship, words, and honesty.

"Talking with him would be a good start. It's like God and me at the moment. I'm still angry toward Him for not saving Shauna—"

Gwendolyn's lips tilted into a tight smile.

"—but God and I are talking and working through it. I've been using your prayer a lot, actually. Help thou my unbelief."

"I'm glad to hear it. But you're working toward reconciliation with the good and perfect Father. Mine is . . ." Her gaze wandered off in search of the right words.

"Broken? Sinful? Struggling?" When she returned her attention to him, he added, "In need of forgiveness. Seeking reconciliation. Trying to become the better man God has called him to be. None of it is easy—for you or for him. Your mother started with letters. Perhaps you should too. It will give you the distance you need, the ability to edit your thoughts when your emotions run high, and the opened possibility for healing."

She shook her head. "I can't ever live with him again. I can't believe Mother is."

"Writing him doesn't mean you have to live with him. You're a grown woman now. You can live anywhere you want. Besides, when the time comes for you to leave Final Chance, I'm still hoping it's my home you come to."

The worry lines on her face eased, and a tentative smile pushed at the edges of her mouth. "Still rushing things, I see."

"Not rushing, just hopeful. It's both easier and harder to walk through life two by two, but I never regretted facing any difficulty when Shauna was by my side. She was my support, and I was hers. Now I hope to be yours, even if only as a friend."

Gwendolyn's eyes grew sad at the use of Shauna's name, but he couldn't be sorry for using it. If they were going to move forward, they'd have to move forward with acknowledging Shauna had been an important part of his life.

They lingered near the tree a few minutes more in weighty silence before he helped her usher the girls inside.

At the door before he left, she gave his hand an encouraging squeeze. "Thank you, Josiah. I'll think on what you said."

It was a start, and no journey finished without first beginning.

CHAPTER 31

ILLNESS HAD CONSCRIPTED MORE THAN half of the girls' ward by Saturday afternoon, and by Saturday night, Wilhelmina had joined their ranks. Gwendolyn lost count of how many trips to the privy she made with girls or made herself to empty chamber pots. Her own stomach turned queasy, but it was difficult to tell if it was merely from the smells she endured or if she'd caught the illness herself. Either way, she never retched and no fever stole her energy, so she pressed on.

But now, as she sat listening to Uncle Percy drone on at Sunday services, she could hardly keep her eyes open. The body warmth of a mostly recovered Tessa curled against her side was lulling Gwendolyn into momentary dozing. She stifled a yawned and forced herself to do another visual check of the girls. Only twelve of the twenty-six were well enough to attend, half of them still lethargic from their recent illness. The other half appeared hale, but a few had slightly flushed cheeks that hinted at a future of joining the girls upstairs.

Superintendent King was incidentally getting what he wanted. Regardless of what she herself wanted, Gwendolyn hadn't ventured into the boys' ward since her search of the records room Thursday night, and it didn't seem she'd be making another attempt anytime soon.

At least he'd resumed his duties over Final Chance. She was too busy with the girls to attend to anything else. Although she'd hardly call him recovered. The man moved as stiffly as a locomotive straining to leave the station. Mouse's "Ghost" would probably think Superintendent

King a fellow specter with how wan he appeared. Light and sound obviously still pained him as he combated the disharmonious choir of children singing with his hands fisted, his eyes clenched, and his teeth gritted. Not that Gwendolyn could blame him. It was a rather atrocious sound, but all were to make a joyful noise to the Lord—or at least *try*.

Finally Uncle Percy ended services with his usual blessing.

"Uncle Joe never came." Tessa's pitiful voice spoke to how unwell she still felt.

"No, sweetheart, I'm afraid not."

Gwendolyn felt the disappointment keenly. She hadn't seen him since Friday, when he'd talked of courting, marriage, and Shauna. Not that she'd wanted to repeat any of those topics, but she did miss him and the immediate joy she felt at finding his eyes on her.

He'd arrived yesterday as a fresh group of girls were making friends with the chamber pots. Gwendolyn had been too busy cleaning up messes and comforting children to go to him.

She brushed Tessa's hair from her face as the other girls slowly made it to their feet and began shifting the benches back against tables. "Mrs. Flowers told him yesterday that everyone in the girls' ward was ill. I'm sure he's just keeping his distance so he doesn't get sick. Go on and join the other girls. I'll be there shortly."

"Hello, Gwendolyn." Mother approached from the row of empty visitor benches as if she were a mouse testing the spring of a trap. "May Aunt Birdie and I help you with the children? Perhaps provide a break for you and the other officers to rest?"

She still might be hurt by the deception her mother had committed, but Gwendolyn wasn't about to turn down help. In fact, she would've begged for it earlier this morning.

"Thank you, Mother. I appreciate it more than you know."

Her tentative smile held a tinge of pain and remorse. "I'll help your Aunt Birdie gather the girls, although it appears she's doing well enough on her own."

They both watched Aunt Birdie as she fluttered about with more enthusiasm than most of the girls had energy for. She practically danced around them as she enticed them with smiles and laughter. After already giving so much love to Gwendolyn and her own, much older children, Aunt Birdie continued to pour out the energetic and unconditional love to all those she met.

Uncle Percy approached with his hat in hand and concern pinching his face. "Are you well?"

"Well enough. There is a lot going on, but I have the support of good friends to help me through."

His head dipped. "I'm sorry, my girl. You know we would never purposely hurt you."

She looked between her mother and her uncle, both undeniably remorseful. "I know, but it doesn't make it easier. Even so, God is good, and I am well."

"What about . . ." His head tilted toward the boys' ward.

"There are no answers yet, but your prayers are appreciated."

"I think while you ladies are tending the girls, I'll spend some time with the boys. See if any of them have spiritual needs or confessions to make."

Gwendolyn blinked. Uncle Percy wanted to get involved? "I don't think that's wise."

"You're not the only one God can call to action. I've prayed about it, and I feel I should. Anything I find I'll share with"—he drew in a breath like he was about to disclose something unpleasant—"your new *friend*, Mr. Isaacs."

She laughed and then kissed Uncle Percy's cheek. The man really did dislike Josiah. "Rest assured, a friend is all he is for the moment."

"And the next?"

"That is yet to be seen, but the possibility is there. So please, both of you,"—she glanced between him and Mother—"strive to get to know him beyond what the newspapers say. I think you'll be pleasantly surprised."

Uncle Percy grunted. "Once I've finished with the boys, you'll find me praying in the receiving room. Between your father and Mr. Isaacs, I've done little else."

He stalked off and joined the boys in returning tables and benches to their correct positions.

Aunt Birdie had the girls already lined up and proceeded to lead the way upstairs like a parade conductor.

Mother took Gwendolyn's arm as they brought up the rear. "You'll have to forgive your uncle. The last time he disapproved of a match that went forward without his consent, it ended badly."

"Do you mean you and Father?"

"Percival has always been protective of me. I don't think any man would have measured up to his standards, and your father was certainly no exception. A man who ran into flames to rescue others without thought to the family he might leave behind never sat well with Percival, even though I still find your father's courage to be one of my favorite things about him. It's one of my favorite things about you as well."

"It wasn't courageous of him to hit you. To rely on opiates instead of facing the pain. Or to leave us and say nothing for so long."

"We cannot judge whether we would have behaved any differently in his position. The pain from the fire is still with him today. Some days it's so bad that he's considered ending his life rather than continuing to face pain."

Gwendolyn winced. She might be struggling with her father's return, but at least he was alive *to* return.

"Those choices to harm us were made during his desperation to escape the pain. It doesn't excuse them or make them right, but with God's help, your father has chosen to break free of his habit despite the life of pain that will come along with that. It's a courage I can't understand.

"He wrote to me for months before I responded. More proof of his courage. You need to understand, he isn't hoping for a second chance at friendship or marriage. He's seeking forgiveness, knowing full well he doesn't deserve it."

Gwendolyn stopped them at the top of the stairs and waited for all the children to turn the corner toward the girls' ward. "And do you believe him? Do you believe that he has really broken the habit? That you can be alone with him and remain safe?"

"That will take time to decide, but I've granted him forgiveness."

"Forgiveness? So quickly?"

"I'd been working on forgiving him long before he ever sought it. Like my faith, forgiveness is a daily decision to choose Christ's way above my own. In addition to praying 'help thou my unbelief,' I've begun to pray 'help me thou to forgive.' But my forgiving him does not mean he has to return to our lives. I'd like to see if God intends restoration, but if bringing your father back into my life means losing you, I'll send him away."

Gwendolyn swallowed past the lump in her throat. She wasn't ready to make those sorts of decisions, and she certainly didn't want to make them for her mother. "Father staying isn't going to make you lose me, but I can't promise I can be in the same room with him yet. You've had months to talk to him through letters. I didn't even know he was still alive until Wednesday."

Mother dropped her chin. "I'm sorry. That is my fault. I should never have hidden him from you. I thought I was protecting you, but you're a grown woman now. I should have given you the choice."

"It hurt to know you, Aunt Birdie, and Uncle Percy kept it secret, but I choose to forgive you. It is going to take me longer to even consider forgiveness for Father, but I promise to try. Josiah suggested—"

"Josiah? I thought you were only friends."

"Friends with a possible future for more, Mother." She smirked. "He's quite ready to declare a courtship. I'm the one who's holding him back. You can be certain I'm not rushing into things."

Mother regarded her with sharp eyes, and Gwendolyn heated under her scrutiny. "I see."

"Regardless of my future with Josiah, he suggested I begin writing to Father like you did. I can't promise Father reconciliation, but I can try to learn forgiveness. If you're willing to play postman, I'll have a letter for him before you leave."

"When did you grow so completely into womanhood, my darling child?"

"I don't know, but I'll never outgrow the need for my mother." Gwendolyn wrapped her in an embrace. "But please pray for me and be patient with me. Move forward with Father however God leads you, even if it isn't how God leads me."

They stood holding each other up with the same strength God had granted them these last seventeen years. Regardless of what role Father played in her future, they had each other and the God who would sustain them through it all.

CHAPTER 32

WELL, THERE'S A FIRST TIME for everything.

Josiah stared up at the stone facade of Saint Mary Magdalen de Pazzi Roman Catholic Church on Montrose Street. Hushed conversations in Italian swirled around him as parishioners climbed the stone steps and passed through one of the three narrow red doors. Thankfully, he'd dressed knowing he'd likely follow Treasurer Wells and his wife to church services somewhere around the city. He just hadn't expected to attend an Italian parish church. So much for hearing a sermon at whatever church he attended—or at least understanding it. Fortunately, he knew how to melt into the background and do his job even with limited understanding. And besides, how different could Mass be from Reverend Ballantine's services?

He waited for the last parishioner to mount the steps and then followed. After passing through the vestibule into the sanctuary, he froze. Instead of the usual hum of congregants chatting while waiting for services to begin, the elaborate and expansive room was filled with a reverent hush. There was a powerful quality to it. Something that raised the hairs on his neck and filled his spirit with awe. No wonder the Wellses attended here.

Red and pink marble columns capped with gilded capitals drew the eyes forward to a large portrait of Jesus on a cross and then upward to three-story vaulted ceilings. Pastel murals of heavenly scenes spread across the front, with a few directly overhead as well. Stained glass windows filtered colored light onto kneeling parishioners with bowed heads. It was breathtakingly beautiful and reminded him of the details that would fill the Old Testament tabernacles.

"*Mi scusi.*" A gentleman stepped around Josiah and dipped his fingers into a bowl set atop a wooden stand. He crossed himself before proceeding down the aisle, hat in hand, to select a seat.

Josiah jerked his hat off and then mimicked the man's movements. He scanned the row of pews until he found Wells and his wife kneeling on the middle left. Good. If he sat in that back pew on the opposite side of an elderly couple, he'd be able to watch the Wellses' exit and follow within seconds. When he tried to slip into the pew, his foot caught on a padded wooded beam. It lifted and then clattered to the floor, causing several nearby heads to turn.

He grimaced. "*Mi scusi.*"

His poor attempt at Italian resulted in the elderly couple smirking and shaking their heads before returning to their bowed positions over a string of beads.

Just as a bell chimed, a young gentleman stopped at Josiah's pew, knelt, and crossed himself before squeezing past Josiah, causing the man to get a quiet admonition from the elderly signora. The congregation stood and then immediately knelt again, leaving Josiah as nearly the last one standing before he dropped to his knees on the padded beam.

Why even stand if he was just going to kneel again? Josiah rubbed his knee and tried to understand what was happening at the front.

The priest faced the front wall and whatever he said was lost to incomprehension. Stillness and silence reigned over the congregation.

When the parishioners then recited together, the words were surprisingly familiar. Latin. Too bad he hadn't studied harder during his university days. Being able to read it was one thing, but understanding what he heard would be another. This was going to be a long morning if he had to dredge up those old lessons.

All throughout the Mass he fumbled to follow the standing, sitting, kneeling, reciting, singing, and reverent silence. At one point, the elderly signora walked over to him, handed him a pamphlet, and pointed to the Latin phrases being recited by the congregation. He was finally feeling like he was gaining an understanding of what was going on when, row by row, parishioners started to exit their pews and join a line moving toward an altar rail in front of the priest. A few in each row stayed behind after allowing the others to pass, and Josiah lifted a grateful prayer.

Going forward would have most certainly exposed him and his ignorance of what was occurring.

Robust notes from the pipe organ reverberated through the sanctuary as parishioners continued forward. Those who returned to their seats bowed in prayer while the choir in the loft above provided an angelic and ethereal quality to the experience.

Wells exited the pew and allowed his black-veiled wife and others to pass. As he turned to reenter the pew, his gaze swept the back. In a room of mostly dark-haired people, Josiah's blond hair stood out like a lighthouse beacon, guiding Wells right to him.

Perspiration erupted between Josiah's shoulder blades as their gazes met. Josiah nodded in acknowledgment and then bowed his head as if in prayer—although he found it wasn't a lie. Panicked phrases flew to heaven as he tried to think how he could escape this mess.

Soon the elderly signora tapped him on the shoulder. "*Mi scusi.*"

Josiah looked up. Not only did the elderly couple stand waiting to be let out, but Wells also stood directly behind Josiah.

Dread clawed at his chest as he forced a congenial nod to the couple as they shuffled past him into the aisle.

Wells leaned forward. "I'd like a word with you, Mr. Isaacs."

"Can it wait until after Mass? I'm not finished worshiping."

Though he made no sound, Wells scoffed at Josiah's claim. "Very well."

When Josiah returned to a kneeling position in his pew, Wells forced him to make room. There'd be no slipping out unescorted, let alone unobserved. Pinned between the young man who'd joined the elderly couple earlier and Wells, Josiah would have to leap over the back of the pew if he wanted to escape. Such a dramatic exit would hardly support his story of attendance for religious purposes.

As the Mass continued, Josiah became painfully aware of how unbelievable his story would be. As the priest led a section of call and response, Josiah had no idea what to say. He'd lost his spot in the pamphlet, and his low mumbles wouldn't even fool a child into thinking he knew what he was saying. His belated crossing himself proved he merely followed the example of those around him. Once the priest's procession passed and the final hymn concluded, parishioners made their own exit.

Following Wells's lead, Josiah genuflected after leaving the pew, crossed himself with the holy water at the door, and then walked into the cool Sunday morning air.

By the red in Wells's face, the man felt anything but cool. "Why are you here?"

"To attend Mass. I should think that obvious."

"What's obvious is that you've never attended a Mass in your life. Besides, your family is Protestant."

There was that. His family was quite vocal about their church attendance, especially whenever Father was up for reelection. "I'm considering converting, so my friend Ignazio invited me here. Unfortunately, we must have missed each other."

"If you're sincere in your conversion efforts, might I suggest a different parish where there are English speakers?"

"Is there a reason you're so hostile to my attending your church?"

Wells's focus shifted to a spot behind Josiah, and his lips flattened. Mrs. Wells and a vaguely familiar man with a craggy face and gray shorn hair descended the stone steps and joined them on the sidewalk.

"Who is this?" Mrs. Wells's manners were far more welcoming as she smiled at Josiah from her spot on the older man's arm.

Wells drew a breath and forced an equally cordial address. "My love, allow me to introduce Mr. Josiah Isaacs. He's our newest board member at Final Chance. Mr. Isaacs, my wife, Isabella, and her father, Gaetano Russo."

Josiah kissed the air above Mrs. Wells's hand.

Signore Russo met Josiah's gaze with hard eyes and produced a handshake firm enough to stand on and leaving no doubts about the sense of superiority and power he apparently felt over Josiah. The man then addressed Wells in rapid Italian with angry, expressive gestures that made even Mrs. Wells wince.

If only Josiah had Ignazio to eavesdrop and tell him what was being said. He thought he recognized the words *investigatore* and *polizia*, but the speed of conversation made it difficult to be certain. A moment later, his suspicions were confirmed.

"I see you at the court, no?" Russo arched thick gray brows. "You catch Colendrino making plenty counterfeit."

It wasn't uncommon for those in the Italian community—especially those with criminal interests—to sit in the gallery during court cases concerning other Italians. They often came to discover who were traitors to their countrymen and who could be trusted to keep secrets. It was one of the many challenges of investigating the growing number of Italian counterfeiting crimes.

"What bring you here? You catch another bad one? You try and catch him?" Signore Russo gestured to Wells.

"I'm just here to attend Mass."

He gave a slow nod. "It was good Mass. You come again. Eat with us. You see, we no bad one."

Mrs. Wells reclaimed the older man's arm and tugged. "Good day, Signore Isaacs." Then to her husband, *"Padre* and I will meet you at *Nonna's.* You can finish talking there. Don't forget the Barolo. Two bottles, please."

She led her father away, and what remained of the after-Mass crowd dispersed, heading toward their homes and the Italian Market.

"Is there a reason your father-in-law was so quick to assume I was here for you?"

"No. It's just the police aren't welcomed here. Good day, Mr. Isaacs. I recommend you leave the Italian district as quickly as possible. Outsiders can risk injury if they offend the wrong person."

"And have I?"

"It's not me you should be afraid of."

With a growing sense of dread, Josiah watched Wells stalk off. The Wellses had called his bluff and exposed that all he held were low cards without matches.

CHAPTER 33

MR. BENSON AND TIM DELIVERED the response to the green goods letter the next morning. After Josiah's quick thank-you for their service and a reminder to Tim of honesty being the best policy, they left, giving Josiah the chance to pore over the letter's contents.

There was relatively little new information to go on. The senders weren't eager to meet in person but were willing should the quantity of purchased counterfeits exceed four hundred dollars. He wasn't permitted to purchase any counterfeits, so they could have required the moon for payment and he could agree knowing the deal would never reach the point of an exchange. The set time was after dark and in a lesser-policed area near the Italian market, which fit with the green goods game being connected to Fantasma.

The question was how to move forward without breaking policy and yet still gain the confidence of the dealers. He flicked the bandalore out and back. He certainly couldn't be the face of Mr. Benson. Anyone connected to Final Chance would recognize him at this point. And if they were connected to Wells or Gaetano Russo, they would likely even recognize him as Secret Service.

Broderick hadn't worked in Philadelphia for more than a year. Even if he'd been observed from the gallery of court hearings, he was the least likely to be recognized. But still—Josiah himself needed to observe the transaction to see if he could identify anyone involved.

The office door opened, and Josiah missed the catch of his bandalore.

"You owe me dinner." Ignazio strutted into the office like a cock in a hen coop. "I told you I can find anyone. Five days, even while working another case."

Josiah caught his bandalore and shoved it into a drawer without winding the string. "You found Hibbard and Wilcox?"

"Of course I did." He dropped into the chair across from Josiah. "Give me your toy. I want to try my hand at it."

"It's not a toy."

He didn't say anything more—just opened his hand and waited for Josiah to deposit it.

Josiah wound the string and handed it over. "It helps me think. Now where are Hibbard and Wilcox?"

Ignazio slipped the loop over his finger and tried an awkward throw that resulted in the bandalore thudding to the floor without returning. "Across the river, hiding out in Darby."

"Darby? He felt it necessary to go that far from his territory?"

"Wilcox has *un amante*, uhh—" He tapped his finger against his temple as if trying to knock the word free. With a snap of his fingers, the bandalore jumped up and then tangled onto itself. "A lover. She's taking care of the boy. Wilcox is out for blood."

Josiah's stomach tied into a knot. The last thing he needed was another threat to Gwendolyn's safety. Wilcox knew that Hibbard had been housed at Final Chance, and he might take it out on anyone who worked there. "Do you know if Hibbard told him who beat him?"

Ignazio looked up from untangling the bandalore. "You must not have seen the boy."

"No. I've only heard of his condition."

"*Che schifo!* He was black and blue with his head all wrapped. L'amante, she had to spoon gruel into his mouth. What kind of *suino* does that to a child?" As always, Ignazio's body spoke as much as his words did. The more agitated he grew, the more the bandalore danced and tangled because of his expressive gestures. Finally he yanked the loop off. "Here. Take it. I cannot talk with it."

Josiah didn't bother to untangle it before tossing it back into the drawer. "How'd you see all this?"

"I may have indicated to Wilcox that we know who hurt Hibbard and would be willing to share a name in exchange for information about his competitor, Fantasma."

"You can't make those sorts of deals, Ignazio. What if he retaliates before we can make arrests?"

"Better he strike one man instead of many, no?"

"But we have no proof of who did it. Only Gwendolyn's suppositions. I will not hand out a death sentence for anyone, guilty or not."

"Even if Wilcox can give us information on Fantasma? He knows who Fantasma is. Or at least some of them. There are many."

A group made sense based on all the offenses he'd heard attributed to Fantasma. "Is Fantasma a branch of the Mafia?"

There was a general fear that the Mafia had set roots in America and were taking over. It was part of the reason there was a growing mistrust of the Italian community. Newspapers propagated stories of Italian crimes, chalking nearly all of them up to the Mafia, though only some stories had any actual connections.

"No, not true Mafia. More like a counterfeit mafia."

Josiah pulled a sheet of paper free from a nearby stack. "What did Wilcox share?"

"*Nulla.* He told me he'd think about it. If he accepts, he'll come here."

"Write down his address. I want to keep eyes on him."

"You can try. I think he's already moved."

As Ignazio complied, Josiah kneaded his brow. Most times Ignazio was a valuable resource; however, this time, he'd gone beyond what Josiah asked and only created more trouble. Now Gwendolyn was in *more* danger at Final Chance. Wilcox was more likely to seek out his own answers than strike a deal, meaning the only loose connection to Fantasma was through Wells. "Do you know anything about Gaetano Russo?"

"Never heard of him, but I can do some checking. Maybe for a dinner with your bella fidanzata?"

"Gwendolyn isn't my fiancée yet, and I wouldn't let you have dinner with her if you brought Fantasma in yourself."

Ignazio flashed a triumphant grin. "Not your fidanzata yet, but you're thinking about it, no? Just like the others."

"Not like the others. They created situations that required a proposal to save their reputations. With Gwendolyn"—he couldn't stop the smile that made his cheeks ache—"I'm looking forward to the prospect of marriage again."

Ignazio leaned back in his chair, a single finger wagging. "Didn't I tell you? *Numero dieci.* When do you see her again?"

"Today. I'm waiting for Orton or Cosgrove to return first. The green goods letter to Tim Benson finally arrived this morning with details for a meeting on Wednesday night." Josiah reached for the missive on his desk and passed it to Ignazio. "Even without Wilcox as a resource, I hope to soon have Fantasma—or at least some of its members—identified."

Ignazio studied the note. "I know this place. Both good and bad for you. There are plenty of places for you to hide and spring a trap."

Which meant the same could be said for Fantasma.

CHAPTER 34

EVEN THOUGH WILHELMINA HAD RECOVERED quickly and returned to her duties by Monday afternoon, she was far from her usual self. And with Gwendolyn, Agatha, and Mrs. Flowers wearing out like the heels of stockings, no one was up to the full mischief the recovered children seemed determined to cause. Now that the number of recovered children had grown larger than those who were ill, it seemed as if Gwendolyn was doling out more punishments than doses of medicine.

"Bábóg!" Cara wailed into Gwendolyn's ear.

That wretched doll was going to be the end of Gwendolyn's sanity. She rocked Cara and patted her back as Wilhelmina scolded the group of girls who'd stolen and hidden it.

None seemed eager to confess or implicate another in the crime.

"I'm disappointed in the three of you." Gwendolyn bounced Cara against her shoulder as she spoke. "Cara is less than half your age, and that doll is her last connection to her deceased mother. Have you no hearts?"

"You're always treating her better than us." Mary was the oldest one of the group and the one Gwendolyn could count on to bully the other children. "She don't do none of the work, but she gets all the best stuff. Quit coddling her. She ain't no better than the rest of us."

Gwendolyn drew a breath and tried to pull something other than frustration from the depths of her empty well. Mary had raised herself for eight years before she was brought in off the street, with no recollection of ever having a mother, father, or even a roof over her head.

While her history normally bred compassion, sympathy, and patience in Gwendolyn, she had none to give today.

"Cara is made to do what she is able, just the same as you. Now where is Cara's doll?"

"I ain't telling."

Before she lost her temper, she turned to Mary's two accomplices. In all likelihood they'd been threatened into participating. "Lottie, Tabitha, do you know where Mary has hidden Cara's doll? Your cooperation will lead to leniency."

Lottie and Tabitha looked at each other, then at Mary, as if deciding who was the bigger threat.

"Keep your mouth shut, or I'll punch your teeth out."

"Mary will do no such thing, and she'll be punished for even threatening it."

Tabitha shook her head and backed away, but Lottie eyed Cara sobbing against Gwendolyn's shoulder. She was the type of girl to care more about others than threats leveled at her.

"Where is it, Lottie?"

Lottie glanced at Mary and edged further away from the girl. "It's in the—"

Mary lunged at Lottie. Wilhelmina dove between them, taking a wallop to her midsection. While Wilhelmina recovered her footing, Mary chased Lottie.

Good gracious. Gwendolyn did not have the energy for this. She dropped a wailing Cara onto the office chair and snagged Mary's arm before she made it out the door. Mary turned her fury at being thwarted on Gwendolyn and jumped at her like a cat with bared claws.

"I hate you!"

Nails scratched at Gwendolyn's face and arms. All Gwendolyn could do was deflect. Though only eleven, Mary was more than half Gwendolyn's weight and stronger than a cart horse.

Wilhelmina slammed the door to prevent Mary's escape and then pulled her off of Gwendolyn.

As expected, Mary turned her vehemence on Wilhelmina.

"You're nothing but a bunch of . . ."

Gwendolyn ignored the scathing words that followed and pinned the girl's body from behind.

Mary's words turned into guttural screams. Though she attempted to reach behind her to claw at Gwendolyn, the angle was too awkward for her to do any real damage.

Gwendolyn fought to maintain control. "Calm down, Mary. I don't want to accidentally hurt you."

Another raging roar ripped from Mary's throat. Her head thrust forward, then back, and slammed against Gwendolyn's face.

A shrill ring pierced Gwendolyn's ears and a nauseating ache traveled up her jaw. She leaned back as far as her neck would allow and avoided the next head strike.

Failing to succeed with her head, Mary pounded the edges of her heeled boots into Gwendolyn's shins.

Each blow sent a line of pain up Gwendolyn's legs, but she refused to let go. To release Mary in this blind rage would mean injury to more than just herself.

The longer Mary fought, the wilder she became.

Please God! Calmeth her spirit before she hurts herself.

Wilhelmina finally pinned Mary's legs but rocked with the force of the girl's attempts to kick.

Officer Bagwell burst into Gwendolyn's office with a wide-eyed Lottie trailing behind him.

Why couldn't it have been Officer Crane? Officer Bagwell would only escalate the situation. Although, could it really get much worse?

Gwendolyn dodged head strikes as she spoke, her words strained and choppy. "We need to get her to the isolation room so she can safely wear herself out."

He exchanged positions with Wilhelmina. "Stop it, girl! Or you'll feel what it is to really get kicked."

The threat only increased her fight.

"You will not harm her." Gwendolyn did her best to glare at Officer Bagwell even as she dodged the wild thrusts of Mary's head.

He said nothing more but shifted to a more robust hold.

With Mary secured, they struggled out of the office and down the hall. Wilhelmina opened the door to the boys' ward and scurried ahead to the room used for isolation purposes. They'd never had to use isolation for a girl before, so they'd never established one for the girls' ward. That would have to change soon.

Once in the room, which was stripped of everything but a mattress, Officer Bagwell released Mary's legs. He escaped out of the room, and Gwendolyn prayed for speed and strength. She dropped Mary onto the mattress and then ran out the door. They yanked it closed before Mary could stop them, but they couldn't get it locked before she started screaming and twisting the knob.

Gwendolyn held firm, keeping one foot against the wall to prevent from falling forward during the instances Mary managed to open the door a crack. After several long minutes, Mary stopped fighting and moved to kicking the walls as she screamed. Officer Bagwell locked the door, and Gwendolyn released her hold.

Everything within her shook. She'd never once dealt with a child so out of control and angry. Had she handled this wrongly? Was there something she could have done differently to prevent this explosion? How was she even to move forward? Once Mary was calm, they'd have to address the behavior, but would it only send her into another spiral and need for more isolation?

"You can leave now. She's secure." Officer Bagwell's voice cut through the chaos of her thoughts.

"I'm not leaving her alone in the boys' ward, even if the door is locked. I will personally sit here to ensure no one"—she glared so that he understood she meant him in particular—"enters her room. She is my responsibility, and that includes doling out the punishments. Thank you for your help in getting her here, but I no longer need your assistance."

"The boys' ward is no place for a woman to hang about. Some of the older boys just might get an idea about teaching you your own lesson."

"Are you threatening the matron of Final Chance, Officer Bagwell?"

Wilhelmina joined Gwendolyn's side and crossed her arms. "I'm more than happy to file a report on her behalf if that's the case."

"It's not a threat. It's a warning. Your girl there was acting like half the boys on this side of the building. Without a strong hand to keep them in line, there's no telling what sort of devilry they'll pursue. We've got a few here that Quincy would be right proud of."

"I'll take your warning into consideration as I wait here. As all the boys are either in lessons or in the workroom, I'll be fine for the time being. I think it best you both return to your duties with the children. Mary is safely in my care now."

Officer Bagwell disappeared into the infirmary and then returned with a chair. He thunked it on the ground outside the door. "I wouldn't leave this chair if I were you."

Without another word, he stomped past the sleeping quarters and down the stairwell.

"Are you certain you'll be safe here?" Wilhelmina glanced around the empty hall like she expected a Quincy protégé to jump out and maul them.

"I'll be safe enough. Aunt Birdie has me carrying this." Gwendolyn pulled Red from the loop she'd attached to her dress and wiggled it. "Besides, you really do need to return to the children. See if you can get Lottie to show you where the doll is . . . Oh, good heavens—Cara!"

"I'll see to her. She's probably still curled up in the chair crying. If it's acceptable to you, I'll have Tessa sit with her for a while in the back of my classroom."

"That sounds wonderful. Thank you."

Wilhelmina left the boys' ward door open to the shared foyer and disappeared into Gwendolyn's office. She emerged again with a still-crying Cara and slipped down the hall toward the other set of stairs.

For more than thirty minutes, Gwendolyn listened to every noise Mary made, envisioning the girl's movements just to ensure she did nothing to hurt herself. Mary stomped the length of the room several times before she tried the knob. When she found it locked, her screamed profanities returned. Along with bouts of kicking the door and walls. How did the girl still have so much fight left in her? Gwendolyn was bone weary.

Eventually all grew quiet. Gwendolyn waited another fifteen minutes before she risked unlocking the door and peeking in. Mary lay in a lump on the mattress, sound asleep.

Thank thee, Father.

She shut and locked the door again.

The entire floor was silent. Completely absent of anyone else save herself. Superintendent King was out on errands, and the boys' ward officers were working downstairs. And Mary should sleep for at least half an hour. Long enough for Gwendolyn to conduct a search of the boys' ward. It was a risk. One that came with potentially dire consequences. But an opportunity such as this wasn't likely to arise again. What if God had allowed Mary's tantrum for this purpose?

She couldn't very well refuse what God had given her, could she?

Of course not, and dallying here debating the matter squandered precious time. If she was going to search, she needed to do it now.

Beginning with Officer Bagwell's room.

Chapter 35

GWENDOLYN CHECKED EACH ROOM OF the boys' ward for anyone who might catch her snooping. It was one thing to be found in the hallways or even the boys' sleeping quarters, but to be discovered in the male officers' personal quarters would be grounds for immediate dismissal. Depending on who found her, dismissal might be the best she could hope for. She fingered Red, trying to steel her nerves. Hiding evidence where only the male officers had access made more sense than hiding the papers in the records room. If she was going to help the children, she had to do this.

Certain the floor was empty of immediate threats, Gwendolyn returned to the door that should lead to the shared quarters of Officer Crane and Officer Bagwell. Her heart pounded, and a cold sweat broke out across her forehead and down her back. After a deep breath to rebuild the resolve she'd had only a few minutes ago, she turned the knob with clammy hands.

It gave way, and she ducked inside.

The small room was a mirror image of the officers' quarters in the girls' ward. One window, two iron beds pushed against opposite walls, and nightstands at their heads. The back wall held two wardrobes built by former inmates, with a single desk wedged between them. There wasn't much in the way of space or privacy, but if the officers switched weeks on who slept in the boys' quarters, there would be only one person in the room at a time.

Now which side belonged to Officer Bagwell? Both were immaculately clean and nearly identical. She examined the nightstand with a book on the corner. Officer Bagwell didn't strike her as a reader, and he certainly was not a reader of Hiram Orcutt's *The Teacher's Manual: Containing a Treatise Upon the Discipline of the School, and Other Papers Upon the Teacher's Qualifications and Work.* He'd never even finish reading the title before tossing it aside. Gwendolyn inspected the other nightstand. The top contained only a half-drunk glass of water, a comb, and a lamp. The drawer, however, was crammed full of grooming supplies. There wasn't room for any evidence to be hidden in there, but she carefully removed each item to be sure and replaced them when her suspicions were confirmed.

The shared desk was also unlikely if only Bagwell was involved, but it contained papers, so she couldn't ignore the potential. She flipped through each blank page stacked in a pile in the corner and opened the drawers on either side of the desk. It appeared that each matched the owner of that side of the room. Officer Crane's drawer was neatly organized with thorough notes, lesson plans, and other paperwork relating to his duties. There was no such organization on Officer Bagwell's side. Interspersed with crumpled paperwork were fashion magazines, catalogues with items of interest circled, and a few terrible attempts at poetry tucked inside a small book. Poor Lord Tennyson would be appalled to see Officer Bagwell's efforts tucked alongside his great works.

While Officer Bagwell's drawer was disorganized and chaotic, his wardrobe was organized by color, season, and accessory. His coats and shirts were easy to feel for paperwork, but other than a few banknotes—genuine or counterfeit, she couldn't tell—in his pockets, she found nothing. She poked at the folded clothes, listening for crinkling to indicate he hid papers within, but she refused to do more. After smoothing out her indentions, she closed the doors.

She made a slow spin, trying to decide what other potential hiding spaces existed. Perhaps she shouldn't be so quick to dismiss Officer Crane's potential involvement. The man might be considerably more likable, but hadn't Long John Silver fooled poor Trelawney and Jim Hawkins?

Someone turned the doorknob.

Scrambling to hide, Gwendolyn dove beneath Officer Bagwell's bed. Her too-big bustle caught, and she had to squish and wriggle her way against the wall.

The door opened.

She froze, though bits of her skirt still pooled at the foot of the bed.

Black polished boots stepped into view at the edge of the door. Their fancy leatherwork paired with the perfect length of the trouser cuffs meant these shoes did not belong to Officer Crane or Superintendent King. Being found by either of them would get her fired, but knowing Officer Bagwell's penchant for fashion, she was in far more jeopardy than a mere firing.

He stepped forward another step and closed the door slowly until it clicked softly.

Gwendolyn held her breath even though in all likelihood he already knew she was there.

Officer Bagwell dropped to one knee, and the weight of his body creaked the mattress as he leaned forward.

This was it. She might be pinned like a mouse in a trap, but she wouldn't go without a fight. Her hand found the awl's wooden handle and gripped it in preparation for whatever attack she could manage in the cramped area.

Josiah appeared in the space between floor and bed frame. "Have you lost your mind? What are you doing in here?"

The breath she'd been holding exploded from her lungs. What a fool she'd been to come in here.

He continued his vehement whisper. "Get out from underneath there, and let's leave before you're caught."

All she could do was nod and silently praise God that it wasn't Officer Bagwell who'd found her.

His face disappeared, and he scooted away.

As difficult as it had been to squeeze under the bed, escaping it was far more challenging. With every movement, her skirts caught on the support rails. It took wriggling like a worm, with arms pressing her bustle flat, to maneuver free. Once her bustle was out, she angled her head and upper body to avoid hitting the edge of the nightstand.

Something black caught her notice, and she froze. Was that . . .

She tugged the book loose from its wedged position between the bed's leg and the nightstand. Her diary. Proof that Officer Bagwell was involved. She finished her escape from the confines of the bed.

Though Josiah helped her to her feet, he looked ready to shake her like a rattle. "What were you thinking coming in here?"

"I wanted to find evidence, and look"—she held up her diary—"he had this hidden beneath the bed."

Josiah pinched the bridge of his nose and drew in a long-suffering breath. "Gwendolyn, do you realize what could've happened to you if I'd been him?"

"Then let's go, before he returns. I have what I need."

"Put it back. If you take it, he'll know you were here."

"But he might not have read it all yet. He may not know you're involved or even that I'm helping the police."

"Or he could have read it all, and it wouldn't matter if you remove it or not." His hands gripped her shoulders, and his tormented eyes pleaded with her. "Please, Gwendolyn. Put. It. Back."

"But the children—"

"Aren't going to be made any safer by its removal."

"What if I just rip out the pages that—"

"No. He already knows an investigation is occurring. Finding missing pages might prompt him to take action against you." When she didn't move, he rested his forehead against hers. "Please, Gwendolyn. I need you to trust me. I can't lose you like I lost Shauna."

The weight of his words draped over her like a winter cloak. The care behind them filled her with warmth, but the choice between herself and the children was unbearably heavy. "Are you certain removing it won't protect the children?"

"Nothing changes for them either way; the only risk is to you."

Denying the truth wouldn't change it. Though it chafed, she submitted to the wisdom God was placing before her through Josiah. *Help thou my unbelief.* "Fine. I'll put it back intact."

His lips pressed a lingering kiss against her brow. "Thank you."

Though she yearned to stand there and relish the feel of his lips against her skin, she pulled away and returned the diary to the position in which she'd found it.

His fingers entwined with hers, and he pulled her into the empty hallway, where her chair remained a sentinel outside Mary's door. Hopefully no one other than Josiah had realized her absence.

"I need to check on Mary."

She tried to step away, but Josiah tugged her back to him and wrapped an arm around her waist. With his free hand, he cupped her chin and lifted it until their gazes met. "Don't ever do that to me again. When you weren't here like Officer Grace told me, I feared the worst. Officer Bagwell isn't with his wards in the exercise yard, and Jude says he's somewhere in here with several other boys in order to 'take care of a pest problem.'"

"I don't know where he is, but he isn't up here."

"Wherever he is, you have to be more careful. Trust me to do the searching. I know these children mean more to you than preserving your life, but your life means more to me than any evidence you could find. We will catch Officer Bagwell and everyone else involved. Don't let it be at the cost of your life. I can't handle losing you too. I've only just begun to dream again."

The pad of his thumb brushed over her lips and sent a tingling thrill through them. His gaze dipped to her lips, and a devilish grin appeared.

Her breath caught. Was he going to kiss her? Worse still, if she didn't stop him, would that make him a rake or her a coquette?

Heat suffused her face, and she struggled with which she wanted more. A taste of what it felt like to be kissed by him or the respectability of restraint.

He brushed his thumb over her lips again and leaned in.

A tingle of anticipation buzzed through her. Should she meet his approach or pull away?

Indecision left her frozen and waiting.

His mouth veered away from her lips, and instead he whispered in her ear. "I will wait to court and kiss you until this is over, but please don't make it an eternal wait. Jesus says none are given to marriage in heaven, and I don't want to miss my opportunity here on earth."

His lips pressed against her cheek in a lingering way that made her feel everything she'd missed by not acting. Her heart pounded, and she wanted to puddle at his feet. No wonder Shauna had married him within a month. He said all the right things and set a woman's heart to spastic rhythms. But no man was perfect, and enduring love was more than words and tingling feelings. She'd do well to remember that and proceed with enough caution for the both of them.

"I really do need to check on Mary." The words came out more breathless than she intended.

The rake's smile expanded until a dimple showed. How dare he enjoy her discomfiture!

She jutted her chin and squared her shoulders. "Afterward, we can figure out what I can do to help your investigation from the inside."

Though she expected to goad him into a frown, he just shook his head and continued to grin. "You're determined, aren't you?"

"If you don't give me something to do, I'll find things to do on my own. Perhaps Superintendent King is hiding evidence in his quarters."

That worked to wipe the smile off his face. "No, Gwendolyn. I promise you, progress is being made. Don't do anything but care for the children. I don't want to worry about Bagwell or King finding you where you shouldn't be."

On that point he needn't worry. Next time she wouldn't get caught.

CHAPTER 36

THOUGH SHE SHOULD'VE SLEPT THAT night, Gwendolyn returned to the records room and continued her search. Although she didn't search as thoroughly as the first night, she still made it through another file cabinet. Unfortunately, it yielded the same. Nothing but a dearth of sleep with which to face the next day and a host of paper cuts.

It was the latter she found most frustrating today. What on earth had possessed her to suggest they make a slaw with the massive amount of cabbages they'd received?

Gwendolyn straightened away from the counter to allow Lottie the room needed to stir the mix of cabbage strips, salt, pepper, and vinegar together. She swiped a drip of vinegar away from the jar's lip, and the immediate sting of it in her cut made her regret the action.

Glass jars clanked together in the pantry, and Gwendolyn frowned. Only adults were allowed in there, and Mrs. Flowers stood near the stove with two older girls. A moment later, Cara waddled out of the pantry with her arms wrapped awkwardly around the neck of a large jar of pickled eggs.

"Put that down, Cara." Mrs. Flowers beat Gwendolyn to the command. "It's too heavy for you."

"I want eggs." She continued toward Tessa, who chopped cabbages at the center table, and lifted the jar. "Tessa, open it."

Before anyone could reach her, the jar escaped her grip and hit the floor. A crack splintered up the side and caused the vinegar water to seep out. Cara peered up with wide eyes and then sprinted into the pantry, slamming the door behind her like it might prevent her from being caught.

What an afternoon. At least a cracked jar was easy in comparison to Mary's outburst yesterday. That was still a challenge Gwendolyn wasn't sure how to overcome. For now, the girl was sentenced to constantly being at either Agatha's or Wilhelmina's side and making rag dolls from the donations too threadbare to be worn.

Gwendolyn snatched a towel from the counter. "Tessa, please retrieve your sister and take her to Officer Grace. Jane, would you please fetch an empty jar and wash it so we can transfer these eggs?"

By the time she finished sopping up the vinegar water, Gwendolyn's fingers screamed at her. May the Lord count her silent suffering toward her reward in heaven. She'd rather have a sunburn than this pain. At least with a sunburn one had the pleasantness of a day outside to reflect on. There was no such joy in last night's search. She tossed the wet towel into the sink, helped pour the eggs into the new jar, and then carried the cracked one outside. The last thing she needed was for it to shatter and cause one of the girls to require stitches. She set the jar at the edge of the growing pile of rubbish and refuse.

"Stop it!" A pained voice cried from around the corner.

By the sound of scuffling feet, yelps of pain, and malicious threats, a fight was underway.

Josiah would want her to return to the kitchen, but how could she ignore the safety of another in favor of her own? The person—or people—who'd attacked Mr. Farwell, Gareth, and Superintendent King hadn't been caught yet. They could have been lying in wait to kill again. Gwendolyn released Red from its loop and clutched it defensively as she edged to the corner. Should worse come to worse, the kitchen door was still open, so someone would hear her scream.

"Let that be a warning. Keep your mouth shut and let your friends know the next time the Ghost catches you, we'll kill you. Got the message, runt?"

The "yes" came out more moan than word.

"Good. Now crawl back to your hole before I change my mind about using you to send the message." The threat ended with the *ptui* of a spit.

Fading footsteps sounded while sobbing whimpers remained behind.

Gwendolyn waited a full minute before she peeked around the corner to the narrow alley. A small, filthy lump of human body curled upon itself. Keeping Red ready for the defense, Gwendolyn rushed to the child's side and dropped to her knees.

"Can you hear me? Where are you hurt?"

The child's face, bruised and covered in dirt, turned toward her. "I found you, Miss Matron." A weak but triumphant smile revealed a missing front tooth.

Gwendolyn's heart wrenched from her chest. "Mouse!"

She returned Red to the loop on her dress and looked over his body. Filth covered his clothes and disguised any blood. Nothing on him poked at obviously odd angles to indicate broken bones, but many had died from what couldn't be seen. She gingerly felt for other indications of injury, but that only caused him to cry out more. He needed care and a safe place.

"Where are Speedy and the others?"

"Hiding. He told me not to come. Said it was too dangerous."

"Obviously he was right. I'm going to get you help."

If she brought him into the kitchen, it would cause a stir that wouldn't escape the notice of the boys' ward—but going to the front would expose them to the Ghost's view. In the end, she decided on carrying him to the back steps. Though he tried to put up a brave front, pain marred his face, and small whimpers escaped as her steps jostled him.

"Wait here. I'll be just inside the door. I'm sending someone to get Mr. Joe."

Once in the kitchen, she waved to Mrs. Flowers. She didn't have much choice but to send the woman for help. Agatha and Wilhelmina were either with sick children or supervising those assigned to workroom tasks. If Gwendolyn left, she'd never make it back in time for the evening meal, and her absence would be noticed.

The woman walked over, her face flushed from the heat of the kitchen. "Yes, ma'am?"

"I need a private word outside."

Before they'd even reached the bottom step, Mrs. Flowers's eyes grew wide, and her mouth fell agape. "Who is he? What happened?"

"I found him in the alley just after he was attacked."

"We should bring him in. Care for him."

"I agree, but he can't stay. I almost lost my job over sharing a loaf of bread. How much more if anyone finds out we've taken on the care of a child not consigned to our charge?" A lie, even if the reasoning she'd provided wasn't necessarily untrue. "I need you to sneak out and go straight to 1506 Arch Street. Inform Mr. Isaacs he's needed immediately. But you need to be careful. I don't like the number of attacks in the area."

"Shouldn't we go to the police?"

"He's just a street child. If they don't turn him away outright, they'll shove him into an orphanage without proper care. Mr. Isaacs will ensure this child receives what he needs. Can you do this?"

"Should I take him with me?"

"No, I don't think so. It will draw too much attention. He needs to be carried, and I don't think you can manage him with the way your leg gives out."

"True enough. But what will you do with him? He can't stay out here alone." Mrs. Flowers peered at the building behind them as if she might find the reason for Mouse's condition there.

"I'll stand here in the door to let the cool air into the kitchen until it's time to send the girls to wash up. When they're gone, I'll sneak him into the pantry."

"Be careful, Matron. Whoever did this to him could come back."

"Go on, and tell Mr. Isaacs to come in through the back. I don't want anyone to become aware of his arrival."

Mrs. Flowers returned to the kitchen, made an excuse of feeling unwell, and then escaped down the hall.

As she disappeared from view, Gwendolyn prayed that Mrs. Flowers would be able to maintain a facade of normalcy and that Josiah would be home or easily found. Then she moved on to prayers for Mouse's health, Speedy's safety, and this incident to somehow provide what they needed to bring this case to a swift end.

CHAPTER 37

"ARE YOU CERTAIN IT WAS Quincy Slocum you saw with Gaetano Russo?" Josiah stopped pacing and gripped the back of his desk chair.

Though Hayden's revelation marked significant progress on the case, it sat like soured milk in Josiah's stomach.

"I'm certain." Hayden punctuated his words with a nod. "And their conversation was heated. Russo's arms were waving everywhere, and he occasionally hit Slocum on the chest. Given Slocum's demeanor, he wasn't happy either, but he didn't retaliate against the man."

"Were you able to hear any of the conversation?" Although, if it had been carried on in Italian, it wouldn't matter.

"Some. Russo's English was passable until he became so angry he slipped into Italian. From what I gathered, Wells is conducting the green goods game by stealing the counterfeits from his father-in-law. Russo had a circular with one of his banknotes sent from someone inside Final Chance. I didn't see who from. Russo wants Slocum to shut it down and punish those involved."

The edge of the chair bit into Josiah's palms. Gwendolyn wouldn't know to send anything to Russo, and she certainly wouldn't do it without telling him about the connection first. That meant either someone within the green goods game had decided to turn on their accomplices or Wilcox had somehow exacted his revenge in a hands-off manner. Either way, the new threat of punishing those inside Final Chance was the same, and it sickened him.

273

"Who did you follow after the conversation?"

"Slocum. Russo insinuated he was going to take care of his son-in-law, and Slocum seemed like the larger threat to Final Chance. Unfortunately, I lost him shortly after."

"When and where did you lose him?"

"About an hour ago near Christian and Tenth Street."

Josiah clenched his jaw. It was anyone's guess what Slocum would do. He obviously worked for Russo, but by the threats made to Gwendolyn and the other bits Josiah had pieced together, Slocum also had his hand in the green goods game. His boss just didn't know it.

If Josiah were Slocum, he'd be scrambling to identify who'd betrayed them to Russo. "He's likely going to make contact with whomever he trusts at Final Chance. My money's on Bagwell or King. I have a room rented in the building across the street from Final Chance, but I think it's been compromised."

"We don't have enough available eyes to keep someone there anyway."

"Not necessarily."

Mr. Ellison wanted to leave, which would allow Gwendolyn the ability to go home to her mother. Perhaps this was a solution that would benefit them all. Mr. Ellison could live close enough to allow for a slow reconciliation without preventing Gwendolyn from visiting her home. Josiah would have a set of eyes with a vested interest in seeing to Gwendolyn's safety.

"If you can watch Final Chance, I might have a—"

The office door swung open, and his butler, Elias, stepped in. The gleam of sweat across his forehead revealed he'd come in a rush.

"You're needed at Final Chance immediately, sir."

Josiah's throat tightened until it choked the breath from him.

"Gwendolyn?" Her name barely croaked out as he gripped the edge of the desk.

"It's at her behest you come. Something about a beaten child."

The breath rushed back into his lungs at the news, even as dread twisted his gut. If he never heard of or saw another battered child for the rest of his life, it still wouldn't be good enough.

"Did she provide any more information than that?"

"Only that you need to come through the back."

A secret arrival then. That didn't bode well.

He and Hayden left immediately. Once they reached the vicinity of Final Chance, Josiah directed the hack to take the back alleys used primarily for deliveries and waste dumping. No matter how carefully he watched their surroundings for a tail, he couldn't shake the feeling of being watched.

At the back of Final Chance, he climbed down from the hack and conducted a visual search. His eyes traveled low and high, pausing at each window of the surrounding buildings. Movement in one across from Final Chance caught his attention, but it was too fast for him to get a good glimpse.

"I saw it," Hayden said from behind him. "I'll send the driver around front as a precaution."

The last thing they needed was another person attacked.

Once the driver pulled away, Josiah knocked on the kitchen door.

Mrs. Flowers opened it with a pan raised and ready for attack. "Oh, good. It's you."

She stepped back and allowed both men to pass.

Once they were inside, she shut and locked the door. "Matron Ellison didn't want to raise the suspicions of anyone in the boys' ward by not attending the evening meal, so she won't be coming."

Anxiety at not being able to see her wound through him, but she was being wise. "I assume the child isn't one of Final Chance's then?"

"No. I don't recognize him, but she wanted you to take him somewhere safe and have him examined by a doctor."

"Where is he?"

Mrs. Flowers opened the pantry door to reveal a small boy asleep on a pallet of rice and flour sacks.

Josiah knelt in the narrow space next to him. It wasn't until he brushed the shaggy hair out of the boy's face that he recognized Mouse. The poor boy had taken a decent beating. Two shiners were already darkening the skin around his eyes. Though someone had washed away the grime on his face, several decent-sized gashes were red and puffy. He'd likely end up with a few scars, and, knowing Mouse, he'd probably wear them with all the pride of an English title.

Mrs. Flowers remained at the door. "She gave him a bit of laudanum, which means he really had to be hurting. She doesn't give it unless absolutely necessary."

That, Josiah well understood.

He spoke to Hayden. "Normally I'd say we need to take him to the hospital, but this is one of Speedy's boys, and so he likely knows information about Gareth. If Slocum sees us leave with him, no hospital will provide him enough protection. I'll have to take him to my house and send for a doctor."

"Considering Elias shoots truer than you, I think the boy will be safe even when you leave your house. I'll head to that room across the street and keep watch until your other man relieves me."

"Thank you." Josiah passed Hayden the key and then focused on Mouse.

After several attempts to wake the boy, Josiah gave up and lifted him to his shoulder. To Mrs. Flowers, he said, "I want you all to be careful. Hayden's watching the building from the front, but somebody who may have malicious intentions is watching from the back."

Mrs. Flowers scoffed like he'd spoken lunacy. "That's not new news, young man. Quincy Slocum's got a room up on the second floor back there. Or at least, if it isn't his, it belongs to someone he frequents. He might have left Final Chance a free man, but he haunts the place like the ghost of a prisoner."

Chills scraped down Josiah's spine. Every time Gwendolyn had walked outside, Slocum could have snuffed out her life. Could still. "Does Matron Ellison not know?"

"I've done my best to keep her unaware. It's safer that way." Her gaze locked with his. "The first time I spotted him, he made sure I knew to keep my mouth shut. I still have trouble with that leg when the weather turns. I'm not ashamed to say I've made a deal with him to protect her."

"What sort of deal?"

"One I'm breaking right now by telling you, so you had better do your job and arrest him, Mr. Secret-Service Man." She arched a brow.

There was no point in hiding it. Anyone criminally connected or otherwise was bound to know by now. "When and how did you learn that tidbit?"

"I've known all along. Elizabeth Carlisle is my niece."

Josiah groaned. Elizabeth was fiancée number five, whom he'd rescued from the obsessive stalking of a man twice her age and size.

"She's a Harris now, by the way. Her husband thanks you for your bravery in rescuing her and your stupidity in not marrying her."

"I'm glad. Now, about Slocum—what do you know that you're not supposed to tell?"

Mrs. Flowers glanced around the kitchen, pausing at each door. "He arranges for the food deliveries to include a packet of letters and counterfeit money. It's my job to ensure Matron Ellison doesn't see it and that it goes straight into the hands of Superintendent King. As long as I do that, she's kept safe."

Proof he could use that King was involved.

Another thought struck him. "Did you write Gaetano Russo about what's going on here?"

"No, but I think that was a name on one of the envelopes Matron Ellison brought down from Superintendent King's office. If so, I mailed it out Saturday."

Superintendent King wrote the letter? Why? Had the beating he received been enough to make him reconsider his participation? Maybe once Mouse was awake, he'd have some answers about what happened when Gareth and Superintendent King were attacked.

"Are you willing to testify in court to all you've told me?"

"So long as you can guarantee me Quincy ends up in jail until I'm dead." She crossed herself. "I'd prefer the good Lord to take me home in my sleep, not welcome me after an act of violence."

"You have my guarantee." With all the warrants out for Slocum's arrest, the boy wasn't likely to see the light of day for decades.

"Good. Evening meal's just about over. We need to get you out of here without being noticed."

Josiah shifted his grip on Mouse in preparation for walking out. "Tell Gwendolyn I'm going to see to Mouse's care and then return as soon as possible. But it may not be until tomorrow."

He would hate for that to be the case, but the hour was already late, and he needed to address Mouse's needs, have Gwendolyn's father switch places with Hayden, and see if Detective Morrows could get a warrant to search that second floor.

"If there's trouble, find a way to signal to the man in the top room in the building across from the girls' ward. No one should go outside alone, and I want all the female officers to be aware of danger from the inside. Do not go into the boys' ward for any reason. Is that understood?"

Mrs. Flowers gave affirmation, and Josiah snuck Mouse out the front into the waiting hack. Sleep would be elusive tonight. He hadn't experienced anxiety this intense since the strange anticipation he'd had leading up to Shauna's death.

Lord, please don't allow this feeling to be a sign of what's coming.

CHAPTER 38

WAS IT WRONG TO WISH that for one night he had God's power of omnipresence? With all that needed to be done at the same time, Josiah could have split into ten different versions of himself and still felt overwhelmed. How was he to prioritize his activities and all the complexities they entailed? Mouse's health, Gwendolyn's security, and Slocum's arrest all seemed equally important and urgent.

If it hadn't been for Elias's less frantic mind, Josiah would have wasted precious time by forgetting about his newfangled telephone and its ability to make things infinitely easier. In the span of a half hour, Josiah summoned the family physician, arranged for officers to watch Slocum's building, and sent word for Detective Morrows to meet him at the Ballantine home.

From there, all progress slowed to a crawl.

Obstacle after obstacle worked to slow his progress. A lame horse. A lack of available hacks. Even an issue with the train blocking the quickest path. Why was it when Josiah was in a desperate rush, everything seemed to work against him?

Lord, aren't You supposed to be helping us through this?

His arrival at the Ballantine house was met with anxiety that only grew as he explained the situation to Detective Morrows and the family. Once he'd been briefed, Detective Morrows shot off to obtain a warrant. Mr. Ellison and Reverend Ballantine, in a rare show of cooperation, agreed to split shifts watching over Final Chance from the empty apartment. They arrived around midnight, but it was past one before Detective Morrows obtained the warrant and enough men to actually conduct the search.

A search conducted in vain. Slocum was gone, and the family he'd been staying with refused to reveal where he'd gone to. The only recourse left was to increase the foot patrol through the area. By the time Josiah collapsed into bed, twilight kissed the horizon.

"Wake up, Mr. Isaacs. Mam says you don't want to be late picking Miss Ellison up."

Josiah rubbed the grit from his eyes and then blinked at the low burning lamp next to his bed. Ever since Shauna's death, it had been his faithful sleeping companion, providing light to illuminate her likeness whenever a nightmare woke him. Though the late morning light relieved the flame of its duty, it continued its dance at the end of the wick.

"Are you awake, Mr. Isaacs? Mam said to be gentle, but I can jump on the bed if that'll help."

Josiah chuckled. "I'm awake, Saul. Just going about it slowly."

"Just don't do it so slowly that you make Miss Ellison wait. Mam says it's a woman's prerogative to make a man wait, but a man better be on time."

"Your mam's a wise woman."

He shifted to view the oval frame next to the lamp, where Shauna's image greeted him with her usual good-morning smile. A bittersweet smirk pushed at the corners of his mouth as he lifted the frame and stared at it. She was such a beautiful part of his past, one that would always have a place in his heart and life. Waking up to her face every morning was something he was going to miss. But it was time to make room for new memories with a different woman. One who'd captured his attention and heart in a way different from Shauna but who was just as special and important to him. He wouldn't pack away all Shauna's photos, but he was ready to move forward. To seek a future with Gwendolyn.

Josiah released a slow breath and slid the frame into the drawer.

Maybe tonight he'd even try to sleep without the lamp. He snuffed out the wick and rolled out of bed.

"How is Mouse? And why aren't you in school?"

Saul grinned like he had an orange peel over his teeth. "Mam said I could stay home if I helped her with Mouse."

He began haphazardly collecting Josiah's clothes for the day like a valet without any training as he proceeded to talk about Mouse. His choices didn't make much sense, and he missed a few critical pieces, but Josiah would fix it when the boy left him to dress. Except for formal family dinners or evening entertainment, Josiah had dropped the habit of using a valet.

Saul continued his childish ramblings. "Mouse doesn't feel like playing much, but we get along great. Did you know a ghost beat him up? I didn't think a ghost could really hurt you none, but that one did him up real bad."

"A ghost?" As in, one of Fantasma's members?

"Mm-hmm. That's what he said anyway." Saul dumped the pile of clothes onto a chair. "Do you need anything else?"

"Just coffee brought into Mouse's room. Once I'm dressed, that's where you'll find me."

"Yes, sir." He saluted and scampered out with more energy than Josiah could muster after ten cups of coffee.

Josiah rushed through his dressing ritual and then opened the pocket door to Mouse's room. The bruised boy lay on top of the covers, playing with two of Saul's tin soldiers.

"Mr. Joe!" Mouse tried to scramble out of the bed, but he yelped in pain when his feet hit the floor.

Josiah scooped him up before he fell and set him back on the bed. A bandage wrapped around his foot disappeared up his trouser leg. Tillie had said something about a bruised bone or sprained ankle or something of the sort.

"Take it easy, young man. We can't have you injured worse."

"Is Miss Matron here too?" The excitement and hope in his voice were endearing.

"Not yet. She's still at Final Chance."

His eyes grew wide, and then he attempted to push Josiah off the bed. "You gotta go get her. She's not safe there." If Mouse had actual whiskers, they'd be quivering in panic to match his voice. "The Ghosts were told to kill you and her like they done Mr. Farwell and tried to with Gareth."

"Slow down, Mouse. It's all right." Even if Mouse's panic did reawaken his own anxiety from last night's failed attempt to catch Slocum. "First off, Miss Ellison is being protected by her father and several policemen outside the building. Inside, she has the support of three strong women, and she carries an awl with her for protection. She's safe for now."

Mouse didn't look convinced, but he stopped pushing at Josiah.

"Second, I need you to tell me everything you know. Who is the Ghost? What happened to Gareth? Where are Speedy and the others?"

"The Ghost is a bunch of boys who belong to Devil Quin. Speedy says they sold their souls to him and do whatever he says so they can live an easy life. He gives them fake money, and they go buy whatever they want as long as they give the change back to him to give to his boss."

"How does Speedy know this?"

Mouse dropped his chin and picked at a thread in the coverlet. "I ain't supposed to say."

"I need to know if we're going to keep Miss Ellison safe. If you're afraid of Speedy, he can't get you here."

"I ain't afraid of him. He's family. It's just that he and Gareth used to run with the Ghost until they got caught by police. Speedy got free, but Gareth got arrested. Speedy didn't know where he ended up until you sent us to Final Chance."

"Do you know where Gareth is now?"

"With Speedy and the others. That fop, Bagwell, made him take the blame for beating some kid. Instead of just putting him in isolation, they wanted to send him to the big prison. Mr. King knew who we were because Miss Matron was feeding us, and he promised to pay us lots if we pretended to attack him and Gareth on the way there."

"King paid you?"

"He was 'posed to, but when we went to get Gareth, the Ghost were there to do the same thing. Gareth didn't want to go back with them, and they didn't like that. We got away, but now Speedy's too afraid to come out of hiding. Even when his friends told us Devil Quin wants you and Miss Ellison both gone."

"And that's why you were beaten. You went to warn Miss Ellison?"

"Yeah." His voice turned as small as his name. "I got spotted. Only reason I ain't dead is 'cause it was one of Speedy's old friends from the Ghost."

"If he's one of Speedy's friends, why didn't he let you go?"

"'Cause Devil Quin was watching from the window."

And he'd seen Gwendolyn bring Mouse in. Between that and the search conducted last night, Slocum would have had no trouble connecting Gwendolyn to the continued crumbling of his plans. He already wanted her gone. How much more desperate would he be now?

CHAPTER 39

"MATRON ELLISON, WHAT ARE YOU doing in here?"

Gwendolyn stopped flipping through files and stiffened at the accusation in Superintendent King's voice. Had it been the middle of the night and she'd been found rummaging through the records room, she'd feel caught and guilty. However, it was the middle of the day, and her reasons for being here were legitimate and related to fulfilling her duties.

"I'm collecting the files of each girl who fell ill during this latest bout to update their health records. If you'd like to examine the files I've removed, feel free to do so."

"If you would have told me you needed them, I would have collected them for you." He stepped closer, and his voice dropped to a level that skittered chills down her back. "I warned you that coming to the boys' ward was dangerous."

She wrapped her hand around Red and turned a forced smile on him. "While I take your warnings seriously, I cannot stop doing my job just because you don't want me here. Feel free to stay with me while I finish collecting my files and then escort me to my office if you're so concerned."

"I did not ask that you stop conducting your duties. Only that should you require something from this side of the building, you come to me to request it."

"I'll keep that in mind for the future, but since I'm here, I'm going to finish. If you'd like to help, I still need the files of Lucette Nel, Danielle Owen, Winnie Thomas, and Betsy Tieperman."

She waited for him either to leave the room, move to the filing cabinet, or get his face stuck permanently in that scowl.

After a glaring showdown, he yanked open a filing drawer.

Keeping him in her periphery, Gwendolyn finished collecting the files from the 'M' drawer and added them to her stack. Superintendent King took considerably longer with the task than it would have taken her, but eventually he added his files to hers.

"Is that everything you need?"

"Quite everything."

"Good. When you need them returned, just put them on my desk." He locked the door behind them and then directed her toward the building entrance. "I recommend you take the shorter way of cutting in front of the building."

"It's raining. Not only will I get wet, but so will the files."

"A little water is better than the alternative."

Farther down the hall, Officer Bagwell called out. "Is all well, Superintendent King? Do you need my help?"

"All is well. I'll be in shortly to inspect their work."

She noted he'd effectively hid her body from view. Was it an act of protection against Bagwell or a tactic to get her outside without anyone knowing so she could be attacked?

The door at the end of the hall shut, and Superintendent King opened the front. "Please, Miss Ellison. You've made my job hard enough."

"Very well." After all, what choice did she really have in the matter?

She hunched around the files and stepped into the steady rain of a duck's heaven. The door closed behind her, followed by a resounding click. She scurried to the other entrance, but it too was locked. With arms full, she kicked at it.

No one answered.

She continued to kick, but the results were the same.

Where was Jane? She was supposed to be organizing the donations room.

An umbrella extended over her head. "Are you locked out, Miss?"

Gwendolyn barely squelched the startled shriek that rose to her throat at the unfamiliar male's low timbre. With as much courage as she could muster, she turned.

A stocky man of middling age stood only a step below her. His face was oddly familiar, though she was sure they'd never met. She'd remember a man who kept his hair cut close to the scalp. It almost made him appear bald. His denim pants indicated he was a laborer at one of the mills, but his presence at this time of day contradicted that.

"I'm sure one of the girls will allow me in shortly."

"By that stack of files, I'd say you work here."

Unease wound its way through her stomach. "I do. We're a house of refuge, here to serve and provide children with a second chance."

"Or a final one." A hard edge cut into his tone, and he put one foot on the same level as hers. His shirt sleeve shifted, revealing a partial tattoo of a woman just above his wrist. "You think beating a kid so bad he can't even eat is giving him a second chance?"

"Mr. Wilcox." Her breath caught.

"So you know who I am?"

She swallowed. Was it a good thing she knew, or did it give him the motivation to do her harm? "What can I help you with?"

"All I want is a name. I know you know it. Who did that to my boy?" He leaned in, putting his face within inches of hers.

She pressed her body against the door, but there was no escape. "Officer Bagwell."

"You! Get away from her!" someone across the street yelled.

Mr. Wilcox pivoted and then leapt down the stairs.

In his rush, the umbrella fell on Gwendolyn's head and then slipped sideways. She shrugged it off, and it rolled to the bottom of the stairs, where her father panted and leaned heavily on his crutch.

"Are you hurt?" He didn't come any closer, just stared up at her with the same fear she'd felt moments ago. "I tried to get to you quicker. I'm just not as fast as I used to be."

He'd been rushing to her? Not just passing by? She blinked against the brightness of realization. Her father had been watching and had come to rescue her. It was almost more than she could comprehend.

He took a tentative step forward. "Gweny?"

"I'm . . . I'm fine." She shook away the shock. "Where did you come from?"

"Your Mr. Isaacs rented me a room up there so I could keep watch if you needed help."

A strange swell of emotions swirled in her chest. She didn't know whether she should be angry or glad that Josiah had enlisted the man she wasn't ready to see to be her guardian.

The door behind her opened, and Gwendolyn fell back onto the foyer floor.

"Oh, Matron Ellison! I'm so sorry. I didn't know you were there. Mrs. Flowers needed me, so I locked the door while I was away." Jane crouched next to her, collecting the damp files that spread across the floor.

"All is forgiven. Please, take those to the receiving room and then bring some coffee and whatever baked goods Mrs. Flowers has on hand."

"Yes, ma'am."

Perhaps she wasn't ready to renew a relationship with her father, but she at least owed him a chance to step out of the rain and have something warm to drink. Gwendolyn ungracefully pushed from the floor. "If you'll join me inside, Miss Jane will bring refreshment."

Father shook his head. "You don't have to. I just wanted to be sure you were safe."

"Please, come in. I insist."

He looked about to decline again, but a hack stopped at the curb behind him.

Josiah stepped out and took one sweeping look at the two of them. "It appears the three of us need to have a conversation."

Or at least two of them. She had no idea what to say to her father.

Gwendolyn led the way into the receiving room and gestured for the men to take a seat. "I need a moment to spread out the files. It appears they've become damp."

"They're not the only thing." Josiah came from behind her and settled his coat over her shoulders.

It wasn't until his warmth enveloped her that she realized how wet and cold she'd really become. Fifty-degree weather was fine enough when dry, but now gooseflesh popped along her skin, and drips of water rolled off her hair.

"Sit. I'll spread the files." Josiah saw her to the settee and snagged a blanket from the chair. He tucked it around her, all the while speaking low enough for only her to hear. "I'm sorry you didn't have forewarning about your father. I didn't have enough people at my disposal to watch Final Chance, but even if there had been, I knew he'd be far more vigilant in his watch."

"All is well. Mr. Wilcox paid a visit, but Father scared him off."

"Wilcox? What did he want?"

"Only the name of the man who beat Hibbard."

He blew out a breath as he brushed a wet strand of hair from her face. "Well, there goes his need to make a deal with me."

"Should I have not—"

"You did the right thing. Your safety takes priority every time." He cupped the back of her head and kissed her forehead. "I'm glad your father was here."

"I'm still here, young man. Unless you two have said vows, I'd put some distance between you."

Embarrassment chased off some of the chill, but it was Josiah's wink and quiet words that really warmed her. "I'm ready whenever you are."

She refrained from saying anything in response, but she couldn't stop the grin. Josiah was as hard to slow down as a runaway train, and she was very much in danger of hopping aboard and accepting the inevitability of a proposal and marriage. Though he moved away, her eyes followed him. It would be difficult to leave Final Chance behind when all this was over but perhaps not as difficult as she once thought. After all, Wilhelmina would make a wonderful matron, and it *was* rather nice to have the love and attention of a man like Josiah.

She blinked in surprise as the word *love* rolled through her thoughts.

Three weeks could not possibly be enough time for that to be true. Maybe the hope of it, but not the actuality of it. Still, hope was a powerful thing.

"Where would you like me to spread these out? Several of them are quite wet."

"Along the back wall will be fine. Will you read the names on them as you spread them out? I want to make sure none were lost outside or in the foyer."

Other than Josiah's voice reading off names, silence reigned over the room. Talking about the case wouldn't be wise. It only took once for Gwendolyn to learn her lesson about Jane's perfect timing to hear things she should not. Circumstances were too perilous to risk Jane hearing about Superintendent King's threats.

The girl rolled the tea cart in a few minutes later, poured cups for everyone, and then excused herself to help with lunch preparations. Gwendolyn didn't even have to ask her to close the door. She'd greatly improved since Josiah's last visit and would make a great servant at a big house when her sentencing ended in a few months.

"There's no name on this one." Josiah rose from his crouched position and flipped to the front sheet. A *V* formed between his brows. "Gwendolyn, where did you get this?"

"The records room."

"I told you not to do any snooping."

"I didn't. I was only there this morning to update the health records of the girls. It's part of my job."

"Then where did this come from?"

She opened the file he handed her and frowned. The top sheet was a partially finished letter.

Dear Sir—No doubt when you receive this letter you will think there is some trap set for you to get you into trouble, but such is not the case. I promise you this is as true as there is a God in heaven. Anything that passes between us will be a sacred secret. I swear. I'll be plain with you. I am dealing in articles, paper goods—1s, 2s, 5s, and 10s—(do you understand?) . . .

"Is this a circular? Like the ones you talked about?"

"That is exactly what it is."

She thumbed through the rest of the folder. Various circulars, responses, and a thick envelope of banknotes were tucked inside. Money? She fanned the bills out and frowned. There had to be hundreds of dollars here. "Are these counterfeit?"

"They are."

All this time searching and finally the evidence rested in her hands. "It must have been one of the files Superintendent King handed me."

"Superintendent King handed that to you?"

"I don't see any other way it could have happened. I certainly hadn't found it."

"If he locked you out, I don't think he wanted it brought back in." Father rose from his chair. "Isn't today your half day off?"

"But he put me outside a full hour before my time. Surely he'd know I wouldn't leave."

Josiah removed the file from her lap and pulled her to her feet. "Well, you are now, and you're not coming back until everyone's arrested. I'm convinced he locked you out so you and the evidence could be easily destroyed by Slocum and his ghosts."

"But the children—"

"Mouse specifically said that you and I are the ones Slocum wants snuffed out. Staying here is dangerous for them and dangerous for you."

Father's crutch tapped against the floor as he drew near. "I'll return to my room and watch Final Chance for trouble. I promise, I'll not fail in my duty."

He stopped in front of her and held her gaze with a clarity she hadn't seen since his opiate habit started. But that didn't change the fact he'd broken many promises he'd meant to keep. She wanted to believe him. To trust that her father was in control and protecting those she loved. But he was still a fallible person. She couldn't trust his promises, no matter how earnest they might appear. Entrusting her children into his hands wasn't something she could do.

But she did have a Father who was in control. A Father who loved these children far more than she herself ever could. A Father who could be trusted no matter what, because He was incapable of lying. And that same Father had promised never to leave nor forsake.

Oh, Father God. Help thou my unbelief. Thou art in control, and I submit to thy will, whatever it may be.

CHAPTER 40

Mr. Ellison exited first and completed a quick survey of the area before signaling it was safe for Josiah and Gwendolyn to enter the hack. Although Slocum didn't seem the type to prefer a gun as a weapon, Josiah wasn't taking any chances. With a speed that bordered a run, they dashed from the building. Josiah lifted Gwendolyn clear over the foot iron and practically tossed her inside. She landed sideways, and he cringed even as he hopped inside.

"I beg your—"

She waved away his apology and readjusted her position. "Where are we going?"

"The Secret Service office. Our plans need to change."

He handed her the file and drew his revolver. The hack rolled forward at far too sedate a pace. Even with the curtain pulled across to protect passengers from the rain, they were an easy target for anyone with a gun. Josiah sat at the edge of the seat and searched for any sign of Slocum or his ghosts through the narrow window.

"What about Mouse? Is he well? What did he tell you?"

"He'll recover with time and rest. Everything else I'll explain at the office. For now, I need to keep my full attention on the street."

"I'm sorry. I'll keep quiet."

With eyes still focused on their surroundings, he reached for her hand with his free one. He squeezed his assurance before letting go in favor of balance and maneuvering. She didn't speak again, but her presence provided a sense of peace even as his muscles remained coiled tighter than a rattler ready to strike.

Thankfully, they arrived at City Hall without incident. He returned the revolver to its holster but rested his hand on the grip as they walked through the ornately carved entrance of the southwest corner pavilion and up the hanging staircase. Even though he led her through the justice department corridors, he didn't trust it to be safe. Until they reached the Secret Service office, his eyes never stopped evaluating, and his muscles never ceased humming with warning.

Broderick and Hayden waited for him and scrambled to their feet when they realized Gwendolyn was with him.

"Miss Ellison, it's a pleasure to finally meet you." Broderick shot Josiah a knowing smile.

Now was not the time for pleasantries. "We need to change our plans. No one is going to show for the Tim Benson exchange. They're dumping evidence and scrambling to cover their tracks." Josiah indicated for Gwendolyn to hand Hayden the file. "For the time being, Slocum's flown into the wind, but we have what we need to arrest Wells, King, and Bagwell now."

Josiah summarized Mouse's information and Gwendolyn's experience this morning. Between that, the file, and what they'd already collected, it was more than enough to take action, and they wouldn't even have to bend the rules about policy.

"I'll work with Detective Morrows on getting the arrest warrants." Hayden tapped the papers back together and closed the file. "We'll need to coordinate the timing of the arrests so news doesn't travel and prompt the others to leave. I think we might have enough against Russo already, but if we can get Wells to turn on him, our case will be stronger."

"How soon do you think we can move?" The longer the delay, the more likely they were to get away.

"A couple of hours at the most. I'll work with the station nearest Wells's home. You and Cosgrove will work with Detective Morrows to make arrests at Final Chance."

"And how do you plan to do that? Just walk in and inform them they're under arrest?" Gwendolyn spoke for the first time since acknowledging Broderick's greeting.

"In a general sense, yes."

"That might work if there weren't children around, but if they suspect you've come to arrest them, they might hurt the children in an attempt to get away. Officer Bagwell in particular."

With the man's violent history, Gwendolyn's concern was a valid one. "We'll either have to lure King and Bagwell away from the children or remove the children from the area unnoticed."

"You'll not get both of them out of the building at the same time. It's against policy. Any attempt to try would only make them suspicious."

"Then how do we get the children out of the way without raising the alarm?" Broderick asked.

Josiah closed his eyes against the words he knew would come next.

"I can do it."

And there they were. He'd have better luck convincing a rock it could float than convincing Gwendolyn not to participate.

"I just need you to wait until after the evening meal. That's when Officer Crane will take the younger boys out to the exercise yard. If I go back now, I can catch Jude outside. He and I will have a plan to get the older boys out of harm's way by the time you arrive with your warrants."

Josiah shook his head. It was foolish and treacherous. "If you go back now, they will know something is going on."

"They don't have to know I'm back. I can sneak in through the kitchen. Mrs. Flowers and the others will help to keep my presence a secret."

"And what if Slocum sees you?"

"You said it yourself. He's flown into the wind. He may not even be around."

"We can do this without you. There is no need to jeopardize your safety."

"They are my children. I won't risk Officer Bagwell harming them."

"I hate to side with her, but . . ." Broderick shrugged. "It helps to have an ally familiar with the layout and circumstances. We'll be in the building and able to step in if necessary."

"It's that *if necessary* part I'm worried about." Just the thought of her being caught in the boys' ward was enough to make his heart pound and sweat bead. Losing Shauna had been devastating enough. To lose both her and Gwendolyn? He wouldn't survive.

"May I have a private word with Josiah, gentlemen?"

Broderick glanced at Hayden with an amused smile. "By all means. We'll go into Hayden's office and start drawing up the paperwork for a warrant." As he passed Josiah, he whispered, "You're doomed, my friend."

Josiah didn't even wait for the door to close before taking control of the conversation. This was one battle he couldn't afford to lose his senses in. She might think it was a good idea, but he could feel it to his marrow it would end badly.

"We can get the children out ourselves. I'm familiar with the layout of the building and can take on Bagwell myself. If he catches you—"

Gwendolyn cupped his face with both hands, obliterating his words and thoughts. Her eyes closed, and for a moment he thought she was going to try to sway him with a kiss.

"Father who art in heaven, innumerable evils have surrounded us, but thy perfect love casteth out all fear. Help thou our unbelief so that we might not be afraid. We choose to trust thee no matter what happens because thou art good, even when circumstances are not. Amen."

She opened her eyes, and the earnest compassion there was his undoing. Unable to restrain himself, he wrapped his arms around her and pulled her to him. Her humble faith bore him up and reminded him to choose to trust. That didn't mean he agreed with her desired role. In fact, he still felt it was a mistake. But peace soothed his fears like a salve.

God, how I've missed this. Thank You.

Though initially stiff, Gwendolyn relaxed into his hold. Her thumbs caressed his cheek as she spoke softly. "I know you fear something happening to me, but I need you to trust me. I know these children in ways you don't. You need me there to keep them safe."

"I need you. Full stop."

Not since Shauna had he felt as if a part of him belonged to another. But Gwendolyn held as large a piece of him as Shauna did. It was more than the physical—though there was a great deal of that. She slowed him down and made him feel grounded. She lifted him up and supported his weaknesses without ever belittling him. He didn't need to know everything about her to know that God had gifted him a second chance at partnership and love.

Josiah drew her hands from his face, kissing them as he brought them to rest over his pounding heart. He could see a whole future stretched before them. Moments like this not just stolen in secret but boldly enjoyed. Flirtations. Kisses. And perhaps, God willing, he could still become a father.

"I know I promised to wait until this was over, for us to have as long a courtship as you needed, but I'm terrible at waiting. I want to spend the rest of my life with you. Not as a friend. Not as a fiancé. But as your husband. Will you marry me?"

Gwendolyn's mouth fell open, and her eyes shot wide.

When she didn't respond but continued to stare in bewilderment, panic set in. "Please say you'll marry me. I love you, Shauna."

CHAPTER 41

GWENDOLYN COULDN'T BREATHE. COULDN'T MOVE. Couldn't think beyond those four words.

I love you, Shauna.

The horror on Josiah's face meant he'd realized what he said, but silence cracked between them like the splintering of ice.

No. Like the splintering of her heart.

He'd called her Shauna. Is that what he saw when he looked at her? Not Gwendolyn Ellison, but Shauna Isaacs, his deceased wife?

Three weeks. That's all it had been. She knew he couldn't love her in that short of a time. And she'd been right.

She stepped out of his hold.

"Gwendolyn, I didn't mean it. I mean I do. I love Shauna. But I love you too."

Her head began to shake, and she couldn't stop it. Nor could she stop the backward step. What had she expected? Romance? Love? A future where she was the cherished wife?

"Mr. Orton!" Her voice came out strangled and high-pitched.

The door flung open an instant later, and both Hayden and Mr. Cosgrove stepped out, weapons drawn like they'd expected trouble.

Well, they weren't wrong. This was just a problem no weapon could solve.

She licked her lips before forcing out her breathless request. "Will you escort me to Final Chance? We've decided on a plan. I'm going."

"Gwendolyn . . ."

The agony of her name on his lips was more than she could handle.

Without waiting for Hayden's answer, Gwendolyn pivoted and fled out the door.

What was wrong with him? "I love you, Shauna" in the middle of a proposal to Gwendolyn? Josiah gripped his hair, knocking his hat to the floor of the hack.

Broderick sat next to him, shaking his own head. "Why did you never tell me about Shauna? You had a wife. A whole life you never shared, even after I told you all the troubles I had with Theresa."

The guilt of keeping one of his closest friends in the dark compounded with the utter agony of seeing Gwendolyn's face when it wasn't her name that fell from his lips.

"Shauna had been dead five years before we met. I already had her locked up so tight that no one knew about her except my family. And they didn't even want to acknowledge she existed."

"I'm sorry. I know that had to be difficult."

"It was. Still is, if I'm honest. I thought my mother had changed, was making progress when she finally started asking about Shauna a couple of weeks ago. Then she outright rejected Gwendolyn. She hasn't really changed."

"Maybe. Or maybe she just needs more time. One month is a quick turnaround for anyone to adjust. Especially for mothers—and you're her only son. That has to make it even harder. Even having known and loved Theresa for so long before we married, it was hard on my mother. How much more so for yours with no prior relationship with Shauna or Gwendolyn? Give her a little grace. And time. It sounds as if all three of you need it."

"I don't think I'll have a second chance with Gwendolyn."

"If she's got as big a heart as you say, I wouldn't be so quick to dismiss a second chance. You, my friend, have always been quick to rush into things. God just might be teaching you to slow down and to put your faith in His timing instead of your own. It's easy to counterfeit faith by putting ourselves as the decider of all things. It might be time to surrender your plans and timelines to God's and see what He has planned instead."

"What are you? A hundred? You must have gray hair hiding under that hat of yours. You're turning into a wise old man."

Broderick chuckled. "My brothers warned me fatherhood would do that. I just didn't expect it so soon."

"Explains why I'm doomed to forever act a child." The pang of jealousy and lost hope cut through his humor.

"Don't give up. God's timing. Not yours."

The hack slowed to a stop in front of the police station.

Josiah blew out a breath as the weight of anxiety pressed against him. He didn't feel that he had much in the faith department, but he'd give what little he had to God.

"Let's just hope God's timing includes five arrests today."

CHAPTER 42

AFTER NEARLY THREE HOURS OF hiding her presence at Final Chance, the time had finally arrived for Gwendolyn to perform the greatest pretense she would ever commit. Pretending nothing was wrong.

The time alone with her thoughts had been insufficient for her to determine if and how she could move forward with Josiah. And avoiding him wasn't an option. Not with the necessity of his role in removing Superintendent King and Officer Bagwell from the premises. So when he arrived with Detective Morrows and Mr. Cosgrove, all she could offer him was a strained smile.

Josiah nodded his greeting but spoke no words. Remorse and anxiety pinched at his normally jovial face, and his eyes declared a thousand apologies within the span of seconds she'd allowed herself to regard them.

Once she secreted the group into the donations room, she only addressed Detective Morrows so that she didn't have to look at Josiah or the keen eyes of Mr. Cosgrove.

"All the girls are in the workrooms with the officers and the doors locked. No one will be wandering the halls on this side. Unfortunately, the rain is preventing the boys from receiving their outdoor time. Officer Crane is supervising the children working in the smaller room next to the boardroom, and Officer Bagwell is with the older children in that long workroom. Superintendent King is working in his office."

Detective Morrows nodded, factoring in the information she'd provided. "I've got a couple of officers outside watching the exits, so no one is leaving the building. But there are only three of us if there's trouble. Who'll be the most likely culprit?"

"Officer Bagwell. I don't think Superintendent King will resist arrest, but Officer Bagwell most certainly will."

"And he's the one with the children?"

"Yes, but I have a plan for that." One that Josiah would not like. "You'll position yourselves on either side of the door, and I'll draw him out. All you'll have to do is grab him."

"Absolutely not." Josiah stepped toward her. "It's too risky."

Mr. Cosgrove disagreed. "All she has to do is speak and then get out of the way. Considering some of the cases we've worked together over the last year, this is nothing."

"You wouldn't call it nothing if it were Theresa."

"Theresa would do it regardless, and by Miss Ellison's determined face, you're not going to stop her either."

"He's right, but I'll concede to hiding in the storage closet around the corner as soon as I draw Officer Bagwell out." Gwendolyn reached for the door. "Shall we go? The sooner this is done, the sooner Final Chance can move forward."

And the sooner she could figure out what her future—with or without Josiah—entailed.

No one spoke as they traveled down the hallway and through the dining hall, but she felt Josiah's eyes on her. It wasn't right how aware she was of a man who only saw another when he looked at her. After she unlocked the boys' ward door, she drew a deep breath and released a prayer that everything would go better than expected.

Outside the long workroom door, she waited while the three men positioned themselves: Detective Morrows on the left, Josiah on the right, Mr. Cosgrove against the opposite wall from Josiah.

Josiah gave her a curt nod, signaling both his displeasure and her permission to knock.

This was it. Finally, the end to Final Chance's troubles.

She rapped on the door. "Officer Bagwell, I need a word with you."

Without waiting for a response, she pivoted around the corner and rushed to the shallow storage closet a few feet away. She swung open the door and ran right into the chest of a taller, stocky body.

A hand vised around her wrist as she pulled away.

"I'd stay quiet if I were you."

In one fluid movement, a knifepoint bit into the soft flesh beneath her chin and forced her gaze up.

Right into the eyes of Quincy Slocum.

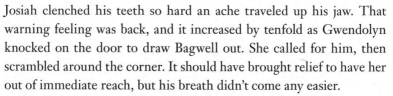

Josiah clenched his teeth so hard an ache traveled up his jaw. That warning feeling was back, and it increased by tenfold as Gwendolyn knocked on the door to draw Bagwell out. She called for him, then scrambled around the corner. It should have brought relief to have her out of immediate reach, but his breath didn't come any easier.

Bagwell flung the door open and stepped into the hall.

"Put your hands up where I can see them," Detective Morrows instructed. "You're under arrest."

Bagwell's head swiveled between the three weapons directed at him, and his hands shot up in the air.

The workroom door diagonal to them opened, and Officer Crane's head poked out. His eyes widened, but his attention was on the storage closet, not Bagwell's arrest. "Let her go, Quincy!"

Quincy? Let her go? Acid sloshed a blistering trail up his throat. It couldn't mean . . . She couldn't be . . . Not again.

Detective Morrows pivoted and directed his weapon toward where Crane stared.

Using the momentary distraction, Bagwell dove back into the room.

Though desperation to reach Gwendolyn clawed at him, Josiah forced his concentration back on Bagwell. There were still children inside, and he was the closest one to handle it.

The door swung closed, but Josiah jammed his foot in the way just before it slammed.

A familiar child's voice squeaked. "No! Stop!"

Jude.

Josiah shouldered the door open.

Bagwell wrenched an arm behind Jude's back and wrapped a massive hand around his throat. "Slide your weapon under that cabinet, or I break his neck."

The man had broken Hibbard's jaw and sent him to the hospital; he'd have no problem snapping Jude's twiggy body.

As Josiah lowered his weapon to the ground, he evaluated his options. There was no shot he could make without risking hitting Jude. Even if he did decide to make a shot, there was no guarantee the bullet wouldn't pass through Bagwell's body and into one of the other children in the room. Reluctantly, he released the hammer and skidded the revolver across the floor toward the cabinet.

"Now step back into the hall with your hands raised."

Josiah complied, and to his dismay he found Detective Morrows also had his hands in the air and weapon on the ground. Broderick had disappeared, likely through the boys' ward door to come at the situation from another angle.

"Keep going."

Josiah backed toward Detective Morrows but froze when he cleared the corner.

Gwendolyn stood in front of Slocum midway down the hall, her chin forced up by the point of a knife. Red dribbled down her neck in a single thin line.

Jude's breath wheezed under Bagwell's grip as they slid past Josiah.

"Looks like we had the same idea, Quincy." Bagwell joined the backward progression toward the exit. "Crane, open the front door."

When he didn't immediately comply, Gwendolyn released a restrained cry of pain.

"If you don't, the blood of two bodies will be on your hands."

Crane glanced toward Josiah, and Josiah had no choice but give his assent.

Crane slunk along the hall wall, giving Bagwell and Slocum as wide a berth as possible. When he opened the door, the coolness of evening swept into the building and flickered the gas lighting.

Josiah took a step forward but was met with denial.

"No following or you'll be tripping over a dead body." Bagwell vocalized the threat, but Slocum's face indicated he planned on leaving a dead body either way.

They crossed the threshold and descended the steps. At the base they split directions—Slocum toward the hack stand, and Bagwell toward Spruce Street.

How the devil was he supposed to choose between his nephew and Gwendolyn?

The moment they were out of view, Detective Morrows scooped his Smith & Wesson from the floor. "I'll go after Bagwell. You go for Slocum."

"Jude's my nephew—"

"And the one who doesn't have a knife to his throat. You're faster than me. Someone has to keep the pressure on Slocum. The moment he thinks he doesn't need a hostage to control the situation, he'll kill her. Bagwell's a fool who the other officers and I will catch off guard."

Josiah swallowed hard. Either path he pursued would mean putting one person he loved in the hands of someone else. Even though, in truth, they were already in God's hands. Not that that brought as much comfort as it should.

God, You said You care. Help thou my unbelief. Help me save them both.

"Slug him hard for me, Morrows."

"It'll be my pleasure."

Josiah retrieved his revolver from the workroom and then sprinted through the dining hall and out the kitchen door. Morrows turned toward Spruce while Josiah ran down the back alley toward Locust. By the time Josiah reached the corner, Slocum had reached the first hack at the stand.

Broderick and another officer stood at a distance, weapons raised. But the only benefit their presence provided was keeping Slocum focused on them and not on who came from behind.

Josiah approached slowly, holding his breath. Before he could get near enough to put the muzzle to Slocum's head, Slocum pivoted to maneuver Gwendolyn into the hack.

"That's far enough. You're not going anywhere with her."

"I didn't realize you preferred your fiancées to be corpses, but I'm happy to oblige." He stepped onto the foot iron and forced Gwendolyn to step on tiptoe to prevent the blade from cutting into her.

"If you kill her, there will be nothing preventing me from shooting you. Let her go, and you at least have a fighting chance."

"You'll not risk her life. I've watched you two. I know how you feel about her." He wrapped an arm around her waist and hauled her inside the hack.

"You pull away and I will shoot you."

"Shoot away, but I'm calling your bluff. Drive on."

When the driver didn't move, Gwendolyn gave another pained yelp. A string of curses followed as the driver was forced to set the horse in motion.

"I'm following behind you, Slocum. Anything happens to her and you're a dead man." He jumped into the next hack.

"Follow them."

CHAPTER 43

THE BLADE PULLED AWAY FROM Gwendolyn's neck, and she gasped. For the last eternity, her every thought had been how to move, breathe, and swallow without accidentally forcing the blade through her chin to her mouth.

"Don't get any foolish ideas. You only stay alive for as long as you're useful." Through the trapdoor, he said to the driver, "As fast as you can to the docks."

He rested the knife on his lap but gripped it so that the point remained directed at her. All he had to do was fling his arm toward her to plunge it into her abdomen, and from everything she knew, gut wounds were painful killers.

But so was a Quincy with the freedom to carry out whatever torture he wanted.

Doing nothing to save herself would be just as fatal and perhaps far more painful. She touched her wet and sticky neck and winced at the sting. The cuts were superficial but proof of how sharp Quincy kept his blade. If she could get it away from him, she might have a fighting chance at getting the driver to stop. Then Josiah would have an opening to intervene.

She dropped her hand to her hip on the opposite side from Quincy and grabbed Red's handle. He hadn't yet noticed the instrument. It might not be as sharp as a knife, nor as long, but the two-inch pointed end could do some damage. And make Quincy really angry.

Timing would be everything.

"You've cost me a lot of money, Matron Ellison. If I don't have to kill you, I might just sell you to make up for my losses."

"What were you doing back at Final Chance? I thought you ran off when the police almost caught you last night."

"Those Nancys didn't have a chance. I hopped over the garden fence, and they didn't catch me sneaking in."

"Why bother?"

The knife twitched on his lap, and she held her breath in anticipation of a lost temper. She shouldn't have pressed for an answer.

"Russo's out for my blood now that he knows I double-crossed him. The only money left is what I hid in that closet, except it was gone when I went for it."

Maybe that envelope of money Superintendent King had slipped into the file was Quincy's. But she didn't dare ask. It didn't matter now and would only serve to anger him further.

He flexed the knife back and forth as he studied the road.

Red slipped easily from the loop, and she adjusted her grip to a stabbing position. If she targeted his hand, he'd have to release the knife. But she'd need to lift her arm high in order to have enough strength and force to accomplish it. And unless his full attention faced away from her, he'd have time to react.

Timing. She had to wait for God's perfect timing.

Frustrate the plans of the wicked, Father. I shall wait to act until thou sayest to act.

Her foot bounced with nervous energy as the hack continued its harried journey toward the Delaware River.

Though Quincy stayed tense, he spent less and less time looking in her direction. The knife remained poised to act, but it appeared he was growing more confident in her lack of ability to fight against him.

"Why are we slowing? Speed up!" Quincy's attention shot to the trapdoor.

With a speed and strength only God could provide, she stabbed the awl into the back of Quincy's hand.

His fingers shot open in response, and he roared in pain.

The knife slipped off his lap onto the floor.

Refusing to let go of Red's handle, she drew it out and plunged it again wherever it would land.

This time she'd lost the element of surprise.

Quincy grasped her wrist and banged it against the wooden doors used to protect their legs from the elements.

"Stop the hack!"

She tried to keep ahold of Red, but after Quincy's third forceful bang, it flew from her hand and landed on the floorboard between the curved fender and the wooden enclosure.

The driver pulled so hard on the reins that the horse leaned back into the britchen as it slowed. It was enough of a change in speed and motion that Quincy leaned forward onto the enclosure door.

"Release the door latch!" she yelled.

The enclosure door released, and Quincy's body weight forced it to swing open.

Bless the driver's quick response. With just enough room to maneuver, she kicked against Quincy's knees and tried for where his wounded hand clutched the door for balance.

Curses filled the space.

He grasped for the knife on the floorboard. "I'm going to slice you to pieces."

His hunched position only made her kicks more potent. Her knee connected with his face.

Guttural rage erupted like Mount Vesuvius. He burst into a standing position, and murderous intent billowed toward her.

He didn't need a knife to kill her. He was going to do it with his bare hands.

She shrank against the bench and crossed her arms in front of her face. Her eyes clenched and her body tensed in anticipation of the blows to come.

A shot fired.

Quincy's full body weight slammed into her, and she screamed.

He made no threats or curses or even moans. He just lay atop her, eerily still.

She didn't dare open her eyes. What if he was dead? But what if he wasn't? Either way, she didn't want to see.

Multiple voices joined the pounding of her heart, but only one mattered.

"Get him off of her!"

Without any warning, she broke into sobs at Josiah's voice. He was here. It was going to be okay.

Hands brushed against her, and the weight of Quincy's body disappeared. The hack dipped once, and then again a moment later.

"Gwendolyn." Her name choked out of Josiah as he dropped into the spot where Quincy had been. His arms enfolded her and squeezed like she was the life buoy instead of him.

She'd never heard a man cry, and Josiah shook with the force of it. Completely undone and vulnerable. She should have been horrified by the display of what society deemed a weakness. But she wasn't, and it wasn't. Josiah was the strongest, most valiant man she'd ever met. His tears weren't weakness. They were the most precious gift she'd ever experienced. His sobs spoke of his love, trust, and care in ways no words could ever communicate. They washed over her and soothed the broken and hurting places, declaring how very personal and important his love for her was.

And it only made her cry all the harder.

She didn't know what the future held for them, but she did know there *was* a future. There had to be. She wasn't ready to declare betrothal or marriage, but to lose him forever would rip a hole in her life. Knowing him—loving him—had changed her. She didn't work in the same independent way she had just three weeks ago. There was a need for partnership, to be able to lean into someone and look to that person for help, answers, and strength.

And not just any someone.

Josiah pulled away, holding her by the shoulders as his gaze swept over her. "What am I doing? You need to go to the hospital, and I need to get to Jude."

Jude. Her stomach vaulted. The last she'd seen him, Bagwell had him in his death grip. Whatever injuries she had were superficial. Nothing in comparison to what Jude may be enduring. She would not go to a hospital without knowing he and all her children were safe.

Gwendolyn tapped on the driver's trapdoor. When it opened, she said, "Take us back to Final Chance with all haste."

"Gwendolyn, your neck is bleeding. You need a doctor."

"It's nothing but scratches. If it were anything serious, I'd be dead by now."

Josiah's chin dipped to a reprimanding angle. "Gwen—"

"Josiah, you can either accept what I'm saying or force me to the hospital and delay yourself getting to Jude."

He yanked the enclosure door into place and leaned his head out. "Cosgrove, we're heading back to Final Chance. Can you deal with things here?"

"I'll meet you there after the coroner arrives. Don't let that driver leave without getting his information and a statement."

Josiah leaned back into the seat and motioned for the driver to turn around. "You're the most stubborn woman I've ever met."

"Just so long as stubborn saves Jude."

"If you don't want to frighten the children with your Marie Antoinette neck, allow me to wipe away what blood I can."

By the time they arrived, Josiah had deemed her neck passable and begrudgingly admitted the nicks on her neck were no worse than his after shaving.

After a frantic search through the swarm of police officers, they found Detective Morrows supervising his new prisoners being loaded into a police wagon.

With the pristine condition of Superintendent King's clothes, it appeared he'd surrendered without a fight. The same could not be said of

Officer Bagwell. By the awkward droop of his head and the sag of his body as two officers lugged him toward the back, the man was incapacitated. A hospital visit would likely be required. Probably a mercy considering the beating he'd obviously endured.

"Where's Jude?" Josiah's voice held an edge of panic.

"Take it easy." Detective Morrows laid a hand on Josiah's shoulder. "Jude's fine. He's inside with his sisters. A little shaken up, but no injuries."

"Then what happened to him?" Gwendolyn pointed to Bagwell.

"You have Billy Wilcox to thank for that. He was lying in wait to get his hands on Bagwell. Something about Bagwell having beaten his son."

No wonder Bagwell was in such poor shape. Revenge packed a powerful punch, especially when the fist was delivered by Mr. Wilcox.

"While we were putting pressure on Bagwell down the alley, Wilcox came out of nowhere and slugged him. Jude got away, and I admit to maybe not having moved as fast as I could have to stop Wilcox. We eventually had to secure him in the wagon so he didn't finish the job."

"So it's over, then? The children are finally safe?" She held her breath, fearing some new bit of information.

"Barring Orton having trouble with Treasurer Wells, I believe everyone at Final Chance is safe."

His words robbed her legs of what little strength they had left. She sank to the ground, and Josiah scrambled to her side.

"What's wrong?" His eyes searched her neck, as if he feared one of the cuts had developed into something life-threatening.

"It's over. Praise God, it's finally over."

Relief washed over his countenance. "Let's get you inside. It's been a long day for all of us, and I want to see Jude and the girls."

CHAPTER 44

THE ABUSE AND GREEN GOODS game at Final Chance may have theoretically come to an end, but the ramifications were leaving Gwendolyn struggling to find her footing. Everyone and everything needed her attention at once.

Although Officer Crane had been cleared of criminal involvement, his lack of observation or reporting of what he did see proved him an inadequate replacement for superintendent. He retained his position because she needed at least one male in the building to contend with the group of boys who refused to recognize her authority. It was yet to be determined whether he would keep it once the board finished the arduous process of hiring new male staff, including a superintendent.

The right to have a voice in the interview and hiring process had been hard-won, but her role in the saving of Final Chance had earned a few champions to her cause. Still, it was an exhausting task on top of her already exhausting list.

Josiah came by every day, and each time she turned him away. She simply didn't have the time or energy to confront the ghost that haunted the space between them.

"What are you still doing up? It's nearly two in the morning." Wilhelmina moseyed into Gwendolyn's office with a glass of water in hand.

"Oh, nothing. Just exorcising ghosts and trying to determine what's real and what's not."

Treasurer Wells's donation ledgers lay before her. While not an urgent task, sorting through them and determining what donations were real and which were the ones Treasurer Wells made under false names was a legitimate distraction. Although she *had* been staring at the same line for the last forty minutes while her mind continued to revisit her last real conversation with Josiah. The one where he'd proposed and then said he loved the wrong woman.

"Well, if the ghosts you're exorcising are in those ledgers, you'll have better luck in the morning. However, if it's something else—which I highly suspect it is—you'll do better talking it out with me. Come on. It's time for some hairbrush curative."

Gwendolyn glanced at the ledgers and sighed. Wilhelmina was right. She wasn't getting anything done this late. Reluctantly, she rose and led the way into her bedroom. There, she passed Wilhelmina a brush and then freed her hair from its pins. They sat on the bed, and Wilhelmina began brushing Gwendolyn's hair.

"Now spill it. Not that you don't have plenty of things to keep you up and worried at night, but something beyond Final Chance is bothering you. Given your consistent avoidance of Mr. Isaacs, I gather it has something to do with him."

"I'm not avoiding him. I just have too much to do."

"Poppycock. If you were on good terms, you would have wanted him here even if he only sat in the room while you worked. What happened? And no skimping on the details." She waved the hairbrush in admonition before returning to her slow, even strokes.

Gwendolyn debated for a moment and then surrendered to the inevitable. Wilhelmina was her best friend, and she needed the wisdom of someone she could trust. She poured out the details of her strange relationship with Josiah, especially those relating to Shauna.

"He's already found his one true love. How could he ever love me as much as he did her? I'm not Shauna. I can't ever be Shauna. The man was standing right in front of me, looking at me, and all he could see was Shauna."

"I can see why you might feel that way, but I think you are coming at it from perhaps the wrong angle." Wilhelmina set the brush aside and split Gwendolyn's hair into three parts for plaiting. "Does anywhere in the Bible actually say that God has created one love for each person?"

Gwendolyn gave serious consideration to the question. There were a few random discussions on remarriage, especially when Paul spoke of young widows, but love really hadn't played into discussions of marriage in the first place. It was always framed as a vow—a willing choice to commit to another person. "I don't know that God really says we are to have only one true love."

"Then you can toss aside the notion that Josiah is only allowed to have one. What if God has chosen to bless him with two? One of them being you. Now granted, there should only be one love while both are living, but Shauna's gone. He's free to love again."

"But I can't replace Shauna."

"Is he asking you to?"

"Don't you think so? He called me Shauna."

"And you've called Tessa Cara. Sometimes we slip and say the wrong names, but that doesn't mean we think they're the other person or that we want them to be. I can't speak from experience, but I imagine falling in love a second time is sort of like working here. Every child that comes through our doors becomes a cherished part of our hearts. Even after they've moved on, we continue to love and miss them. Our hearts aren't limited in love. They grow and expand to make room for the new loves without pushing out the old. Just because Josiah loved Shauna as his wife doesn't mean he can't love you as his wife as well. But . . ."

Wilhelmina tied a ribbon at the base of Gwendolyn's braid and then turned Gwendolyn toward her. With a compassionate smile, she squeezed Gwendolyn's shoulders.

"But you and Josiah do need to talk about Shauna and work through her part in his life. It's not fair of you to ask him to act like she never existed. She did, and he loves her. But it sounds like he loves you too. Marriage is hard work, and if that is in the future for you, it's best to tackle this before making a vow. Because if you can't move past the insecurity of sharing Josiah's heart with Shauna, then marriage would be a bad choice for both of you."

⁂

If it weren't for the swirl of activity related to closing the Final Chance case, Josiah might have gone mad over the last week. He'd hoped to have a conversation with Gwendolyn by now to determine where they stood. Although her consistent avoidance of him might be his answer. He desperately clung to the hope that the repercussions of losing three employees was the cause rather than his accidental slip of Shauna's name.

Josiah trudged into the office after seeing Broderick and Theresa off at the train station and slumped into his chair. He didn't even feel like tinkering with his bandalore.

Get ahold of yourself. She just needs time. You've prayed about it. Now leave it in God's hands.

The pep talk did little to motivate or soothe him.

At least the case was going well even if his personal life wasn't. Wells hadn't been able to fight the arrest as his father-in-law had gashed his face so badly he'd been laid up in bed when Hayden arrived. Wells, once recovered enough to speak, turned on Russo, providing the how and where of his money production. The group of "ghosts" had scattered without Slocum's leadership, although Speedy and Gareth had been able to provide some help in rounding up a few.

It was King who'd ultimately revealed the details of an operation that had been going on for six years. What had started out as a temporary way to save Final Chance from closing became a lucrative business that Wells refused to abandon. Stealing the counterfeits from Russo had made it a low-cost endeavor for them. Until Slocum—a former dock mate of Russo's—recognized the counterfeits and took over the operations through blackmail. It wasn't until Bagwell was added to the scheme that things turned violent. Had it not been for his abuse of the children alerting Gwendolyn to a problem, the green goods game may never have been discovered.

And there he was again. Back to Gwendolyn.

Josiah pinched the bridge of his nose with increasing pressure, as if that might squeeze her right out of his mind.

When someone knocked at the door but didn't enter, Josiah rose to his feet and opened it. No one stood there, so he stepped into the hall to glance around. A few doors down, Gwendolyn frowned at the lettering on a door.

"Are you lost?"

Gwendolyn spun toward him. "Oh, thank goodness. I've knocked on four doors trying to remember which one was your office."

"It would help if we had something other than a number on our door to indicate who we are. Come on in."

Though he feigned nonchalance, his heart pounded in his chest. She'd sought him out. Or at least sought out the Secret Service office. If she'd come across more evidence in her duties, she might just be delivering them. After all, it wasn't even her day off.

"I can't stay long. There aren't enough people to cover all the duties, even with members of the Ladies' Committee coming every day. But I needed to see you."

He regarded her wan and exhausted face. Perhaps he'd been too quick to assume her reasoning for rejecting his visits. She had a lot of responsibility weighing on her and no one else to help her bear it. He wished she'd allow him to come alongside her.

She accepted the proffered chair, and he sat in the chair across from her. "I'm always happy to see you for however long I'm allowed. I've missed you."

"I've missed you too, even if it is my fault that you've not been invited in."

The admission emboldened him, and he claimed one of her hands. "I've understood. It's a difficult time at Final Chance, and I've tried to stay out of your way."

"I don't want you to stay out of the way." She popped to her feet and paced as she worried her hands. "But a lot happened last week. Your proposal being one."

He didn't know whether to be encouraged or discouraged by her words. Especially considering where that proposal had led.

"I'm not ready to marry you, Josiah. I'm not Shauna, and I never will be."

"I know you're not Shauna, nor do I want you to be." He clasped her arms and stopped her pacing. "Look at me."

When she reluctantly did so, tears reflected the grief and pain she felt.

"When I said 'I love you,' it was the first time I've said it to anyone other than her, and her name just rolled off naturally. It doesn't mean that I don't love you, Gwendolyn, because I do. I do love you, Gwendolyn—" He paused, realizing for the first time he didn't actually know her full name. "What *is* your middle name?"

She chuckled and palmed a tear away. "See? We don't even know that about each other. How can you truly love me? How can you be sure that you're not just seeing Shauna when you look at me?"

"For one, you two look very different. Sound different too. In fact, you're more different than you are alike. Only Shauna can be Shauna, and only you can be you. And I love you, Gwendolyn Mystery-Middle-Name Ellison. I don't need a long time to know I want you as my partner in life. And it's not because I need someone to take Shauna's place. I've had ten years to do that if that was what I wanted. I want you because you are you, and you've totally captivated me."

Her eyes closed, and she drew in a long breath as if drinking in his words. After an equally long exhale, she clasped his hand and offered a rueful smile. "You may not need a long time, but I need more. I need courtship, a chance for us to get to know each other outside of this case. I need a chance to see and know who Shauna is. To see if you really do have room to love both of us."

That last bit was utter ridiculousness to him, but he could tell it wasn't for her. This is what Abigail had warned him about. The need to move slower, allowing Gwendolyn the chance to grow comfortable with his past and accept the place it still had in his present.

"Then I'll court you for as long as you need to understand what you mean to me. You might have to help me go slow, but I'm willing."

"Really? You'll go slow for me?"

"I promise to try, and you can rein me in when I'm going too fast."

She laughed a full, hearty laugh. "You're like a runaway train, Josiah. There is no slowing you down."

"Then you'll just have to pray that there are plenty of tracks ahead."

"And so I shall. Thank you, Josiah, for understanding." She squeezed his hands. "And it's Olivia, by the way."

"I like it. It'll sound especially good when you change the last name to Isaacs."

"Josiah . . ."

"I'm not rushing, just flirting. You'll soon see it's one of my favorite things to do."

"Then I suppose I'll have to brush up on my skills." She smiled at him, and the earlier grief and pain was replaced with a tentative joy. "I really do need to leave, but please, come by. We might just be sitting in an office in silence while I work, but I'd love to have you there."

"Shall we go then? You have work to do, and I have a chairman to convince to give leniency to your courting clause."

"You don't have to go with me now. The threat is over."

"The threat may be over, but this is my first day officially courting you. I'm going to walk you to your door, Miss Gwendolyn Olivia Ellison, and I plan on flirting with you the whole way."

CHAPTER 45

May 14, 1886

AN ENTIRE YEAR OF COURTSHIP. Three hundred sixty-five days of both absolute torture and sweet memories. Josiah never thought he'd make it, but he'd do it all over again for Gwendolyn.

Please, God, don't hear that as a challenge.

He fingered the ring box in his pocket, unaccountably nervous, as he watched Gwendolyn play tag with Oscar and Luella Darlington on the Rittenhouse Square lawn. It wasn't as if they hadn't talked about marriage. They had. Quite a bit, in fact. Both about their hopeful one-day marriage and his past one with Shauna. Gwendolyn had even helped him pack away her pictures and set up a small corner on his library shelf where those memories could be revisited as he needed. But the more time passed and the more memories he created with Gwendolyn, the less often he'd felt the need. He might have hated her wisdom in waiting, but it had been wisdom indeed. They needed time for healing and forging strength into their relationship with each other and their families.

While she was still working through reconciliation with her father, they'd reached a point where her parents' remarriage no longer kept her from home. The year had been good for his nieces' and Jude's acceptance of Gwendolyn as well. They'd completed their time at Final

Chance last month, and now that they were home with Conor, they fully embraced Gwendolyn as one of their own. His own mother and father had finally begrudgingly accepted Gwendolyn as their future daughter-in-law. It would take more time for them to accept her as an equal in character and worth, but the open hostility had faded. He'd learned to release their rejection of Shauna into God's hand and to move forward in his faith. Yes, the learning to wait for God's timing before marriage had been worth it.

But hopefully that waiting was over.

He realized now how presumptuous it was of him to bring in Andrew Darlington and Broderick Cosgrove, along with their families, for a wedding he hadn't even proposed for yet. He was certain of his feelings and even hers, but if this was one of Aesop's fables, she'd be the tortoise and he the hare.

"You're a dolt." Andrew's blunt words did not bolster his confidence. "Had I known you hadn't proposed yet, I would have postponed the trip until you were certain of a date. I'm not likely to be able to ask off for so long a period again. I may have reached detective, but I'm the bottom rung."

Josiah shifted his gaze from Gwendolyn to the Bailey & Co. ring box. He'd gone for the best, wanting her to know how much he cherished her, but Gwendolyn was not a woman to be bought by diamonds.

"Then I suppose if she says no"—his chest constricted at the thought—"when I finally convince her to say yes, we'll have to make a visit as part of our wedding trip."

He would be as patient as she needed. Even if it killed him. Which, if they continued at this speed, it might.

"Don't let Darlington work you up. She'll say yes." Broderick rubbed three-month-old Catherine's back as she wiggled and began to fuss. "Now go work that silver tongue of yours and get an answer. Theresa's holding back lunch until she can reveal all the special treats she packed in anticipation of congratulations, and I'm not sure how much longer Catherine can last."

Broderick walked away and joined Hayden at the spread of blankets where Theresa and Felicity attempted to teach Martha Orton to be gentle with her little brother.

Andrew charged into the game of chase and swooped Oscar into the air. He set the boy back on the ground and offered an arm to Luella. After a few words with Gwendolyn, the trio of mother, father, and son departed on a sedate walk along the asphalt path and blooming trees.

Gwendolyn smirked at Josiah as she approached. "It appears as if I've been forced out of our game of chase."

"Haven't you had enough of running by now?"

"Possibly. It depends who I'm running from." She tilted her head at a coy angle. "If it's from you and you promise to give chase, then I shall endeavor to run to that grove of trees and allow you to catch and kiss me."

Before he could convince her otherwise, she pivoted and did just that. He shoved the ring box deeper into his pocket and caught up to her before the grove. However, he waited to catch her around the waist until they'd fully passed into the seclusion provided there.

She laughed and panted as she laid her arms atop his. "It appears you've caught me."

"Have I? Have I really caught you?" He stared into her copper orbs that danced with mirth, searching for any hesitancy. Any indication that he was rushing ahead of her again.

"Oh, Josiah." She caressed his cheek and blinded him with her sunshine smile. "I am yours for as long as God allows."

His throat bobbed, and he fumbled to retrieve the ring box one-handed. He almost dropped it, and she stifled a chuckle. "This isn't funny. I'm trying to ask you to marry me."

Her laugh burst forth and tears sprung to the corners of her eyes. "Then ask me already, so I can say yes."

He did drop the box then. "What? You'll marry me?"

"I don't know, you haven't asked."

"You torment me." But he dropped to a knee to retrieve the box and opened it for her to see the solitaire diamond. "Gwendolyn Ellison, you would make me the happiest of men if you would consent to marry me between now and next Friday. Will you put me out of my misery now and say yes?"

She dropped forward into him and wrapped her arms around his neck, laughing all the while. "I love you, Josiah, and I'm so glad I know you well enough to anticipate your plans. Yes, I'll marry you next week. Mother will be finished with my dress over the weekend."

"Your dress?"

"When you told me you'd invited Andrew Darlington and his family for a visit, I suspected your goal." Her eyes twinkled with amusement.

"So I gave it away, did I?"

"You did, but it allowed me time to make plans of my own. Chairman Abernathy gladly accepted my resignation last week. Why do you think I've had this entire time off without his having a conniption? My last few days at Final Chance have been helping Wilhelmina to transition into her role as matron."

"And you kept it secret?"

"I'm just glad I was right. It would have been awkward to explain why I no longer needed you to pick me up from Final Chance. Now, are you going to kiss me or not? You've thoroughly caught me, and I expect a kiss to match."

"Your wish is my command."

He leaned in and captured her lips in the same way she'd captured his heart—fast and thoroughly. And like the flirt she was, she turned it slow and lingering. He'd learned from her there was a richness and depth to love that could only be found through testing and patience. It was the hardest year he'd walked through since Shauna's death, but it had been the richest too.

In the end, God had exposed his hidden broken heart and restored it, not with gilded filigree but with the solid foundation of faith, hope, and love.

Acknowledgments

THANK YOU, JESUS, FOR GETTING me through another story. Especially this one. May your name be glorified always.

To my family, thank you for always being my cheerleaders. I love you all. To my besties, there would literally be no ending for this book. Thank you. To Martha Hutchens, Grace Hitchcock, and Kathleen Denly, your support and encouragement mean the world.

Thank you, Rhonda Ortiz, for your invaluable help with ensuring the Catholic Mass scene was accurate. Any mistakes are my own.

I am so grateful to Patrice Doten, Kendell Hopper, and Kim Spille for their insights into the struggles of life as a widow/widower and re-marriage. I pray that I was able to honor your experiences realistically. Where I have failed, thank you for your grace and mercy.

Thank you to my Kregel team for believing in me; my agent, Tamela Hancock Murray, for encouraging and praying for me; and my amazing Kregel editor, Janyre Tromp, and copyeditor, Lindsay Danielson. Thank you to all those on the Kregel team who design, distribute, and help market my book so well. God bless you all.

And thank YOU, reader, for choosing to read my book. I pray you were blessed by it.

Author's Note

Dear Reader,

Thank you for choosing to read my novel, for I know there are many other ways that you could have spent your time. I pray that you were blessed with entertainment and encouragement. Like with Josiah, Gwendolyn, and me, there are going to be seasons of doubt in your walk with Christ. Doubt doesn't make you an unbeliever or make God love you less. Take your doubts to Him and ask for His help. He'll never turn you away. I pray that at the end of your season of doubt, you will stand firm with faith stronger than before.

There is only so much space in a book for me to share with you what I've learned. I'd love for you to visit me on my website, join my newsletter, take part in my annual reading challenge, and/or hang out with me on social media. Find all the details for connecting with me at www.crystalcaudill.com. Thank you so much.

Until next time,

Crystal

Discussion Questions

1. Throughout this story conflict arose from the paradox of serving others while considering oneself superior. Where did you see this play out? How did this affect behaviors and the relationships involved?

2. Once Josiah realized he was ready to love again, he jumped right in, but Gwendolyn needed more time. What unique struggles did Gwendolyn's and Josiah's relationship have due to his being a widower? Do you think it was important that they addressed Shauna's part in their relationship instead of moving forward like she didn't exist? Why or why not?

3. Josiah's family claims a history of knowing who they will marry from almost the beginning. Do you believe love at first sight is possible? Why or why not? How does one know if it is infatuation or real love?

4. Instead of facing his doubts, Josiah chose to ignore them. How did ignoring those doubts affect his relationship with God? How has confronting or ignoring doubts in your own life affected your faith?

5. Gwendolyn wrestled with her faith despite knowing all the right verses, hymns, etc. How did you see her faith sustaining her even through her doubts and struggles? What verses and/or people do you turn to when your faith needs to be encouraged?

6. The prayer Gwendolyn leans into, "help thou my unbelief,"

comes from a desperate father in Mark 9:24 after Jesus confronts him about his unbelief. What do you find powerful about that prayer? How does that prayer have the potential to change a person?

7. At what points do you think Gwendolyn acted out of faith, and at what points do you feel she acted out of fear? What did those moments of fear reveal about her faith? Can fear ever be used to grow our faith?

8. Mr. Ellison was a hero turned addict. How did this addiction change him and his view of himself? How did his addiction affect the rest of his family? If you were Gwendolyn, how would you have reacted at his return?

9. Gwendolyn and her mother eventually learned to forgive her father. How did that forgiveness look different for each of them? Does forgiving someone require trusting that person and/or allowing that person to return to a place in your life? Why or why not?

10. Mr. Ellison told Josiah that the hardest truth he had to learn to be content with was that faith is founded on declaring God Lord of his life, even when the answers don't come. How does one learn to be content with not having answers? How has struggling with not knowing the why to situations affected your faith?

Historical Notes

Houses of Refuge

Houses of Refuge were the predecessor for juvenile jails, with the idea being that children needed to be protected from hardened criminals and given a chance for reformation. Youth under the age of twenty-one who were abandoned, convicted of a crime, or homeless could be referred to the state-run Philadelphia House of Refuge or private variations by the order of a mayor or judge. Children stayed there for at least one year, and their days were highly regimented and aimed toward moral, intellectual, and physical improvement.

Ban on Buying Counterfeits

Early in President Cleveland's administration, a new solicitor assumed office and almost immediately forbade the use of Secret Service division funds to buy counterfeit money. He claimed that buying counterfeit money from a counterfeiter incited the counterfeiter to commit a crime. Since operatives routinely purchased counterfeit notes to gain the trust of criminals and to infiltrate their counterfeiting organizations, this new policy struck a devastating blow to Secret Service operations. Investigations throughout 1885 were crippled to the point of seriously jeopardizing the Secret Service's effectiveness and mission. Through the persistent work of Chief Brooks and Operative Andrew Drummond, the ban was lifted in December 1885. I wanted to show the struggles of the operatives as they attempted to do their job while having their primary tactic forbidden from use.

Green Goods Game

The green goods game was a con played against other criminals and thus went largely unreported. Even so, the scheme was widely known throughout the late 1800s, and newspapers frequently printed sample letters and stories of those who succumbed to the lure of easy money. Since the green goods game rarely included actual counterfeiting, the crime fell under mail fraud and thus the Postmaster General's purview. By having real counterfeits included in my story, I was able to finagle this scheme into falling under Josiah's caseload.

The Opiate Habit

During the late nineteenth century, the United States dealt with opiate addiction at epidemic levels. Roughly 1 in 200 Americans were addicted to opiates. Opiates were largely unregulated and widely prescribed, and pharmacists sold them to individuals who self-medicated for physical and mental discomfort. But those who suffer from addiction are not just numbers. They have friends and families who love them but struggle with all the consequences that arise from addiction. This story only showed a glimpse of one such family. Being an addict doesn't make you a bad person, but all sin does have the power to destroy. If you or a loved one suffers from substance abuse, please seek help. You can call the SAMHSA National Helpline at 1-800-662-4357.

HIDDEN HEARTS
OF THE GILDED AGE
SERIES

COUNTERFEIT
HOPE

CRYSTAL CAUDILL

COUNTERFEIT
LOVE

CRYSTAL CAUDILL

COUNTERFEIT
FAITH

CRYSTAL CAUDILL

KREGEL
PUBLICATIONS